Journey of the Rose

Twisted Rose Saga - Book 2

Bonita Clifton

Cozy Corner Press

"We are all broken. That's how the light gets in." – Ernest Hemingway

for Kevin,
because you make my world real,
and without your knowledge, insight,
and trippy imagination,
this book wouldn't be possible.
I love you

xo

CHAPTER 1

Prologue

Triple Bar C Ranch, Wyoming
Early Spring, 1888

T he figure of a man materialized from the shadows, sudden and without
a sound.

For a hair of a second, she questioned the accuracy of her eyesight. By the time
Emmy Bartlett glanced over her shoulder, he was upon her; no time to brace her
stance, poise for an elbow jab, or thrust a knee into a tender part. No time to
scream or defend herself.

Her washcloth fell into the soapy water as a sinewy arm looped around her
upper body from behind, winching her away from the wash basin. Legs mimicking an awkward swimmer's kick, her boot heels skidded across the linoleum.
The man dragged her from the bathing room, heaving her flush to his frame as
he traversed the kitchen, first to the left and then to the right, grumbling words
she tried to understand. Through the doorway, he pulled her into the dining
room. The stench of old sweat, dirt, and manure snaked into her nose, and she
swallowed a gag.

"*Stop!* What is it you want?" she cried.

He didn't respond. Squirming to the side, Emmy sunk her teeth into his forearm, clawing with both hands and breaking fingernails. The man expelled a curse, swinging a hand around to strike her cheek. An explosion of numbing pain squeezed her eyes shut and tears rolled down her cheeks. She felt the pressure of material crammed past her lips, wedging into her mouth.

"You'll do as I say. Hear me?" every syllable emphasized with a powerful jerk. She coughed against the wad in her mouth, unable to form words, nodding in understanding. "Anybody else in the house? Where's the old couple? If I get a surprise, I'll kill'em, sure as I'm standin' here."

Emmy shook her head. Estelle and Henry lived in the big house with her and, as far as she knew, were busy down at the chow house. Every other Wednesday, they took the wagon into Gunn Pass City for supplies, the return trip lasting into nightfall as they enjoyed helping Cookie with the organization and storing of provisions. In his younger years, Henry worked on the ranch first as a cowhand, then as an assistant foreman. That was before a traumatic leg injury put an end to his bronc-busting days. Nowadays, Henry kept watch over the main house, occupying himself with odd jobs and repairs. Estelle was a godsend in caring for Mama. At roughly the same age, the two women had grown close. Few women lived at the Triple Bar C Ranch back in the beginning, or since the murder of Charles and Katherine Chase in this very house back in '68. The only adult females were herself, Mama, Estelle, Hanna, and a few cowhand wives. Sadly, Mama's mind had grown weak and she often didn't recognize her own daughter, let alone her good friend.

Emmy's thoughts raced. With any luck, Henry and Estelle wouldn't return to the main house anytime soon. What worried her most was Mama, tucked into her bed in an upstairs bedroom. If she woke, she wouldn't understand what was happening and the possibility filled Emmy with terror.

Her captor gave another jerking squeeze of his arm, forcing her to keep up with his stride. An icy dread crept into her body. Who was he and what did he want? Was it something to do with the range wars creeping closer to the borders of the Bar C Ranch? Did he intend on raping her? She swallowed at the lump in her throat, a surreal dawning settling in her gut. *Think!* Is he armed? A glimpse of steel glimmered at his waist and her hopes soared. At least the pistol wasn't in his hands—but what about a knife?

"Where are important things kept?" he demanded hot and damp on her ear. "Heard you got a safe somewhere. Where is it, sweet one?"

A modicum of relief swept through her. He only wanted valuables and money. She tried to speak, the cloth in her mouth making it impossible. Laughing at her effort, he dragged her squirming form past the stairway before aiming down an unlit hallway.

"Calm down and I won't hurt you. I expected you to be an ugly spinster, not a comely young lady," he grumbled. "Maybe if I didn't come out so quick you would've had more clothes off—a visit to your bed might put you in a friendlier mood, eh? Wish I had the time."

The man craned his neck to see past the shadows. As he reached for a crystal doorknob, the toe of his boot caught the ornate leg of a rustic pine coat rack positioned outside of the door. Growling, he pitched to the side. Emmy thrust an elbow into his ribcage and stomped a sturdy boot heel on the top of his foot, twirling from his grasp as he yowled in pain. He made a grab for her, fists closing on air.

At that moment, Emmy glimpsed his features. He was at least a head taller than her, the breadth of his beefy shoulders twice as broad. Dark hair snaked out from a gray cavalry-style hat, his black eyes flashing with anger. What looked to be a scar shimmered white beneath a scruff of beard. One thing for certain: she didn't recall ever seeing him before.

"C'mere!" the man roared with a lunge, limping back up the hallway to catch up.

But it was too late. She yanked the cloth from her mouth, rounded the bend, skirts flowing behind as she passed the dining room table and aimed for the kitchen, feeling the vibration of his angry footfalls gaining behind.

"Get back here!" the man bellowed.

Please stay asleep, Mama ... Emmy ducked into the kitchen and pulled the door shut. Then came a thump and crash of glass shattering followed by a curse.

"When I get a hold of you, I'll snap that pretty little neck," he groused. "Should kill you for that! Think you broke my foot...."

Emmy snatched up the Winchester rifle kept tucked into a cubbyhole by the back door, in case a bear or other dangerous critter got too nosy. Hands shaking, she chambered a round and brought it to her shoulder, training it on the door. Then she waited. If she heard any movement on the stairs leading to where Mama slept, she would shoot him dead without remorse.

A full minute passed. The sound of footfalls faded, and Emmy toed open the door, easing the barrel of the rifle out first. Glancing both ways, she focused on the parlor. Had the man gone? A chilly evening breeze blustered, and the lacy parlor curtains billowed into the room. Cautious, she made her way to the open door and poked her head out to scan the porch.

Not a soul in sight.

Only the soft snuffle of an animal paired with the tippy tap of canine claws on wood. Perplexed by the open door, the diminutive black, white, and tan terrier peeked around the corner. Dottie earned her keep by monitoring the rat and mouse population alongside the barn cats—or that was likely the impression the terrier chose to convey. To Emmy's knowledge, no one had ever observed Dottie with a rodent. Upon spotting Emmy, Dottie's tail whipped excited circles in tandem with a wriggling hind end, and with a snort of joy, she touched her nose to the ground and darted to Emmy's side. Tongue lolling eagerly, she awaited a scratch.

CHAPTER 2

Broken

Middle of July, 1888

D ressed in black muslin, Emmy pushed to her feet, brushing grass from her box-pleated skirt and swiping a rogue tear from her cheek. Never one for sewing, she had purchased the mourning garb from Fanny Picard's dress shop in Gunn Pass City. However, she ignored the lace handkerchief Hanna had laid out for her that morning. The ranch foreman's wife was a good friend, so helpful since Mama's dementia set in. But Emmy flat-out refused to tuck a hankie into her sleeve, or to carry a reticule with said hankie. Old ladies did that. Besides, it was a bother.

Angry at everyone and everything the morning of the funeral, she had stalked from her bedroom, leaving the handkerchief folded upon the dressing table. Simple solution. She wasn't going to allow herself to cry.

Rogue tears didn't count.

It wasn't that Mama didn't approve of tears. Quite the opposite, she encouraged them. Cleansed the soul, Rosannah would insist with an infectious chuckle, and unhealthy to hold all those feelings inside to fester and rot. Precisely the reason Emmy refused to weep. As per tradition, anything her mother told her to do she bucked, going her own way. One could say she sported a stubborn streak. Why stop now, she reasoned. Oh dear, she must have been a nightmare to raise. Good thing she and Mama had grown so close after Papa passed, when Emmy was only a young girl.

Mama was gone now, and that meant Emmy was in charge. The Triple Bar C ranch was in her hands, all two-thousand acres of it.

The idea terrified her.

All by yourself. No room for feminine tears going forward, so best to get it out of your system now.

As much as she loathed the concept, Emmy squeezed her eyes shut, crumpled her face and willed herself to cry. For once, it actually worked. A swell of stowed-away grief blossomed in her throat, snatching the strength from her legs. On a hill above the big yellow house, she once again sank into the swaying grass beside a mound of fresh black soil overflowing the new grave in the family plot. Cupping her hands in the fine material of her skirts, she buried her face and sobbed from her heart, shoulders quaking. Now, she wished like hell she had tucked that damned stupid hankie into her sleeve.

Too hardheaded for your own good, that's what you are. Mama emphasized that very thing at least once a week. One more detail she was right about.

For a good ten minutes, Emmy wept, a chest-heaving wail, ridding herself of an accumulation of tears from all those months prior to Mama's death, beginning in early winter and lasting well into the first month of summer. She mewled for all the grief she had given Mama over the years. Plenty of that. And for all the laughter and camaraderie they shared despite their disagreements.

"Rosie, dammit!" Emmy choked out, pounding a fist onto the black dirt with a thump. Then, clutching her skirts, she mopped up the river of tears dripping from her chin. Eventually, a purged sensation rose inside, and she sat back on her heels, dissolving into a silly hybrid of laughter and anguish, hiccupping in between.

When angry, Emmy would address her mother by her given name. Mama's second love, Bud Tipsword, the previous ranch foreman, had passed on years ago, but when he was alive and got aggravated, the most he could utter was, "Rosie, dammit!" before drawing her into a tender bear hug. They cherished one another like no two people Emmy had ever known. Except for maybe Colt and Madison when they were here.

Emmy's father, Doc Bartlett, cared for her and Mama, too, and was a steadfast provider, though he was reserved and less demonstrative. Not nearly as jolly as Bud. And he worked all the time. Emmy remembered loving her father and the modest pink clapboard house the family shared—window boxes bursting with summer flowers. It served as their home on one side, an office and examination room on the other. Though Rosie lacked formal training, she functioned as a nurse to Doc Bartlett's patients in the humble little town of Gunn Pass City.

All that was before she and Mama came to live at the Triple Bar C Ranch. When Papa died, the Bar C owner, Colton Chase, proclaimed they always had a home at the ranch. Papa had served as the Chase family doctor, and Mama had midwifed Colt Chase into existence. Emmy's lips twisted into a half-smile, recalling numerous renditions of the heartwarming story of his birth.

"Figured I'd find you up here."

Embarrassed, Emmy dabbed away the tears and pushed to her feet long before her old friend got close enough to offer a hand.

"Miller, it's you."

"Expecting someone else?"

"Nobody but you would interrupt a lady's mourning without a second thought, so probably not."

He tipped his head back and laughed. "I've always enjoyed your humor, Emmy."

"You weren't so high on my humor that day in the schoolyard when I stuck a grasshopper inside your lard sandwich."

The gaiety on his face vanished, replaced by a green veil of disgust. For the locust as well as the nasty lard sandwiches in his lunch pail, all because of Pa's gambling away the family's money.

"We were eight," Miller pointed out, Adam's apple bobbing. "And it was one of those gigantic locusts. Stunned me that you picked the dang thing up in the first place."

Emmy shrugged. "Never been much of a girly-girl."

"The girl is now a woman, just as tough."

"You don't say?" She planted a hand on her hip, though she didn't feel so strong right then.

"Now, now. I only meant you're not the prissy type. You are capable. You have grit."

"Might be so. I do wash the grit off … every now and then." With that, she brushed a lock of sandy brown hair from her forehead and pushed past him, ignoring his outstretched hand. She picked her way down the hill behind the sprawling yellow ranch house and climbed the back porch steps. Miller followed.

"That I do appreciate. Washing off the grit, I mean."

Emmy lunged at the door handle before Miller could reach it. The last thing she wanted was to give him the impression she approved of his recent notion to court her. They had been friends since grade school. *Ick.* It was the same whenever he dropped by for a visit, whether it be ranch business or Mama's funeral feast.

Just as his arm came around to grab at the door, she flung the screen open, almost knocking the bucket-sized hat from his head.

"Now why you gotta go and be so independent, Miss Emmy? You know I'm serious about us."

She watched as he adjusted his hat back into place. Where did he get that thing, anyway?

"There is no us, Miller. We've been friends ever since we were kids and that's all good and fine, but—"

"But what? We are adults now."

"Exactly. High time you acted like it," she finished, slinging a tired, peace-making smile over her shoulder.

"I've been acting mature since Pa died."

"Six months is hardly long enough. You're more familiar with the inside of a jail cell than you are with your own house." She walked to the coat rack and removed the black lace flat cap from her head, hanging it on a hook and smoothing the chignon at the back of her head.

"Now that's not fair, Emmy. You must remember I've given up the bottle."

"Forgive me. My mouth gets ahead of me at times," she said.

Perusing the extravagant varieties of foodstuffs lining the countertop, brought by well-meaning neighbors and friends, she lifted a checkered cloth from Helen Riley's cherry pie and broke off a piece of sugared crust, popping it into her mouth. Chewing but not tasting. Staring past Miller's burly shoulder, she recalled how she and Mama used to stand at the kitchen wash bucket, side-by-side every evening after supper, gazing out the window while washing dishes, chitchatting about the day's happenings.

The dratted burn started up behind her eyes again and she presented her back to Miller so he wouldn't see.

"That's why I find you so attractive, Emmy."

"My verbal indiscretion?" She arched a brow, rooting under another cloth for a nibble of cornbread.

"Nope. Your honesty. We make a good pair."

"Miller...."

"Yes?"

"We won't ever be a pair of anything."

"But we have to!"

"We don't have to anything. We are neighbors, and that's all."

"Can't you tell I'm asking for ... your...."

"Spit it out. For my what?" Aggravated, she spun around to face him, hands planted to her hips.

"Your ranch, it's—"

"My ranch? You're asking for the Bar C?"

"No! Emmy now, don't be disagreeable. Your mama wanted it this way. Us, together."

"Mama didn't want any such thing."

"But our spreads back up to one another. Don't you know what that means?"

"I have an idea." She blinked, picturing two wide backsides touching. On any other day it might strike her as humorous. But not today.

"Only stands to reason we join up and make our relationship legal. We'd have the biggest spread in Wyoming and Montana put together. Maybe even Texas!"

Emmy exhaled a defeated sigh, shaking her head.

"Miller, I'm tired. It's been an exhausting and emotional day. The Bar C is the most I can handle right now. Besides, when I marry, it will be for love, not the acquisition of land."

Just then, the kitchen door from the parlor hallway swung open. In rushed Helen Riley along with two others from the Crooked Creek Presbyterian Church in Gunn Pass City: twin sisters Mrs. Florence Jenkins and Miss Joy Warner. Joy was the eldest of the two by one minute and proprietor of the Flower Emporium, having never married. Apparently, she didn't care to share her land either, or never found a love that made it all worth it.

Smart woman.

"Emmy, there you are!" Helen said, stepping up for a quick embrace. "I believe we are the stragglers. Most everyone has gone home except for the menfolk gabbing down at the barn. How are you faring, sweetheart?"

Pressing the woman's cool hands between hers, "As well as to be expected. I'll be fine in time. Thank you so much for everything you've done, and for attending Mama's services."

"Rosie was a dear friend and a kind spirit," Helen said. "We are here for you. Don't forget, choir practice every Monday and Thursday. We'd be overjoyed if you joined our humble group. Be good for you to get out and away from all this on occasion." Both Florence and Joy bobbed their heads in agreement.

In turn, Emmy wrapped the sisters in tight hugs. "I appreciate the invite, and I'll consider it. Though my warbling might scare off the ravens."

All four women laughed. The treacherous fowl had multiplied over the years to become the town's faithful mascots, fond of the monolithic cottonwoods encircling the churchyard.

"Those birds are a nuisance. Would do well to frighten a few of them off," Joy said. "You could always stop by my garden and help with pruning."

"Shush, Joy," Florence barked. "Always trying to recruit free garden help. Why don't you hire one of those Carlson boys? They could use some quality work to do. Might get their minds on something besides causing trouble. You know what the Lord says about idle hands."

"I won't allow a delinquent to snip my blooms!" Joy shot back, aghast.

Helen rolled her eyes. "There's plenty of food to see you and Zak's family by for a while. I'll make sure my sweet Dibbs stops by in a few days to check on you."

Dibbs Riley did little of anything without Helen's blessing and would undoubtedly show up in exactly two days' time. Emmy would bet her life on it. She escorted all three ladies to the front door as the summer sun began its descent behind the jagged Teton range.

"Thank you, ladies," she said with another hug, waving as Joy's black carriage with the flashy red interior bounced out of sight, the three women chattering as they went. Turning, Emmy almost slammed into Miller's barrel chest.

"Oh. You're still here. Please, help yourself to the food, then I would like to be alone."

Miller's eyes brightened. He hustled back to the kitchen, snagged a plate and piled it to overflow with fried chicken, vinegar'd cabbage, and a heaping mound of prairie beans simmered with ham hocks, topping it off with fresh onion and horseradish from the garden. Emmy watched the man pour a tall glass of cider and take a seat at the kitchen table, polishing off the entire plate without so much as the blink of an eye.

When he sat back in his chair and patted his puffed-out midsection, Emmy counted her blessings she wouldn't be near him over the next several hours. Surely the gases grew by the second. He scooted his chair back and stood with a satisfied groan.

"I'll be outta your hair now, Miss Emmy. You'll consider my offer now, won't you?"

Emmy frowned, shaking her head. "I don't recall there being an offer. As far as that goes, I don't want an offer."

He ignored the comment, saluting the brim of the monstrous hat as he turned to exit. "I think you'll see my side of things soon enough. We've been friends for a long time. It's high time we were more." With that, he spun on a boot heel, mounted his bay horse, and was gone. Perplexed, she watched him ride off into the sunset, the image far removed from the romanticism of her girlish fantasies of long ago.

Suddenly, Emmy recalled the letter.

Yes, the letter. She undid the top buttons on her dress, fishing inside her camisole to retrieve the envelope. It was where she kept important things.

She went to sit in the parlor rocking chair, grappling for a semblance of comfort despite the corset Hanna had guilted her into cinching around her middle.

"Proper ladies wear them to funerals, weddings, and church," Hanna had explained in her brusque Prussian accent, as if everyone in the entire world accepted that as an undisputed fact.

Emmy relented, seeing as how it was Mama's funeral at a church.

Oh, how I despise corsets!

One more thing to be obstinate about. Although Rosie also cared little for the torture contraptions, never giving her grief for choosing not to wear one, even at a barn dance or when a prospective suitor came to call. The last thing Emmy wanted was to put on false airs. If a man was interested in what she had to offer, then he had best be wanting her the way she was. Not because of a sheath of boned satin and strangulating ties cinching her middle—trimmed in delicate lace to conceal its tormenting qualities.

Funny thing, she found no interest in those prospective suitors, no matter how good, kind, attractive or moneyed they were. They were boring. Right or wrong, she entertained grander dreams. One more reason to assume she alone was responsible for the ranch, for she didn't share the popular notion of marrying to obtain a man's help with the land.

Emmy held the letter in her hand a moment before unfolding it, then settled in to read it once more.

Just in case you missed something in the first ten.

Colt had given the letter to Rosie before disappearing ten years ago, instructing her to pass it on to Emmy when the time was right. His plan was to leave the Bar C to begin his life with Madison, the mysterious woman who appeared at the ranch one summer day with a bump on her head—the one he claimed was his wife. Would they visit? Surely, they would, Emmy had reasoned, clinging to hope.

At long last, when Emmy turned 19 and prepared for college, she was tired of waiting and so packed a bag, announcing her intentions of traveling to Colorado Springs to find the couple. She recalled Madison speaking of the city as her hometown. She and Colt might have several children by this time, she reasoned. Why hadn't they written? Rosie had begged Emmy not to go, said it wasn't wise or safe for a woman to travel alone—not to mention the unlikelihood of finding them.

Emmy insisted. Though she had enjoyed the scenery and fine food, she returned a week later, downtrodden, baffled, not having learned anything about their whereabouts. In her early teen years, she had loved Colt the way a girl loves a first crush, with all the force of a youthful heart. But when Madison appeared, one only had to look at the couple to see how much they cared for one another. Emmy watched that love grow and came to cherish Madison as a sister. Then, for the happy couple to disappear....

She lifted the paper and read:

Dear Emmy,

If you are reading this, then I bestow my deepest condolences. Rosannah served as the mother of the ranch after my mother passed, Bud the father, and you, my brave little sister. I love and admire you all and I always will. I regret I can't be there now to explain everything. Rest assured, Madison and I are safe, along with an expected little one I learned about not long before I left the ranch.

You are now the owner of the Triple Bar C. The safe in my office contains the deed and other paperwork, as well as several bank accounts established in yours,

*Bud's and Rosie's name along with funds to keep the ranch flourishing for years to
come. Now that Rosie and Bud are gone, they are yours. You are a smart lady and
will know how to run a cattle ranch. Keep trustworthy hands by your side, treat
them well, and you will not go wrong.*

*You will notice I specified in the deed that the ranch shall go to Madison Chase
and our child upon your death. I know this doesn't seem logical, most likely odd
and impossible, but here is where you will need to trust my judgment. My injury
may well take my leg in the end, but my mind remains very much intact.*

*Don't try to find us, or to follow us. Now is the time for faith. Your life is only
just beginning, despite what you must be feeling right now. Carry on and may you
have a beautiful and prosperous future.*

With love and respect, Colt

Emmy lifted her gaze, heavy tears once again filling her eyes. She pressed a
fist to her lips. She had been correct in her suspicions—Madison was with child
when they disappeared, and they now have a family of their own.

Emmy folded the parchment and returned it to the envelope, tucking it
back into her camisole. Between this letter and her bizarre dreams, she simply
didn't know what to think. The wording in the letter was odd, and so were the
dreams—palpable, realistic, always the same:

Horses plodding along an indistinct trail, unclear of who sat in the saddles,
a plethora of roses on either side marking the way. Clouds moved in. Lightning
snapped. Horses broke into hefty gallops, despite the trail being steep and rocky.
No matter how Emmy struggled to slow her mount, Obie—at least she thought
it was Obie—the horse ignored the reins and continued upward. Then came a
break in the trees. A mind-bending flash of sunlight. Finally, she glimpsed the
faces of those who rode beside her, only somehow, now they were ahead of her,
welcoming her. Colt and Madison, astride their mounts, smiling.

On cue, she woke up at this point in the dream every time.

Chapter 3

Lonesome Loser

Triple Bar C Ranch, July 2019

K ade Stockton froze, recognition clenching his gut.

Pale gray, the rattlesnake slithered through powdery dirt, vague charcoal patterns striking a glimmer in the afternoon sun. As big as his wrist, the sleek reptile coiled at the base of a boulder and readied to strike. A juvenile jackrabbit hovered within a cluster of sagebrush, whiskers twitching, striving to blend into the landscape.

Little late for that.

In a tightening of muscles, Kade advanced two agile steps and raised his shovel into the air, arching a blow, his aim mere inches in front of the snake. In the same micro-second, an all-too-familiar vision splintered into his brain, unwelcome, dimming the world around him. He squeezed his eyes shut to rid himself of it.

A bearded face smeared in sweat and dirt, black devil's eyes zigzagged in red veins, a bloodied turban on the soldier's head. The weight of the Afghan commando pinned him to a spiky rock wall, sharpened with remnants of a recent bombing. A string of foreign words spat out between clenched teeth, some he understood,

Afghan slang, most gibberish to his ears. The soldier rammed his head back into the rocks, again and again.

Focus. Breath hitching, Kade struggled to shake off the tormenting vision. The shovel blade pierced the soil inches in front of the reptile, prompting it to strike at the steel. The jackrabbit exploded from the brush, bolting a serpentine pattern into the rippling prairie heat and out of sight.

"Run, Forrest, run..." Kade murmured, a forlorn smile indenting his cheek beneath dark brown beard stubble.

With long strides, Graham Stockton rushed to his son's side, his own shovel poised to put an end to the snake with a well-placed thrust.

"No, Dad, don't." Kade held out a gloved hand. "It's a grey ghost. Remember the time we were hiking in the back country near Cheyenne, came across that rattler? What was I, barely 16?"

Graham chuckled. "Something like that. You think this is one of those?"

"Pretty sure it's a big female. I remember looking it up when we got home, finding out the species was endangered."

"Yup. Think I still have the rock prints in my ass from the hard ground on top of that plateau where we decided to camp. Stupidest place in the world to pitch a tent." He laughed at the memory, his profile striking an older version of his son.

"Now that was Sean's idea. What was he, ten years old? Convinced he'd spot aliens from the top of that plateau." Kade wondered if his younger brother's alien fetish was still a thing at the veterinarian school he attended in Idaho. "All I saw was giant mosquitos eyeing my veins all effing night. I do four tours in Afghanistan, and those suckers hold the record for draining the most blood."

"Sure am glad you're home, son." Graham's expression turned into a questioning squint when Kade snared the thick snake with his shovel blade, flinging it across a ravine. The weight of it crinkled the low shrubs as it slithered off.

"Every creature has its purpose, don't you think?" Except for maybe camel spiders, he thought, cringing.

A content smile eased across the older man's face. "You always did have a soft heart."

Kade expelled a long sigh. "Not feeling so softhearted these days."

After six years as a combat engineer in the U.S. Army, he prided himself on his job skills. Still, a man didn't see and experience what he had and not carry deep scars. Afghanistan may be a world away from where he now stood at the southeast border of the Triple Bar C Ranch, but like it or not, war still lived in his blood. Every day—every muscle in his body tensing at the memories. Too many nights he woke up in a cold sweat with a growl on his lips. Mortars and screams echoing in his head.

At some point he came to accept it as a necessary evil he must live with. Despite months of therapy, sitting in front of sensible psychologists with soothing voices and empathetic eyes behind conservative glasses, scribbling notes on legal pads. Words of encouragement and assurances came easy. As far as relief? Not so much. Since he'd been working on the Bar C Ranch this past year, the night terrors had eased somewhat, yet resurfaced when he least expected it.

Kade attributed working with the horses as being the most effective therapy to date. There was something about earning a thousand-pound animal's trust, enough so that it welcomed a human to climb onto its back. When Dad had contacted him a day after he was honorably discharged from the Army, informing him of an open position at the ranch where Graham worked as stock manager, he came close to declining the opportunity. What experience did he have training horses, and for a real ranch, one the size of the Bar C?

Other than being assigned to an experimental mounted specialty unit in its testing phase in Afghanistan, he didn't have much experience with horses. He learned by being tossed off a 17-hand quarter horse a half-dozen times. Definitely the hard way.

"Hey man, wanna go hang out with the horses?" his commanding officer had asked a few months after he graduated from advanced combat engineer training. "With an above-average aptitude, I think you've got what it takes. You do like horses, right ... being from Cheyenne and all?"

"Sure, what the hell. Tried most everything else," Kade had said, aware of his illusory cowboy image. Tori always said he had a certain persona, attributing it to the long-legged confidence in his walk. Two weeks later, he was presented with unit orders.

"How's it going with that yearling—what do they call him?" Graham asked.

Hooked on 70s-era music, Kade tapped an ear pod, lowering the volume of the rock anthem Lonesome Loser, then reached for the wire-stretcher. He looked up from the new fence post he was muscling into position. "Twins call him Tumbleweed, and from my secret sources, I suspect it'll stick," he replied, referring to Colt and Madison's little ones.

Graham laughed. "Sounds appropriate to me."

"He'll be a good horse for the kids. We're working on ground manners and trailer loading now. He breezed right on through the basics of lunging. Took him a while to figure out how I was able to 'touch' him when he was clear across the paddock. He's extra smart though. I could see the cogs throwing off steam when he looked at me." Kade chuckled, squinting up into the glare to see his dad staring off into the north pastures where a couple dozen head of cattle grazed on a hillside.

"What's on your mind?" Kade asked, though he figured he knew. Graham looked down, weariness reflected in his eyes. He scrubbed his jaw, then bent to retrieve a fence post, passing it to his son.

"Ah, nothin'."

"It's Mom again, isn't it?"

"No need to go into all that."

"Why in hell do you even allow her the space in your head?" Kade growled, struggling to temper his irritation. "She doesn't deserve it."

"She's still your mother, no matter what she did."

"Except she hasn't been a mother to me or Sean in what ... 16 years? What kind of mother up and deserts her entire family, when her sons are barely old enough to know what the fuck is going on? I mean, I knew, but Sean sure as hell didn't."

Little brother Sean was in his last year of vet college, always top in every class, so it came as no surprise he would graduate next spring with honors. He deserved the success. Growing up had been tough for them both, but most challenging for Sean.

Their mother deserted the family when Kade was fifteen. Ran off with some truck driver delivering to the grocery store she managed. He pushed to his feet and took a breath, taking his frustration out on the wire, contracting the stretcher as hard as he could and bunching the chest and bicep muscles under his shirt.

Finished, he said, "Sorry, Dad. I'll shut up."

"No, you're right. I don't dwell on it. 'Cept when something makes me think of her when things were good, ya know?"

"Yeah. I get it."

Kade's thoughts shot to his ex-wife, Tori, and the day he returned early from what was to be his final tour of duty. He had intentions of surprising his wife—instead was greeted with the sick feeling of walking into his own home, his own *bedroom*, and discovering her in the arms of the one guy he thought was a friend. Any wonder Kade re-upped for another tour of duty the following week? All he wanted was to go back to a place where he could go numb and not have to face reality—in a hot, dirty corner of the world where nothing existed except hard reality. Ironic. If he hadn't gone back, would the rest of his team be alive today—would Wyatt be alive?

"Hey, son, Sean called last night. He starts classes next month. He's thinking of coming up here to spend a few days before then."

"Sounds great. Be good to catch up." When Kade looked up, Graham had that faraway expression on his face again. Sure would be nice if his dad met a good woman. Was there such a thing? His boss, Colt Chase, got lucky. His wife seemed to be a fine woman, and he supposed they were out there, just few and far between. He wouldn't be putting his trust in one anytime soon.

Thoughts of Christmastime five years ago entered his head. He had come home for the holidays to surprise Dad and Sean, catching a lift with a buddy as far as Fort Collins, then hitching a ride with a trucker up to Cheyenne. In uniform, he stopped into his favorite coffee shop to warm up while awaiting Dad to come in from a nearby ranch where he worked as stock manager.

Kade had been sitting at a table near the window, scrolling through his phone when he looked up and saw her standing outside by a bench, hugging her arms against the cold, snow flurries starting up around her. She wore a thin coat and a sock cap, her blond hair poking out underneath. He would know those eyes anywhere.

Kade blinked a few times, then stood up, tossing a bill on the table before walking outside.

"Ma?" he said, tentative, moving closer with a sensation of stepping out of his own body. How many years had it been? Her face, drawn with lines, was thinner than he remembered as a teenager. It appeared she didn't recognize him at first. Squinting, she sucked a final drag from her cigarette, then eyed him through tendrils of smoke before dropping it on the pavement and grinding it out with the toe of a sneaker. She looked him over, head to toe a few times, spearing his eyes at the last pass. A flicker of recognition brought those blue eyes to life. The ones he remembered.

"Kaden?" she said in a voice raspy from too many cigarettes and who knew what else.

"Yeah, Ma, it's me." What did one do in a moment like that, embrace? Laugh? Slap each other on the back? Say, hey, good to see you, been a long time, what've you been up to, so this is what you look like now? None of those things had struck him as remotely appropriate. Those eyes swept over him again, focusing on his shiny black boots, then up to his face.

"Army?"

He nodded, "North Carolina. Bragg."

"Always knew you'd be all patriotic and such," she had said, rocking back and forth on thin-soled sneakers. She fidgeted with her hands, digging into her pocket for another smoke.

"No, Ma, don't light up now. Let's go inside, it's colder'n shit out here. I'll buy you a cup of coffee."

"Always told you not to cuss," she mumbled, shrugging thin shoulders while walking beside him to the restaurant door.

Kade didn't remember his mother ever reprimanding him for cussing. Maybe that was the problem—never heard her, never listened. He recalled overhearing arguments between Mom and Dad before she left. Her words, something about Dad never listening to her.

Inside, amongst the clatter of dishes and hushed conversation, they sat across from one another at a booth with two cups of brew between them. Curls of steam filled the awkward space. He watched as she tore open and dumped three, maybe four packages of sugar into her coffee, drinking it fast, clasping the cup tight like she craved the warmth. At the time, it made him feel good, as though he were doing something to help his mom out. She kept fiddling with the collar of her coat, which only served to draw attention to the yellowish bruise on her right cheekbone, highlighted by the glare from the window.

"You good?" she asked.

"Getting married," he answered, at the time missing his cute blond-haired fiancée back in Carolina waiting for him and making plans for the wedding of the century. What a farce that turned out to be.

"What're doing that for?" his mom asked with a disdainful curl of her lip, the most emotion he had seen out of her.

What did he expect—congratulations! A joyful squeal? A hug and a kiss?

Kade slammed back a swallow of coffee then, looking at her straight, aware of the shake of his hand as he fit the coffee cup back onto its saucer. "Is your life so much better now than with us and Dad?" he asked, gaze focused on the bruised side of her face. Once again, she shifted in a feeble attempt to hide it from view.

"I'm getting by," she said, demeanor becoming defensive. "There are things you were too young to know. Your dad was able to do a better job than I was."

"How—how can you say that? Everybody needs a mother. Sean needed a mother!" He tried to continue but felt sick, wanting to vomit all the words he had swallowed over the years. *Why had she left? Why hadn't she at least tried to contact him or Sean? All he wanted at that moment was her side of the story.*

She lifted her chin and glared down her nose, "You think you have all the answers because you wear a pretty uniform? You don't know the half of it, Kaden."

"Then why don't you explain it to me?" If anyone had cause to be angry, it was him. But there she was, on her feet in a huff, zipping up her coat and fumbling through pockets for what he figured was her contribution to the bill.

"No, Ma, it's on me, remember?"

"This all has me a little upset and it's a long way home. Mind giving me a lift?"

"I'm not driving. Hitched a ride with a trucker."

She sighed in agitation, tapping a foot and scanning the restaurant again; anything to avoid looking at him, he supposed.

"How about a few bucks then, so I can get a cab."

The old teenage anger, hurt, and sadness reared up inside, grabbing at him and squeezing. Somehow, he managed to push it down while plucking a twenty from his wallet.

Her eyes lit up. "That's good," she said, snatching it from his hand. She made to leave, pausing long enough for a time-worn look to flicker past his. "Nice to see you, son. Take care." Eyes glazing over with priorities he wasn't privy to, she left, leaving him in the wake of a faint aroma of alcohol.

An assemblage of replies had stuck in his throat then. On one hand, he wanted to kick her ass. On the other, curling up into a ball and crying like a hurt little boy sounded infinitely better. Kade figured he would have been much better off had he not run into her that day.

The roar of an engine sounded at the rise, snapping him from his doldrums. He set the wire stretcher aside and stood, brushing the dirt from his pants.

"Hey, Chase, how's it going?" Graham called out as Colt pulled up astride a beefy 4-wheeler. He switched off the motor.

"Northwestern quarter looks good," Colt said. "Though I did run across a couple rotten posts by the old creek bed. I mapped them out. Looks like one of the heifers dropped a calf in the south pasture. I didn't want to get too close with this machine and stress her out."

"Mercy," Graham said with a wince. "Little late for that nonsense. I'll get over there and check it out."

"You boys wrap it up for today," Colt said. "Why don't you two come on by the house for a bowl of Angela's chili and cornbread. Heard a rumor there's

chocolate cake, too. Ever tasted her cooking? You'll kick yourself if you miss it."
Colt grinned, gave the men a so-long nod, and fired up the quad ATV. He jetted
off and over the hill, back the same way he had come.

The men's eyes sparkled, meeting in a hungry challenge.

"Buck's wife knows how to cook," Graham voiced unnecessarily.

"Oh, I'm already down," Kade said, having tasted the foreman's wife and
Colt's mother-in-law's pot roast a few weeks back. Both men hurried to toss the
fencing tools into the dump bed of the quad. "Get in. Let's go check on that
calf first, then I'm having me a bowl of chili. Maybe two."

"I'm right there with you." Graham hopped in the other side as the engine
fired up. Kade slammed it into gear and hit the gas.

CHAPTER 4

Strange Magic

July, 1888

E mmy woke up with another monster headache. Two evenings past, a group of renegade riders had thundered through Bar C land. Bouncing out of bed, she pulled on a wrap and grabbed the Winchester, rushing out to the front porch. There, across the creek, were the bobbing torches of riders yipping and hollering as they rode through rows of bunkhouses. Two split off from the others and splashed through the water toward the house. Men emerged from the bunkhouses with their own responses, firing rounds into the air and calling out words she couldn't decipher. It was pandemonium.

Shots sounded, and she levered a round into the chamber of her rifle. As they neared, the light from a torch illuminated what would be their faces, only they wore what looked to be flour sacks on their heads with holes cut for eyes, nose, and mouth. The lead rode a piebald paint horse.

Emmy descended the porch steps with angry determination, and took a stance at the bottom, thrusting the butt of the rifle to her shoulder and firing into the air.

"I know that's you, Tom Carlson!" she had cried out. "I'd recognize that pretty paint horse anywhere. Get off this land or I'll...."

The whoops and hollers from the trio drowned out her threats, but that didn't mean she didn't intend on carrying them out. Sheriff Townsend would hear about this. Those Carlson boys were getting too big for their britches, however there were more than three men on horses that night. Who were the others? The riders circled the house in a cacophony of hollers, exiting the opposite side and dashing back across the creek, light from the torch bouncing in the night.

Out of the dark, a man came racing toward her. By the light color of his hat and a long-legged gait, she had recognized him to be her old friend, now the Bar C foreman.

"Zak!" she called out as he neared. "Who are they? I recognized Tom Carlson's horse."

Tom had been so proud of purchasing that horse a while back. The middle brother of three, he wasn't unruly as the others. Not that they did anything worse than disrupting and vandalizing, which was bad enough, but that night it appeared he chose to follow the path of his siblings.

"All three of the Carlson's I suspect," Zak answered between puffs of breath. He stopped beside her, pistol at the ready in his right hand. "There are several others though. No idea who they are. You alright, Emmy?"

Emmy's thoughts went to that night last spring—the unknown man in the house who accosted and threatened her, then disappeared. No reason to think he was among these riders. She had turned to see Estelle and Henry standing on the front porch, eyes round in the misty moonlight, Estelle with a shawl gripped tight about her shoulders.

"I'm fine," Emmy verified.

"Get back in the house," Zak said. "We've got it handled. I'll talk to Townsend tomorrow."

It had been hours and two cups of sassafras tea before Emmy, Henry or Estelle had been able to get any sleep that night. The next morning, they learned Helen's husband, Dibbs Riley, was shot and killed while attempting to scare off intruders at their place by firing a shotgun into the air. A bullet from one of the riders struck him square in the chest, killing him.

Had it been the same gang? Had the Carlson boys graduated to murder?

Helen and Dibbs' homestead wasn't far, a few miles to the east. The news hit Emmy hard. Less than a week after Rosie's death, they would be burying Helen's husband, and for what? She, Henry, and Estelle had spent the entire next day at Helen's place, sitting with her and her sons. Senseless is what it was.

Now, Emmy hunched over the kitchen table nursing a mug of extra strong, black coffee, cradling her forehead on the heel of her hand. Even when she had managed to sleep, the bizarre dreams continued. If only she could make sense of them—riding a rocky trail, an unusual rosebush under a tree at the top. It reminded her of the marbled pink roses Joy Warner took pride in cultivating, keeping the bush separate and protected with a sturdy picket fence at the rear of the Flower Emporium.

After dreaming, Emmy would wake sitting straight up in bed, one hand at her heart, the other fist clenched as if still holding the stem of one of those thorny roses. Funny, her palm even smarted with the phantom sensation.

Now that she thought about it, the trail in her dream was like the one Colt used to enjoy traveling—a favorite ride when he desired alone time, sometimes disappearing for days. Emmy frowned in thought. She hadn't ridden in that area in years. A rockslide took out a portion and she never ventured back. Maybe today was as good a day as any to give it a try. There must be an alternate route to the top. With all the turmoil of cattle rustling and outlaw gangs, a bit of peace and quiet would do her good.

It being Sunday, she usually attended church, but the lure of nature won the argument in her throbbing head. With Dibbs' funeral planned for early next week, she would stop by the Riley homestead on her way home and check on Helen and her two teenage sons, now the only help Helen would have on the land.

An hour later, Emmy sat astride Obsidian, a.k.a. Obie, her black mustang with a white star on his forehead and one blue eye. Five years before, she had nursed him back to health after he showed up on the ranch lame and hurting.

A shy yearling, he remained hidden in the cover of trees outside the corral fences where he would nicker to the other horses, running off whenever anyone approached.

Eventually, she gained the colt's trust with sweet grain and an occasional apple. It took months, first introducing him to a brush and then grooming until she was able to nurse the abscess on his neck. Then after a time, she managed to get him under the saddle. Sound and strong, Obie was the best horse she had ever had.

She clicked her tongue. "C'mon, boy. Let's take a ride into the hills. I've got the last bit of Helen's cherry pie for me, and some carrots for you. We'll have a picnic." At the sound of her call, Dottie came flying around the corner in a puff of dust. "You can go, too, girl," Emmy promised. Once Emmy was seated in the saddle, she extended a leg for Dottie to scamper up to her favorite perch, at the front of the saddle behind the horn.

A burst of yips at her side announced the arrival of sibling yellow retrievers, Sage, and Brush. They trotted alongside, stopping every now and again to shove a curious nose into a bush or tuft of grass, then bounding to catch up. Gray hair sprouted at their muzzles, and they weren't as energetic as they once were, but remained as loyal as ever.

Passing by Zak and Hanna's cabin, Emmy waved to five-year-old Beatrice and three-year-old Julie. Dressed in their Sunday dresses, they sat cross-legged on the front porch, intent on bouncing a tiny rubber ball in a game of jacks as they waited for their parents and baby brother Eli to finish dressing for church.

"Morning, girls. Tell your mommy and daddy I'm riding up to the ridge this morning for some peace and quiet. How about we fry up some chicken for dinner when you all get back from church?" She was answered by a cheering chorus of giggly girls as she disappeared into the trees, waving as she went.

Emmy and Obie picked their way around the old rockslide, swales of grass, and little pine trees now growing from nooks and crannies. They arrived atop the expansive ridge a short time later.

The rolling sea of fertile mountains surrounding her fed her soul as much as the crisp air nourished her lungs. Wildflowers splashed color over the grassy basin—paintbrush orange to purple iris dotting the dusty green sage, the entire picture framed by pine trees and massive boulders. But the subtle flower that caught her eye this day was elusive, situated on the opposite side of the trail and tucked under the limbs of an old spruce tree.

Astride Obie, she paused, "Just like in my dream!" The shade of pink was quite unique. Even the rose garden behind the house had nothing that rivaled this one.

A lump formed in her throat, instigated by a déjà vu and conjuring a well of emotion associated with the dreams. A gray jay cackled from a low branch, skittering from one end to the other. Obie tossed his head and began to prance, anxious to move on, she supposed. His hooves thumped the ground impatiently.

"As good a place for a picnic as any," she announced, extending a long leg out of the stirrup for Dottie to scamper to the ground. Emmy swung from the saddle behind her. Still clothed in black, this dress was lighter and less cumbersome than the mourning habit had been, although now she wished she had worn trousers like she usually did when riding. Considering the recent deaths, she didn't think it appropriate.

After removing Obie's bit, she left him ground tied near a spruce tree where he proceeded to rip at a patch of sweet grass, a sure sign he felt relaxed. A breeze whispered through the pine trees as Emmy unpacked the miniature picnic, choosing a spot beneath the spruce where she could sit and contemplate the troubling situation on the ranch. Sage and Brush turned in indecisive circles before plopping to the ground nearby, panting in expectation. Dottie chose to curl up beside her.

"I brought two biscuits. You three will have to share." She tore it into pieces, amused as three sets of eyes shifted one to the other and back again, determining who would score the first bite, deciding harmony to be the best option.

The soda biscuits disappeared in one long unified gobble.

Laughing, Emmy nibbled on the cherry pie, the tartness pinching her tongue. Helen Riley tended to skimp on sugar, though her creations were delicious in their own way. The wind picked up then. A gust here, a swirl there, dirt, pine needles, and leaves making her sneeze.

"Mercy," she said, wiping her eyes. "Wouldn't you know, the wind has to come along and mess with our picnic." She caught hold of the edge of the red cloth she had spread on the ground and secured the ends with rocks.

When she righted herself, the thorny, scraggly vine with the unique rose swayed over her shoulder. Mindful of thorns, she touched a velvety petal, stirring up a seductive scent. It filled her nose, resulting in a second violent sneeze, causing her to accidentally snap the bud off its vine.

It dropped into her open palm.

"Whoops, looks as though you were meant for me." She tucked the bloom into the thick twist of hair at the back of her head.

In a manner of seconds, a bolt of lightning slammed to the earth at the edge of the clearing, reverberating into her core. Alarmed, she let out a scream as a crash of thunder followed. Obie reared, pawing at the air. When he hit the ground, he dashed off at a full gallop, disappearing into the valley below.

"Oh no! Obie!"

Emmy tried to push to her feet, but couldn't, as though a great weight pressed her to the earth. Another sound pierced the air: her own screeches in tandem with Sage and Brush's yips. Dottie wormed her way into Emmy's lap as the ground swirled, picking up speed, so fast she couldn't even fathom, causing her stomach to grip her ribs for stability.

Limbs, leaves, and dirt shot past.

One moment Sage and Brush were right beside her and the next they had vanished into the fray. With a cry for the dogs, Emmy crouched to her knees and covered her head, holding onto Dottie, with no concept if she were still upright. Nausea expanded her gut. She clutched at her head with one hand, her midsection with the other. A discord of jumbled voices pierced the air, joining with other sounds she couldn't define, easing in and out of her head.

Am I going crazy?

The earth shook as if it prepared to roll out from beneath them all. Somewhere in the distance, she heard her horse whinny. *Obie!* Stomach pitching, the ground fell, or so it seemed, and Dottie frantically began to dig her way under her skirt.

Then everything went black.

CHAPTER 5

Beautiful

Triple Bar C Ranch, 2019

Clothing drenched and strength drained, Emmy changed into one of Madison's flannel nightgowns and a soft robe. She wiggled her toes in fluffy pink slippers, thinking how wonderful they felt. After getting her to nibble on a bit of food, they sat in the parlor, decorated so differently from what Emmy knew. They now called it the living room. They visited, shared, and reminisced until long past dark.

Neither Madison, Colt, nor Emmy wanted to call it a day for fear it would all turn out to be a bizarre dream: That terrible storm, their description of Emmy materializing from the trees, skin pale, a terrified look in her eyes, hair wet, strands over her shoulders and what remained of her chignon dangling down her back.

"I must have looked a sight," Emmy said, giggling now, though at the time she had felt terribly ill. Colt and Madison had rushed up to catch her as she weakly sunk to her knees into the damp pine straw, sobbing at the realization that the couple stood before her. Was this real, or another dream—had she found her old friends after all these years? If so, where had they been? Sage, Brush, and even Dottie wound happy circles around the trio, tails slicing the air, licking Emmy's face in unison.

The dogs are here. But ... where is here?

Madison plopped down on the settee beside her and clasped Emmy's hand. "I *know* how impossible this seems. Remember the first day you saw me on the ranch? I felt how you must be feeling now. As difficult as it is to fathom, this is the 21st century. It's where I come from, and this is the world Colt and I chose to live in. We had to make a difficult choice when I got pregnant with the twins. That's why you didn't see us anymore."

"So, it was that ... *rose?*" Emmy asked. "I've been dreaming about roses, the trail. About seeing you both again. It's all so difficult to digest. The house and land look different, but wonderful just the same. But, if I am existing inside those dreams, I admit I rather like it,"

"Hurts my heart that your mama passed on, and Bud a few years back," Madison said. "But I'm so happy to hear about Zak and his family. Three little ones?"

Emmy nodded. "They bring such light to the ranch. Much like Charlie and Katie. My goodness, I still can't believe you had twins!"

"Sometimes we can't either," Colt reiterated in typical dry humor, entering the room with two mugs of hot tea for the ladies. They thanked him and he leaned in to deliver a kiss to his wife before taking a seat in an easy chair across from them. "And you, Emmy, grown into a lovely young woman with a ranch to manage. Are you up for it?" Colt asked.

"Yes. I think so. But I am a bit scared. There's so much to think about and plan for. Before Bud passed on, he had taken ill more often, and that's when he started to teach me about the ledgers and how things were managed day-to-day. He encouraged me to enroll at the university in Bozeman soon after. At the time, I didn't understand why he was teaching me. When he was gone, Mama continued the lessons. I'm so thankful she did. I feel somewhat prepared. However, I didn't expect...."

"Go on," Madison urged. "What is it?"

Emmy sighed. "It's ... I suppose, pressure from people."

"What people?" Colt and Madison voiced in unison.

"The usual requests from neighboring ranches, trading supplies, water rights, fencing, and the like. Zak oversees the hiring, which I'm thankful for. One of the bulls broke through a section of the fence twice now, making his way over to Riley land. A few heifers seem to have caught his eye." They all laughed, "And, well, then there are the men."

"Men?" Colt's gaze narrowed.

"Coming around ... to court me, I s'pose." She cleared her throat then, wondering if she should tell them of the man who attacked her in the house. She hadn't even told Zak about that, even though she knew she should have. It only reflected her inadequacy. If she had been a man, would that have happened?

"Ohhh," Colt and Madison voiced in unison, gazes connecting in a twinkle.

"That's to be expected," Madison said. "You're beautiful, smart, and eligible."

"Let's not forget wealthy," Colt added. "Only stands to reason the men will come out of the woodwork. Keep your wits. No sudden decisions and set your standards high. Anyone in particular?"

Emmy shook her head. "I'm not interested. At least not yet. Miller Johnson got it in his head that we're betrothed. Ridiculous. I never said anything to give him that impression."

"Miller, eh?" Colt whooshed out a breath. He leaned back, folding his arms over his chest and shaking his head. "I can think of better matches."

"There's no rush, Emmy," Madison said. "I remember when you were only going to settle for a rich rancher who loved to travel."

Both women laughed at the memory and for the first time in months, Emmy felt happy and at ease. Young with her entire life before her. More like herself.

"Did I really say that? Seems like an eternity ago. My childhood self was living in a fantasy world. I still want to travel. London. Paris. And I love reading about the steamships crossing the oceans. Maybe someday," she vowed. "However, I'm in no frame of mind for a man, or romance. I can't fathom marrying because it's a good monetary decision. There was a time when women were required to do so. But times are changing. I'm capable of running the Bar C by myself, thank you very much. I'll marry only for love. If I never fall in love, then I won't marry. Simple as that."

Recalling the letter penned by an elderly Emmy and delivered to Madison over five years ago, her heart thumped a painful beat. The letter had been a sagacious ode of remembrance and gratefulness—an old woman's rich life experiences. A local rumor had it that Emmy never married. Madison made a mental note to find that letter and read it again.

"It's been an eventful day. Bet you ladies are as bushed as I am," Colt said at last, sensing Madison's train of thought. He pushed to his feet and placed a comforting hand on his wife's shoulder. "It's all good, Sugar. Let's continue our conversation in the morning."

Sipping the last bit of tea, Emmy walked her cup to the kitchen sink before retiring upstairs. Madison stood in the kitchen grinding beans for the morning coffee, setting the timer on the pot as Colt shuffled up from behind. He slid his arms around her waist and drew her into a secure hug, and she leaned into him with a sigh.

"I'm having trouble," she confessed.

"Figured as much. Talk to me."

"The way Emmy's life turns out," she began, voice low. "There are things, I mean ... do you think maybe we should tell her? She mentioned steamships. *The Titanic?*"

Colt shook his head. "No. She survived the sinking, we know that. No rash decisions. A lot happened today. Remember our promise to never meddle in the timeline? We wouldn't even go through her possessions for fear of ... something."

She nodded, "I know. It's just so hard. And what about the picture?"

"The picture," he repeated with a sigh. "No, it's too much to think about too soon. Let's get a good night's sleep, and we'll discuss it in the morning."

As always, this wonderful man had a way of making her feel safe and secure like everything was as it was meant to be. She tilted her head back and looked up at his face, his neatly trimmed beard tickling her cheek.

"I see a gray hair," she pointed out.

He grinned, turning her around to brush a kiss over the smile on her lips, folding arms around her and squeezing tight.

"Mm. Love you, Sugar."

The first thing greeting Madison the following morning when she crawled from bed and padded downstairs was the idyllic vision of Katie and Charlie outside by the cottonwood tree, each with a tight grip on one of Emmy's hands. Charlie pulled her along, pointing upward and likely showing her where his dad would be building a tree house for their next birthday. Impressed, Emmy nodded and followed along. Sage and Brush chased one another amongst the reeds, while Dottie darted between them in flashes of black and white. All three splashed in and out of the creek.

"The kids sure are enjoying their Aunt Emmy," Colt said, moving to stand by his wife at the window. "Warms my heart."

"Mine, too, but why did you let me sleep so long? It's after nine."

"You needed it. Besides, you looked so damn cute all cuddled in a warm ball. Didn't have it in me to wake you."

"I'm happy she's here, Colt. I don't know what to do first. I suppose starting with breakfast is always a good choice." She ducked out of his embrace in the direction of the kitchen, and he followed.

"Think I'll take her down to the barn later and show her the black mustang Kade discovered grazing outside the fence line by the corral. Still dressed in full tack."

Madison stopped mid-stride, waffle maker in hand, "A mustang horse?"

"A beautiful one, too. One blue eye, a white stripe in his mane, and a star on his forehead. A bit fiddle-footed. My guess is he's the horse she lost in the storm."

"I hope so, that's awesome. Thank goodness Kade caught him. She'll be thrilled!"

Later that day, Emmy beat Colt out to the barn. When he mentioned one of the hands had located Obie, she couldn't wait, thankful he had been found. She gave him a generous scratch behind his ears, then led her horse around the corral several times, eyeing his gait for lameness. At last, she brushed the dust from her black skirts, noting how everything she wore needed a good washing after that drenching rain the day before. Though Madison had offered a change of clothes in the form of a blouse and denim trousers, it didn't feel right to forfeit the black. She was still in mourning, after all.

With intentions of pilfering a few carrots for Obie, she led him into an empty stall and removed his rope harness, then exited the barn through the man door at the back. A sound caught her attention and she paused to listen. The velvety sounds of a baritone voice and the soft notes of a guitar. Surmising it originated from a cabin positioned where the carriage house used to be, curious, she crept closer, circling around to the back where the sounds were clearer.

Picking her way along a skinny grass trail, she peered around the corner. A man leaned back on two legs of a wooden chair, head down, a doe-color Stetson hat concealing most of his features, except for a stubble of beard along a strong jaw. He strummed a guitar, humming along, inserting words now and again:

> *"...how you could be anything but beautiful.*
> *And I know that I will never change*
> *Rain or shine, for such a long, long time..."*

The music stopped.

In one lightning-swift move, the man looked up and came out of the chair, propping his guitar to the side of the building.

Startled, Emmy took a step back. "I-I apologize. I heard music and thought to see where it was coming from. Please pardon me."

She dipped her head in apology and turned to leave, noticing he was quite tall. He wore a black shirt that fit close to his body, accentuating a variety of muscles, though her attention fixated on a splash of blue-green artwork beginning at his elbow and extending up and over a bicep, disappearing under a sleeve.

"Hey, it's all right," he said. "Reflex is all. You must be the lady who got caught in that storm yesterday."

Emmy paused. "Yes, that's right."

"Think I saw you in the window."

"Oh," was all she said, cheeks heating. "If you'll excuse me, I must tend to my horse." His eyes pierced her like chips of blue ice.

"It was a wicked one. The storm I mean. Name's Kade Stockton."

He extended his hand and she reciprocated with a shake. "Emmy Bartlett."

"Pleasure to meet you, Emmy. Found your horse this morning out by the blackberry bushes behind the corral. Still had his tack on, and a cut on his fetlock. Missing a shoe. At least I assume he's your horse. Black mustang?"

Emmy nodded. That mesmerizing blue gaze lingered, his perusal making her uncomfortable. She must look quite strange compared to everyone else. She smoothed her skirts, more out of nervous habit than anything else.

"I noticed he had a new shoe. I appreciate your care of Obie, doctoring the cut and all. I couldn't help but notice, it's purple," she said, referring to the color of the medicine.

"That's the antifungal. Best thing for a cut like that."

"Anti....?"

"Fungal. Antiseptic. Don't want an infection." He folded his arms, drawing her attention to his sun-browned and lightly furred forearms. Shifting his weight, he leaned against the corner of the cabin.

"You're referring to a contamination of the wound?"

Those eyes probed hers. He nodded, a smile teasing his lips. Was he mocking her?

"I see. Well, thank you again. I was on my way to the house for a few carrots."

He pushed his weight from the building. "No need. I'm happy to show you where everything is, including carrots."

Kade set his guitar inside the cabin, then crossed in front of her to lead the way. Emmy followed, passing the tack room, and stopping at an adjacent doorway. He pulled out a ring of keys, inserting one and twisting, ushering her inside an expansive room where feed and medicines were kept. An ice box as large as the one in the kitchen stood sentry in the corner. Kade swung it open, grabbed a bag of carrots and passed it to her. This room alone was larger than the entire kitchen back in her time.

"Here you go. Don't feed him too many now, or he'll get fat." He winked.

Emmy blinked. "Are you the cook, Mr. Stockton?"

Kade shook his head with a chuckle. "There'd be a death toll if I were. Why do you ask?"

She smiled, shrugging. "Maybe that's why you seem to mistakenly think carrots will make my horse fat. Are you ... the ranch foreman?" she ventured a second time.

"Nope. My dad claims that title. I've only been here since being discharged from the service a year back. Enjoying the peace and quiet of ranch life until I figure out what I want to do next."

"Oh, I see. Service?"

"Army. Hired on to work with the horses. Sometimes I wonder who gets the most out of it, me or them."

"Horses can be medicinal," she agreed.

Curious, Emmy studied the color varieties of buckets, bags, and boxes lining the shelves. She glanced out the doorway to a wall lined with hoses, silver knobs, and brass handles. The entire setup overwhelmed her.

Kade watched her, inclining his head toward Obie's stall "I noticed your boy is a bit skittish. If you like, I can spend some time with him. Likely the storm got him agitated."

"Obie came to me as a feral horse. He showed up at the ranch near those bushes where you said you found him—" She caught her words, backtracking. "What I mean is, a similar area at my ranch." She cleared her throat, "He was traumatized. A shy colt, alone, too thin, with a sore front leg and an abscess on his neck. I nursed him back to health and trained him until I could ride him. When necessary, he's right as rain and steady, but can be as excitable as a youngster."

"Impressive. He's a handsome boy."

"I've been riding since before I could walk," she blurted.

The cowboy paused, glancing up from the feed bucket, those eyes beneath a dark brow causing her breath to hitch. She felt all the world like a dolt. Why did she go and say that? She supposed she didn't want him thinking she didn't know what she was doing. After that freakish storm, no wonder Obie was skittish!

At the sound of grain sifting into buckets, Obie began to pace inside his stall. Likely he caught the sweet aroma of molasses. Emmy thanked Kade for the carrots and headed to her horse.

"Let me know if you need anything else," he called after her. "Or if you'd like to hose him off." He indicated the area with smooth gray floors covered in a green carpet-like cover with holes for the water to drain. Her gaze lifted to the red hoses suspended from a metal contraption on the ceiling. He flipped a switch then, and rows of overhead lights flickered on.

Emmy squinted, looking away. "I only walked him around the property a bit. A wash-down won't be necessary. Sh-sh, it's all right boy," she crooned, entering Obie's stall and offering up a carrot. He snatched it from her palm and stomped an impatient hoof for more, not unlike a spoiled child. She gave him two more of the tiny carrots from the interesting clear bag and turned to leave, running right smack into the tall cowboy again outside the stall door.

"If you'd care to go on inside the house, I'll get this boy fed."

"I enjoy doing this sort of thing, Mr. Stockton."

"Kade."

"*Kade,*" she repeated, dragging his name out and emphasizing the D. There wasn't a call to be so witchy, she knew that. But things were confusing right now, and she didn't need an over-confident ranch hand making it worse. Especially one who flaunted bare arms, all muscled and inked. And smelled so ... nice. "I am perfectly capable of handling my horse."

"Suit yourself."

As he turned and walked away, Emmy caught herself staring at the subtle bulge of muscles on broad shoulders, and his dungarees so flagrantly displaying tight hips. Strange the way everyone wore abbreviated clothing here. He disappeared into the room where the feed was kept.

"Are you always so bossy?" she called out.

He stuck his head back out. "Suppose so. Don't mean anything by it. Must be the military background. Need to do it right the first time, otherwise may not get a second chance."

"I see. And your way is always the right way?" Emmy exited Obie's stall, sliding the latch into place, and then testing it. Her horse had been known to work them loose, only to be discovered half a mile away dilly-dallying in a clover patch.

"I like to think things through."

"Thank you again, Mr. Stockton, for caring for my horse. I would appreciate it you fed him some grain," Emmy said, turning on a heel and heading toward the huge double doors, skirts swishing about her legs. Whoever he was, he certainly had a way of making her feel inadequate.

CHAPTER 6

Auntie Em

Out of breath, Madison burst into the back door of the kitchen.

"Colt?" she called out. Seeing Katie and Charlie at the dining room table coloring, she went to them and placed a kiss on each forehead.

"What's that for?" Charlie asked.

"Because I'm your mom and can kiss you whenever I like." She smiled down at him, ruffling his hair.

"Momma, we are coloring hippopotamuses," Charlie explained. It was his favorite word this week, and he used it as often as possible.

"Not me," Katie added, expression focused and intense. "Me coloring a baby sloth."

"*I am* coloring a baby sloth," Madison corrected. "So, where is daddy?"

"He's working in his office," both chimed in at once.

"Color a pretty picture for me, okay? I'm going to talk to Daddy."

Moments later, Madison found her husband behind the double doors of his office at the end of the hallway, an expansive room that didn't look much different than it had a hundred-plus years before. A massive oak desk sat before rows of bookshelves. Rich paneled walls glistened in the solitary light upon the desk. Curtains ruffled in the breeze from an open window.

"I'm sorry to bother you."

"Couldn't bother me if you tried, Sugar," Colt responded, looking up to catch the distress on his wife's face. "What's wrong?" He came out of his chair and approached all in one movement. She met him halfway, falling into his arms.

"I went up the hill. To the cemetery. It's been nagging at me since our conversation last night."

He set her back at arm's length, searching her face, "And? What did you find?"

Her words were low as she tried to keep the tremor from her voice. "Emmy's headstone is different. I stared at it, thinking I must have lost my mind. I have an awful feeling, Colt. What can we do?" Knees weak, she stepped out of his embrace and sank into an easy chair. Absently, she worked the toe of her sneaker across what appeared to be an old bullet hole in the floorboards, repaired, sanded and stained to blend in. She wondered why she hadn't noticed it before.

Colt chewed his cheek in thought, "What are the dates—on the headstone?"

"Yesterday," she replied, so faint he had to step closer to hear. "In 1888."

Madison pressed a finger to her lips, still staring at the oak floors, scarred with over a hundred years of everyday life. If Emmy were here with them now, alive and well, how could it be that the headstone even existed at all?

"Let me see the picture again," she asked, looking up at him.

Colt went to the desk drawer and drew out a ragged paper sleeve, yellowed and watermarked with age, removing the vintage photo inside. Its condition was far from ideal, moisture and heat having taken its toll. A random crease marred the center, and three corners were dog-eared—the fourth gnawed by rodents. He passed the photograph to his wife. Madison held it, studying it like she had many times since Buck discovered it inside an old steamer trunk in the attic of the carriage house, during the remodel a few years back.

The photograph was clearly 19th-century. A native American on his paint pony. But it was the man who stood beside the horse that interested her. He was quite handsome, with an impression of dark hair beneath a light-color hat, and pale-hued, striking eyes. His smile was broad, admittedly a bit blurry. Did he move when the photographer took the photo? Even beyond a lack of focus, a dimple was evident on his right cheek.

The first thing Buck noted about the picture was, "Looks a bit like Graham's boy. Wonder if he had family in this area way back when?"

Madison studied it for a long while then shook her head, "I can't help but think the same thing you do about this picture. But there's something else," she added, slipping the cardboard-like photo back into the sleeve.

"I'm listening."

"I dug out the letter Emmy wrote as an old woman. The one the lawyer delivered to me that day back when I was pregnant and feared I had lost you forever. I needed to read it again. But, "she paused, taking a breath, "... it wasn't there."

Colt stepped closer. "What do you mean it wasn't there?"

"I found its envelope, but the pages of the letter were blank. I don't know what to make of it."

The sharp chime of the doorbell shattered the silence.

"Are we expecting anyone?" She came to her feet and Colt stepped around her.

"Wait here," he said.

Old habits. Making certain all was safe, he would insist she remain behind while he checked to see who came calling. When Madison peeked around her husband's broad shoulder, she caught sight of a black and gold Teton County Sheriff's vehicle from the front window. She moved around to stand beside him as he swung open the front door.

"Good morning, sir," greeted a law officer. "I'm Deputy Dillard with the Teton County Sheriff's Office."

He wore reflective aviator sunglasses and the usual khaki and brown civil servant uniform, a clipboard and envelope in his hand. A lady deputy stood beside him. Colt knew several of the deputies that worked in the department, those who routinely patrolled the area. Dillard didn't look familiar.

"Morning, Deputy. How can we help you—everything all right?"

"That's what I'm looking into. May I have your name, sir?"

"Colton Chase, and this is my wife, Madison."

"Mr. Chase, may I ask how long you've been residing here at the Johnson Ranch?"

Colt and Madison glanced at one another in confusion before looking back.

"I'm sorry, but this is the Triple Bar C. The Johnson Ranch was—" He intended on stepping onto the porch so as to point to the southwesterly direction, but the deputy lifted a hand to stop him.

"Please remain inside the doorway, if you don't mind, Mr. Chase."

Colt halted, finishing with a frown, "—used to be south five miles or so, but it's all houses now. Sold off in parcels. What's all this about, Deputy?"

"This here *is* Johnson Ranch property, Mr. Chase. There isn't a record of you or your wife having permission to live here. Now, I don't know how long you've been here, but there are laws against squatters."

"Squatters?" Colt and Madison parroted in unison.

"This is ridiculous, Deputy," she continued. "We've lived here in this house, on this land, for well over a hundred years. This is *our home!*" Then, realizing the context, she amended, "What I mean is, the Chase family home."

"I'm not sure who you are, but all that will be sorted out in a court of law. Right now, I can advise you to retain an attorney for legal counsel. What I have here is an order to vacate signed by a judge." He held up the envelope and pushed the clipboard forward. "I'll need both your signatures right here."

"This is a enormous mistake. Who sent you here?"

Deputy Dillard studied Colt from behind mirrored lenses before looking down to flip through some pages on the clipboard. After a moment he looked up again. "An Elmer O. Johnson is the petitioner and owner of this property. If you possess a lease or legal document giving you permission to occupy this property, your legal representative will want to see it. Take note of the date noted in the paperwork. We will return then and make sure the premises have been vacated. Have a good day, sir."

"Wait," Colt said, and Dillard paused. "Who is the acting Sheriff of your department?"

"That would be Sheriff Tim Wilson. Is there anything else?"

Colt sighed. "No. That's all."

With that, both deputies swiveled on the heels of glossy black boots and trotted down the porch steps, entering the Dodge Charger and leaving the dumbstruck couple to digest the bizarre information. Katie and Charlie wormed into the doorway as the police interceptor rolled along the circle driveway and disappeared over the rise.

"Daddy, what did the policeman want?" Charlie asked, head poking out between them.

"I'm hungry, Mommy," Katie added, looping arms around her mother's waist. Bending down, Madison tucked her daughter's blond curls behind an ear before scooping her into her arms, clutching the little girl as if never intending to let go. The family shuffled inside, and Colt shut the door, locking it for good measure.

"What ... just happened?" she asked.

"Give me a minute," Colt responded. He ruffled Charlie's hair, sending him into the kitchen. "Finish coloring a picture for me, son, and we'll make your lunch in a bit."

"Okay, Daddy! It's really pretty."

Charlie broke into a run. Katie wiggled until her mother set her feet to the floor and she followed suit, their chatter echoing from the dining room.

"I'm confused. Isn't the sheriff's name Orson Black?" Madison asked. "And didn't you have lunch with him a month or so ago?"

Colt's gaze grew weary as he looked at his wife, the aqua eyes he loved so much starting to mist over. "You're right. I've met Sheriff Black several times. No idea who Tim Wilson is."

"I don't understand. And Johnson Ranch? What was that about? Wait." She pushed fingers to her forehead to quell the building pressure. "Could it possibly be what I'm thinking?"

Colt ripped open the envelope, unfolding the paper inside and skimming the contents before passing it to Madison.

"A repeat of the freak thunderstorm. Emmy's appearance. The dates somehow changed on the headstone. And now the ranch," he said, pacing the length of the room, to the stone fireplace and back again. "Something has gone terribly wrong with the time line. Maybe because Emmy came forward in time, thus her death occurred in 1888." He shook his head, "I hate to say it, but it's possible Miller Johnson, or rather his heirs, own this spread."

After spending time with Obie, and then taking a quiet stroll with the dogs around the garden and east pastures, Emmy entered the house via the newly constructed mudroom, passing by the arched doorway into the dining room. The youngsters sat at the rectangular table, busy drawing with waxy chalk pencils in a rainbow of colors. What had Katie and Charlie called them? It was another C word....

Her musings were interrupted by the sound of conversation in the front parlor, and she aimed in that direction to greet her hosts before continuing upstairs to freshen up. Pressing closer, she hesitated in the shadows. The serious tone of Colt's voice gave her pause.

"*Miller Johnson?*" Madison said. "Didn't Emmy speak of him last night? I think I remember him from the ranch rodeo. Wait, didn't you find him passed out in the barn the next mor—?"

"One and the same," Colt finished, tone scalding. Determined strides took him to the bay window where he pivoted, retracing his steps. "He had the youngest Woods girl with him all night. Caused all sorts of issues with her family. Miller isn't a kid anymore. Something has gone very wrong. There's only one thing to do. I've got to go back."

At the tense words, Emmy pressed her spine to the wall, the coolness reminding her to breathe. *Did he mean return to 1888?* She would not stand for it! She reached into her skirt pocket, fingers closing around the very same rosebud from yesterday. Had she only been here twenty-four hours? It seemed much longer. She looked at it, expecting to find the flower squashed, mutilated, wilted. The truth widened her eyes. How could it be? It appeared as fresh as it had been on the vine!

"No, Colt—there must be another way," Madison pleaded, hot on his trail as he paced.

"If there is, I can't think of it right now."

"I won't let you go. You have a family now. What if you can't get back home?" she asked, tears welling at the terrifying possibility.

"If I don't go, we don't have a home."

Little feet clomped down the hallway, jarring Emmy from the drama unfolding before her. Not only was she stunned, but she also felt sneaky hovering behind the lip of the doorway. She stepped into the open then. Whatever the source of their upset, she must find a way to help.

"Auntie Em!" the twins crowed, bounding up to grip her skirts with little fists made for sculpting mud pies and drawing pictures.

They dissolved into giggles whenever they called her that, and Emmy wondered why they found it so funny. She squatted to their level and pulled the two wriggling children into her arms.

"Come now. Give Auntie a big hug. She needs it right now."

A moment passed and their parents stood beside her, too. When she straightened, she opened her arms to the woman she had grown to love, pulling her into a vehement embrace.

"I overheard," Emmy said. "Whatever's wrong, I promise to help however I can. There's a solution, I know it! This is all my fault, isn't it?"

"No," Colt and Madison voiced in unison.

"If the time continuum is this fragile, something was bound to happen eventually," Colt said. "We'll figure it out."

"Why is everyone crying?" Katie asked, her tone much too serious for a five-year-old. Arms akimbo, she glared first at her father, and then the others.

"The *girls* are crying," Charlie corrected with a roll of big green eyes.

"Sometimes girls and boys both cry," Colt explained. "And if you two don't get busy washing up for the midday meal, I may cry, too. Now git." He gave a play lunge and the twins squealed, racing down the hallway. He looked to Madison and Emmy, "We have some serious discussing to do. First, let's make a hefty batch of peanut paste and jam sandwiches. At this point, I need sustenance as much as the twins do."

CHAPTER 7

Revelation

After an evening meal of tacos, then baths followed by story time for the twins, the sun ducked behind spiky granite peaks, leaving a magenta glow in its wake.

"This table has witnessed a lot of history," Madison noted, sitting down beside Emmy. "I remember joining the family for supper that first evening with the Chase household in 1878. The fried chicken and mashed potatoes were to die for."

"I could eat tacos every day," Emmy gushed with a laugh. "The spices, oh my. I love chili pepper!"

Madison grinned, turning wistful.

"Your mama was an amazing cook, and everyone was so kind to me—well, except for Garrett. He didn't like me from the beginning. I was so angry with Colt that night. But, you know, I loved him—even then."

"I wasn't very kind to you, not at first." Emmy bowed her head, "and I'm so sorry about that. I understand now."

"You were young, confronted with this strange woman. How could you? But we grew close." Madison smiled, her green gaze lifting to Emmy's hazel one.

"Like sisters."

Colt meandered into the kitchen in his sock feet with a bottle of Sonoma Valley merlot in tow. Shirttail hanging loose and wearing a close-cropped beard these days, he was as handsome as ever. Emmy didn't miss the weariness in his rich brown eyes. After the dire news the sheriff had delivered, Colt had grown pensive, retiring to his office for several hours, while she, Madison, and the children worked in the garden. Something Emmy and Madison both shared—a need to keep their hands busy when a problem required working out.

Emmy felt for this strong man who used to run the ranch she grew up on. *How could this have happened?* How was it she had come to be here in the first place, only for the Chase family to discover the ranch doesn't belong to them anymore? That awful storm had made her dizzy and nauseous—and though the sickness had faded along with the thunder and rain, the discombobulation remained.

Colt rummaged through a drawer for a wine screw and pulled free the cork, lifting four glasses from the cabinet shelf. He joined Emmy and Madison at the table.

"Trust me, something stronger is mighty tempting," he vowed with a lift of an eyebrow as he sat down. He poured three glasses before setting the bottle to the side, both women thanking him.

"It's clear what needs to be done," Emmy said. "I must return home. It's possible, isn't it? I mean, with my disappearance, Zak, Hanna, Henry, and Estelle, all of them will be looking for me. I'll be considered dead, don't you think? That's the only outcome I can think of."

"Let's not jump to conclusions. You can't go back with the unrest that's going on," Madison said.

"With what I've learned, I know what needs to be done. Once I'm back, I won't be considered ... dead." She focused on her lap and clasped her hands. "I saw my headstone. The dates."

"Oh no! Emmy, you shouldn't have gone up there," Madison said.

She looked up. "I had to! I assume the dates were different before I got here. Those details aren't easy to digest, but harder to ignore. I will make certain everything returns to normal. Only then will this be the Bar C again!"

"That's all well and good," Colt said, pushing a hand through his hair. "But what happens when the range wars close in? Who's to say it won't trigger something else? Emmy, if anything were to happen to you, *now* we know the ramifications. Miller Johnson found a way to acquire this ranch. Whatever happened, it was something I didn't consider five years ago when I put everything together. This afternoon I backtracked my actions, pinpointing a couple of things I might have missed. If anything, this is my fault.

"There's something else," Emmy said. Both Colt and Madison looked up, waiting. Gathering the courage to speak of it, she stood up with an inhale and walked to the window over the kitchen sink. So familiar, and yet not. Every now and then she saw figures of workers passing under huge lights illuminating the barn. "I suppose I was embarrassed by my vulnerability. There was a man—he came into the house one night."

Madison gasped, "What happened?"

"He attacked me from behind—"

"Any idea *who* it was?" Agitated, Colt came to his feet.

"At the time, I figured it might have been someone associated with the Carlson boys. I never found out one way or another. Suppose I just wanted to erase it from my mind." She hugged her arms, moving back to the table. "If I didn't speak of it, then maybe it wasn't real. Silly, I know. I wasn't hurt, other than a few bruises. And my pride. I don't think the man's vision was good. He had me from behind, like this." She demonstrated. "He wanted me to open the safe, but he stumbled on the coat tree outside the office door. I took advantage and stomped his foot."

Colt snorted, "I can think of something better you could've done with your knee. What happened then?"

"I went for the rifle, but when I came back, the front door was hanging open and ... he was gone."

"Did you get a good look at him?"

Emmy shook her head, "Only saw dark hair. He was dirty. A gray hat, bushy mustache, scar on his chin. And like I said, I don't think he could see well."

"That's terrible, Emmy. I'm so sorry you had to go through that," Madison said, lost in thought as she studied the swirl of burgundy liquid in her glass, taking a sip. "I have an idea." She tapped a fingernail on the table in thought. Both Colt and Emmy looked up, waiting for her to finish. "Colt, you and I first got together in the year 1878."

"How could I forget?" A warm smile spread over his jaw.

"So that was almost six years ago for us," Madison pondered. "And yesterday, Emmy moved forward from 1888. The math is jumbled; doesn't make sense. The roses hold secrets we can't begin to know. We haven't seen a rose up on the ridge in years. And, Colt, you're right, we don't know what is set in motion for the future—or rather, the past. Wait! Research—that's what I'll do!"

On her feet, Madison disappeared down the hallway, returning a moment later with a flat black book. Emmy scooted close, watching her lift the lid on a wondrous object to peer inside, her face bathed in a blue glow. Eyes wide, she watched in mounting excitement as Madison's fingers flew over the black and white letters without any effort at all.

"I saw a demonstration of a Caligraph typing machine at the county fair a few years back. Is this like that?" Emmy asked. She loved all these new contraptions and wished she didn't have to go back so soon.

"More or less. This is called a laptop computer. It gathers information, types words, computes like an adding machine, and communicates all over the world like a telephone."

"All inside there?" Emmy asked, propping elbows on the table and pillowing her chin in her palms. Tentative, she reached out to touch the blue light with the pad of an index finger. "The paper is inside there?"

"Yes, ma'am. It's not actually paper. It's called a screen and responds when you touch it. See, like this." She placed a fingertip on the screen's surface, highlighting letters in blue, enlarging and then shrinking pictures. Emmy laughed at the mesmerizing movement of the images. "It performs the same way as paper when you write on it or take photographs."

"Now isn't that impressive. I wish I had one of those at Montana University. What are you using it for now? I apologize if I'm being nosy. Mama used to tell me to button it up or tend to my own knittin' when I asked too many questions."

Madison placed a hand over Emmy's and squeezed. "I've missed you so much! You nosy? Never. Curiosity is an admirable quality. Now, what I'm doing is looking up the history of the Wyoming range wars."

"So, it's like a library in a box." An expression of wonder crossed Emmy's face as images and text rolled past. The speed of it made her eyes cross. Colt moved up behind and the trio continued discussing recorded history. "This is amazing. It's like the history books from school."

"I don't want you to be upset by any of this information," Colt said, looking out the window and heading to the back door. "Things must seem surreal to you right now."

"But I need to know. Though I feel I'm cheating by looking at this. Peering into the future of my neighbors, the people of Wyoming ... even myself."

"It's valuable information. Similar to how a change of ownership of the Triple Bar C seems to have occurred in the last 24 hours, so could recorded history. Take it with a grain of salt."

Men's voices echoed from the direction of the mudroom construction project, and Colt excused himself. What had been the kitchen door opening to the wraparound porch, was now an entrance into a mudroom with plans of children's backpack storage, along with seating benches and racks for muddy shoes and coats. Paned windows lined two walls, retaining views of the garden, pastures, and the big red barn from an extension of the porch. She heard Kade Stockton and the ranch foreman, Buck Epson, had joined forces to get the room finished and painted before the start of the school year. It was to be the first year of kindergarten for the twins.

Emmy leaned back in her chair just in time to see Kade Stockton enter the space with an armload of cut lumber, depositing it into a corner. He stood several inches taller than Colt, as well as an older man who followed him inside with what looked to be a toolbox.

"This'll do it for the shelves on the left side," Kade explained. "We'll start tomorrow afternoon. Should have them up in a few hours, give or take. I think cabinets along this wall would be a nice addition. That's up to you, though."

Colt laughed, motioning them inside, "I'll discuss it with the boss. Come on in."

"Leave it to Kade to go and suggest more work for us," the older man interjected with a hearty guffaw. He deposited the toolbox into the corner and both men wiped their feet at the door.

"Anything to keep you busy, old man." Kade's lips hitched into an abbreviated smile.

He does have a nice smile. But that's neither here nor there.

"Can I get you two something to drink?" Colt offered. "Opened a bottle of wine; you're welcome to join us. I'd like you to meet Emmy Bartlett. You could say she's somewhat of a little sister to me."

Emmy gazed past Colt to the older man in a plaid shirt with hair a shock of silver and eyes a cheerful blue. She had to look at him twice. He reminded her of Bud, and for a moment she thought she had seen a ghost. She nodded, "A pleasure."

"Nice to meet you, Emmy." Buck stepped forward and extended his hand for a firm shake. "Ah, no wine for me. Just finished the last of Angela's chili leftovers."

"I'm amazed there were any leftovers to be had," Madison said.

"Extra good this time, too. She even made another batch of jalapeño cornbread."

Kade entered the room a few steps behind Buck. His tall form filled the doorway, contemplating the room first before lingering on her. She shifted away from Buck's merry gaze, lost in the ranch hand's moodier one. His eyes seemed indigo in this light. Somehow, he made her feel as though she were being dissected. When Colt started to introduce him, Emmy spoke.

"I believe we've met, Mr. Stockton. Nice to see you again," she lied. Even more than the man's apparent arrogance, something else made her uneasy. Maybe it was his size, tall, rugged. Or the way he looked at her, like a wolf eyeing its prey.

"Likewise," he responded with a lift of his chin, voice commanding in this small space.

She broke his gaze, and though he wasn't in her line of sight, she continued to feel him.

"All right if I pour myself a cup of that coffee?" Kade asked, indicating the half-full glass pot. "Can I pour you one, too, old man?" He glanced at Buck, a twinkle in those eyes.

"Naw," Buck said. "You go ahead. Too late for me. I'll take a glass of water though."

"Of course, Kade. Help yourself," Madison said. "Sorry, the coffee is from breakfast. You'll have to pop it into the microwave."

"Not a problem," Kade said.

Curious, Emmy's directed her focus back to Kade Stockton. Hard not to do since his persona filled the entire room. From a full, dark head of hair to pronounced shoulders and arms—and that shirt, why it was downright indecent. More like a pared-down union suit hugging his body, she thought. Eyes clear and alert under a heavy brow. What ghosts did they conceal?

A capable hand fisted the coffee pot handle, and he filled his cup then opened a black cabinet, setting the cup inside. The door clicked shut. He brushed a long finger across a panel at the front and it lit up with a humming sound. Transfixed, Emmy stared at the checkered light illuminating the cup going around in circles like a tiny merry-go-round.

The resulting *ding* made her jump, snapping her out of her stupor. Flustered, she realized Kade was watching her watching the cup. Hot blood stung her cheeks, and his mouth lifted into a succinct grin. She looked away.

After he retrieved a glass of water from the colossal white ice box that dropped ice from outside the door, passing it to Buck, the two men pulled out chairs and joined them at the table. Emmy thought how strange it was ... the comfort of *her* table. Only older. In the same kitchen. Almost.

With this man sitting at it.

"Don't want to interrupt your work here," Buck said. "I'm sure you kids are catching up. We'll be on our way soon."

"Nonsense. We welcome the company," Madison said, glancing at Colt for confirmation, and they shared a long look.

"Since you're here, there are a few things you two should be aware of," Colt expanded, drawing another look from his wife. She nodded and touched his arm.

"How's that?" Buck asked, expression turning serious. "Something going on?"

"Nothing too obvious right now, but there are some people who seem to think the Bar C belongs to them. Legal ... loopholes, you might say."

"*Who?*" Buck asked, brows drawing low. "I grew up nearby and know just about everyone."

"Came as a surprise, and we aren't aware of the details yet. You may have seen the Sheriff's car here earlier."

"Saw it drive off," Buck said.

"Bottom line, I need to figure out a few things. I wanted you both to know. Kade, if you'll pass the information on to Graham, I'd be obliged. Don't mention it to any of the hands. I'll most likely be gone for a few days—"

"Colt," Madison interrupted, eyes wide, "we talked about this. I won't let you go! There must be another way."

He reached for her hand. "I'm sorry. Still not for certain what needs to be done, but a decision must be made soon."

"But what do you hope to accomplish?" Madison asked.

"Won't know until I get there. Things need to be stabilized. Set right. Who are the men terrorizing the Bar C? They need to be put in their places. And if that means in the ground, then so be it."

"Maybe it's Miller Johnson's family line." Madison theorized, eyes first on Colt and then to Emmy.

"Old Man Johnson died a few years back," Emmy explained. "Agnes, his wife, passed some time before that. All that's left of the immediate Johnson family are Miller and his two older sisters. They married into the Merrick's out of Billings, Montana." She shook her head in thought, "Miller speaks of growing his holdings as big as the Merrick Ranch. I get the feeling he tries to compete with his sisters, or with the Bar C. Maybe both. I don't see why he needs to compete. He raises sheep, a different thing altogether."

Emmy came to her feet, unable to tolerate the confusion and pain in their eyes. She went to stand by the back door, hugging her arms tight as she watched Sage, Brush, and Candy gambol across the yard, Dottie darting in between their legs and rolling in the grass.

Craziness. Their lives are upended, and it's all my fault!

She returned to the table, wringing her hands as she walked.

"I refuse to allow you to go back, Colt," she said. "I can manage what needs to be done. It's my responsibility now. Let me do what I need to do. With the knowledge I have, I can make certain nothing happens to the Bar C. There, it's settled. I'm heading up to the ridge at first light."

"No, Emmy," Colt insisted, "I stand a better chance, with the help of Zak and the sheriff—"

"Is it because I'm a female?"

"Now you know that's not the case."

"*You know me, Colt!* If it weren't for me, you'd be minus a leg. *You're* the one who taught me how to shoot. And you know I don't take any bull...." she paused, tempering her language, aware of Buck's and Kade's eyes upon her. She had been told the ranch foreman and his wife knew about the time travel. But when she glanced at Kade, the expression on his face alarmed her.

Does he know about the roses on the ridge, too?

"This is none of my business," Kade interjected, focus breaking away from Emmy and landing on Colt. "I don't know what's going on, but clearly this is serious. You know my background. If there's something I can do to help out...."

The conversation bounced back and forth, and the next thing Emmy knew, Kade had offered to help her get home safely. Judging by the way he spoke, he hadn't an inkling where *home* was. When she attempted to butt in, both he and Colt acted as if she weren't even there.

Damn men!

"Listen here," she upped the volume, stepping closer and slamming her hands to her hips. "You two can hash things out back and forth until the cows come home. But I, for one, am not cowering down from those outlaws, whoever the hell they are! Believe me, I have a few questions for Miller. As soon as I study Madison's library-in-a-box a bit more, I plan on heading home with Obie and the dogs. I caused this mess, and I'm going to fix it!"

At that, Madison jumped up from the table. "Well now, who's down for popcorn?" she asked with forced glee. "Emmy, let's get you in front of the TV and we'll settle in and watch The Wizard of Oz. Remember I promised to explain why the kiddos call you Auntie Em? Now come on. It'll be fun!"

Without allowing a chance for rebuttal, Madison dragged the reluctant woman down the hallway and away from the ample amounts of androgenic hormones in the kitchen. Stumbling behind, Emmy glanced over her shoulder to see Colt, Kade, and Buck leaning in close for more conversation. She didn't have a good feeling about this.

CHAPTER 8

Don't Look Back

Madison wanted popcorn, or so she said. Clever idea to get Emmy out of the conversation for a bit; she looked rattled, and for good reason. Her description of the situation at her place angered him. Death and destruction, people helping themselves to things that weren't theirs. It was as if he were having an out-of-body experience when he volunteered to accompany a stranger home.

The conversation had ceased, everyone glaring at him as if he had just sprouted horns. Emmy stopped her nervous pacing—floating across the kitchen floor in that long dress, chewing a thumbnail. She stiffened, hazel eyes flashing at him like fireworks. He couldn't tell if she liked the idea or was considering wrapping her hands around his neck.

Colt and his wife hadn't been so quick, both interested in what he had to say. It eliminated the necessity of Chase himself making the trip back to ... wherever.

Not like Kade had a lot of responsibilities. No wife or children. Tori got the house, boat, and dog. Not much in the way of family ties, except for Dad and Sean, and they had their own lives. Bottom line, he was expendable. What better time to have a little adventure, check it out and see how he could assist.

Sure, he'd go 'back in time.' He remembered training missions in the Appalachians and the hollers of West Virginia. Had hiked through remote villages in Afghanistan that looked to be straight out of the 1800s. It did explain Emmy's strange mode of dress and the severe bun knotted at the back of her head. At first, he thought she may have been from Mormon Row, the Amish community near the iconic Moulton barn. Few folks remained at the settlement these days, but there were some traditionalists.

Then Colt mentioned 1888. Nobody laughed. Kade wasn't convinced, but what did he have to lose? Always had been the first one to enter the spook house on Halloween. And so, it was. Back to the Triple Bar C Ranch—the 1888 version.

He packed a compact army-green backpack with a few essentials, changes of clothes, shampoo, toothbrush & paste, deodorant, and a bar of soap—doubtful he'd find his favorite brand where he was going, amused at the thought. And of course, his iPhone, fully charged with a secondary battery pack, a plethora of maps and history articles downloaded for reference. He ducked out the door of his cabin before dawn, grabbing his guitar in afterthought.

Kade and Emmy rode in silence up the switchback trail to a place known as Rosebush Ridge, the 'magic' place he'd been told about. He chose to ride Skitter, the amazing sidestepping wonder—a hefty part-Arab palomino gelding with an affinity for randomly stepping to the side. And he did it with such grace. Having crafted a sling that fit on the side of a saddle for his guitar, he was good to go.

Kade's thoughts focused on the woman riding in front of him. The weighty light-brown braid queued down her back, swinging with the rhythm of her horse. Had a touch of blonde in it when the sun grazed it. Did she ever unravel it? Of course, she did. That first morning he had seen her in the window looking down at him, her hair undone. Must be a chore to wash it, he thought. Had to be down to her hips.

He tried not to think about those either, though he'd have to be dead not to notice her curves, despite being hidden under a long dress. He caught himself studying her shapely behind dipping first to one side and then the other in the saddle, beneath yards of depressing black material.

Intriguing eyes, too. And lips. For a woman over a hundred years old.

Kade groaned inwardly. How old was he, fourteen?

Good thing history was one of the few subjects he managed to reap good grades in, along with math and home economics, that is. Home Ec only because he knew if he laid on the charm thick enough, the girls tripped over one another to help with his homework. All that was ancient history, before he got himself kicked out of school altogether for a stupid senior prank, ending up in cold-ass Kansas for basic training.

"You have a family," Kade had said, agreeing with Colt's wife. "Just let me know what I need to do, and I'll take care of it to the best of my ability."

Was he crazy? Who does this?

In a perfect world, a show of force went a long way, stand up to the intruders, calm a few tempers, and with any luck, settle at least a small portion of the Wyoming range dispute. He remembered bits and pieces of the range war history. Not only was it a bunch of Texas hoodlums—it also included corrupt politicians and state government. Ranchers were stuck in the middle. He loved history. Read everything he could get his hands on back when he was a kid. Turn down a chance to live it? No way.

Besides, a stint in the simplistic time of 1888 sounded intriguing. He was always up for a challenge, feeling sure he could handle a horde of outlaws with a grudge. How hard could it be?

After coming to an agreement with his boss, the two men shook hands and Colt thanked him for his sacrifice—not only for military service but for stepping up to set things straight with the troublemakers.

"Oh, one more thing," Colt had added before the two men retired for the night. "A friendly warning, don't be surprised if your stomach gets all twisted on the trip back, and you lose your chow."

Emmy broke the silence, interrupting his thoughts. "I think it's around this rock."

Steering Obie around a massive boulder, the three dogs trotted alongside, their own demeanors serious. One of the retrievers moved ahead and planted his butt next to an ugly bush underneath an even uglier pine tree. He panted in a come-hither way.

"This it?" He reined to a stop behind her, dismounting his horse.

Emmy looked at him as if she could stare a hole right through and keep going. Couldn't blame her for disliking his presence. From his perspective, she wasn't an overly affable woman herself. But he had a job to do and was accustomed to being disliked for one reason or another. They should get along fine. Besides, whatever created that haunted look in her eyes was likely something to which he could relate.

Kade watched her slide from the saddle, ramrod stiff, in a flounce of equally stiff black skirts, marching over to that spruce tree. He wasn't convinced. But that didn't stop an icy fear from inching into his gut.

"Can I help with something?" he offered, striving to relax as she crawled on hands and knees in the pine needles, fanny bobbing side-to-side.

"Ah, here it is." She sat up with a vine in her hand, the origin embedded in the bark of the tree. A half-dozen perky pink rosebuds dangled from it.

"That's it?" Kade asked, and she nodded as if she weren't quite sure herself.

"Are you ready?" she asked.

Hell no.

Not waiting for his blessing, she pinched off a random bud and tucked the vine back under the tree before scrambling to her feet, ignoring the hand he held out. She marched back to her horse, face a mask of austerity as she snatched up the reins and swung back into the saddle as if she had done that very thing every day of her life. Must admit, she had a talent for riding horseback in a skirt. He watched her remove a foot from the stirrup and extend her leg, exposing an old-fashioned boot and frumpy stockings. The little black and white dog she called Dottie took a leap and scampered up, wiggling into a gap between the saddle and her body.

The two retrievers stood alongside, alerted to something he hadn't become aware of yet. Looking around, Kade mounted his horse. Just in time. A threatening bank of thunderheads rolled in their direction, gliding over peaks, blackening the sky. He stared in awe, cringing as they neared and exploded overhead just like Colt had told him they would. He then found himself fighting a spooked horse while covering his head with a free arm.

"Hold on!" he called out, wondering if he meant the words for her or himself.

Lightning spiked from the clouds, scorching the grass nearby.

Time travel. Yeah, right.

Wind buffeted, picking up dried leaves, pine needles and branches, swirling them through the air, the rain falling in a deluge of blinding sheets. Then came a sickening lurch of what he could only describe as the earth moving. Skitter whinnied, rearing up on two legs and it was all Kade could do to stay in the saddle. A deafening whir of voices filled his head, causing his ears to pound to the beat of his heart.

The world around them upended and went black. When Kade regained consciousness, he lay slumped forward on his horse, rain dripping from his hair and chin. He opened his eyes, focusing on his horse below him munching on a patch of grass. Stomach lurching, he dropped from the saddle and crawled to the nearest bush where he got sick. A moment later, Emmy knelt beside him and placed a hand on his shoulder.

CHAPTER 9

Should've Been a Cowboy

1888

K ade drove his shovel into the dirt, glancing toward ranch foreman, Zak Tompson. Skeptical pale blue eyes surveyed him from beneath a discerning brow and a sweep of dishwater blond hair, tamed by a beat-up western hat the color of tobacco. Kade went back to shoveling, and when he looked up again, Zak's stare threatened to burn a hole in his forehead.

"You got something to say? Spit it out."

"Don't know where Emmy found you at. Sometimes I think you're a little crazy, is all," the foreman replied.

A grin sliced across Kade's jaw, white against two days' worth of stubble and prairie dust. "Only a little? I consider that a damned nice compliment."

Gazing away and into the vacant horizon, he lifted his Stetson and mopped the sweat from his brow with a bandanna, tugging the hat back into position. He stuffed the bandanna into a back pocket. If Emmy hadn't told her foreman where she found him, then he sure as hell wasn't going to fill the void. That was her job. As for him, he still wasn't completely convinced, his chest clutching when he allowed himself to think too hard about it. The Bar C ranch was the same, and yet it wasn't. Far more rustic, and fewer buildings. There weren't any bathrooms unless you counted the few outhouses dotted around the bunkhouse area.

When he had climbed to his feet in the meadow that morning after the nasty storm, which had spiraled out of nowhere with speed like nothing he had ever experienced, Emmy had knelt beside him and touched his shoulder. Waiting, she rose to her feet alongside him.

"It's all right. Take a moment to catch your breath," she had said before stepping away, those eyes sweeping over him. "I think ... we're back."

"You okay?" he asked, for lack of anything else occupying the odd vacancy in his head. Who the hell is okay after what just happened? At the same time, disbelief and a sense of disappointment descended on him. Like Christmas morning after learning Santa didn't exist. This wasn't real either. *Yes, it is,* a voice inside argued. *Now get on your horse and stop acting like a weenie.* Not appearing overly bothered, Skitter had stood a few feet away with a stubborn tuft of grass wedged between his lip and the bit, eyes half closed.

Emmy had acknowledged his question with a slight nod, then turned to inspect the lifting fog before swinging astride her horse and waiting for him to do the same.

Kade's head still swam in dizziness, and he felt numb. Disoriented. The forest growth looked different, sparser, and yet the same. He half expected Buck and Colt to come walking out of the cover of the trees, laughing, and giving him a clap on the back. *Can't believe you fell for that!*

And then, they had ridden in silence except for the cheery chirps of birds, single file down the trail until the trees opened into a vast ranchland as far as one could see. Like a vintage photograph that had been colorized. He brought Skitter to a halt and could only stare at the familiar—so different. People had rushed up to Emmy, women clothed in long dresses like hers, with smiles of relief, asking questions all at once. Eventually, those curious eyes rested upon him, and he was introduced as someone who was there to help. Was he—there to help? At that moment he wasn't even completely convinced of where he was.

Zak's voice brought Kade back to the moment.

"I can't claim to know your past, but this ranch is my responsibility, Stockton. My job is to ensure the safety of the stock and the men."

"Which is what you're doing, am I right?" Kade asked. "That and the protection of the ranch owner. Not to mention your own wife and kids."

Zak bristled at the newcomer's mention of his family.

"How will a series of channels along this valley keep anyone safe? If anything, it's creating a good place for a horse to break a leg. Emmy's likely to get herself and her horse killed while on one of those morning runs she does. Ever seen her do that? As fast as she takes Obie around the fence line, the last thing she needs is to run smack dab into a ditch. One of these holes will end up a grave for both of'em."

"Emmy's morning rituals will have to change. I'll make sure of it."

"Reckon you will, since she hired you all special like."

Zak tore his gaze away, the sole of his boot crushing onto the step of the shovel. Kade wondered if the ranch foreman envisioned his neck under that blade. A morbid grin itched the corner of his mouth.

He couldn't blame Zak for taking exception to his sudden appearance. According to what he had learned from the bunkhouse grapevine, Emmy had disappeared a few Sundays back. Had she gotten turned around in the mountains after a terrible thunderstorm? Maybe she had gotten hurt. Zak pointed out she'd been gone almost a week, had everyone searching, scared to death. Even her horse and the three dogs had vanished. Kade estimated two and a half days, but accuracy wasn't the point. Who knew how the time continuum worked anyhow?

He had learned a few things since arriving in the 19th century: Zak ran the place alongside two lesser-ranked foremen, all under Emmy's lead; Zak had worked the Chase family's Triple Bar C Ranch since he was a teen, back in the glory days of the illustrious gunslinging hero, Colton Chase. Back when Emmy was a young girl.

Kade could indeed imagine Colt as a gunfighter, but envisioning the starchy lady rancher as a young girl was a different thing. He figured Emmy to be five or six years his junior. The old-lady bun she wore was a fashion statement at this point in history, he supposed. He soon realized it to be a necessity for a woman working on the land.

He leaned on his shovel and surveyed the horizon.

"I'll explain to Emmy," he said. He needed to chat with her anyway. "However, it's up to you to advise the rest of the hands that the southwest forty is off limits, so as to prevent anyone from falling into one of these things. Got that? No one besides us and the few men helping to dig these holes needs to know about the trenches. Can I trust you to handle that?"

"Just what are the plans?" Zak asked. He didn't much care for this man's familiarity with his old friend. He dropped the shovel at his feet and lifted his hat to scrub the sweat from his forehead. "From my perspective, we've got an army of thieves threatening what's left of our herds. After the last two harsh winters, it's a damned miracle we have any cattle left. Lost almost every calf that year. We're finally getting the numbers back up and can't risk losing more. I used to ride this range alongside Colt Chase when he owned the place. He's done gone with his family now, but he taught me well. What are these trenches for, anyhow? You plan on killin' and buryin' the rustlers? We don't need the law comin' down on the ranch."

"From my research, it's more than a band of rogue rustlers. It's an organized coup originating two states south. Texas to be exact, and they won't stop until they get what they came for. I don't plan to kill anyone that doesn't need killing, but I suppose that's up to them." Kade stepped closer, propping his arms on the handle of the shovel. "They want more than cattle, Zak—they want the entire ranch. And I've been hired to make sure they don't get it."

"Naw, I don't think that's the case." Zak shook his head. "Maybe you're talkin' 'bout Miller Johnson. His Pa died a year back. Since Miller took control of the Johnson ranch, he's been more aggressive with Emmy. Had designs on her since they were both school-age, and it was innocent enough. But she doesn't mince words, says it like it is. Always has. Tells him no every time he comes a-callin'."

Kade considered this new information. "You make it sound like he's after her hand in marriage," he said, grateful the shadow of his hat hid his scowl. Colt had mentioned the Johnson dude, and he already didn't care for the guy. Protecting Emmy was a priority. If she was like a little sister to Colt, then he would see to her best interests.

"I reckon he is. Johnson ranch borders the Triple Bar C. I heard Old Man Johnson helped out when the Bar C was first homesteaded by Colt's folks. Johnson's ain't a small parcel, but not nearly the size of the Bar C. If Miller and Emmy were to marry, combining lands is an attractive option for both of em. You been here nigh on two weeks. A lots gone on in past years. Emmy used to be sweet on him."

A niggle of icy anger filled his gut. The last time he experienced that sensation, a woman was involved, but for an entirely different reason. No matter the context, he didn't like it and shook it off.

"Hey, boss, look here."

The call shook Kade from his thoughts. A man crested the rise astride a hefty sorrel horse, an arm swaying above his head. Kade discouraged any of the hands from referring to him as boss. That was Zak Brown's position, and he didn't need any more resentment from the foreman. He thrust the blade of his shovel into the soil.

"What is it?" Zak asked.

"Dead calf over the rise," he responded in a Mexican accent, reining up beside them and pointing.

"Dammit, another one? What happened?"

"Too small. My estimation is, the heifer standing over the calf is less than a year."

Zak shook his head, "Shame. Let's get it buried so we don't attract wolves or bears. Gather more of the boys and drive the herd to the north."

"What's all this?" The man squinted through the afternoon sun, referring to the men busy shoveling.

"As soon as I find out, I'll fill you in," Zak said. "Stockton, this here is Rainero, best tracker I've ever known. Not much gets past his keen eye."

Kade leaned in to shake the newcomer's hand. "Name's Kade Stockton, nice to meet you."

"Rainero Ignacio Estéban Mansilla. My pleasure," the man said with a wide smile.

Kade pondered for a bit, then, "How about I call you Scout?"

Rainero tilted his head back in laughter, "Scout it is, Señor Kade. What's all this?" he asked then, inclining his head to the trenches. "Looks like an embankment. Are you cutting in a choke point?"

This man knew what he was talking about all right. "Sure is."

"Need some loblolly," Scout advised. "Take a machete like this," he paused to demonstrate, "make points and then line up like a fence. Too far north for loblolly pine up here, but spruce trees might work good."

"I agree. I like your train of thought, Scout," Kade said. "We're going to pile the dirt on the far side of the trench."

"We gonna sit and wait for the rustlers to strike again?" Zak asked. "And how do we know they'll come up this particular draw?"

"Up there," Kade said, pointing to the crest of a grassy mesa, "is what we'll call the honeypot. The trenches divert traffic up the draw, the only way to get to it."

"A honey—what?"

"Honeypot is bait," Scout interjected.

"The herds are the bait," Kade elaborated with a nod to Scout. "Where we are now is the choke point, due to the narrowing of the passageway to get to the other side. "We'll use that over there," he continued, pointing to an imposing rusty orange bluff of rock. "The goal is to stop whoever tries to cross this draw."

"And how do we stop them? Outside of the trenches, I mean."

"Never my first choice to take a life, but a man must protect himself, property, and loved ones. Bands of thieves ride these hills. They take what isn't theirs and murder those who stand in their way. It's happening to your neighbors, good people. You told me yourself, rustlers have breached the boundaries of the Bar C and taken a good twenty head of prime beef. They'll be back, more aggressive each time. If we don't show 'em what we're made of, they'll take everything until they control this entire spread."

Zak nodded in understanding, thinking he should have taken steps earlier. This newcomer made some good points. The last thing he wanted was to put Emmy, Hanna, and his children in danger, and he would be doing just that if he didn't take a stand. He folded his arms and exhaled. "You have my cooperation, Stockton. I'll call a meeting at the bunkhouses tonight. I hope you'll come down with instructions."

"Sure, I'll be there."

Zak grabbed up the shovel and concentrated on starting a new trench ten feet away.

"Hey, Scout," Kade said, stopping the man as he began to ride off. "How about we have a talk after dinner? Few things I'd like to go over with you."

"Sure thing," Scout said, nudging his horse forward and disappearing over the rise.

Kade didn't bunk down with the others, selecting the upper level of the carriage house instead. It stood where his cabin was in the modern day, situated behind the big red barn, making it easy to tend to the stock last thing at night and first thing in the morning. Besides, his night terrors weren't something he chose to subject to anyone else, and he appreciated his privacy.

He sliced his shovel into the dirt, slinging two heaps onto the growing mound, pausing to focus on the silhouettes of a half-dozen men hard at work within the long shadows of a setting sun.

CHAPTER 10

Stand By Me

"Thank you, Detective," Emmy said, rising from a porch chair and extending her hand.

Nicholas Grayson, a WSGA—Wyoming Stock Growers Association—range detective assigned to Johnson County, followed her lead and stood, stretching long legs before closing her outstretched hand between his with a gentle shake.

"My pleasure, Miss Bartlett. It is Miss...?" he asked in a flash of white teeth.

She nodded. "All the more reason your presence provides peace of mind. There are plenty of men here at the Bar C, and I'm more than capable of handling a weapon. But I'm sure you'll agree, better if it doesn't become a necessity. Something needs to be done about the violence."

"I completely understand. I'll be riding the county line and commiserating with other landowners in these parts in the upcoming weeks. Your offer of a bunk, whenever I'm nearby, is much appreciated. The Triple Bar C is the largest spread in the county, if not the northern parts of the state, and I suspect I'll be in this area often."

"I insist," Emmy said. "You're welcome at the bunkhouse, as well as in the old cabin on the other side of the creek. It's a bit worse for the wear, though. It was Mama and Bud's place when he was alive. After he passed, Mama got lonely and wanted to stay here in the big house with me. Their place has fallen into disrepair, I'm afraid."

"That's too bad. Maybe I'll get the opportunity to help with some repairs in my spare time. If there is any spare time, that is." He laughed, pressing a black hat with a snakeskin band upon his head. She accompanied him to where his gelding stood tethered, tail swatting at flies. After mounting a gray horse that matched both the man's name and his steely eyes, he tapped his hat goodbye. With a push of a heel, his horse broke into a trot for the strip of road leading off the land and to Gunn Pass City.

Emmy turned, gasping to find herself nose to chest with Kade Stockton. She took two brisk steps backward, "You have a knack for sneaking up on a person."

.

"Um, thank you?" he responded dryly. "No sneaking about it. Came around the house when I didn't find you in the kitchen. You were so taken with the lone ranger there, I'm guessing you failed to notice."

"First of all, I'm not taken, as you reference it, with *anyone.* And why do you expect me to be in the kitchen?"

She skirted around him and marched up the gravel walkway, lifting her skirts to mount the porch steps. Kade followed.

"Just happens to be the room you're usually in when I need you. Emmy, I get the distinct feeling my presence irritates you, but for the record, I didn't come here to annoy you. I work for Colt Chase. I'm hoping to assist with your situation. After that, I'll be out of your hair."

Emmy halted at the top of the steps and rotated to face him. From this perspective, they stood at eye level, those icy-blue orbs of his stripping away her defenses and making her forget whatever it was she intended to say.

Get a hold of yourself!

She cleared her throat, pushing her palms down the front of her apron. "First off, you work for me now." A thick brow cocked up at that, though he didn't say anything. Was he mocking her? "That came out wrong. I've been tense with all that's going on. I do appreciate your willingness to help, but...."

She moved to stand by the planter pots lined along the railing. He followed, too close by her estimation, but when she looked over her shoulder, he wasn't close at all. Simply her imagination.

"That night at Colt and Madison's place—well, this place," he clarified, inclining his head to the house, "You weren't keen on my helping out. Were adamant about my not coming here at all, and I want you to know that I get it. Would feel the same way myself."

"You weren't supposed to be involved in that conversation. As I recall, you more or less inserted yourself."

"You're right. When I sat down and the conversation was going on around me, I did insert myself. My bad. I apologize. But in my defense, when I offered to help out, I was under the impression you lived nearby at a different ranch. Not the Bar C a century and a half back in time!"

"Nothing personal, Mr. Stockton—" she interrupted.

That's a lie. It's all about personal, isn't it? He makes you uncomfortable. No matter how far away he stands, it's like he's under your skin.

"Kade," he corrected.

"Kade. After Colt's advice," she tried again, "I thought on it long and hard. I only agreed to your accompanying me because I couldn't let Colt come back himself and risk being killed."

"Ah, I see. Okay if I'm killed, that it?"

"I don't want anyone killed!" she blurted, flustered for having fallen for the bait. His eyes sparkled. He was joking, toying with her.

You're in charge here. Don't let him see your weakness!

"The point is, I fail to see the need of either one of you being here. When Colt insisted, well, I have a lot of respect for him. Even though I agreed to your accompanying me back to my own place—*time,* I mean, this is something I can handle. With the assistance of the hands—men who know the land, have worked the Bar C for years, and the neighbors, Sheriff Townsend, well, I have plenty of help. Dropping your entire life to come back here was unnecessary."

"Like I said, I get it. As for my life, not much to drop. Can't ruin what's already in a shambles. And not much in the way of family."

She hugged her arms even though the sun was warm, and there was hardly a breeze to cause a chill. Was that a flicker of remorse in his eyes?

"Isn't the assistant foreman, Graham Stockton, your father?"

"He is. All I have left except for a little brother, Sean. He's in college in Idaho. They have their own lives, and all of them will be there when I return."

"I see."

Kade cleared his throat. "So, you called in that range detective?" he asked.

"No. Detective Grayson was assigned to Johnson County by the governor, being that innocent people have been killed. I hope he gets to the bottom of it sooner rather than later."

"He doesn't realize the gravity of the situation."

"And how would you know that?" Emmy found it difficult to carry on a conversation with those deep-set eyes scrutinizing her every move. Unsettling. Causing her to stumble over her words.

"Let's call it a hunch," Kade retorted.

"Some special knowledge from the future?" she asked with an edge of sarcasm. It was all still so unreal.

He looped thumbs into his pockets and shifted his stance again, attention focusing across the far range where cattle milled on a hillside. The high noon sun cast a glow over his face, the chiseled line of his jaw beneath a scruff of beard. Rich brown hair curled slightly over his ear. And one of those tight shirts again. Laundered white, it displayed every shape, dip, and mound on his torso, the sleeves barely large enough to accommodate bicep muscles. The flex of those muscles disarmed her most of all.

"Let's just say I don't believe the detective understands the gravity of the situation, or that he will take the right approach," Kade explained. He faced her again. "I wanted to ask you a question." She nodded and he continued, "Is there anything I should know about the happenings of late? You know, things that have taken place out of the ordinary. Like, the death of your neighbor. I'm sorry to hear about that, by the way."

"I appreciate it," Emmy said. "Dibbs was a good family man."

"The more I know, the more I understand what's going on, and what needs to be done. Things I need to pay attention to."

"I'm sure Colt told you things, gave you instructions?"

"He did. But I haven't had the chance to talk with you. Maybe you could provide insight as well. Descriptions of anyone you may have seen, that sort of thing."

"I see," she said, chest tightening to the point of being painful. Had Colt told him of the man who came into her home and attacked her? Why else would Kade be questioning, trying to pull it out of her like this? She couldn't bear to speak of it anymore! The feeling of it happening all over again came back when she did.

"Emmy, are you alright?" Kade took a step closer.

"It's warm out today is all." She faced away from him in favor of the potted mint, plucking a velvety leaf and pressing it to her nose. It helped with the lightness of her head.

"If you think of something, let me know. I'll let you get back to what you were doing. Also, I wanted to let you know I'll be going into town. I'd like to use a horse and buckboard."

"You mean Gunn Pass?" Emmy's eyes widened when she shot him a look over her shoulder.

"That's the nearest town, right?"

"Yes, but is that wise? Aren't you afraid someone will see you?"

"I'm afraid a lot of people will see me while I'm here. Not like I'm invisible or anything."

Kade laughed creating a dimple on a stubbled cheek. It wasn't as though he laughed at her. More like a private joke only they could share. His humor prompted her to smile along, and she felt the twist in her chest ease a bit.

Suddenly shy, Emmy looked down. "You're not invisible, but you are unusual. I suppose it's your clothes."

More than his clothes.

She took in his entire height, from dusty boots to compact hips encased in faded dungarees. And those wide comforting shoulders. His lazy sapphire gaze rested on her, and the smile faded.

She looked away, pretending further interest in the potted herbs, stroking a mint leaf between a thumb and forefinger, and making a mental note to water the poor things. He sure had an annoyingly confident way about him. Made her want to pull her hair out. Or something.

"I'll be sure to dress appropriately, if that makes you feel better," he promised.

"Why are you going into town, if you don't mind my asking?"

"Supplies."

"Have you asked Zak or some of the others? We have a storehouse out behind the barn. Maybe you can—"

"A few items down there I can use, like gunpowder, dynamite, and blasting caps. But I need more. Saltpeter, for one, and ammonium nitrate. Some sort of fertilizer."

She frowned. "Explosives?"

"Don't worry. I won't blow up anything that doesn't deserve it," he clarified with a wink, mouth hitching into a smile of sorts. Deciding to forgo the stairs, Kade swung first one long leg over the railing and then the other, jumping to the ground. Determined strides ate up the yard as he aimed toward the barn.

"Fertilizer? But—"

"Yep. For your rose garden," he slung over his shoulder,

Absently bringing fingertips to her nose, Emmy inhaled the crisp mint scent as she watched him walk off, realizing she had mutilated the leaf between her fingers as they conversed.

She circled the porch toward the back door, passing the window where a delectable aroma of German *bratkartoffeln* rolled from the kitchen.

"Hanna?" she called out, pulling open the screen, pleased to see a crock wrapped in a checkered cloth sitting upon the counter.

Without Emmy's notice, Zak's wife had dropped off a helping of the fried potato, bacon, and onion dish—but not the *correct* type of bacon, Hanna was quick to point out in her infectious accent. *Bauchspeck* was what one needed to create the dish as it was meant to be done. Ritually, Zak would cup Hanna's face between his palms and profess the dish was as delicious as she was beautiful. In response, Hanna pouted, insisting it wasn't, meaning therefore, she wasn't beautiful, either. And so, it would go round and round until the couple dissolved into mutual laughter.

Emmy was happy Zak had found such a perfect mate in the only Shaffer daughter, a family of Prussian immigrants homesteading a spread to the east. Hanna's younger brothers, Lukas and Micah, worked as hands on Bar C as well, while the eldest, Klaus, remained on the family farm. The young men were two of the most loyal workers they employed.

CHAPTER 11

Never In My Wildest Dreams

Kade glanced over his shoulder to see her cross the porch and aim for—yes, the kitchen. She did have a cute little sway to her walk. He didn't enjoy telling an outright lie, but she didn't need to know all the particulars. Not yet anyway.

Without the option of hopping into his red Ford F-250, crank up some 70s classic rock or country, depending on his mood, and cruise on into Jackson on a supply run, he would have to rethink a few things. In his century, he recalled the town of Gunn Pass being nothing more than a few skeleton buildings rotting in the wind and sun.

His thoughts turned to that detective. From what little he heard of the conversation, the man seemed more interested in the Bar C mistress than apprehending criminals. And the way he glared at Kade before swinging up onto his horse, he had a hunch it wouldn't be the last time they crossed paths.

That night in the Chase home, after Madison had whisked Emmy out of the room, Colt had explained the entire scenario: The odd rose. The wicked storm. His own stumble into the future, and how his wife had entered his life.

Then, how both had pushed forward to live in modern times, even though Colt had grown up here on this very ranch in the mid-1800s. Coming from any other man, Kade wouldn't have believed it. Still almost too much to accept. He recalled Colt and his wife enjoying periodic rides up to an area they called Rosebush Ridge. They liked it up there, was special to them. Now he knew why. *The roses.*

And when Emmy stumbled onto his cabin wearing a startled expression of uncertainty and hurt, it resonated with him. On a gut level, Kade knew why he had returned with her. Boiled down to more than the range wars. The haunted look in her eyes struck a chord, as though he peered into a mirror of his own soul. Silly, he supposed. Sometimes he could be an emotional sap. Everyone has ghosts, don't they?

The hamlet of Gunn Pass City grew in the horizon. Nearing, he slapped the reins, steering the buckboard toward what looked to be the main street—and trying not to gawk too obviously.

Becca Wilkes charged out the door of Wilkes Mercantile, letting it slam behind with a clatter. Broom in hand, she smacked at the rodents zigzagging two paces ahead.

"You little...! Get out of the grain. And take your family, too!"

Whack, whack, went the broom, always a hair behind the tiny offenders, until they escaped with a wiggle into a hole in the boardwalk.

"Got lucky this time. Don't show your little pointy noses around here again or you'll regret it!"

Inhaling in satisfaction, she leaned on the broom handle and swiped a sleeve across her brow. A hot one today, she thought. Then, she caught sight of a man watching from a wagon across the street. Not anyone she recognized. He stepped down from the buckboard and looked up to read the sign swinging in the breeze over her head before approaching the boardwalk.

Becca smoothed her skirts and wiped the dust from her face with her apron, then as an afterthought, crammed a loose strand of hair into the twist at her nape. Just her luck a handsome stranger would mosey into town on cleaning day. She knew everyone in these parts, but this man didn't look at all familiar. The unpredictability of the range wars came to mind and a wary prickle tingled her spine. Father had warned her to be extra vigilant.

"Good day, Ma'am," he said with a lift of his hat, stopping at least ten feet away. "Kade Stockton is the name. I work at the Triple—"

"Bar C!" Becca finished with a sigh of relief.

She recalled Hanna Tompson mentioning the newcomer at church last Sunday. Hanna told her all about how Emmy disappeared for a full week, then reappeared alongside a man, without much of an explanation of where she had gone or who the man was. Speculation was, he was a hired gun from Hoback, the next sizable town to the northwest—a town no respectable person would claim to be from, or at least that's what Becca had heard. Not that she had any personal knowledge of the place.

This man did have an air of dangerousness about him.

All that aside, Becca wondered why Hanna hadn't made mention of Emmy's companion being so handsome. A man who looked like him shouldn't be lost on any woman, no matter how married she was. Jaw strong and square, skin healthy, cheeks pinkened from the heat of the ride. A dark curl lopped over his forehead when he removed his hat. Becca made note: she must quiz Emmy the next time she saw her.

"Word gets around in this area," Becca added in explanation, gifting the stranger with a cheery smile.

"I'm sure it does. I see you're waging war on the local mice population."

"Oh, never mind this." Waving a hand through the air, she propped the broom to the clapboard building with a little chuckle, face flushing hot. Not because he was fine-looking, she told herself, but because he was a stranger to town and should be welcomed properly, not by a crazy woman chasing mice with a ratty old broom. "My name is Becca Wilkes. Please, do come inside. Is there something I can do for you? Wilkes Mercantile is our family store. We have almost everything a person could want or need in these parts. Except for that new Chantilly lace sewn with black silk thread that's all the rage in Paris. I don't suppose you would be wanting any of that."

She laughed, opened the door, and motioned for him to follow. Most every woman in the region, at one time or another, had requested the lace. She really should investigate putting in an order.

Kade followed the tails of her drab brown skirt, the click of sensible shoes on wood. He pressed his hat back onto his head and looked around, studying the interior of the building like a little kid in a toy store. There wasn't a spot unoccupied with some manner of food, tool, knick-knack, utensil, bolts of colorful materials, hats, rows of shoes, walking canes, and even furniture. Jars of sugary creations lined glass-topped cabinets. Ham hocks swung from rafters, and ropes of tobacco dangled above gunny sacks bursting with coffee beans. Curiosity got the better of him and he lifted the lid on a wooden barrel to see plump pickles floating in a vinegary brine. The entire building permeated warm goodness and he inhaled.

"I expect I can do without the lace," Kade said. "But I do have a list of items I am looking to purchase, if I may." He smirked inside, thinking he sounded like an idiot. To come across as proper, considering the time period, he realized if he wasn't behaving like himself, what's the point? He needed to relax. Nobody knew he had just waltzed across a time barrier. He pulled a paper list from the pocket of a button-up collared shirt, the only one he brought. He unfolded it, holding it out to her.

Becca snatched it up, ticking off each item. "Yes, yes. Hm, not so sure about this."

"Which one?" he asked, leaning in. She flashed a sparkly-eyed look and snapped a wink. Her complexion glowed and he took a step back, wondering if he'd gotten too close. Apparently not, since she adjusted herself in his direction and moved even closer, pointing at the word 'fertilizer'.

"Manure?" she questioned. "I'm sure you have plenty of that back at the Bar C." That brilliant smile flashed again, enhancing her clear brown eyes, and he detected a big whiff of feminine pheromones billowing in his direction. She wasn't miserable to look at, but the last impression he wished to give was that of interest. In any woman. At all. In the entire world, as far as that went.

"Um, the fertilizer I need is supplemented with certain chemicals."

"Hm, you don't say? I'm not familiar with it, but that doesn't mean we don't have it. I can check with Father. He's in the back."

"Appreciate it. What about the other items?" Kade took the chance to move away, busying himself with perusing the aisles.

"We have everything else in supply. I'll fill your order right away, Mr. Stockton. Give me a moment and I'll be right back."

In a swish of skirts, she ducked behind a display case topped with a brass and marble cash register, then vanished behind a canvas sheet serving as a door.

While waiting, Kade milled about, finding additional items of interest: covered glass shelves lined with Havana cigars, another with health-inducing tonics and hair products promising vigor and shine. Canisters lined more shelves labeled oolong and imperial tea, spices, and even gunpowder. He was studying a vertical display of coffeepots, scrub brushes, and stove cleaner when Becca reappeared from behind the canvas.

"I have everything right here," she announced, logging the items in a ledger before wrapping each in brown paper. "Father said we have the fertilizer, the ammonia, um, ni—"

"Ammonium nitrate," Kade finished.

"That's it! How many bags did you want? You are a very smart man, Mr. Stockton. I wouldn't have had any notion of mixing it with soil. So thoughtful of you to help Emmy with her gardening."

Becca grinned again, another coy wink of a brown eye setting him on edge.

"Yes. Gardening. For her roses. She has beautiful roses." There he went again, babbling.

"Why yes, I'm sure she does." She pressed fingers to her lips to stifle the laugh. "Is there anything else you would like to purchase today?"

"I'll take one of those wire brushes, and how about a few cinnamon candies and licorice ropes ... and may as well throw in a cigar while you're at it."

With purchases packaged and tied in twine, Becca punched the keys on the cash register and tallied up the final cost while Kade watched.

"That will be three dollars and sixty-three cents."

Kade reached into his back pocket, stopping abruptly. He couldn't very well pull out a debit card or a twenty-dollar bill now could he? Why hadn't he thought of this before? A wave of heat climbed up his throat.

"Shall I put it on the tab?" she inquired.

His expression lifted. "Perfect. Do you mind? I seem to have forgotten my wallet."

"Not at all. We've kept a running tab for the Triple Bar C as long as I remember. Don't you worry none. Go on ahead and pull that wagon around back and Father will help load the fertilizer."

Kade scooped up his purchases and headed for the door, Becca close on his heels.

"Will you be coming into town often? Do tell Emmy hello for me, and that I'd love to see her. We really need to catch up."

"I'll be back ... sometime. I don't see Emmy every day, but when I do, I'll be sure to tell her. Thank you again for your assistance."

Becca leaned to a wooden pillar and watched the man hoist himself up to the buckboard seat, marveling over his athleticism. What exactly was his and Emmy's relationship? Such fine form and long legs. Those thigh and arm muscles were something else. And his eyes, like winter's coldest ice, put her composure in danger. The wayward thoughts triggered a blush. When Mr. Stockton was situated and looked back in her direction, she flashed an eager smile and waved goodbye.

Kade touched a finger to his hat and snapped the traces, driving the single horse and wagon down Main Street, making a left to circle back up behind the store to pick up his goods. Well, that was awkward, yet weirdly entertaining at the same time. He could get used to this simple lifestyle.

CHAPTER 12

Becca Pays a Visit

"Becca Wilkes! I haven't seen you in a month of Sundays." Emmy raced onto the front porch and greeted her good friend, drying her hands on her apron before giving her a hug. She set her back for a good look. "My, but you look ravishing! Your dress ... and I don't believe I've ever seen your hair in that style before. It becomes you. Is the hat new?" Her smile fell as her eyes widened, "Oh no. *Did someone die?*"

"No, silly. All is well, Emmy. I missed seeing you at church these past weeks, and I worry about you out here all by yourself since your mama passed. This ole' dress has been in the back of my closet for a year at least. I needed an occasion to wear it. We must catch up!"

Emmy's expression turned skeptical.

"Nice try, but I'm far from alone. And a dusty cattle ranch is hardly an occasion for a fine gown."

"Come now. Dozens of hardy men and only Hanna and Estelle for women-folk? You need a bit of womanly chitchat. Never a bad time for a comely gown. Remember the Spring Blossom dance? We must've been no older than fifteen. Seems so long ago now. That pink flowered dress your mama sewed up for me to wear; I loved that dress! A sad day when I outgrew it."

"I remember," Emmy said, nodding. Becca's mother had passed when she was very young and though Russell Wilkes was a doting father, Rosie, Helen, and several others from church took every opportunity to make sure Becca received womanly care. No substitute for a mama, Rosie always said.

Becca had always been shorter than Emmy, her boyish shape following into her teens. Womanly curves didn't develop until after their school years, but when she bloomed, it seemed to happen overnight. Eligible men from miles around took notice. Surprisingly, she hadn't married yet, as much as she loved children and caring for others. That was it, Emmy surmised, Becca's papa needed her, and that took up a good portion of her time—keeping their home in order, as well as tutoring her younger siblings, Bart and Merry. Not to mention helping run Gunn Pass's only mercantile.

"You were brave enough to ask Easton Ryker to go with you to that dance. As I recall, you had quite the infatuation." Emmy grinned at the memory, bumping a hip to Becca's with a coquettish wink.

"Gracious, don't remind me! Can you believe I considered him the most handsome thing this side of the Snake River?"

Emmy tapped a finger to her chin in thought. "As I recall, he was."

"Pfft. Maybe so, but he was a work in progress as far as hygiene. Why he had enough dirt under his nails to sod up a house and barn to go with it."

Both women dissolved into laughter.

Lifting rich burgundy skirts that complimented the red highlights in her auburn hair, Becca twirled to show off her dress one more time. "No telling if I'll ever get a chance to wear this again. Now, take me inside and we'll set up a proper tray. I brought cinnamon glazed cake." She gave the basket on her arm a little shake.

Micah Shaffer busied himself at the corner of the big red barn, hammer in hand and nails between his lips as he repaired a broken shutter. Shirtless in the late morning sun, he had taken to imitating Kade's distracting habit. She could only hope Kade wasn't somewhere nearby without his shirt on.

Emmy stood on tiptoes and waved to get Micah's attention.

"Micah, would you mind haying and watering Becca's horse, please?"

"*Ja*, Fraulein, I get to it right away."

"And put on your shirt," she added. "Thank you."

"*Ja, ja*, will do." Snapping to attention, he set aside his tools, working his arms into his shirt while racing toward the buggy. He unhitched the bay mare from the buggy and led her to the watering trough.

In the kitchen, Becca chattered about the latest happenings while slicing the cinnamon cake into perfect slivers. Emmy set the kettle on to boil, and retrieved dishes from the hutch, placing two delicate plates, the teapot, and cups on a tray. All done, she lifted it and headed for the door. If Becca took the trouble to dress up for this impromptu occasion, the least she could do was break out Rosie's green and ivory bone china.

"Let's enjoy the outdoors before the afternoon heat sets in," Emmy said. "The weather is beautiful today, don't you think?"

As they took seats in two wicker chairs beside the swing, a table in between them, she set the tray down and filled the cups from the teapot. Nibbling on slices of cinnamon cake and sipping tea, the two women conversed about Pastor Simmons and the church choir, which Becca had been a part of since their school days—the main reasons Emmy didn't care to participate. Not that she would ever tell Becca that. Her friend had a crystalline voice and never missed a note. Self-conscious in that department, Emmy knew she couldn't compare.

They talked about Helen and her boys, and the hardships they would face without Dibbs to take care of the family, which consequently, brought up the subject of his funeral.

"So unlike you not to attend poor Dibbs' services, and then I heard you turned up missing! You must tell me what happened! Naturally, we all were worried sick, what with you feeling poorly after Rosie's passing. Whatever happened?" Eyes wide with questions, she set her fork across the plate and shifted to better face her friend.

"I wasn't missing. It was all a big misunderstanding." Emmy nudged a too-large bite of the gooey cake around on the plate with her fork.

"A misunderstanding ... but how? The girls told Hanna and Zak you rode off into the woods that morning and never returned!"

Emmy forced a chuckle, "That's a bit dramatic." Heartbeat thudding in her ear, she paused to grasp her thoughts, stabbing fork tines into the sticky confection on her plate and lifting it to her lips. "It was a planned ride. You see, I know of a family, they live out there, um, that place out beyond ... oh, you know where I mean." She shoved the bite into her mouth and chewed. Slow. Giving herself time to think. Either that or choke to death. She nodded as she chewed, raising an approving brow at the deliciousness of the cake, though the flavor eluded her.

Becca's forehead crinkled, head tilting, "I'm not sure I do."

"They are a small, tight-knit family," Emmy went on after a long swallow and thorough dabbing of a napkin to the corners of her mouth. "They keep to themselves. Out by that town. Hm, what is it—Hoback? That's it! Hoback. The town. Colt knew them well. I recalled him saying we could call on them should we need help. I figured with all this talk of range wars, the rustling, and then Dibbs being shot, well, *something* needed to be done!"

For a moment, Emmy feared if Becca's frown got any deeper it might remain on her forehead indefinitely.

"What did you do?" Becca asked. She had always heard there were nothing but gunfighters and loose women in the town of Hoback. At least that's what the gossips said. Was Kade Stockton a gunfighter? A shiver of excitement shot up her spine.

"I brought their toughest son back with me. To help. He fought in the war, you know."

"You don't say? Which war?" Becca's eyes rounded in interest, and she stabbed a final bit of cake, raising the fork to her lips.

"Um, the Civil War, I believe." Emmy nodded, cramming the last bite into her mouth, savoring, chewing, then killing more time to blow on her tea, cooling it enough for a big gulp. She rolled her eyes to the porch ceiling in consideration, noticing cobwebs beginning to form in the corners. "Oh dear, would you look at that? Spider webs. I'll fetch the broom—" She set her plate on the tray with a clatter and came to her feet.

"Wait, did you say the *Civil War?*" Becca asked.

Emmy nodded. "Um, yes. Their son is quite knowledgeable about … war things."

"I see," she said, calculating the years in her head. *Was he a toddler when he joined up?* "So, correct me if I'm mistaken. He *is* the man who accompanied you when you returned from being missing?"

"I wasn't missing."

"But—"

Just then, Kade burst around the corner causing both women to swallow their words and look up. At least he wore a shirt, Emmy thought, even though it was reminiscent of abbreviated long johns and left little to the imagination.

"Excuse me. I'm sorry to interrupt the ladies club." He paused, eyes alighting once, and then twice on Becca. "Miss Wilkes?"

Becca set her teacup to its saucer and bounced to her feet with a smile and a curtsy, followed by a giggle. "Why, Mr. Stockton, I had no idea I'd see you here! A pleasure, once again."

She extended a gloved hand and Kade stared at it as if it were something dead and he wasn't quite sure what to do with it. At last, he clasped it within both his and delivered a gentle shake. Becca giggled again.

"Please, do join us," Becca said. "I baked a cinnamon cake with the most delicious glaze—"

"Mr. Stockton," Emmy pushed out between her teeth as she came to her feet. She pressed closer until her shoulder skimmed that hard chest. "I didn't realize you two had met. It's too bad you can't join us. However, I know how much work needs to be done before the supper hour. Was there something you needed?" she asked, glaring up at him with a bevy of unspoken sentiments.

"I thought you might be in the kitchen."

"Of course you did." Emmy scowled.

"I need vinegar. Preferably white vinegar. The kitchen is typically where it's kept, and I thought to check with you since Cookie is plum out down at the bunkhouse. He usually has ample provisions, except as it turns out, vinegar."

Though the words were understandable, it took Emmy a moment to digest his meaning. The tight dusty pink shirt sculpted the breadth of chest muscles, making them impossible to ignore. Nothing about the color was feminine. Quite the opposite, emphasizing the danger in those intense blue eyes. This man would be the death of her! Glancing at Becca, she caught her friend's gaze raking over the new arrival like a starving feline readying to pounce on an over-plump rabbit.

"Mr. Stockton," Becca purred, "this coming Sunday is the annual pig roast social. It takes place directly after church service. With you being new to the area, we would be honored if you might consider attending. It will be a grand time, and you'll have an opportunity to meet more folks from town, and—"

"Your invitation is very kind, Becca," Emmy interrupted with a dismissive flutter of a hand, "but I doubt Mr. Stockton attends church."

Taken aback, Kade interjected. "I go to church. Sometimes."

"Oh? My apologies. I didn't realize—"

"Since you're from Hoback," Becca interrupted, placing an inquisitive hand to his rigid bicep, "are you familiar with the church there? I have a cousin nearby and she gushes about the pastor."

"Cousin?" Emmy leaned in to secure Becca's attention, lifting her fingers from Kade's arm. She couldn't have either one of them getting the wrong impression. That would be disastrous. "I thought your cousin and her husband were homesteading a plot of land near Hamilton?"

Becca blinked. "Might be Hamilton. Either way, the pastor there delivers thought-provoking sermons, and to my knowledge, it isn't far from Hoback—",

"Hoback?" Kade's brows lowered. He shot Emmy a look.

"Your family farm is near there," Emmy explained sweetly, angling him a meaningful glare. "I doubt there have been many opportunities to attend church services, with your farm being *so far* from town."

It was one thing for him to accompany her back home with intentions of defending against interlopers. Quite another to take liberties, inserting himself into her business and social life. At the very least, he could take an obvious cue on when to fabricate a lie to cover his own damn tracks. Not like it had been her idea to bring him here! Granted, the church social was Becca's invitation, but

Kade's over-eagerness in town yesterday most likely gave her the idea in the first place.

Kade shifted his stance, his expression thoughtful as he latched his thumbs into his pockets. "All the more reason I should accept Miss Wilkes' kind invitation."

"I'll direct you to the vinegar now," Emmy announced stiffly. Becca made to follow, but Emmy stopped her. "No, dear, don't trouble yourself. Sit back and relax. I'll be right back."

"Are you sure? I can help…"

Emmy plastered a smile on her face and shook her head, marching around the corner in a spin of black skirts. Kade nodded a polite farewell to Becca before following the Bar C matriarch to the back door.

Once inside, Emmy proceeded to the pantry, bending over and shuffling things aside in search of a jumbo-sized jar of vinegar she recalled seeing not long ago. This pantry needed organization. Rosie kept things so neat and tidy, and it all went to hell in a handbasket when she fell ill. Now, it held memories, and she didn't have the gumption to pick up where Rosie left off.

Curtains of dried spices hung from twine and strung along a wall, secured with hooks: bay leaves, sage, oregano, thyme, dill weed, rosemary, mint, and tufts of lemongrass; even dried rose petals. Spotting the clear jar of vinegar, Emmy wrestled it from under a sack of coffee beans. Rising and turning, she found herself less than a ruler's length from Kade's beefy arm. He held a small jar in his hand, those piercing eyes studying the contents. She couldn't even scoot around because his shoulders blocked the pantry opening.

"Excuse me." Something about the swirl of heady scents made her feel dizzy. Or, was it just him?

He replaced the jar to the shelf, pointing out, "You did suggest I follow you."

"I didn't mean quite so literally."

Despite the aromas of spice and coffee, she smelled him. His warm skin; the pleasant musk of a working man, and a spice all his own. She focused on the drawing on his bicep—ink trailing over the mountains and valleys and recalled reading of ancient tribes of peoples tattooing intricate designs on their skin. She tilted her head a skosh to better see: Vibrant purples. Greens and gold. Teeth. Or claws. Hard to tell. It disappeared under a shirtsleeve....

She blinked, why was she in here? Oh.

"Your vinegar," she said, pushing it into his chest. At the same time the kitchen screen door squeaked open.

"Emmy? Is everything all right? Mr. Stockton? Kade?" Becca's sing-song lilt and the swoosh of satin skirts filled the adjacent room.

Kade gripped the hefty jar in large capable hands, both exiting the pantry in one fluid movement.

"There you two are," Becca said, folding her arms. She looked first at Emmy and then at Kade. "This may be forward of me, but what year were you born?"

"Now Becca," Emmy said, "isn't that a rather personal question?"

"I don't mind," Kade began. "Nineteen—" He bit his tongue and amended his words. "What I mean is, I'm twenty-eight." Kade lifted the jar of vinegar into the air. "Exactly what I needed. Thank you, Emmy. This should do the trick. Good day to you again, Miss Wilkes." Like a cyclone late for a date, Kade whirled out the door and leaped off from the porch two steps at a time, aiming for the barn with long strides.

"You may call me Becca..." she called out. Baffled, she faced Emmy, tilting her head in question. "Now whatever do you think got into him? Civil War simply doesn't make sense."

"Have you ever tried Mama's chokecherry jam?" Emmy ducked into the pantry for a fresh jar, dropping it into Becca's basket and helpfully shoved it into her arms. "You will love it."

"But I can't take your mama's jam. It's for you."

"There's plenty. She would insist you take some home to your father and the children." She snatched up a potholder, the closest thing within reach, and began to fan her face. "This hot weather is something else."

"I imagine it was a trifle warm with the both of you inside that tight pantry," Becca commented with the arch of a penciled brow.

The pantry was tight—the shirt even tighter.

"Mr. Stockton is a nice man," Becca tittered on, "though he isn't quite what I imagined coming from a rough community such as Hoback, especially a remote farm. He's quite educated, I found. About all sorts of things."

"Oh?" Emmy decided she didn't want details, "I apologize, but do you mind if we postpone the remainder of our visit for another time? I have a bit of a headache."

"Well, I—"

"You're a dear. Would you like for me to wrap the rest of your cake to take with you?"

"No, the cake is for you, and maybe Kade would care for—"

"I'll return the dish to you soon, and Micah will fetch your horse. Is that a new little bay mare pulling your buggy?" Without waiting for an answer, she whisked Becca down the hallway and out the front door. "She's a pretty thing. I don't recall seeing her before. Isn't that funny? We see things and don't see them at all, even when they're standing right smack-dab in front of us."

"I've had Belle for a few years," Becca explained.

Emmy jabbered on until Micah had Becca's horse once again hitched to the wagon, going as far as to help her up to the seat and handing her the traces. Ah, Micah was a godsend. Though Becca was one of Emmy's closest friends, she didn't think she could bear to answer one more question. And if that question had anything to do with Kade, she may slap the woman silly. So, her friend simply felt like baking a cake, dressing up, rouging her cheeks, curling her hair, and donning her finest hat to drop by for an impromptu visit? Likely story. What ideas had Kade put in her head?

Emmy waved goodbye, calling out, "Belle is a beautiful horse!"

Becca shook the traces, steering the two-seater buggy away from the house and along the grassy lane. Emmy watched the conveyance bounce over the hill and disappear before she turned to focus a curious gaze on the barn. Micah once again busied himself with a second damaged shutter. She skimmed the horizon from the carriage house along past the corrals for a sign of Kade, but he was nowhere in sight.

"What in the world did he need vinegar for?" she muttered, striking out in a brisk walk toward the barn with intentions of checking on Obie. The day had gotten away from her, and she hadn't yet checked the wound on his fetlock. It was healing nicely, and the return from the future hadn't seemed to irritate it, but you couldn't be too careful about those things.

Satisfied with Obie's progress, she gave him a quick currying, combing out his mane and tail before opening the corral gate so he might exercise in the pasture. Thrilled at his newfound freedom, the black mustang tossed his head, snorted, and kicked up his heels before racing out to join the other horses.

Emmy put away the grooming tools. As she left, she passed the narrow alleyway between the barn and the carriage house, spotting Kade at the far end, slowing.

He sat on his haunches with arms in a bucket. Rather than proceed to the house, curiosity got the better of her and she turned down the walkway. At three or four steps in, as though sensing her approach, he rose to his feet and spun around in one fluid motion. Steely eyes held an unfamiliar darkness, the flint-like shimmer stopping her in her tracks.

CHAPTER 13

Vinegar & A Shower

L ost in thought, Kade scrubbed a cast-iron joint with a wire brush, his reflections going to Becca. She looked different than yesterday, decked out for something or other, he figured. Never had seen hair quite as tall, or a hat so large—the sun didn't have a chance of touching her ivory skin. And then there was a big ole swoosh of peacock feathers dancing merrily in the breeze.

And where in hell is Hoback? The name was vaguely familiar. He didn't care for being left in the dark, and if Emmy planned to create stories around his appearance, then she needed to let him in on it. The more he stewed over the entire scenario, the more irritated he became.

The crunch of gravel sounded from behind. Instinct kicked in and he dropped the pipe into the bucket, coming to his feet in a simultaneous pivot.

Emmy stepped back with a squeak, eyes widening.

"Hey," he said, gruffer than intended. He snagged the rag from his shoulder and dried his hands. "Not wise to sneak up on a person. Didn't mean to startle you."

His demeanor softened slightly at the sight of her and those beautiful eyes; now if she wasn't so grumpy all the time. He pitied the man she ended up with, even if it turned out to be the Johnson dude Colt told him about.

She took a breath, "I wanted to inform you that I turned Obie out. His injury is healing, and he's anxious for exercise." When he didn't offer a response, "I expect I'll be able to ride him soon."

"Not wise to do that either," Kade said. He lifted his hat and pushed fingers through his hair, then returned to the vinegar and cast-iron soup.

"And why is that?" she asked, turning her nose up at the pungent aroma hovering in the air.

He squatted, back at work with the pipes, aware her glare might be burning a hole in his back. "Plans are in the works for the southeast corner of the land, which means it's off-limits for now. No livestock or horseback rides until further notice. As far as riding anywhere else, check with me first. Got that? It's important." He shot a serious look over his shoulder.

"And that's it?" she asked.

"For now, yes."

"When did you plan on telling me this? I came close to saddling up a few moments ago."

"No you didn't. My intentions were to discuss it with you earlier, but you had company."

"Well, Becca is gone now. And I certainly did intend to ride! How would you know what my objectives are?"

"Obie's leg is improving, but you know as well as I do, best not to push it."

Emmy blustered, "We do have other horses."

"Either grazing far out in the northern pasture or working. You don't usually ride any of the others. Obie is your favorite."

"How would you know what horses I prefer? Clementine happens to be one of my favorites, too, and—"

"Clementine is due to drop a foal in the next few weeks. I doubt you planned on taking her out for one of those breakneck runs you enjoy." Straightening, he stretched out his tight muscles with a grimace. He dropped the brush into the bucket and dried his hands again, facing her. "By the way, where is Hoback? And were you intending on informing me of where I'm supposedly from?"

"It was an impromptu comment to Becca. She asks too many questions. In the future, I will try to advise you of such things."

Emmy sighed, likely deciding civil conversation was pointless. He supposed he was being somewhat of an ass. Difficult enough trying to formulate a plan in this strange world without continually butting heads with the lady in charge.

Abruptly, the wind picked up, sending the tops of the pine trees swaying. A dust devil whipped grass and dirt into the narrow space where they stood. One minute she looked at him, and then the next her skirts ballooned into the air. She batted them down while clutching at her face.

"What is it?" Kade closed the gap and took her by the shoulders, trying to look into her face.

"Something flew into my eye," the words more of an exasperated growl, rather than the girlish whimper he might expect.

"Hold still now. Tilt your head back," he said, impressed when she obeyed and didn't argue. "Take your hand away so I can see." He applied pressure to her arm until she dropped it to her side.

"I'm trying, but it hurts. I can't...." She let out another groan of frustration, and he smoothed the hair and tears from her face.

"Give it a moment. Now, try to open it again."

Eyelids fluttered.

"Think I see it." A black speck floated near the lash line. Slipping a hand behind her head, he leaned in. With the other hand, he reached into a back pocket and pulled out a bandanna, wiping the moisture and dust from her cheek.

"Can you open a bit?" he asked.

"What is it—a rock? A boulder? Feels as big as..."

He tried to resist a smile, "Hold on now."

"Don't be sticking those vinegary fingers in my eye!" she wailed.

Kade chuckled, "Just so you know, I'm not using my fingers. The bandanna came from my pocket and is clean. Relatively speaking, that is. Only blew my nose on it twice."

Her shoulders shook in mirth, one hand sailing up to smack him lightly on the shoulder. "Not comforting. And I do hope you're kidding."

There it is, he thought with victory, confident her smile had to be in there somewhere.

"Hey now, don't beat up the hand helping you. Try again." She blinked, able to open halfway and he tried a delicate swipe along the lash line with the cloth. Her eye was plenty red and irritated, but he figured he'd gotten most of it out. "How does that feel? We'll need to flush it with water if it's still there."

Emmy blinked twice, three times, looking around. "I think ... it's gone. Thank goodness."

Kade leveled his gaze to hers again, inspecting first one eye and then the other. "Sure? All good?" Then, "Man, your eyes are gorgeous," he blurted.

Both took simultaneous steps back and his hands fell to his sides.

"Um, thank you. I'll be fine now," she said.

"Have any problems just let me know. In a pinch, I've assisted medics."

"I'll keep that in mind. My father was a physician. That was years ago, but I picked up a few things."

"I didn't know that."

"Doesn't matter really. I need to get back to the house." She backed up, adding in afterthought, "By the way, what's that putrid concoction you're brewing up over there?"

He motioned her to the bucket. "Have a look. I rummaged around and found some pipe and metal connectors not in use, from the out-sheds and whatnot. Some had quite a bit of rust and corrosion."

Curious, Emmy stepped in beside him, bending over to study the murky and odorous steel soup. "I've heard vinegar helps remove corrosion."

"Supposed to." He reached in and pulled out a large piece of cast iron with numerous bends.

"What do you plan on doing with that?"

"See that barrel over there?" Her gaze followed where he pointed. "Got this bright idea to create me a shower. Bring the piping over here and on up ... see, like this," he said, indicating the roof of an outbuilding. "And being that barrel will sit in the sun all day, the water will get warm. It's a matter of pumping it up to a higher level so it flows down. If I do it right, I think it'll be a pleasant alternative to sitting in a tub. I miss showers."

Emmy nodded, intrigue furrowing her brow. "I remember seeing the modern showers. Even though Madison demonstrated one, I didn't try it. I wasn't confident with how it worked, and besides, I think I prefer baths." She cleared her throat. "Well, isn't this an odd conversation to be having alone, with a man?"

Kade shrugged. He dropped the pipe back into the bucket, the movement cording the muscle of his arm and revealing the green and blue ink on a bicep. He squinted as the sun fell across the metal roof of the hog pen and he turned to block it. "Figured out a spot at the back of the barn to set it up. Don't worry, I plan to hang tarps for privacy."

"I should hope so," she murmured, so faint, he wasn't exactly sure she said anything at all.

"Would you like a tour? I can show you how it's put together. If you're interested. Of how it works, I mean. Might be of some use to you after I'm gone."

"Oh, yes. When you're gone. That won't be necessary," she declined with a dip of her head. "Thank you again, and a pleasant day to you Mr. Stockton."

Her exit hit Kade with an unexpected pang of disappointment. He felt certain she would appreciate his genius technology of ratcheting a conglomeration of odds and end pipes together so that a pitiful flow of water might make it through without leaking out along the way. Chuckling at the ridiculous thought, he realized her approval meant something. Why, he couldn't be sure. She did have a curious way of making his own problems seem less consequential. Like a fresh breeze wiggling for space under his skin. He didn't quite know what to make of it.

Lifting his gaze, he took a moment to appreciate the feminine swish of her skirts. When she disappeared, he sunk his arms once again into the vinegar water, wondering if she would ever call him by his given name.

∞

Her eye still hurt a bit and felt scratchy. Could be a phantom pain, the remnants of embarrassment, or merely a memory of opening her eyes to his watery visage looming so close above. The kindness of his touch as his hands supported her neck. An unexpected comfort, and at one point she caught herself leaning into him, aware of the wisp of warm breath on her cheek as he spoke. The faint scent of mint, a hint of coffee, and the meticulous stroke of a cloth wiping away her tears. How was it those big hands could be so gentle?

So near, when she managed to focus, his concerned eyes took on an array of jewel tones, azure to cobalt. But it was the lines of concern surrounding them that struck her and gave her pause. What was in his past? Likely best not to know.

He would be leaving soon, only here to somehow use his superior war prowess to protect the ranch. Obviously, he didn't like her, and she wasn't fond of him either.

Emmy upped her pace in the direction of the house. So much to do, and hopefully, Estelle could help. Time had gotten away from her. If she planned to attend the church social, and she did—no way would she permit Kade to mingle with the townspeople without her being there to intercept any problems—then she needed to get busy with the berry cobblers she intended on baking.

As she walked with purpose, unbidden came an image of a rugged, well-formed man with moody eyes, standing buck-naked beneath a stream of water. All wet, soaped up, and such.

"Dear God," she muttered under her breath, quickening her step.

For as long as she could remember, dense thickets of blackberry and gooseberry brambles flourished near the easternmost corrals, where the sun shone fiercely in the morning and disappeared by noon to leave a welcome ridge of shade. Emmy moved along the fence line, plucking only the ripest berries, and tossing them into one of two large baskets looped over her arm. As for gooseberries, only the unripe green ones made it into a basket. The occasional sweet red one she popped into her mouth.

This would be the first year making pies, cobblers, and jams without Mama, unsure she had the heart to tackle the job. However, offering Becca last year's chokecherry preserves made her realize she couldn't dismiss a tradition so important to Rosie. Besides, it would be a shame to let the berries waste away. Not only would they attract bears, but everyone enjoyed the final product with blackberry cobbler being her absolute favorite. Later, in the kitchen, she pumped a bucket of water to rinse the bounty of fruit. Maybe she had been overambitious. Not only was there plenty for the cobblers but also enough for a hefty supply of jams and several pies.

The idea of Kade attending the social made her cringe. What if he said too much or the wrong things? How could she even hope to control the outcome of that whole mess—not like she could babysit the man.

It took a couple of days before Emmy was able to admit it wasn't Kade she worried about. Becca was her biggest concern. They had been friends long enough for her to know when Becca took an extra interest in someone, and when Kade was around, she had the look. Not only that, but Becca was also a bit too interested in where he came from and how he came to be at the ranch. She must try and discourage her.

Detective Grayson mentioned he sometimes stayed at the hotel in Gunn Pass. If he showed up to the social, she wanted to pay him a visit. Things had quieted down. No raids. No random riders blazing through the land with torches and hoods, firing weapons. Something was brewing; she felt it. If he knew something, it was only fair that he shares an update.

The following Sunday morning, two large pans of cobbler rested on the counter to cool. Sage and Brush sat at attention on the back porch as Emmy stepped out to spread freshly washed t-towels on the railing to dry in the sun. She preferred to wash up immediately after so things didn't pile up. Both dogs' heads shifted in unison as she passed.

"You two don't even like blackberries," she teased. "Suppose I'll have to find something you do like, eh?" Two furry tails thumped in synchrony. She entered the kitchen again with Dottie on her heels, the terrier plopping onto her bed in the corner. "And where have you been, girl? Out checking on the pigs and chickens, no doubt."

"Miss Emmy, the baskets are packed with picnic supplies. I'll wrap the pans, and Henry is readying the horses."

"Thank you, Estelle. I'll run over and see if Hanna, Zak, and the girls are ready."

First, she stepped into the washroom to check her appearance in the oval mirror above the wash basin. She had taken extra care with her hair, going so far as to ask for Estelle's help in curling and arranging it into an artful chignon with soft curls cascading down her back. She leaned close, making sure the faint rouge, eye kohl, and lipstick weren't too gaudy. It had been a while since she bothered with such things. Becca may have inspired her to pick through her wardrobe for something other than black as well. The relief of color, a spray of tiny pink flowers on dark blue muslin, was a needed change from the depressing black mourning attire.

The dress alone brought her extra cheer, though it was almost too small for her at the bodice. Mama had made it at least seven years ago, and it showed its age. A good excuse to visit Fanny Picard, Gunn Pass's newest couturier. Splaying fingers across her middle, Emmy admired the cinch of her waist despite the detested corset. No matter, it was church. She could suffer for a few hours.

Grabbing a wrap in case the weather changed, she checked on Hanna to make sure they were almost ready, then went on down to turn Obie out to the pasture. Inside the cool dusk of the barn, she hung halter to a hook and turned to leave, an unusual sound making her pause. The gush of water. Had something broken? What in the world, she thought, making her way to the back.

It happened so quickly. She rounded the corner and abruptly skidded to a halt, reaching for a wooden support beam to steady herself.

There, poised stark-naked underneath a cascade of water stood Kade. Her hand flew to her mouth. Frozen, all she could do was study every intriguing bulge and curve of his body, slick with a white dowse of soap. He scrubbed, then moved under the stream and let water sluice over his head. Shoulder and bicep muscles bunched as he pushed fingers through his hair. Emmy couldn't make her eyes wider if she tried. Perfectly formed buttocks, paler than the rest of his body, melded into muscled thighs.

Move. Go! What are you waiting for?

Refusing to blink, she studied the trickle coursing over fuzzy legs and bare feet, draining into a gutter that directed the flow outside. Ingenious shower, as he called it.

Amazement morphed into horror when he rotated to face her. With a strangled gasp, she shuffled into the shadows, peeking around to see that he scrubbed his face, his eyes closed. She sighed with relief.

Get out while you can!

Whether weighted by rocks or having taken roots, for some reason she couldn't move her feet. Muscled chest sprinkled in brown hair, a flourish of green, vibrant blue, gold, and purple ink in the form of a dragon coiled over his shoulder. Fire-breathing, it slunk along his upper left arm, dropping over a muscled pectoral muscle to slither past the ripple of his abdomen. She tilted her head, following the mesmerizing ink over a hipbone, then lower, where ebony hair beaded with moisture, and....

She stifled a gasp and shuffled back, a heel striking the pillar and throwing her off balance. When she moved forward, her other foot bumped the sharp edge of a crate and she winced with pain, "Oooph!"

Slapping a hand across her mouth, she flattened her body to the wall, remaining still until the water ceased to fall from the pipe. The tacky sensation of a spider web caressed her cheek.

Eww, hate spiders! Thick, humid silence. Watery footsteps.

Thankful of no eight-legged occupants on the web, as soon as Kade disappeared, she set her feet in motion, brushing off remnants of the web as she went. She exploded from the double barn doors and into the sunlight.

"There you are. You look like you've seen a ghost. All okay?" Zak busied himself with adjustments to the carriage wheel, angling a look up at her.

"Very well," she chirped, blinking against the brightness and passing him by at a brisk clip.

"All right if Hanna and the girls ride along with you? I'll ride with Kade and the others."

Emmy rotated to face him, the image of Kade's naked body burned upon her retinas. She forced it away with a series of rapid blinks. "Sounds perfect, yes," she said, leaving Zak with a puzzled look on his face. And then she was in the kitchen on her knees, rummaging through the ice box for the gallon-sized Mason jar of rosehip tea. Unscrewing the wide-mouth lid, she gulped it directly from the jar and leaned back into the cool stability of the plaster wall. Her eyes slid closed.

"Dear God in heaven, I'm a nincompoop," she lamented. "Should have known better."

The most perfect image of a naked man I've ever seen. Have I ever seen a naked man? Never was a man I cared to see naked....

Scrambling to her feet, she raced upstairs to powder her nose and fix her curls, placing a straw hat upon her head. She smoothed her dress and adjusted the crisp white collar to allow her gold locket to drape over it. Downstairs again, she inhaled a fortifying breath and stepped out beneath the brutal Wyoming sun, unsure if she would ever be able to look Kade Stockton in the eye again.

CHAPTER 14

Roasted Pig and Church

E mmy snapped the traces of the shiny black Phaeton carriage, pulled by two sorrel quarter horses. Hanna sat beside her, baby Eli in her lap, shaking a wooden rattle to occupy the squirmy toddler. The girls, Beatrice and Julie, dressed in blue checkered dresses, were perched on the cushioned back seat, swinging their legs and watching the scenery pass by.

"Mommy?"

"Ya, Beatrice?" Hanna swiveled around to face her daughter.

"How many more minutes?" she asked, cramming a barley curl back into her bonnet. "My hair is getting all mussed."

Hanna tipped her head back and laughed, "Patience, dear, we've only just started. Enjoy the countryside. Why, look at that field rat over there, and another ... there!" She pointed, "See? Lots to discover if you take time to look." Both girls giggled, bouncing in their seats as they counted prairie dogs, some with heads poked from their burrows while others stood sentry.

Emmy laughed along. Looking up, she spotted Kade catching up to them, riding his palomino gelding alongside Zak, Lukas, and Micah. As all four passed the carriage, Kade rode last, posture casual in the saddle. He touched the brim of his hat with two fingers in greeting. He looked nice today, she noticed, thankful he chose to cover up his arms. *And the rest of him.* Though his off-white shirt stretched tight and showed off too many muscles. She caught herself focusing on the sway of his hips in the saddle.

"Mighty fine seeing you out and about, Miss Emmy."

Startled from her musings, Emmy guiltily shifted her gaze to the left.

"Hello ... didn't hear you ride up, Miller."

"Lost in your thoughts again? I know how you like to daydream. Better keep a watch on the road," he teased.

"You know no such thing. I haven't daydreamed since my school days," she lied. "Besides, Minnie and Juniper know the way to town by heart. They don't need me to show them."

"What kind of gentleman would I be if I didn't offer to drive you to church? Pull on over now. I'll tie my mare to the back. She'll pony along fine."

"Not necessary, Miller. I'm doing well on my own." As soon as she spoke the words, Kade glanced back. Was that a frown under the brim of his hat? "On second thought, sounds like a fine idea."

She pulled the horses to a stop. While Hanna moved to the back to sit beside her girls, Emmy scooted to the right. As soon as he secured his horse to the back, he took over the driver's seat with a shake of the traces.

"Mighty fine weather isn't it, Emmy?"

"We could use rain."

"Heard the wheat and oat crops are suffering down south, not to mention the recent loss of stock. Not easy surviving these days. I have a notion it's only going to get worse. It's the range wars I'm talking about, Emmy. Nasty stuff. Given any more thought to my proposition?"

Emmy didn't miss Kade's second glance back. The pale-color shirt he wore didn't allow him to blend in. Not much about him blended in, she thought. She looked at Miller again and dissolved into a laugh as if he had told the funniest joke ever. When he gave her a perplexed look, she elbowed him in the side.

"Now come on. We aren't school kids anymore. Let's not talk about doom and gloom. And I'm not up for any of your propositions; told you that before."

"One of these days you'll see the wisdom in what I'm offering. Yup, won't be long and you'll see."

The idea of the Bar C becoming Johnson Ranch in the future was something she couldn't fathom and wouldn't allow. Emmy knew she must sit him down for a talk. But now wasn't the time. She wondered what had gotten into him lately. He stared ahead with a sour expression on his face. Why couldn't he just be her friend, like old times?

"Heard about you bringing in some help," he said with a scowl in Kade's direction.

"You must mean Mr. Stockton."

Miller shot her a pointed look.

"Mr. Stockton is well-versed with war-type things. He's here to help out."

"Hired hand, eh?"

"You could say that."

"Maybe I should rephrase—a *hired gun* perhaps? Shouldn't you discuss those sorts of decisions with me before hiring someone like that? It's dangerous."

Emmy sighed, rolling her eyes. "Hired gun? Where in the world did you hear that?"

"Whole valley talkin' about it. You ain't that stupid. You can't think he would go unnoticed?"

Emmy bristled, her gaze narrowing in his direction. She clenched her fists to keep from slapping him.

"Don't talk to me in that manner. It's nobody's business *who* I decide to hire. And he's not a gunslinger. Is he carrying pistols? If he were gunslinger, don't you think he'd wear them on a trip away from the ranch?"

The first buildings of Gunn Pass City came into view over the rise. The group took a right onto a well-traveled side road and pulled up to a white clapboard building with a modest steeple. The lane opened to a peaceful setting with a gazebo on a pond, a stone-paved path circling through cottonwoods and stately evergreens. A covered pavilion housed tables and chairs, and an enticing aroma of roast pork drifted in the morning air. Pastor Simmons stood at the top of the church steps with a broom in his hand, waving to the group as they rode in.

They waved back as a group of rowdy cowboys came riding up from the opposite direction, whooping and hollering in a plume of dust.

"I hope the Carlson brothers don't cause problems," Emmy said. "Who's that with them?" She eyed each one carefully, always looking for any resemblance to the man who attacked her.

Miller ignored the question, though kept his eye on the Bar C's newest hand as the group of riders headed to a pole barn in the distance.

"We'll talk more later," he told Emmy, expression somber as he steered the horses into an empty spot beside Helen Riley's conveyance. "I'll help you ladies inside with that basket of food. I'll come back and tend the animals."

"One of the hands can do that, Miller. No need to trouble yourself."

"Nonsense. Plan to head over to the barn and say my hellos to the boys anyway. May as well introduce myself to your new employee. Least I can do since we're neighbors, ain't that right?"

Emmy begrudgingly accepted his help as she stepped down from the carriage, unable to shake the sick nervousness his words provoked.

"Check on those Carlson boys while you're at it," she threw over her shoulder, "got a feeling they're up to something." She, Hanna, and the children made their way to the church steps where Pastor Simmons welcomed folks at the door.

"So happy you came, Emmy! How have you been faring since your mama's passing? We've missed seeing you on Sundays."

"Still hard, but each day gets better," she said, squeezing his hand in a warm greeting.

"Happy to hear it. I see Mr. Johnson is helping out. Running a ranch the size of the Bar C is too much for a woman alone, don't you think?"

Pastor Roman Simmons may know the scripture backward and forward and be soft-spoken and kind, but he didn't know anything about her situation, and she wasn't in the place or frame of mind to explain it to him. Not today.

After a lengthy sermon and much singing, Emmy stood, stretched to her tiptoes a few times, to loosen up and attempt to find Kade, thinking she had seen a flash of white in the back row. Shuffling from the sanctuary along with the others, her ears still rang after Becca's amazing solo. That girl sure could carry a note.

"Emmy!" Becca rushed to catch up. "How did you like the sermon today? I thought the feast or famine theme was appropriate, didn't you?"

"Enlightening to be sure," Emmy agreed, adding, "Your solo was beautiful!"

"Was it?" Becca asked, leaning in close. "I worried I would mess it up, and with Mr. Stockton possibly in attendance ... so, he is here, isn't he?" She rested a hand on Emmy's shoulder, but her eyes busily scanned the pews.

"I suppose so. Somewhere." That's it, she must detract from any more conversations between Kade and Becca. It was too dangerous. What if he said something he shouldn't? And to think he might be welcoming her interest. Entirely too much to contemplate.

Parishioners made their way to the pavilion, gathering in conversation and preparing for the feast. Children screamed with joy and dashed about in a game of tag. The men talked amongst themselves or carried supplies for their wives, while the women laughed and chatted, busy spreading cloths on tables and lining them with various offerings.

"If the flies get into my fruit compote I will just die," Millie Banks said. "One time a horse fly dove into it and resembled a blueberry. It was horrifying. My Jasper ate the darned thing. 'Course his eyesight hasn't been good for years."

"Let's make sure it stays covered," Emmy offered, securing a cloth over the bowl. "Where's Hanna?" she asked, looking around.

"*Ja,* here I am. Late as usual. Keeping up with those girls will be the death of me," she said, laughing as she rushed by with pink-cheeked baby Eli on her hip. Zak and the girls followed with crockery brimming in potato dumplings.

Emmy arranged her blackberry cobbler between Florence's chocolate cake and Joy's cherries jubilee, which contained copious amounts of brandy and typically vanished before the main course—which is why she made three hefty bowls full: a second one hidden away until after the dinner, the third for herself to enjoy at home. Helen dropped off a basket of her famous sticky buns before racing off to deposit a pot of snap beans and bacon on the center table. On her way past, she slapped Bernie's hand away from Joy's cherry jubilee. The spoon flew out of his hand.

"No, you don't, Mr. McCrutcheon! You will be polite and wait like the rest of us."

"A taste was all I was after," he responded sheepishly.

She harrumphed, muttering under her breath, "A taste'll knock you on your ass."

Emmy hid a grin, admiring the feisty ladies. She finished folding the napkins and arranged them alongside the silverware, a flash of white snatching her attention. Menfolk milled about the yard, gathering in conversation—all except for Kade. He stood apart from the others, thumbs latched onto his pants pockets, engaging in a serious one-on-one with Sheriff Lloyd Townsend. Even though the shade from his hat blocked his eyes from view, she detected tension in his jaw. He spoke with something specific on his mind. What business did he think he had with the Gunn Pass sheriff?

"Word is, you're a hired gun. Not for certain where you hail from, Mr. Stockton, but I don't want any trouble. From you or anyone else."

"Where did you hear that? Wait ... word gets around in these parts. Am I right?" Kade asked. Then it occurred to him. Becca Wilkes. Emmy told her he came from a town full of gunfighters and loose women. What town was that, anyway? Started with an H...

"Came down from the north. Hoback way, think that's what I heard," the sheriff added.

Hoback. That was it. Kade clenched his teeth and took a breath.

"Never been to Hoback," he corrected. "Eastern Wyoming is my home." He didn't know if it were wise to change Emmy's story, but he didn't know a damn thing about Hoback and didn't want to be caught in a lie.

"Oh?"

"Trouble isn't my idea of entertainment. I do plan to do my job, however."

The sheriff gave a considering nod, "And what is your job, if you don't mind my asking?"

"Colton Chase hired me to help protect the Bar C land from those intent on trespassing and taking what isn't theirs."

"I see. Chase left these parts several years back. He was a close acquaintance of mine, but hasn't been heard from as far as I know. Where's he at these days, anyhow?"

Kade considered his answer carefully, remembering Colt's wife speaking of Colorado.

"Northern Colorado," he said.

Townsend smoothed an abundant salt and pepper mustache with his fingers, "Sure would like the opportunity to sit down with him again and chew the fat. The entire family left a legacy on this corner of Wyoming. Except for the younger brother, Garrett, that is. Shame about those murders years ago."

Kade pushed his fingers into blue jean pockets, uncomfortable with a conversation he knew next to nothing about. He glanced to where the women were setting out the food, picking Emmy out of the group right away. She stood taller than the others, face younger than most. She lifted her head in his direction and he looked back at Townsend.

"I heard talk of a murder," Kade said, recalling conversations reverberating through the bunkhouse grapevine, something about a grisly murder inside the main house in the 1860s. At the time, he didn't think much about it. "My guess is the bad memories prompted Colt and his wife to make a new life for themselves elsewhere. With the threat of range wars breaking out throughout the state, he asked me to help watch over things."

Lloyd nodded, slanting him a serious gaze surrounded with wrinkles of experience. Likely easygoing if you were on his good side. Black and gray waves peeked from a light-colored felt hat. He was average size, but nothing about him came across as weak, and Kade imagined plenty of menace behind that demeanor if provoked.

"Can't blame him none for that," the sheriff said, exhaling a sigh and shifting his gaze around the crowd. "Reckon we both should mingle a bit. A pleasure to meet you, Kade. Remember what I said."

"Likewise, Sheriff. I'll do my best." Kade gave a firm shake to the man's outstretched hand. Turning, he almost ran into a barrel-chested man wearing a hat reminiscent of Hoss Cartwright's. Bonanza was a favorite 1960s retro western when he was growing up.

"You're a difficult one to single out," the man said, holding out his hand until Kade reciprocated, delivering a robust shake. "Name is Miller Johnson. I own the spread butting up to Bar C's southeastern border. Emmy mentioned hiring a new hand with all the ruckus brewing in the Wyoming territory. I don't know what to make of it myself. Wanted to let you know I'm available to help with anything you may need. And your name is?"

"Kade Stockton. Pleasure, Mr. Johnson."

"Aww, just call me Miller, since we're practically working together, eh?" When Kade only stared at him, "You know, neighboring spreads and all. Besides, won't be long Emmy and I will be making it all legal. We may as well get used to seeing one another."

Kade tilted his head and played dumb, "Not sure I understand what you're saying."

"Emmy hasn't mentioned it? Since you're hired help, she likely didn't see the need. But since a church weddin' is in our future, which makes me your boss, I thought it only fittin' to introduce myself. Like to get to know my employees, get my meaning?"

"Ah, I see," Kade pushed out the words slowly, guessing Johnson was full of more bull than roamed the ranch. Now he knew why Colt didn't think so highly of the man. He radiated smarmy all the way from the bone. "To keep things clear, Mr. Johnson, like I explained to the sheriff, I don't work for Emmy. I'm here at the request of Colt. Not much probability of you being my boss."

Miller's smile drooped. As he opened his mouth to respond, a woman rang a dinner bell from the pavilion, signaling the start of the meal.

"Food will be served soon, folks," she called out. "In case you haven't smelled the goodness, Mack Bertand's prize-winning hog is roasting in the fire pit. We're getting all the fixin's ready up here, so start working your way up!" Schoolmarm Maryann Fletcher rang her brass bell again before dropping it back into her pocket. Conversation buzzed as folks made their way toward the feast.

"Dinnertime! Woo-hoo, can't wait to taste Emmy's cobbler," Miller said.

Kade wondered if cobbler was the only thing he wanted to taste. Nope, he didn't like the man one bit.

With anxious strides eating up the churchyard, Miller charged off and Kade followed, thinking the man's too-small pants may pop a button or two after he ate a meal, and he didn't want to miss it.

"Mr. Stockton—Kade, there you are!"

A feminine hand looped around his arm and latched hold as Becca fell into step beside him, her friendly smile and brown eyes greeting him. He bent his arm in accommodation.

"My, don't think I've ever felt a muscle quite that enormous," she said, squeezing and releasing his bicep as they walked.

"Afternoon, Becca." Kade suppressed a laugh, thinking he needed to get his mind out of the futuristic gutter. Was he blushing? His face felt extra hot.

"Thought I'd never get to talk to you. You're awful popular today."

"It has been a whirlwind," he agreed.

"See, I told you it was an excellent idea to come. More than half the town is here. Over there is Fanny Picard. She's a talented French seamstress who owns a dress shop in between the Chinese Laundry and Joy's Flower Emporium. Her designs are positively to die for! If ever you feel the need to find an ideal gift for a beloved, for example, she would be the one to speak to. And naturally, Joy's flowers would be a classic gift as well."

"I'll keep that in mind," Kade said.

"And over there," she added, lowering her voice conspiratorially, "is Vernon Fletcher, Maryann's little brother. Not so little anymore. He has an eye for me."

A lanky cowboy leaned, arms folded, against a support beam talking to another young man.

"That isn't a good thing?" Kade asked. "We don't want to give Mr. Fletcher a mistaken impression," he added, thankful for the opportunity to reclaim his arm.

Becca's eyes crinkled in laughter beneath her prim sunhat, one quite a bit smaller than the one she wore the other day. She nudged his shoulder impishly. "Nonsense. I don't care what he thinks, and I'm not interested anyhow." She wormed her fingers around a bicep once again, taking a place in the food line forming alongside a row of tables.

A thin woman in a starched pea-green bonnet shuffled ahead, and he noticed she studied them from the corner of a dark, beady eye, finally turning to face them.

"Well, hello, Miss Becca. Lovely song you sang in today's services. Who's your friend?" the woman asked with a curious head tilt.

"Thank you, Joy! This here is Kade Stockton, the newly hired, um, hand at the Bar C Ranch."

"I see. You two seem quite familiar. I can't imagine how you've come to know him so quickly, Becca." With a demure flutter of eyes, Joy dipped her head to Kade, "A pleasure, Mr. Stockton."

"Likewise," Kade responded.

She presented her back and resumed her previous conversation while he searched for a way to extricate himself from the tricky situation. Johnson was toxic enough, he didn't need Vernon Fletcher on his bad side, too. The moment the notion entered his head, he saw the man's stare melting into him like honey on a hot biscuit. All inconveniences he didn't need.

"Where's Emmy?" he asked Becca, focused on the pavilion.

"She's somewhere. Don't worry yourself. Likely she plans on having her meal with Miller. Those two are sweethearts, you know."

"So I've heard several times today. You and Emmy are close friends, right?"

"Since we were eight or nine. Attended school together."

"And she told you that she and Miller have a thing?"

"Thing?" she asked quizzically.

"Sweethearts."

"You don't understand," Becca said.

"No, suppose I don't, but I get the feeling you're going to tell me."

Becca laughed, then twisted her lips thoughtfully, gaze roaming the sky as if to snatch the perfect words from the air. "He has always been sweet on Emmy. All of us were in school together, back when Miss Crabtree was our teacher ... before the accident."

"Accident?" Joy spun around like a tightly wound top, eyes rounding, "What accident? Is everyone all right?"

Becca reached out to pat the elder woman's shoulder, shushing her, "Old news, Joy. Nothing to worry yourself over." She shifted positions between the nosy woman and Kade, whispering, "Nothing happens here that Joy doesn't know about. She writes the Morning Joy column in the Gunn Pass Telegraph, reporting on anything and everything she can dredge up. *Keep that in mind,*" she emphasized, lips thinning with seriousness.

"So, what accident?" Kade murmured with a shake of his head.

"That's neither here nor there. Miss Crabtree fell off her horse when she went to shoot her rifle from his back, and he shied. Injured her hip. Sad story. Anyway, Miss Fletcher took over classes after that. Point is, everyone has speculated all these years that Emmy and Miller would end up together. A lingering fondness, you could say. I don't claim to predict the future, but if I had to, I'd say sooner or later those two will marry. Only makes sense, doesn't it?"

"Johnson ranch does border the Bar C," Kade muttered to no one in particular.

"Hm." Becca took one of his sun-bronzed hands between her pale white ones, fluttering her fingers over his knuckles. "My, what large hands you have."

Kade averted his gaze and was mid-eye roll when she grabbed his attention. There, in the direction of the pond, almost invisible in the glare of the sun, Emmy balanced two platters of pork as she picked her way from the fire pit through tall swales of grass in the direction of the pavilion. And judging from a trio of attentive ravens staring her down from their perch on a dead limb, they had little intention of allowing her to pass.

"Excuse me." Kade yanked his hand from Becca's grasp.

"But ... don't go!" Becca propped hands to her hips while admiring his agile weave through the folds of hungry churchgoers.

"Oh no, you don't, bastard birds!" Emmy muttered, blowing a loose curl from her cheek as she made her way along a graveled path. Skirt snagging on a protruding limb, she was jerked to a stop, using the toe of her boot to free herself. "Don't think I don't see your beady eyes on this meat. Mind your business, and I'll mind mine."

"Could you use a little help?"

"Lord almighty Jesus, you scared me." Skidding to a stop, startled kaleido-scope eyes lifted to his.

"Not Jesus," he clarified with a chuckle, "however, I am here to assist. Woulda been happy to walk to the fire pit with you."

"You were tied up."

He snorted, "Nothing so important it couldn't wait. Saw you looking at me. Just curious, do you ever ask for help?"

Those eyes flashed, cheeks flushing a mellow pink.

"I'm a capable woman, Mr. Stockton. And I wasn't looking *at* you. Not on purpose, anyway," she said, pushing a platter of pork into his waiting hands.

"Never said you weren't capable. Wow, smells amazing. We'd better get it to safety before the ravens launch an attack." The aromas of roast pork, fennel, onions, and caramelized fat set his stomach twisting into a loud growl.

"Agreed. Before your stomach escapes and breaks into a run, beating us both."

Kade laughed as he led the way, the nosy ravens ruffling glossy black feathers and heckling judgment as they passed. At the pavilion, they teamed up, shoul-dering a path through crowds to arrange both platters upon a table alongside a myriad of other food choices: pinto beans, shredded cabbage and peppers, bread, cheeses, green beans, parsnips, carrots, and a half-dozen varieties of pota-toes. A line of eager parishioners had formed behind.

"Thank you for your help. May as well find your place in line, Mr. Stockton."

"I'm more than happy to help serve."

Without waiting for an invitation, Kade snatched up a pair of tongs and took a place in between Helen and Maryann, who pulled Kade right into their conversation.

Emmy snapped her jaw closed and reached for a serving spoon.

CHAPTER 15

Dance With Me

E mmy dabbed her mouth with a napkin and stood. Stacking as many plates as possible, she excused her way to the worktable and took a place beside Hanna, already busy scraping plates into an empty crock of what had been her potato dish.

"The dogs will get their share before the hogs and chickens," she said.

"I'll make sure Dottie gets first choice, before Sage and Brush get a hold of it," Emmy said with a laugh, "I feed her inside to be on the safe side."

"When it comes to food," Hanna said, "I've seen Dottie handle her own."

Both women were laughing when Wilbur Judd, along with Florence's husband, Barney, took the floor armed with a harmonica, banjo, and fiddle.

"Move the tables and chairs aside, folks, if'n you want a bit of music to work this food off," Barney boomed, his baritone ideal for calling a square dance. Wilbur's daughter, Faye, not much older than ten, took to dancing in a twirl of skirts, heels clicking as soon as the music began. Thunderous clapping and stomping boots sent vibrations through the floorboards.

"My, we'd better hurry!" Hanna said as Zak latched hold of her arm and escorted her onto the designated dance floor, tables pulled to the side to make room.

"Ya know if it hadn't been fur Cotton-eyed Joe
I'd eh been married long ago..."

Emmy clapped to the beat, watching her old friend and his merry wife skip and kick to the second strain, blending into the couples bouncing past. A grip on her shoulders shook a dose of reality into her mood when Miller ushered her into an opening.

"No," she protested, slapping his hands away. "There's food to be tended—"

"Plenty of time for that later," Miller insisted. "You've been working since we got here. Time for a bit of fun."

"But—" She had no choice but to fall into step lest she risk being trampled.

Left foot tap, scoop, and cross, grapevine shuffle.

"...took my gal away from me, carried her off to Tennessee.

I'd eh been married forty years ago, if hadn't a-been for Cotton-eyed Joe..."

Miller's arm clamped about her waist, forcing her to do the same to keep her balance.

"I'm serious, Miller. I need to set out desserts."

Ignoring her plea, he tugged her in close, a hip rubbing hers as they hopped.

Right foot scoop and cross, grapevine shuffle.

"C'mon now, Emmy. It's been ages since we danced. Don't want you to forget how." He laughed in that booming way of his. "Remember back in '78? I think it was a rodeo at the Bar C, we left 'em all slack-jawed at our square-dancing prowess."

"That wasn't me," she squeezed out between a kick and a cross.

"Well, who in tarnation was it, then? Think I'd remember the fair maiden I was dancing with."

"According to my memory, it was Myrtle Woods after you both emptied a Mason jar of moonshine brought in by her visiting cousins from West Virginia. After that, I don't think either one of you had dancing prowess. The stares likely came from onlooker embarrassment."

Miller didn't speak for a bit, his brow knit in deep consternation. "Myrtle Woods, eh?"

"Her papa wasn't too happy about her not returning home that night. Then Colt found you both passed out behind the hay bales in the barn the next morning. You were still indisposed and feeling a bit green, as I remember. Colt escorted poor Myrtle home. After a stern lecture, he made sure you found your horse."

Miller's frown deepened. "That so? Whatever happened to Myrtle?"

"Married the youngest Howard brother not long after. Moved out to the Mount Ivan area and started having babies right off. I hear the oldest boy doesn't look a thing like the others." She angled a pointed stare.

"Huh." Miller swallowed, his Adam's apple bobbing.

"Last I heard, they're homesteading a substantial chunk of land. I'm surprised you didn't know."

"Reckon I heard somethin' along those lines. A man doesn't always recall unimportant events in his life. Now, as for you and me—"

"Spin 'round and switch directions, folks!" bellowed Barney in between strains on the harmonica.

Tap, cross, shuffle. Spin.

They reversed direction, and she now faced Kade's hefty shoulders encased in crisp cotton. He and Becca danced ahead of them, his cuffs rolled to expose a suntanned forearm looped about her slender waist.

Had the two been dancing behind them this entire time?

Emmy lost her rhythm. Topping it off, she stumbled while trying to catch up with a few unplanned hops and in the process, slung her free arm around Miller's waist for balance, just as Kade glanced over his shoulder. A question formed in his eyes beneath his doeskin hat.

"All okay back there?" he asked, mouth hitching with concern.

"Don't be falling!" Becca added with a flip of her hair, giggling, "Remember that time—"

Kade said something close to her ear, and she diverted all attention back to her dance partner. Emmy's mouth pressed into a stern line of irritation. All she wanted to do right then was to go home and stick her head in a bucket.

"Right as rain, isn't it, Emmy?" Miller asked, placing an impromptu kiss on her forehead. "We are in the company of church folks. Don't want to give anyone the wrong idea."

She pushed at his chest. "For Pete's sake. There's nothing to get the wrong idea about!"

Cheeks flaming hot, she envisioned her escape and ducked out of Miller's grasp and making a run for the dessert table, where a few ladies had already begun to serve.

No such luck. Miller's arm darted out with the speed of a frog aiming for a fly, snagging hold of her hand and reeling her back in.

The first strains of the fiddle floated across the rotunda and into the summer air.

"C'mon now, Miss Emmy, be a shame to miss the square dance," he said, locking her to his side when the calls started.

Bow to your partner, do-si-do, bow to your partner do-si-do...

From the corner of her eye, she spotted Becca latching onto Kade and dragging him back onto the dance floor. She predicted he didn't know a lick about square dancing, but she was wrong. He appeared to know exactly what he was doing. And he was good at it.

Circle your partner, high and low...

When Kade glanced in her direction Emmy managed a smile, but when his cheerful grin crinkle those eyes, she lost count. Again.

Up to the middle and come right back.

Circle to the left, now circle to the right.

"Dammit," she mumbled, scurrying to catch her feet up to her body, her sore toe beginning to ache.

"Aw now Emmy, don't be discouraged. Been a while since you danced, I suspect."

"I *know* how to square dance," she assured him. It's just that her toe reminded her of the bucket, and the bucket reminded her of....

"The key is to pay attention to your partner."

"You don't say," she retorted.

Forward and back...

Vernon and Maryanne danced up to touch hands, though Vernon couldn't seem to keep from craning his neck in Becca's direction. Emmy followed his gaze to see Becca's mouth close to Kade's ear.

Swap your partner!

Kade then locked Emmy into the curve of one arm and took her for a swing. "Having a pleasant time?" he asked.

"Yes," she breathed between beats, "but I intended to remind—"

Swap your partner, do-si-do...

Zak swooped in this time. Miller would be next. Craning her neck painfully, she pinpointed Kade. How long would it be to get back—

Swap your partner!

With a bounce and a sigh of disappointment, she was once again sucked into Miller's girth.

"Tired? I should see you home."

"That isn't necessary, Miller."

Gents swing out and ladies in...

Inside out and outside in...

At long last, the dance ended. Emmy felt a tad motion sick, seeing double after all the neck craning going on. She aimed for the dessert table with her duties in mind, only to be diverted by another tap on her shoulder.

"Mr. Stockton is a lovely dancer," Becca ventured with a wink of a big brown eye.

"I hadn't noticed." Emmy rubbed her arms, remembering the too-brief heat of his touch on the small of her back. Gaze darting back to the dancers, she spotted a flash of his light-color shirt as he led young Faye Judd around in some sort of jig, the young lady giggling her head off.

Becca retrieved a lace fan from her sleeve, wafting it at her face and neck. "Think I'll hop on over to the church and freshen up a bit." Then she pointed out, "Father is setting up his photography equipment by the stream, under the big oak tree. I plan to attend for a bit. Mr. Stockton promised to stop by and have his photograph made. Isn't that grand?" she gushed.

"He what?" Emmy shot back. "I mean, that sounds delightful."

"Emmy, you're not feeling poorly, are you?"

"I'm fine, why do you ask?"

"You seem a bit out of sorts is all. Save some of your cobbler for me?"

"Of course," Emmy promised, patting Becca's hand.

With that, Becca dashed toward the church, still fanning her face. Becca had always been outspoken and trusting, and Emmy hated to think of her heart being broken. Kade's mind must remain on his job. The last thing she needed was for him to forget why he was here in the first place. She couldn't blame Becca for being interested. He was a fine-looking man. Too fine. The image of his nakedness, soaped up and dripping wet, wormed into her mind. She shook it off. Maybe if she gave the impression that Kade was her love interest....

That's a bad idea—not to mention terrifying.

She started for the dessert table, cringing at the hot touch at the base of her spine, spinning around with her hands on her hips and intentions of giving Miller a firm no. She stopped short at Kade's chest. Eyes lifting, she lost herself in a heavy-lidded gaze. His body felt overheated, the heat radiating into hers, a glimmer of sweat on his brow.

"May I have this dance?" he asked.

"Why?" The response fell out of her mouth before she realized it, the music slowing into a lazy fiddle waltz as dancers coupled around them, talking as they swayed.

Kade's lips twisted, "I'll pretend you said why yes, Mr. Stockton, I would love to dance."

Without allowing her a chance to say no, he drew her into the curve of his body with a firm arm, his other hand clasping hers. He swayed to the catchy beat with a spin, deftly steering her to the middle of the floor.

"Aren't you tired?" she asked.

"Not really. I have amazing stamina."

The wink of an eye sent her insides to fluttering.

"I had intended on serving the, um, desserts," she explained.

"It can wait. The way you were eyeballing me a moment ago, I thought you had something to say. Figured I'd keep it natural and ask you to dance. That way we can talk, and nobody will be the wiser."

"That'll keep the tongues from wagging," she responded glibly. "And I wasn't 'eyeballing' you, as you put it."

Smooth as silk, he steered her into another spin, the rhythm increasing almost imperceptibly. She only stumbled once when he lured her into an unfamiliar backward step, though he caught her by supporting her back with his hand, those eyes pinned down into hers with such intensity she almost forgot what she was doing.

One-two. One-two-three. One-two...

She shot a glance over her shoulder.

"Ah-ah. Keep your eyes on mine," he insisted, arching a brow. "I won't steer you wrong. This is called the two-step." An embracing lift of his arm and controlled push to her waist sent her into a twirl and pivot.

"Oh ... me! Ouch..." she squeaked as he reeled her back, flush to his body, drawing her indecently close. To his warmth.

"I didn't hurt you, did I?"

"I ... stubbed my toe earlier is all."

"I'll be more careful," he promised, voice a low rumble against her ear.

So dizzy, she wasn't sure if it was from the spin, his velvet words, or the overall delicious feel of him. They fit perfectly, she noted, marveling at how their legs moved in tandem, like a well-oiled machine. She was learning new dance steps and couldn't be more pleased. An earthy spice scent emanated from the skin at his collar, drawing her in, and she found herself leaning in closer for an inhale.

And then the song ended.

Wilbur announced a refreshment break and Emmy reluctantly stepped out of the circle of Kade's arms. He thanked her and she responded with a bashful nod of assent. Feeling disoriented, she figured most likely they were being stared at, deciding the only thing to do was pretend ignorance: Joy's jaw almost dragged the floor. Hanna bobbed up and down excitedly, a wicked sparkle in her eye. Miller propped himself up to the wall, his expression rivaling a thunderhead.

In one last try, Emmy aimed for the dessert table.

Helen Riley stood on the far end; eyes rimmed in red as she desperately attempted to focus on creating perfect slices of carrot cake. This was her first social activity since Dibbs' passing and the entire county knew how the couple loved to square dance.

"Helen, allow me to help." Emmy placed a hand on her shoulder and scooted in. The older woman looked up with a pained smile.

"Step right on up, sweetheart."

"Looks like the pies and cobblers could use some dividing." Snatching a knife, Emmy inserted it into a gooey purple confection.

A line began to form, and she set to work slicing and serving, in between glances toward the grand old oak tree by the stream. There, Russell Wilkes had set up his photography booth. With a casual sling to his stance, Kade positioned himself first in line, admiring the handsome paint horse belonging to Tate Spirit Wind, a Lakota native from the Teton band. Tate often brought items for trade into Wilkes Mercantile and was also compensated for allowing his horse to be photographed during special functions. The children loved it and it had become a tradition over the years.

Becca sidled in close by Kade's side, speaking animatedly, likely explaining how everything worked. She had a passion for her father's cameras—and so it appeared, the subject about to be photographed.

Not 15 minutes later, a whooping and hollering split the air from the direction of the barn. Knife still in hand, Emmy turned to see Miller, Vernon, Zak, and Lukas racing across the churchyard in the direction of the barn, with Kade leading the pack.

Hanna set the baby down with instructions to Beatrice and Julie to watch after him, taking off in a run across the yard after Zak. Emmy followed suit, sprinting after the others.

CHAPTER 16

Bullies Behind The Barn

K ade ran his hand along the paint's smooth withers, finding his sweet spot and scratching. Blue eyes studied him from a white face. A jet-black mane flowed over a hefty muscled black and white neck, two eagle feathers nestled there.

"You want a photograph with the horse, Mr. Stockton?" Russell asked, stepping up beside his daughter.

"Yes, he does!" Becca piped in.

"Let the man decide for himself, Rebecca."

"It's just that I love Tate's paint horse. He's so ... majestic."

"Stunning, that's for sure," Kade agreed, admiring the horse as he circled around the animal. To his surprise, behind the horse, an old man crouched in the shade of a low-slung branch, practically out of sight. Clearly native Lakota, he wore leather leggings and moccasins covered in elaborate bead art, an ornately stitched and beaded shirt, his silver and black hair hanging in queues from beneath a banged-up tan cowboy hat. Stripes of muted red paint decorated his face.

"This here is Tate Wind Spirit," Russell said. "He enjoys bringing his paint horse around for folks to have their pictures made, especially the children.

Tate wore a stern yet pleasant expression, and though he didn't exactly smile, he gave a serene nod. Deep crevices lined a weathered face, and faint webs of experience outlined sparkling ebony eyes.

"I'm honored Mr. Wind Spirit," Kade said, extending his hand. Tate didn't respond at first, merely studied first his face and then his outstretched hand as if it were something foreign. Finally, hooded eyes lifting, he reached out and took Kade's hand in a firm two-handed shake.

"Haŋ maške," he said.

Hello my friend.

Kade's chest expanded, memories of his childhood friend and Army buddy, Daniel Springeagle, entering his mind. Having grown up close, they joined the Army on the buddy system and shipped off to basic training together. Years later, Kade would refuse the bonuses offered if he reupped, but Daniel stayed on with plans of pursuing a career in medicine, intending to return to the reservation as a doctor.

"I'd like a photo with your fine horse, and I'd be exceptionally honored if you would sit astride."

Both Becca and her father shot uncertain glances at one another, then at Tate, who appeared to be considering the request. For a moment Kade wondered if the elder understood English. Then he spoke.

"I'm an old man. Why?" he asked with a lift of his chin.

Kade grinned, crossing his right arm to thump his chest with a fist the same way he had seen Daniel do many times, "You are Lakota. Pride doesn't age, my friend."

Tate studied him again, finally giving his answer with a pensive nod. The corners of his mouth curled up as he rose to his feet and stepped forward, almost eye-to-eye in height. He must have been a formidable warrior in his day.

"We have met before this day," Tate said with certainty.

"That isn't possible. I'm not from here."

Tate's face crinkled with a broad smile, and he tapped his temple with a forefinger, "Yes, you are. You will see."

He took hold of his horse's lead rope and a hank of mane at the withers, and with the litheness of a younger man, took a step and swung upon the horse's back. The paint tossed his head with a snort, stomping hooves as if to say, let's get this show on the road.

Kade blinked. "Whoa. I'm impressed."

"Me as well," Russell added, scuttling to the tripod for final adjustments, turning knobs and sliding levers. Becca dashed up to Kade and gripped his shoulders, tweaking his stance. Head concealed under a black cloth, Russell called out, "Hold still!" followed by a big *poof*. The horse snorted and clomped a hoof.

All of a sudden, a disturbance echoed from the direction of the barn, and Kade looked up, racing in that direction.

"What's going on?" Becca cried out, head bobbing around the hedges before joining the crowd following Kade.

"What you got there, Kraut?" Larry Carlson asked, pale whiskers jutting from the point of his chin. At the age of 19, he stood a full head taller than the 14-year-old boy cramming something shiny into his pants pocket. The boy moved away from a carriage belonging to Russell Wilkes.

"None of your concern," Micah said in his distinctive accent, shoving a protective hand into his pocket and breaking into a jog.

"Not so fast. Let's see what the little Kraut-boy has in his pocket. Don't they share where you come from?"

Brothers Tom and Edson followed, intercepting Micah before he reached the corner of the pole barn. Larry reached out and snagged hold of his shoulder, spinning the boy around.

"Lemme see what's in the pocket." Tom and Edson moved in close beside their older brother, shoving Micah first to one side and then to the other.

"Mind your own business," Micah said, stumbling to avert a complete tumble to the ground. "I'm doing what I was told."

"Well, aren't you a good little Kraut-boy."

"Stop calling me that, Carlson."

"Or else?" he mocked, tipping his head back and laughing. "What you gonna do about it, huh?" He leaped forward, swiftly dipping his hand into Micah's pocket and removing a silver flask. He darted away in time to avoid the boy's angry counterattack. "It's ours now, Kraut-boy. See? Should've shared when you had the chance. Now you won't get none."

"Not mine and not yours either. Belongs to Becca."

"Don't you mean her pappy, Old Man Wilkes? He may not take too kindly to a Kraut stealing his possessions. Maybe you should thank us for taking it off your hands."

"Call me that one more time and I'll—"

With a growl, Micah broke free of Edson's hold, charging the eldest Carlson and diving directly into his midsection. Larry whooshed out a lung-full of air and fell back, flinging the flask into the air as he went. The flask twirled, falling to thump Edson on the top of the head.

"Damn you, Larry! That hurt." He swiped off his hat and rubbed his head. "Good thing I had on my hat."

"I didn't do it!" Larry grumbled as he and Micah engaged in a spirited tussle on the grass. While Edson occupied himself with his throbbing head, Tom took the opportunity to snatch up the flask lying in the dirt.

"Welp, belongs to me now," he affirmed with a guffaw.

"Like hell," Edson growled, leaping onto his brother's back, clinging there until they both dropped to the dirt, writhing, and punching in a ball of arms and legs.

A dusty pair of Lucchese boots stepped up within inches of Larry and Micah, a hand descending to grip the back of the older youth's his neck, squeezing.

Kade yanked him off his younger counterpart and to his feet.

"Ow, ow, ow! That plum hurts!" Larry whined, legs wobbling like a broken puppet.

Kade strengthened the one-handed grip, shaking his head as Larry squirmed.

"C'mon mister, let go. Ai-ain't done nuthin' to you."

"Micah, you okay?" Kade called out to the long-legged youth scrambling to his feet, snatching up his hat, backstepping as he pressed it onto his curly mop of blond hair.

"Yessir," he said.

"Mind telling me what's going on here?"

"Becca wanted—" Micah began, words drowned out by the others.

"Tend to your own business and let go of Larry!" The youngest brothers ceased fighting and advanced in confident strides. Mud streaked their clothes and faces from a residual puddle. Dragging Larry alongside with a face screwed up in pain and boots scrambling across gravel, Kade met them in the middle. He glared at first one Carlson brother and then the other.

"Not letting him go until I get an answer. Who's talking first?"

Larry whimpered and Tom fidgeted.

Kade focused on the flask in Tom's fist, not missing the pistol grip poking from the waistband of Edson's suspendered pants.

Quiet hovered in the air, an ominous click sounding across the way.

"May want to reconsider your actions, Carlson," Sheriff Townsend said in his intrinsic drawl. "Sounds like a reasonable request to me. Best to answer the man." One shoulder propped to the doorway of the barn, his stance was casual as he leveled his revolver on the middle brother.

"W-we only wanted a little taste," Tom explained, referring to the flask.

"Becca asked me to retrieve the flask from the carriage, Mr. Stockton," Micah explained. "Doing as I was told."

Becca exited the forming crowd and Kade glanced up.

"That true, Becca?"

She nodded, "Yes, I'm sorry, Micah. Irresponsible of me."

Kade frowned, shaking his head at the inconvenience of it all. "Doesn't belong to you, does it?" he said to the older boys. "Give it back to Micah and I'll let go of your brother."

Tom swiftly did as he was told, while Edson snatched up Larry's hat and pushed it into his older brother's hand. Kade gave Larry a push, sending him skidding across the gravel, face reddening with embarrassment. He rubbed his neck, sheepishly working his hat back onto his head.

"You three want to spend the rest of the day in the hoosegow?"

"No, Sheriff," all three chorused.

"Best you head on home then. Where's your ma? Bet she'd be surprised knowing you three decided to attend church services this fine Sunday," Townsend said, knowing full well none of them had set foot inside the church, only showing up for the festivities afterward.

The three lanky youths bowed their heads, Tom screwing the toe of his boot into the dirt. "I dunno. She was in bed when we left. Had a tad too much wine last night."

"I see," Townsend said, holstering the pistol and levering his weight from the building. "How about you three wrap up some fixings for your ma and git on home." Aware the family harvested grapes and made wine along with other meager crops, the sheriff also knew Butch Carlson had passed away in a mining accident several years back. His wife Peggy lost her zest and took to drinking up a good share of the proceeds, letting the fields waste away and the boys run wild. A sad situation all the way around.

"Yessir," all three mumbled in unison, hedging a wide berth around a sea of gathered onlookers, especially the stranger in the white shirt.

Becca trotted up to Kade, "Stupid of me, and I should have known better. A nip ... or two, sounded celebratory," she explained with a shrug.

"I get it," he said, "Glad nothing bad happened." He adjusted his hat against the sun, intending on heading back up the hill. "Whoa." He caught himself with an automatic step back, lifting his hands in defense of a silver knife blade smeared in purple goo. "You didn't like the dance?" he asked Emmy. "I hope that's cobbler on that blade."

She looked at her hand and lowered the knife. "Was serving cobbler," she explained. "When I heard the commotion and saw you—I mean, *everyone* running down here, I neglected to put it down. I should finish serving. Care for some?" Without waiting for his answer, she was gone.

Humor itched Kade's lips and he bit his cheek, walking slowly and studying the precise, feminine sway of hips under a pretty flowered dress, telling himself he only noticed because it was the first time to see her in anything but black. Absolutely the only reason. Though she *was* cute—which reminded him of the feel of her body beneath his hands as they moved to the music, the supple touch of her hands. He purposely rode near her carriage hoping they could talk, find out how her eye was doing, and maybe learn more about her. But Zak's wife and kids were in the carriage, too, and it didn't seem like the best time. Becca was yammering something or other in one long continuous sentence as they walked. He didn't hear a word of it.

Then, "Mr. Stockton?"

Becca excused herself as Kade pivoted to see the sheriff following along.

"Sheriff," he said, clearing his throat. Not okay for someone to approach without his being cognizant. He needed to get a grip.

"Grateful you showed up when you did," Kade said.

"You had it handled. I was simply there for decoration" Townsend said, his wry smile white under the gray mustache, eyes teeming with humor. "Carlson boys find trouble every now and then. Usually harmless, 'cept they're getting older, and I worry what they may get caught up in. Their ma never got over losing their pa, so not much support there."

"I see. That's tough."

"Wanted to let you know I appreciate your stepping in."

"Not a problem. Don't want to encroach, but I'm happy to help where I'm needed," Kade said.

"You let me know if there's anything you need up at the Bar C. I know things have been tough on Emmy with Rosie passing, and now with all this unrest. Had hoped Johnson might step up since there's talk about them tying the knot."

Kade frowned. With every passing day, it became harder and harder to imagine Emmy with Johnson. "I'll do it. One more thing. That range detective—what's his name?"

"Nicholas Grayson. He arrived in town a week ago. Governor Moonlight assigned him to Johnson County, why do you ask?"

"He was at the Bar C talking with Emmy. All she told me was that he would be helping out. Don't think she's keen on my presence, but I wanted to let Grayson know my duties here.

"That's odd. I'd expect she'd be happy to have your help. But with Johnson vying for her hand, maybe she figures he should be the one stepping up. I reckon he's got his own fish to fry, what with his ma and pa both gone."

"That's what I heard. Aspires to grow his ranch, I hear."

"That so? Well, I'm sure Emmy will come around and realize you're here to help. She did say those riders haven't been back since you arrived. She suspected Tom Carlson to be one of them. That's exactly the sort of shenanigans they get into, and I've had talks with all of them. Don't expect it to happen again. However, things are heating up down south. Hear bands of outlaws are heading up this way to take advantage of the unrest. You need to keep your wits about you. Already been a few murders in the next county over, another on the Riley place. Too close to home."

"I heard about that. Unfortunate." More than rogue bands, Kade thought, wishing he had access to Google, or at least a modern library and more of those history books and magazines he used to like reading. At least he had a few saved on his iPhone.

"Well, I'll be. Look over there." Townsend bumped his hat up, squinting into the distance. "Why don't you go have a talk with the man yourself?"

Kade followed Lloyd Townsend's gaze, temporarily sidetracked by Emmy standing at the dessert table. She had done her hair differently, lifted into a net at the back with golden brown curls escaping along her slender neck and around her face. Imperfect. All the moreso after their dance. He liked it, focusing on her fingers as they tucked the strands back in place, unsuccessfully. He preferred disarray. Kinda sexy. The notion caught him off guard.

Something caused Emmy to break into uninhibited laughter, a part of her he hadn't witnessed before. What a riveting smile. Her fingers fluttered to her ear, once again fiddling with disobedient hair, and her lashes lowered shyly. Who had made her laugh like that?

A man moved into a shaft of sunlight, and Kade's expression went hard, hackles prickling his spine. Engaging her in conversation was none other than Detective Grayson.

"Miss Bartlett seems to have a good head on her shoulders." Detective Nicholas Grayson lifted his glass, studying the swash of amber liquid before downing a hefty swallow.

"That she does," Miller Johnson agreed. "Emmy and I go way back. Always been close. Only logical we tie the knot and make our little romance legal."

He rested a casual boot across his knee and poured two shots of whiskey into glass tumblers, replacing the half-empty bottle on the scarred oak table. The chair creaked when he leaned his weight into it. The Roundhouse Saloon and sometimes Opera House had the reputation of being the liveliest place in Gunn Pass City. However, this Sunday afternoon was relatively quiet, with only a couple of patrons drinking at the bar, while some cowboys dealt faro at a corner table. A smoky haze floated through the room. The occasional hurdy-gurdy gal strolled past, passing out smiles and anything else a gentleman may require.

Grayson chuckled, "We must grab hold of the opportunities when they present themselves. Lost my wife a few years back."

"I'm sorry to hear that, Detective."

His expression grew wistful. "She was a beauty."

"I bet. What happened if you don't mind my asking?"

His eyes closed as if conjuring a memory.

"Remains a mystery. Could've been a freak accident. Maybe not." He focused on his glass again, swirling the contents as he considered his words. "I arrived home after being gone a few days working a case. Found my five-year-old daughter, Nancy, sitting at the base of the stairs beside her mother's lifeless body. A basket of laundry lay spilled and scattered."

He pressed his lips together. Never would he forget Meredith's lifeless face. Like an angel. So peaceful. Except for the blood under her fingernails. Something about that didn't add up. She wasn't bleeding anywhere. Grayson inhaled, continuing, "If not for the whitish cast of her skin, one would assume she was merely asleep—"

"Except for the fact she lay crumpled at the foot of the stairs," Miller interjected in a booming voice.

Grayson frowned, studying the crass man across from him before continuing. "Nancy told me she couldn't wake her momma. Saddest thing I've ever witnessed."

Miller fidgeted, expression screwed into one of repugnance. "Why, that's downright terrible," he said. "How long had little Nancy sat there with her momma?"

"Maybe the entire afternoon."

"Some bum luck there. So, she was doin' the laundry and fell down the stairs, eh?"

Grayson eyed the man across from him, slamming back the last of the whiskey in his glass. "Broke her neck."

"Damn." He shook his head, "And your daughter?"

Grayson nodded, "She has adjusted, and we are close. I'm gone so much of the time. Her aunt and grandma help care for her. I have my sights set on sending her to a private boarding school in Helena."

"A mighty fine idea."

"Private schools cost a pretty penny, but my hope is I'll be able to tie up the loose ends by the start of the new year," he added, watching Johnson's reaction.

"I wish you well, Detective."

"Appreciate that."

"Glad you could join me for a drink after all the church festivities. Sometimes men need to get away from the womenfolk. Working on all this rustling and range war business, I feel like we're old friends, eh?"

Grayson paused, the niggle in his gut intensifying. Something about Johnson hadn't set right with him from the beginning. The sheriff didn't have issues with the man, but he wasn't as confident. He glanced at the whiskey bottle. Never drank much before losing Meredith; didn't care for the taste, but a lot has changed in recent years. Besides, he hoped Miller would let down his guard. The man wasn't overly smart. Shouldn't take much.

"I take my job seriously, Johnson. Don't usually mix it in with personal affairs." Sometimes those lines had a way of blurring, he added to himself.

"Completely understand. It's serious business, what's going on around these parts. Take for instance, that Kade feller."

Grayson's gaze lifted, "Stockton?"

"The new Bar C ranch hand. If that's what he is. I, for one, have my doubts."

"Why is that?"

"Something fishy is all I'm saying," Miller elaborated. "Don't trust him. He shows up out of nowhere. Emmy says she hired him to help with the rustling and terrorizing that's been going on. Then she said Colton Chase did the hiring. Not to mention Chase hasn't been around in years. So where did Stockton come from? I'm not so sure he doesn't have ulterior motives."

"You don't say." Grayson straightened in his chair, rubbing his jaw in thought.

Miller leaned forward. "Not to horn in on your job and all—but if it were up to me, I'd be checking him out. Fact is, if you're open to earning some extra greenbacks, I might have a job for you myself. Have my own holdings to watch out for with my place backing up to the Bar C, and I've got my suspicions Stockton is up to no good." He noticed the detective downing the last of the liquid in his glass and reached for the bottle to fill his glass.

"Your suggestion is not something I am at liberty to do," Grayson said, thinking this might be easier than originally thought.

"Nonsense. What about your daughter there, Detective? I'm talking about funds to get her started off right in that private school in Helena. A mighty fine opportunity."

Grayson held his glass up to a ray of afternoon sun casting through a plate-glass window, considering the amber liquid for several seconds before downing a final slug. His expression twisted at the burn. Good thing he held his liquor well. Opening his eyes, he glared directly into Miller's.

"You pique my curiosity," he said.

"Emmy offered you a bed at a Bar C bunkhouse should you need it, right?"

"Yes, she did."

"She's hospitable that way. Take her up on the offer and do a little extra investigating. Simple enough. Pick through Stockton's personal items. Get a feel for who he is and where he's from. Question some of the hands." Miller wagged a finger in the air, "Not only do I suspect he's up to no good, but I've also seen the way he looks at Emmy. That's my woman, Detective. I sure as hell don't want some high'n mighty gunslinger moving in on my territory."

"*Gunslinger?*" Grayson's gaze narrowed. This is something he hadn't considered. He attached a drunken lilt to his speech to aid the ruse.

"There are rumors. Point is, if he's up to no good, it needs nipping in the bud. He might be a wanted man!"

Grayson listened intently. He needed time to think, peace and quiet. And Miller disturbed the process.

"Not only is it outside of my duties and ethics," he said finally, "but I don't have the time for your personal inquiries, Johnson. Not my problem if Stockton takes a shine to your woman."

With the man's words having developed a distinct slur, Miller took the opportunity to push the issue. "C'mon now, don't forget about that private school. Just think how little Nancy would flourish in a place like that. Being without a mother, hell, I can only imagine what challenges she will face—"

Grayson pushed back from the table and stood, chair scraping the wood-planked floor.

"Listen up now."

Grayson paused.

"How about we get together to discuss specifics? Ride on out to my place and I'll introduce you to some of the boys I've rounded up to help with these wars. A man has a right to protect himself and his land. Need a few extra men at the ready in situations such as these. Townsend said himself there's rumors of bands of roving thieves and murderers riding up from Texas."

"I'll be in touch, Johnson. If you'll excuse me, been a long day. Good evening to you." With a tug on the brim of his hat, he turned for the exit, a purposely exaggerated wobble to his gait. Who exactly had he gathered up? This could be interesting.

Miller called after him, "And if you change your mind about the little extra job I mentioned, I'll have a down payment for you. How's that sound?"

Batwing doors swung shut in Grayson's wake. Miller relaxed into his chair with a chuckle, satisfied the troubled lawman would come around to serve his purpose.

As soon as Grayson left, Amos Timms stood from a table in the back, his frizzy reddish hair resembling a halo around his head beneath his hat. He approached Miller from the corner table full of card-playing cowboys, one an employee of the Bar C Ranch.

"He sure didn't stay long," Timms pointed out, folding his lanky frame into the chair the detective had vacated.

Miller grunted. "Tell me something I don't already know."

"I 'spect you have him right where you want him."

"How's that?"

"Give him time to ruminate on the idea. Hit him up again in a few days."

"I don't have a few days."

"Sure you do."

Annoyance flashed on Miller's face. He clutched the bottle and finished off the whiskey.

"Seth and his boys won't show up for a good week. And you're expecting Clive Monroe to come down from Montana. He and his cohorts should arrive soon after. We can step up the raids. Clive already knows the layout of the place. If the Bar C boys aren't shittin' in their britches by then, I guarantee they will be."

"Yeah, well Clive's worthless as far as I'm concerned. Who's the Seth feller?"

Amos leaned in, "You forget, I worked with Seth in Texas. He's got quite a reputation. Carries a guttin' knife and noose in his pocket just for sport."

Miller shook his head. "I need time to think. You're getting ahead of yourself."

"Don't go gettin' soft now. You're in this neck deep—"

Miller exploded out of his chair, circling Amos's throat gripped by meaty fingers before the man could register what was happening. Amos strangled a swallow. Two men glanced their way from the bar to see what the commotion was about.

"Don't start acting like you're running the show. I call the shots. Not you, and not those hillbillies you call friends. Your job is to play it cool, play cards with the Bar C boys and keep tabs on our friend. He's our only source of information at this point. Make sure he doesn't get all loose-lipped. Got it?"

Amos's scuffled for a foothold under the table, attempting a nod. A gurgle sounded in his throat and Miller relaxed his hold, the man slumping into his chair, rubbing the red marks on his throat. He watched the doors swing back and forth, the clomp of his Johnson's boots fading aw

CHAPTER 17

Cobbler For Two

E mmy plopped a hefty ball of dough onto the well-floured tabletop, pulling the rolling pin from the drawer. She looked up to see Estelle fiddling with the new pump recently installed.

"Still leaking?" Emmy asked. "Maybe Henry can take a look at it."

"He's the one who got it started leaking again," she bemoaned. "The man knows how to fix almost anything on the range but can't do a blasted thing inside the house. Wait. I have an idea." She dropped the dish towel and headed for the door. "Mr. Stockton will know how to fix it."

Emmy blinked, shaking her head. "Wait." She set aside the rolling pin and nudged a lock of hair from her cheek with her wrist. "Why ask him? Mr. Stockton, I mean."

Estelle spun around. "Why he's an engineering marvel! Surely, you've seen the standing bath he designed for himself in the barn?"

Seen more than that.

"A wonderful thing for those in a rush," Estelle continued. "Everyone is talking about it. If it wasn't already too late, I'd encourage him to enter his design into the county fair. Come along," she encouraged with the motion of her arm, "I'll show it to you."

Show her what? she thought, envisioning a finely muscled male backside.

"For heaven's sake, I've seen him in it. I mean, the shower. I've seen *the shower.*"

"Shower? That's an ideal description. A rain shower! Does he know you named it?" Estelle asked, vanishing out the door.

Emmy rolled her eyes and went back to the dough.

Keep your mind on the cobbler.

She snatched up the rolling pin. Thrust. Pull. Repeat. Thrust. Pull. Repeat.

At just the right thickness, she cut strips, gently peeling them from the floury surface, to arrange them artfully in a crisscross pattern, pinching to seal in the final step. She went to work on another ball of dough, first dashing to the stove to stir the filling, then back to the table to pick up the rolling pin.

Another ball of dough hit the table. Grip. Pinch. Grind. Roll. Thrust. Repeat.

"Take it easy. Not sure what you're trying to kill, but I think it's dead."

Emmy glanced over her shoulder to see Kade's broad-shouldered form filling the better part of the doorway. Thankfully he wore clothes. Barely. One of those union suit shirts again. The corner of his mouth hitched up in a hello-grin and she greeted him with a nod as he entered.

"Good day, Kade."

"And a fine day it is," he agreed, slinging a work rag over a shoulder and crossing to inspect the pump handle.

Honestly, Emmy didn't know what irritated her more about this man: his cavalier attitude, the way he walked around in those underwear shirts showing off his muscles, the dramatic ink on his biceps, or the risk he took of being seen, shamelessly showering stark-raving-naked in the middle of the barn? Well of course he showered naked. Maybe it was the annoyance at her own inability to eradicate the image from her mind. An Italian statue carved from marble came to mind. All right, so he hadn't exactly been in the middle of the barn. More like a far corner behind a tarp—a private area she had known full well he occupied, one she shouldn't have been nosing around anyway.

Thankfully, he's none the wiser.

Estelle trotted into the kitchen a few steps behind Kade, pointing to the newfangled swan-neck water faucet positioned over a white porcelain bowl. It had a pump feature on the side like the old pump. It drew water from the well, the porcelain bowl disposing of the excess through a drain feature at the bottom, sequentially taking the waste along a maze of galvanic pipe cleverly installed along the walls and under the floorboards. The waste was dumped into a basin of river rock and pine straw for filtration located uphill from the vegetable garden. The tub and washbasin in the bathroom functioned in a similar fashion.

The new Crapper commodes were installed before Mama passed, one upstairs and one down. It worked under an entirely different concept, put in after a cistern, fed by a spring, was placed on the hill behind the house. The commodes flushed into a dedicated cast-iron pipe system and routed the waste outdoors, depositing it into an underground cesspool where the old outhouse still stood. Emmy considered the Thomas Crapper commode to be about the best invention ever. According to the history books she loved perusing, it wasn't the first toilet ever fashioned, nonetheless much appreciated as far as she was concerned.

"You see how it drips all the time?" Estelle pointed out. "I'm no expert, but I don't think it's supposed to do that."

"You got that right."

Kade tinkered with the fittings on the handle, pulling a wrench from his pocket to test first one bolt and then another. Arm muscles flexed and rippled with his tinkering, and after a few moments, the dripping ceased. He returned the tool to his back pocket and pulled the rag from his shoulder to dry his hands. "Should do it. Let me know if it starts up again."

"I certainly will, Mr. Stockton," Estelle gushed, all bright-eyed. "I knew you could fix it!"

A man's voice called Estelle's name from down the hall.

"Be right there," she answered. "Henry is painting trim today. I'd better go see what he wants." She excused herself and disappeared.

"You know quite a lot about indoor plumbing," Emmy said, at the stove stirring the bubbling purple brew. She faced him, wiping her hands on her favorite apron, a wash-worn yellow cotton with tiny white flowers. As usual, Kade's tall presence had a way of intimidating, though she trained her focus to his face with the mature intention of ignoring imaginings of his naked body—and the probable birthmark above his left butt cheek. It did little good. Thick chestnut hair, his white grin, the angle of his jaw. And those lips. She wondered what it would be like to kiss them.

Damn those lips.

"Nope, not really. Common knowledge where I come from," he said. He made a growling sound in his throat. "Smells great in here. I cook some. Anything I can help with?"

Is there anything you can't do? You could kiss me into oblivion. That would help a lot.

"No need," she said, clearing her throat. "I'm utilizing the rest of the berries." She scrubbed her palms down the front of her apron for the second time. "Can't have them going to waste. Plan to put up jams and preserves in a few weeks, but for now, it's a cobbler and gooseberry pies."

"The bears will be disappointed."

"What's that?" she asked, losing herself in the blue depths of his gaze.

"I'm teasing. Don't need bears nosing around the bushes, do we?" He seemed to cringe at his words, and she thought his neck reddened.

"You're right about that." With potholders, she aimed for the cast-iron kettle half the size of her upper body.

"Let me get it," he insisted.

"I'm perfectly capable—"

"Believe me, I know. But may as well use me if I'm here." Kade took the potholders from her grasp and lifted the pot from the heat.

Visions of using him filled her imagination. The thought struck her, he would leave eventually when this violence was over, and she wasn't looking forward to it.

"You can place the pot right here." She adjusted a heat trivet near a wood counter workspace. The oblong supper table was lined with pans, a line of dough balls wrapped in cloth, neatly arranged dough lattice, a sack of flour, and a rolling pin awaited her return.

"The aroma is amazing," he said. "Could've found my way up here with my eyes closed. You know, my grandma had a secret recipe for blackberry cobbler."

"A secret? My."

"Made Dad, Sean and me promise not to share it with anyone, except for our offspring. Keep it in the family, you know."

"I see. And ... do you have children?" she ventured, holding her breath at the anticipated answer. She heard talk of being married once but didn't know anything about what had happened to his wife.

"No kids. I'm not good dad material."

She frowned, "Nonsense. You are a bit intense, but it doesn't ... what I mean is, I'm sure you'd be a fine father."

"I pity the poor kid that gets me for a father," he said in a strange but funny voice, winking with a jovial laugh, obviously referencing something from the future. He went on to say, "Methinks your cobbler skills are way better than your psychology skills."

She laughed along, his chuckle forcing an obligatory boyish dimple in his right cheek and crinkles at the outer corner of his eyes.

Please stop with the winking. It makes my belly go all wiggly.

"My little brother, Sean, is a better candidate. Think I mentioned he's in graduate school in Idaho. Plans a career in veterinary medicine."

"That's wonderful! I would've been interested in attending medical school for the purpose of treating animals. Not a proper choice for a woman, at least that's what I'm told." She shrugged. "But I could do it."

"I'm in total agreement," Kade said.

"I don't understand the restrictions on women, even though it worked out better for me than most. Agriculture suited my needs on the ranch, seeing as I would be taking over the ranch. I don't suppose there is much difference in actuality. I learned how to treat livestock. There was only one other woman besides me at Montana Collegiate Institute."

"Says a lot about your drive and desire to educate yourself. Impressive in this era, you should be proud of what you've accomplished. It does get better for women. In my time, I mean."

"Yes, I saw." Emmy smiled, turning away so he wouldn't detect her blush. *He* existed, which was enough. It annoyed her, the effect he had on her. The way he looked at her, spoke to her, stood near ... had the predictability of making her pulse race.

She sprinkled more flour and placed the dough ball onto the wood surface, thinking of all that had happened in the past year. By the time she graduated the previous spring, Mama's mind had mostly taken leave of her body. Emmy wondered if she had ever comprehended her having earned the agricultural degree she worked for. Whenever she spoke of it, Mama seemed to understand—she would beam, and tears would well in her eyes. But the next time Emmy brought it up, it was forgotten, and she would ask why Emmy was not at school in classes.

Deep inside, Emmy knew Rosie was proud. No one, except for maybe Zak's family, and Becca, had helped her to celebrate her achievements. Not even Miller. During her first week home from Bozeman, he had shown up only long enough to share a meal she had spent half a day cooking. The memory brought on a disturbed frown. He completely disregarded her interests and accomplishments.

Kade's voice lifted her from her thoughts. "Here I am watching you do all the work."

He washed and dried his hands and had looped an extra apron over his head, tying it in the back, biceps flexing at the movement. His sky-blue shirt set off the color of his eyes and the frilly apron made him look a little ridiculous. She grinned.

"You have a strange way of speaking, Kade.

"So do you."

"I certainly do not!" She rummaged for a second rolling pin from the sideboard drawer and pushed it into his outstretched hand.

"Yes, ma'am. You talk like a pioneer woman."

"A pioneer woman? What in the world does a pioneer woman sound like?"

"You."

Emmy laughed, "Well, you talk like a-a..."

"An ass?"

"I wasn't going to say that!" she said, flicking a bit of flour in his direction. "But you do make a valid point." She dabbed a tear from the corner of her eye with the back of her hand. "Does everyone in the 21st century talk like you do?"

"It gets worse, trust me. I much prefer your style." The room grew unusually silent, the only sound the dual squeaking of ancient wood rolling pins. She wasn't sure but suspected at least one of them had been handed down from her great-grandmother on Doc Bartlett's side.

"You do?" she asked finally, looking up.

"The future world is a pretentious place. There may be more creature comforts, but the simplicity in this era is the best. Your straightforward honesty is refreshing."

"Even when I pepper it with an occasional curse?" she challenged.

He laughed, a cheerful sound that filled the kitchen before his tone lowered, "Especially then."

She shook her head. "I try to be good. Honest. I used to blame my indiscretions on the fact that I lived amongst cursing men, so it wasn't at all my fault."

"And how far did it get you?"

"As far as the washbasin to get my mouth washed out."

Laughter boomed again. "So, I'm guessing the soap in the mouth didn't work?"

"Cursing is my weakness," she responded, completely distracted by the flex of corded arm muscles with every stroke of the rolling pin. The space they occupied on this side of the table was compact, every move creating the danger of contact. A brush, skin to skin. More than once they touched.

"Is it now? I tend to think it shows you have passion. Lots of passion."

Kade's neck and face flamed hot. Why did he go and say that?

Shit, you're an idiot, Stockton. What are you thinking, talking 'passion' with a 19th-century proper lady?

Bravely looking up, he fell into eyes the color of a churning gray-green ocean, rimmed in black lashes. Those lashes batted a few times.

"What I mean is," he tried, "a passion for whatever it is you set your mind to doing."

Emmy jammed a spatula underneath a sheet of dough and skillfully transferred it to the pan. "You're right," she said. "I do possess a passion for all I set my mind to. Now, tell me more about the future, Kade. Like those intriguing telephone music boxes that light up and fit into your pocket. And sky transport machines. Can't think of what they're called, but Katie and Charlie showed me a book and told me all about them."

"Airplanes," he confirmed.

"Ah, that's it. I cannot imagine what it might be like to fly across the skies so high in the air. Frightening, but exciting all at the same time. I only saw pictures."

When she glanced up, excited and serious, those orbs now glimmered a welcoming warm gold in the muted light of the kitchen—made even more endearing by a daub of flour on the tip of that cute nose.

Kade's smile faded.

What he longed for was to pull her against him and dance her around the kitchen, like they had at the social. Only slow. Kiss the flour from her nose. Kiss her lips.

"See, you have a passion for learning, too," he said instead, this time not caring about his word choice. He lifted his hand and Emmy shied away.

"Hold still. You have flour on your nose."

"I do?" She fumbled with a corner of her apron.

"I've got it," he said, leaning in to brush the white dust away with the pad of his thumb. "All gone. I can see your freckles again."

And those rosy lips. How would they taste under his tongue? As syrupy sweet as the bubbling berry goo smelled. He would never know. Was the oven radiating the heat, or was it simply her closeness?

"Thank you," she replied breathlessly. And then she twirled away, gone, busying herself once again with the rolling pin and another shapeless blob of dough.

He joined her in rolling, humming an old Seals & Crofts song. A tattered handwritten cookbook lay open on the countertop, and once he had finished with the last of the dough, he moved to look at the food-stained page.

"Grammy Barnes' recipes," Emmy explained, glancing over her shoulder. "Mama's mother. She cooked for Yankee troops in southern Missouri, I'm told. I didn't know her. Mama married late in life, and I was an only child after my father brought her out west. Anyway, those are Gram's and Mama's recipes, compiled over the years."

"Mint leaves," Kade murmured. He admired the pride and raw history reflected in her eyes. He could get lost in those hazel eyes. Already had.

The last thing you need in your depressing life is the complication of a woman.

Emmy shrugged, "Unusual, maybe. But it does add freshness. An earthy spark."

"I agree." He looked away with a need to break her gaze before he embarrassed himself and started drooling. "You know, when I tasted your cobbler at the church social, it reminded me of my grandma. Only I didn't know why. Mint was her secret ingredient. One of them, at least."

Emmy folded her arms, seemingly quite pleased at the compliment. "What a coincidence! I'm happy you approve."

"I do," he said, clearing his throat. "Approve."

Slightly too much. Colt would have his hide if his Bar C boss were aware of the lurid thoughts bouncing around in Kade's head: involving those inviting lips, amongst other things, and the gooey blackberry filling. Too long since he'd been with a woman. Yep, that was the *entire* problem.

"Maybe you could teach me that dance. What did you call it—two-step? Someday, I mean. Not now, we're cooking and, in the kitchen—"

That's all it took. Grasping her floury hand into his, he ignored her protests and led her into the open area. Setting her in position, he placed a hand on the small of her back and drew her close, a chance to look into those eyes.

The vanilla-berry-woman scent of her filled his nose and he took her for a twirl around the modest space until he had her giggling.

The back screen door flung open.

"Oh—what do we have here?" Hanna asked, eyes bright at the vision of the two cooks dotted in white dust and clad in ruffled aprons, waltzing around the kitchen.

CHAPTER 18

The Bear Chase

Inside the barn, Emmy tightened the cinch on Obie's saddle, looping the excess leather into the O-ring before placing a seasoned western hat upon her head and securing the stampede thong under her chin. Reins in hand, she led Obie outside.

The beige cotton shirtwaist soaked up the late July sun, its heat blossoming into her shoulders. She tucked it tighter into her faded blue riding dungarees held up by a coppery-brown belt with a silver buckle. Placing both reins in one hand, she inserted a boot into the stirrup and hoisted herself into the saddle. Obie danced in anticipation, eyes round with excitement. She stared across the plains where she usually took her morning rides, steering Obie to the west instead, where towering pines swayed heavily in the breeze.

"We'll have to make do with a mountain ride today."

Obie snuffled in approval, dipping his head to snatch a tuft of grass.

"None of that now. You'll have plenty of opportunities for snacks along the way."

"Fraulein! Nice morning to ya." Micah called out as he approached.

"Good morning, Micah. Please call me Emmy. Really," she encouraged.

"Ja, Fraulein Emmy," he responded with a wide grin. Thick blond curls reached for the underside of his hat as ocean-blue eyes snapped in wit.

"What can I do for you, Micah?"

"If it's alright, I'll be heading out to ride the line with Kade. Zak gave his approval. We'll take our bedrolls and camp along the northern borders."

"I see. Why are you camping?"

About that time, Kade meandered from the corral leading his horse, saddle propped on his shoulder. Something about the man caused her breath to hitch. An unhurried, purposeful walk, head down until he decided to look up. His icy-blue gaze snagged hers and held, and she remembered the feel of his arms around her, leading her in a dance, even though it was cut short.

"Emmy." He nodded in greeting. He slowed to a stop beside her.

"Micah says you're riding the north line and will be gone until tomorrow?"

"Yes, ma'am. I'd like for him to ride along."

She didn't want to be overly nosy, but the ranch was her responsibility. When he didn't offer anything more, "Is there a particular reason why?"

"Need to familiarize myself with the lay of the land. Haven't explored the northwestern border. At least, not in this time."

Flustered, Emmy glanced at Micah to see if he picked up on Kade's words. He wasn't fazed. She wondered if it mattered to keep their journey through time a secret. If people knew, would they think them crazy, or would there be a fray of excitement, crowds beating tracks up the ridge to find a magical rose of their own?

A troubling vision entered her mind: hordes of invading tourists on elaborate rose-hunting expeditions. She frowned, not liking it at all. It happened when President Grant signed the protection act, establishing Yellowstone as a national park. Ever since people ventured into the beautiful park in droves to take in the magnificent scenery and wilderness. Some lacked respect, and through ignorance got themselves killed in the process—falling into the canyon, over a waterfall, or into a hot sulfur pool. Gored by bison, elk, or mauled by a bear.

Emmy's thoughts raced. She blinked, locking another gaze with Kade, wondering if he had already told someone.

"One of the boys spotted a break in the fence over Colbert's Gulch," Micah said. "Thought we could fix it up while we were out there."

"Maybe hang out for a night, do some fishin'," Kade added, inclining his head to a pair of bamboo fishing poles propped to the fence.

"Ah, fishing," she said, smiling. "Sounds fine. Obie and I are heading in the same direction. Thought about getting him out for some exercise."

"May as well ride along, at least for a bit," Kade offered. "I've packed plenty of venison jerky, beans, and hard sourdough biscuits. Plums for dessert. Yum."

"Don't mind if I do," she said, thinking to herself she would be home by dinner. "While you two are saddling up, I'll take Obie around the meadow a few times. He's chomping at the bit—"

She barely got the words out before the hefty black mustang took his cue and broke into a sleek run. Emmy melted into the horse's rhythm, woman and horse becoming one until it was hopeless to determine where one ended and the other began.

At the north fence line near Colbert's Gulch, the trio split up to search for the breach. After several minutes, Kade called out to the others.

"This must be it. Not as bad as I worried it might be. A washout must've taken two posts out of the soil. We'll have it fixed in no time." He walked to where Skitter waited, pulling out a cast-iron barbed wire fence stretcher from a saddlebag. He and Micah made their way down the soft banks and set to work.

Emmy rode out further, following a break in the trees to where a tributary of the Snake River, the Little North Fork, entered the land. It would later split into two again, creating the creek flowing beside the big house. She dismounted, allowing Obie to drink before strolling along the banks in search of wild mushrooms and herbs hiding in the proliferous alpine grasses.

The breeze quieted. Conifer and aspen leaves stopped their chattering and whispering, and Emmy paused to look around, inhaling and thinking how beautiful it was here. A patch of columbine rested at her feet, and she knelt to touch the velvety petals.

A noise brought her out of her reverie, and she straightened.

Familiar yet indistinct, it sounded like a calf bawling for its mother—a calf in pain. Cocking her head, she heard it again, only this time closer. Then she saw its origin. On the opposite bank, the reeds swayed wildly. A dusty-brown bear cub, large for its first year, split a gap in the scrub and lumbered up the soggy bank, legs moving like paddles and nose to the ground.

Hot panic shot through her veins. She scanned the banks for a sign of the cub's mother, recalling the recent story of a fur trader mauled to death after inadvertently stumbling onto a sow and her cubs. The young bear's bawling intensified, and it lifted its nose into the air.

"Shh, little one," Emmy said under her breath, striving to keep a wary eye in all directions at once. Quickly, she mounted Obie and heeled him into a trot to where she had left Kade and Micah, keeping watch on the tall grasses where bears like to root for grubs.

Out of the scrub, she nudged Obie into a canter.

Rounding a bend, at last, she caught sight of the men, wildly waving an arm over her head, not daring to yell and thus draw unnecessary attention.

Heads down and busy with repairs, neither Kade nor Micah saw her approach. But up the twisting turns of the gulch directly behind them, something saw them. So large, it could only be the mama bear. To Emmy's right, in the cover of trees, a second cub gamboled along the trunk of a pine.

Kade and Micah worked halfway between.

"Oh, God!" Emmy breathed on what little breath clenched in her lungs. She reached for her trusty Henry rifle and rested it across her thighs, securing it with one hand as she rode.

Mama bear rose to her back legs and sniffed the air. A grizzly. Apparently locating the whereabouts of her second cub, she dropped to all fours and disappeared. Where did she go? All Emmy saw as she approached the men were flashes of brown patterned within green foliage, intentions obviously set on getting to her baby.

"Kade! Micah!" Emmy screamed now, reining Obie into a sideways skid. "Bear ... behind you!"

At the same instant, their horses caught the scent of the bruin and bolted to the left, dashing across the less rugged landscape and disappearing into a wall of mesquite and juniper. Both men dropped their tools and clawed at the crumbling walls of the wash to get to solid ground.

Emmy knew what she must do—distract mama with the first cub. As though Obie read her mind, he lifted his nose, the whites of his eyes glistening. He blew, tossing his head wildly in the negative.

"We don't have a choice," she argued, reining him around. More than happy to face the opposite direction of the grizzly, Obie bounced onto his hind legs and prepared to run. Emmy thwarted him, "No—not yet, boy." Unhappy, Obie's hooves clubbed the dirt as he pranced from side to side.

Kade and Micah made it above the wash, Kade with his fist bunched into Micah's shirt to keep the youth from taking off after his horse. "Never run from a bear," he said. "Makes you look like a tasty meal. Raise your arms and make yourself as big as possible."

Micah nodded and followed Kade's lead, raising his arms while backing up slowly, facing the confused bruin now barely 25 yards away. Reaching a border of trees, the grizzly stopped, bouncing once again to her hind legs and sniffing.

Emmy glanced over her shoulder, "She smells us, Obie."

Heart twisting with each panicked beat, she recalled a time when a bear cornered her between the outhouse and the back porch when she was barely six. Rosie had charged out the door beating a pan with a spoon, yelling and flinging every curse word a six-year-old shouldn't hear, and inserting herself between the bear and her only daughter. Emmy clenched her jaw at the memory.

The cub let out another bawl and ducked into the reeds.

Emmy threw the rifle lever forward, slamming a round into the chamber and bringing the stock to her shoulder. Steeling herself for a sharp kick, she squeezed her finger, firing into a downed aspen tree close to where she had last seen the first cub.

Obie startled at the loud boom.

In a burst of splinters and dust, the first cub shot out of its hiding spot and cried even louder for its mother.

Shoulder throbbing, Emmy yanked the reins and steered Obie in a circle. That's when she saw mama grizzly drop to all fours, passing by cub number two and lumber directly towards them. The race was on. Amazing how fast something so big could move, Emmy thought inanely. Gratified knowing the grizzly steered clear of Kade and Micah, she once again cradled the rifle across her lap and leaned forward, digging heels into Obie's flanks--a needless action, for her horse was already galloping.

"Go, boy! Run as you've never run before."

They raced into the embankment of willows. In one side and bursting out the other, leaping over a fork in the river. The huffing sounds from behind grew louder. Rounding a grove of pine trees, they were forced to slow, picking their way down a rocky slope before barreling powerfully up the other side.

Emmy chanced a glance behind to see flashes of the grizzly between the trees on the other side, contemplating its course. She urged Obie on, worried about her old friend. The stress of being chased along with the heat of the summer day had him lathered. His breathing was labored. He needed to rest, but it was far too dangerous to slow down now.

"Only a bit further," Emmy coaxed.

Consoling Obie or yourself?

A game trail led to the right. Easiest to navigate for them, but also easier for mama bear, too. She nudged Obie to the left, into a forest thick with conifers and underbrush, instantly worried she had made the wrong decision. If her sense of direction hadn't failed her, up to the crest of this hill and back to the north, would take her in the direction of Kade and Micah.

She glanced back again and saw no sign of the bear, praying the bear had tired of the chase. Surely, she wouldn't leave her cubs to fend for themselves for too long.

They paused at the top of the crest. Instead of a meadow as she had expected, it was a maze of cylindrical sandstone boulders. Medicine Springs. This was all wrong! She'd gotten completely turned around. Nothing to be done about it now.

Must continue onward.

Horse and rider trotted into the cover of the tight formations, forcing them to slow, weaving one way and then another. It became unclear which way to turn until an outcropping of red sandstone rose before them.

Dead end. Obie skidded to an abrupt halt.

Kade fixed his gaze on the horizon in hopes Skitters hadn't hightailed it back to the barn. Micah located his horse hanging out in a patch of sweetgrass and now rode horseback, while Kade walked alongside, alternating his focus also on the opposing hills for any sign of Emmy. This hiccup would add another day to this little adventure, and he already felt things were falling behind schedule.

They had returned to the fence line for a few more tweaks, then gathered the tools, certain Emmy would be right back once the bear rounded up her babies and disappeared. But there had been no sign of her.

"I'm a tad bit worried," Micah voiced for the second time. "Emmy isn't accustomed to this part of the land. It's rugged. I suspect there's a chance of crossing paths with unfriendly natives."

"And don't forget the bear chasing her the last time we saw her," Kade added, the pair locking worried gazes.

Natives. First time considering that lovely possibility. To his knowledge, the Lakota were peaceable peoples, but not all bands thought the same. And Shoshone lived in these parts too. This isn't Kansas anymore, Dorothy. Sure, Emmy's a fine horsewoman, but repeating it over and over in his head wasn't doing jack shit for the sickening tightness in his gut.

"That big ole' sow had a family to tend to. Don't imagine she'd chase Emmy too far, not as long as she stayed on Obie." Micah's brows knit. When he spoke again, it was with forced lightness. "*Ja,* she rides well. I expect her to be along any time now."

"Yep, me too," Kade muttered on the cusp of a growl. She'd better damn well be all right. He scanned the horizon again for a sign of Skitters. Damned horse.

Afternoon shadows glanced off the ragged Teton peaks as they traversed the level prairie and they upped their pace. Even though it was mid-July, a sparse veil of snow graced Grand Teton's rocky face, the majestic mountain resembling a grumpy old man with a white beard.

The diatribe in Kade's head darkened with every breath. It was all he could do to keep from ordering Micah off his mount, leaving the boy behind while he tore off into the hills to find her. She could have been thrown from her horse. Lying injured in a ravine. Or worse. Colt had given Kade one responsibility—well maybe a few more. No matter. So far, he hadn't proven himself worthy of any of them.

Emmy had only begun her duties with the ranch. It was a big responsibility, and she showed amazing spirit, courage, and determination. He had never known a woman with her honor, one who lit up a room as she did. And her stubbornness. Damn, but she could be stubborn. If something happened to her, he didn't know what he would do. Not only was he assigned the duty of protecting the Bar C, but defending the matriarch was part of the deal as far as he was concerned.

Fuck.

Hadn't he lost enough in Afghanistan? Two good buddies killed right in front of him, falling at his feet, and a third because of his poor decisions. Then there was the Humvee struck by a bomb, his teammates so new, he barely knew their names. Not a single logical reason why he should have come back from that war alive.

None.

"Micah, give me your horse. I'm going to find her. She could be injured somewhere." Kade motioned for Micah to dismount.

The boy did as he was told, passing the reins to his elder and Kade swung into the saddle, steering the horse toward the ridge. He paused to assess its face. The opposing side of a craggy hill was where Emmy would likely be. It wasn't easily accessible from here, not with the loose gravel and the steep grade.

"Kade! Micah!"

A crystalline voice shattered the peaceful mountain air. It came from the top of that ridge and both men looked up, hands shielding their eyes from the afternoon sun.

"There!" Micah pointed excitedly. "It's Fraulein Emmy! See, I told you she'd be all right."

"Thank God," Kade muttered, swinging an arm above his head.

Returning an exuberant wave, she vanished into the trees, several minutes before she reappeared with Obie exploding from a clearing at full gallop. She slid from the saddle and jumped to the ground without waiting for him to come to a complete stop. First, she raced up to Micah, who met her halfway, wrapping him in a tight hug.

"Goodness gracious, I'm so happy you're safe; don't think I've ever been so terrified."

"We were scared, too, but are fine, Frau—I mean, Emmy," Micah returned the hug and patted her back awkwardly.

"I wasn't scared at all," Kade lied with an expression of relief. Emotions he couldn't even identify surged through his veins, and it felt as though the sun had risen for the second time that day. He relinquished Micah's horse and dismounted just as she flung her arms around his neck, squeezing. He reciprocated.

"Don't lie, Stockton," she voiced into his collar. "Your nose will grow like Pinocchio's."

"Whoa. Developed a bit of attitude after your adventure, eh?"

Hey, she dropped the mister in your name. Baby steps.

Though he tried, he couldn't bring himself to let her go. Not yet. Not when this phantom emotion surged through him for some damned reason. The bear, her disappearance. That would shake anyone up, right? When he should have been loosening his hold, instead, he tightened it, rocking her to and fro, burying his face in her hair and neck, breathing in her scent. Woodsy with feminine fire, uniquely her.

She leaned back just enough to scan his face and he noticed a tiny tear squiggling down her cheek. She swiped at it.

"Kade ... are you sure—"

"Right as rain." He leaned away to fix his gaze on her face, still not letting go.

"I worried about you most of all," she confessed, untying the scarf from her neck to wipe the dust from her face. And blot the tear, clearly hiding that move.

"Now why is that?" he asked.

"Because you—" she paused, realizing Micah was in earshot. "You're new here, is all."

"There are bears where I come from, too."

"They aren't as big and scary as they are here," she teased.

"Hm-mm. You lost your hat," Kade pointed out.

"You try to outrun an enraged mama grizzly and see if you don't lose your hat."

He chuckled, dipped his head, and took a step back. He let his hands slide along her arms, giving her the once-over. "Seriously. You *sure* you're okay?"

"I'm fine, and thankful both of you are safe. I don't know what I would do if..." she paused, cramming the scarf into the pocket of her skirt.

"Here, let's get you some water." Kade reached for Micah's canteen and passed it to her. "Where the hell did you go, anyway? You saved our lives."

She tilted her head back for a long drink before passing the canteen back, then she flattened her palms to her thighs and leaned forward, obviously still grasping her bearings.

"I-I did what I had to—distracted mama bear. You were right in her path. Did you see the second cub nearby the fence line where you two were working?" In sudden realization, Emmy straightened, glancing back to where Obie had parked himself under a shade tree. "What if she's still following me?"

"Don't fret. Nothing is out there," he said, hoping he spoke the truth. He circled an arm about her shoulders. "Let's get Obie to the stream. He's a hero, too."

"I got turned around, up there," she explained, pointing at the higher ridge. "The goal was to lead the bear away from you two, and every time I looked over my shoulder, she kept pace. Then when I didn't see her anymore, I headed south, or what I thought was south. Somehow, I ended up at Medicine Springs."

Kade knew the Springs well. The modern version anyway. Was a nice place to go for some peace and a dip in the thermal waters.

"Medicine Springs is still there?" *Now that's a dumb question.* "What I mean is, I've been there a few times."

They shared a knowing look for a sliver of a moment, and that's all it took to lose himself in her eyes, the many colors reflecting in the soft gray. A breeze caught a lock of her soft brown hair, threaded with gold, and blew it across her face. She lifted it away. All he wanted at that moment was to press his lips on hers, taste her.

"Used to swim up there when I was younger," she said. "It's a sacred spot and the natives frequent the area. But I didn't remember the rock formations being so confusing; backtracked after hitting a dead end, and around every corner, I expected to run into her. Never seen a grizzly sow so big."

Emmy hugged herself, glancing over her shoulder. When she faced ahead again, she slanted a palm to her brow and squinted. "Isn't that Skitters?"

"Damn," Kade said. "Imagine that. The ornery cuss didn't head home after all." He thrust two pinkies between his lips and let go with a shrill whistle. The piercing sound lifted his horse's head. He broke into a trot in their direction. The gelding appeared to have a slight sidestep even as it came toward them. Goofy horse. Brought a smile to his face.

"Little bit of sugar goes a long way." When she slanted him a confused look, he explained, "Sugar cubes."

"I agree wholeheartedly," she replied.

Unsure, but he could almost swear her sexy gaze traveled from his eyes to his mouth, and then back. All it took to get the testosterone humming through his veins.

"How about we head back," he said.

"I can't let yours and Micah's fishing trip get ruined. The house isn't far. I'll be fine."

"And the fish will be there tomorrow or the next day. Seriously, we'll head home."

"Kade, no," she said, resting her palm on his chest, and shaking her head. "I'm heading back. You two enjoy your break."

The simple touch instigated that phantom emotion to flood through him, and he realized he had placed his hand over hers.

"Be safe," he said.

"I will. I have to be."

CHAPTER 19

Rendezvous

Micah pulled a sizable cutthroat trout from the brook, freed it from the steel hook, and lopped it into a basket atop two others.

"Look at this one. Biggest yet!"

"Awesome job, Micah. Probably a good idea to stop now. Don't want to get more than we can eat in one sitting."

"Yessir. Good eatin' tonight though."

A noise prompted Kade to glance over his shoulder where he saw a doe foraging along the side of a grassy berm. Just as he was about to brush it off, the doe spooked, jetting off and disappearing. Something on the other side of that hill had startled her.

"Micah," he said. "Go on over to camp, quietly now, and mind the horses. I'm going to have a look on the other side of that rise."

Micah looked up, "Something wrong?"

Kade crossed a finger to his lips and shook his head solemnly. "Hope not. Go on, stay there and keep the horses calm."

"Yessir," Micah dipped his head in understanding, snagged the basket of fish, and picked through the grass to where the horses grazed within a roped remuda between three trees.

Kade crept to where he had first spotted the doe. Immediately, he detected the murmur of voices followed by the distinct snuffle of a horse. Squatting to his haunches, he leaned forward and silently traversed up the hillside on all fours. He paused at the top to remove his hat, then stretched out flat on his stomach and positioned behind a tree. The crest of the hill gradually slid into view.

One man on horseback waited at the far side. Four others, also astride horses, were closer, backs to him as they lined up opposite the first man.

"Gonna introduce your friends?" the man in the distance called out as he kneed his horse into a slow approach.

"Told you I had some new blood. This here is Seth Baxter from Fort Worth and a few of his boys. Clive Monroe and his men aren't here yet. Reckon you know Larry."

Kade recognized the first voice, though at a loss to place it. Shoulder aching with his odd position, he shifted, unable to fully see a face from his unfortunate angle. Carefully, he braced a palm to a boulder and went to adjust, pushing with his right foot. A twig snapped. His eyes squeezed shut. *Shit!* Almost two years out of the Army and he's losing skills, he thought with irritation.

"Who's out there?" a voice said.

The six riders with their backs to him swung their mounts around in a one-eighty, drawing weapons at the same time. Firearms cocked simultaneously and he shrunk flush to the tree, heart thudding a vicious beat down his spine and into the earth.

"Who's there?" came the call again, impatient.

Another recognizable voice—Larry, the oldest Carlson brother. Boy. Man. Whatever the hell he was. For sure a coward who liked to pick on those younger and weaker than himself. Should have squeezed the runt's neck harder in the churchyard that day, Kade thought in a flash of irritation. Hindsight.

Another doe and two youngsters exploded from the brush, darting into a clearing and leaping out of sight in graceful serpentine patterns. An explosion reverberated through the air, penetrating the forest with waves of sound. Kade cringed, not moving a muscle.

"Hellfire!" someone barked. "Only a deer. Gonna shoot your own damn self with that thing. Holster it before I cram it up your skinny ass."

Grumbles of displeasure and the scuffle of hooves.

Kade gradually released the breath locked in his lungs as he watched a shiny black beetle hard at work navigating rusty pine straw, wobbling past his thigh before disappearing into a rotten log.

"You boys afraid of a few deer?" came the first familiar voice from behind, a chuckle tailing his words.

Kade would recognize that cheeky laugh anywhere. *Miller Johnson.* What business did he, or any of them, have so close to the borders of the Bar C land? About that time an eighth rider approached, a contrasting voice inserted into the fray, this one clear and concise.

"Gentleman. What's going on here?"

"Where you been, Detective? Thought you done gone and lost your way."

Kade's frown deepened. *Grayson?* His focus bore an invisible hole into the ground, unseeing. How he longed to lean in, take a chance, and see the face belonging to the new voice, though common sense wouldn't allow it.

"Understood we were to be meeting at your place, Johnson. I was on my way when I heard the shots. This is the outer edge of Bar C land. You aware of that?"

"Damned good at your job, Grayson." Miller laughed, though he was the only one. He cleared his throat and continued. "A little joke to lighten the mood. Anyhow, these men are here to help with the current situation. Easier to congregate on this side of the creek seeing as how the boys are coming up from the south. I'm certain Emmy wouldn't mind."

Miller proceeded to name the new arrivals.

"Amos here is one of my top hands. I'm considering promoting him to the Johnson Ranch foreman. Ain't that right, Amos?"

Muffled conversation and the shuffle of movement.

"Next to Amos is Larry, the oldest Carlson boy. Some of the others are fresh in from Paris, Texas. They erecting a tower in Texas, too, or is that only for France?" Miller guffawed at his joke, the others not uttering a peep.

"Anyhow," Miller continued, "I put them on the payroll for five dollars a day. I'd say that's a handsome sum for men of that caliber. Am I right, Detective?"

Grayson's gaze seemed to narrow as he quietly surveyed each man Miller identified. A few more sauntered from the cover of trees on horseback.

"This is not something the Wyoming Stock Growers Association is apt to authorize. Not the way to go about it, Johnson," he said finally.

"Does it matter?" Johnson shot back. "The WSGA is getting a kickback. We all know that. I'd say that's all they care about. Now about you, Detective, since we're on the same side of this little war, I'm thinking we need to be setting a few ground rules. Just to keep things straight, you understand."

"Mr. Johnson, I only follow the orders coming down from the Governor."

"That's right fine. You know who doesn't follow the Governor's orders? Emmy Bartlett, the new matriarch of the Triple Bar C."

"I'm familiar with Miss Bartlett."

"I'm sure you are. Heard you stopped by when you first arrived here in the region. Emmy and I will be married soon, and I'll make sure she begins to follow orders then."

"I wasn't aware. Of a marriage that is. Congratulations are in order."

Miller's chest puffed, "Why thank you, Detective. You see, there was an incident a few months back. A man attacked her in the house when she was all alone, was lying in wait for her. I heard about it after the fact, and it's only by the grace of God she wasn't hurt!"

"Was this man ever apprehended? Sheriff Townsend didn't mention anything about it."

With a silent inhale, Kade pushed with knees and elbows, hoping for a glimpse of Miller's face. Good thing he wasn't any closer; something about the man made him want to smack the crap out of him. They were speaking of the assault on Emmy that Colt had mentioned. Kade had attempted, unsuccessfully, to bring it up with her. His own fault. He just didn't feel like it was his business, but the time had come to make it his business. Whoever attacked her was still on the loose. Time to stop being delicate about it. He needed the truth.

Is she or is she not planning to marry Miller? Hasn't told me anything about that, either.

"Um, don't think Emmy made a report. That's how she is. A private sort. Probably feels like she can handle it herself. When we're married, she'll have my protection and we won't have to worry about it."

A few moments passed before Grayson spoke. "What's the story behind the Bar C? I hear Colton Chase is on record as the owner. What do you know about that?"

"Your records may not be accurate, Detective. Chase left the state. Craziness if you ask me. Up and signed the deed over to Emmy's mother. Something else you may not know. Before she passed...."

Miller's voice quieted to almost a whisper, and between that and the scrape of horseshoes to gravel, and muffled voices from the others, Kade strained to hear, only making out a few scattered words.

Dammit, what are they saying?

"...soft in the head. Thought it best ... my name ... don't forget, there's money in it for you."

A cackle sounded from someone in the group and Kade hunkered further into a soft bed of mulch behind the rotted tree trunk. The beetle, or a close relative, thrust a stickery leg up out of a tiny hole, popping out and wobbling off in a huff. Or at least it looked that way.

"Must be that deer again. Keep hearing something behind that brush over there," someone voiced. "I say we go have a look. Fresh venison for supper don't sound half bad."

"They teach you how to shoot deer down in Texas?" another said, instigating a round of laughter and conversation.

Time was up. Kade couldn't afford to be discovered. Quietly as possible, he crept back down the hillside and climbed to his feet, stepping parallel through the gulch, then up the other side, running into Micah halfway back to camp.

"What are you doing out here?" Kade hissed, tone sharper than intended.

"Uh, you been gone a long while. Thought I'd better check," Micah whispered.

"No time," Kade added, urging the boy around. "We're going to have company if we don't get out of here."

"But what about camp?"

"Moving it further down the river. Saddle up as quick as you can and let's get on it."

Emmy sunk into the tepid water of the clawfoot tub. There wasn't yet a reliable means in place to heat the water properly for a comfortable bathing experience, as it currently relied on the heat of the stove, and when it wasn't being used, then the water didn't heat. It was a work in progress, and so she made do. An equally tepid cup of sassafras tea sat on the stool beside her. She reminisced over the day's happenings, sliding further into the water until it lapped at her ears.

The bears. Micah. And Kade.

A memory of his embrace. The intensity in which she had returned it. Almost as though she were trying to pull him inside her skin.

All she knew was, after the chase, seeing him and Micah far below the bluff, made her heart lift and her hopes soar. Kade was a difficult one to figure out, maybe because of different time periods. He filled her with what she could only describe as longing, a longing for something she wasn't sure of.

A sharp rap on the front door caused her to jump.

Estelle's sure footsteps descended the stairs and crossed the parlor to the front door. Then came the muffled sound of voices. With a slosh of water, Emmy cut her bath short and stepped out, scrubbing dry with a linen sheet. She heard Estelle's footfalls approach.

"Emmy dear, that detective ... Grayson is it? He wishes to speak with you. Shall I wake Henry?"

"No need to disturb Henry. The water is cold anyway, and I'm finished. Tell the detective I'll be out shortly."

"Alright. Call if you need us." Estelle's footfalls faded down the hall and eventually up the stairs.

Emmy pulled a cotton gown over her head and worked her arms into a vanilla damask dressing gown, checking the mirror, then adjusting the combs that kept a relatively tidy mop of hair under control. Working her feet into slippers, she left the bath closet, padding her way into the parlor. Through the expansive front window, she saw Detective Grayson's form at the top of the porch steps, his back to the door.

She tightened her robe and opened it.

"Good evening, Detective."

"Miss Bartlett." Grayson swung around and stepped up, removing his hat in the same movement. "I'm sorry to have disturbed you, and without notice."

His gray eyes swept over her, instigating her fingers to provide further adjustment to the ruffled neckline. "I trust there's nothing wrong?"

"Been a noteworthy day, but yes. As well as can be expected. Again, I apologize for disturbing you so late. I wonder if your offer still stands?" When she didn't immediately answer, he went on. "A bed for a night or two?"

Emmy nodded, smiling, "Of course, Detective Grayson. If you will make your way down to the main bunkhouse, let them know I said it was fine for you to stay as long as required." Emmy poked her head around the oak door, noticing a glowing lantern upon a hook at the barn door, a host of tiny moths and other night bugs fluttering in the halo of light. "It looks as though someone is still in the barn."

"I'll mosey on down. Appreciate the hospitality. When you're available, I'd like to sit down with you for a conversation. A few things need working out."

"Absolutely. I've had an eventful day and I plan to sleep in tomorrow morning. I trust that works out for your schedule?"

"Oh?" When she didn't elaborate, he continued, "I hope things weren't too trying. The heat doesn't help when we are trying to get work done, does it?"

She shook her head, "No, it does not. Well then, we shall speak soon. Good evening, Detective." She pressed the door shut, leaning against it until the sound of his footsteps faded. Something about his demeanor set her on edge though she couldn't quite put a finger on it. She hoped he wasn't saving some kind of bad news for tomorrow.

CHAPTER 20

Grayson Snoops

N icholas Grayson crept along the corral fence toward the great red barn silhouetted against the night sky. He paused long enough to scratch the neck of a handsome chestnut mare, a wobbly-legged filly nuzzled close between her legs in search of a teat.

"Certainly are a pretty girl," he complimented in a hushed tone before moving on.

The air had cooled in the wake of a purple dusk, daylight only a memory. And the light played tricks, creating shadows out of nothing as clouds rolled over mountain peaks. He wondered if they were in for a storm.

Nick looked up to scan the three roof eaves. The structure was massive, he thought, as he walked the circumference of the old-style Dutch construction. Sturdy, he surmised this barn would stand for at least a couple hundred years, maybe more. An elaborate weathervane perched on the cusp of the tall roof, a rearing horse with a wind-torn mane.

Nick passed through a second doorway at the rear of the barn, assuming it led to an attached carriage house. Cautious, he surveyed his surroundings before going inside, making certain no one else loitered about. Carefully, he eased open a man door and stepped inside, pulling it shut with the hushed sound of recently oiled iron hinges.

The air surrounding him was thick and cool, aromas of tanned leather and neat's-foot oil filling his senses. Quietly, he stepped past a phaeton carriage, remembering it from the church social—at least it appeared to be the same one in the near absolute darkness, polished and well taken care of.

Earlier, he had joined the cowhands for a late meal and conversation, a few stragglers sitting about playing cards. Lucky for him, he ran across several who liked to talk. Nick was careful not to strike up any undo notice, at the same time keeping a watchful eye on everyone. One never knew who may end up proving useful.

His prime focus was to keep the topics light and friendly. When Zak Tompson passed through the chow hall, stopping to say hello, Nick asked a few friendly questions, even volunteering to help repair a leaky roof above the porch on the main house. The least he could do to repay the favor of allowing him to bunk down. Perfect arrangement. Not only would it allow him to observe the daily activities of the hands, see who came and went, but it also provided an opportunity to keep an eye on the ranch mistress.

Lucky woman to have such a fine spread of land bequeathed to her and her alone. At least that's what he had been told: But there was a catch, one Nick would have never known about if he hadn't paid a visit to the Beckett Law office in Gunn Pass City. Wasn't even a planned visit. More like an afterthought. Nick had merely intended on asking a couple of questions of the old barrister, but the man turned out to be more accommodating than expected.

Years prior, Glen Beckett had drawn up legal paperwork for the entire Chase family, back when Charles and Katherine first homesteaded the Triple Bar C. And the man loved to chat. The unrest on the entire upper Wyoming rangeland was particularly troubling since Beckett's daughter's family had a place in the region and feared for their livelihood. A common story in the region. Nothing unusual there, and frankly none of it was Nick's business. Beckett's daughter's place was a county over, out of his jurisdiction.

Nick made the excuse of pressing appointments to tend to, but Beckett insisted on telling him about the strange wording in the paperwork drawn up by the eldest son, Colton Chase before he disappeared from the area ten years before. Said it had been bothering him lately, and being that Nick was a state lawman, he wondered if he could have a look.

At that, Beckett snagged Nick's attention.

He scanned the documents. Indeed, the wording was odd. Why would Colton Chase deed the family property to a woman of middle age with the stipulation it goes to the woman's only daughter, Emily Anne Bartlett, at her demise, then back to Chase's wife and child at Emily's passing? Illogical to say the least. Beckett spoke highly of the Chase family and said it had always struck him as a curiosity. It had slipped his mind until recently when Miller Johnson stopped by his office with a few questions. That combined with the unrest in the region, he thought Nick may like to know about it.

Bottom line, one man's curiosity didn't constitute a broken law. Nick had thanked Beckett politely, with intentions of filing the knowledge away in case it was needed. And he would have, except one last thing continued to nag at him: Clearly, Emily Anne Bartlett was the sole heir to the Triple Bar C property and cattle operations. Then why had Miller Johnson conveyed an entirely different story? Something about the elder Bartlett woman changing the will. Could she even do that after Colton Chase had specifically stated to whom the property would be deeded? Johnson seemed mighty bitter about the whole situation—namely the appearance of Stockton. Which begs the question: Exactly *who* was Kade Stockton in all this?

Fortunately, on this evening, Nick didn't worry about accidentally stumbling into Stockton. Zak Tompson had been more than accommodating, divulging details including Stockton's preference to bunk in the carriage house. Tompson even mentioned his whereabouts that very night—he and one of the younger hands, Micah Shaffer, had gone on an overnight fishing and property line trek. Wasn't expected back until the following day. The fact was, it may even be longer than that, according to Zak's rendition of some trouble with a grizzly that afternoon. Near as he could tell by Tompson's description, Emmy had accompanied them initially, returning before dusk. No wonder Emmy looked exhausted. Fortunately, no one was hurt in the grizzly encounter.

Nick knew he hadn't needed to stop by the house for Emmy's permission to bunk down. His request was confirmed the week before. All he needed to do was to show up at the bunkhouse.

No, he wanted to see her. A personal reason.

Something about her struck a chord and he couldn't quite shake it. She was a uniquely beautiful woman, but it wasn't just that. She sparked his interest. Something about Emmy Bartlett reminded him of Meredith. Made the ache in his heart start up all over again. Not something he wanted to rehash but couldn't seem to walk away from either. She had the same coloring, and pale brown hair; struck him as independent and a bit aloof. Hard to read. He understood why the woman might be a challenge to some men.

Like Miller. Or Stockton. Even himself.

Grayson's thoughts turned to the rough men Johnson had introduced earlier. When he had first agreed to meet Johnson at the edge of his property line, he hadn't expected anyone else to be there. Supposedly they had freshly arrived in the state. There to discuss security tactics. Or so Miller had said. Nick wondered why Baxter's horses were loaded down with packs. Weapons, maybe? And who was Monroe?

Johnson had insisted he knew of an upcoming invasion from the south, a group of ex-lawmen and ex-military. Somewhere close to 35 men were supposedly making their way up from Texas to join forces with the homesteaders. Where did he acquire that knowledge?

Grayson focused on the task at hand, scanning his surroundings once again from a paned window, making certain no one was around before ascending a skinny set of stairs. Predictably, it led to a caretaker's living quarters. After talking with a few loose-lipped cowpokes in the chow hall, he learned Stockton suffered from nightmares of the war and would wake up screaming. Nicholas didn't buy it. Which war? He had a unique way of speaking, and when he asked around, none of the locals had any inkling of who Stockton was or where he had come from. Never heard of him before.

Maybe a stroll through his quarters and a peek through his belongings would shed some light on the man's background. Grayson may not agree with all the political officials in Wyoming, but he took his job as a state lawman seriously, and if Stockton were up to no good, Emmy Bartlett, for one, needed to be aware.

As for Miller Johnson, the second-generation sheep rancher seemed overly anxious to learn more about the outsider. Worried about the interloper moving in on the woman he had his sights set on. Seemed more than that to him. From the start, something about Johnson hadn't set right with Grayson, not since the first time he met him. From that first introduction, he pegged him as one of those blowhard types. An annoying gnat compared to a flesh-hungry horsefly. One got in your business and annoyed, while the other chomped into the flesh until a man yelped. From the get-go, Grayson pegged Miller Johnson as an irritating gnat. Men like him didn't have the balls or common sense to get out of their own way.

Grayson's plan all along had been to investigate Stockton, the obvious horsefly in the ointment. But when the 'Gnat' resorted to bribing a law officer, now that put a new slant on things. Let Gnat think the extra cash he offered would assist with a private school for a daughter he didn't have.

Oh, Meredith was factual—his wife. Murdered senselessly by a wanderer he vowed to find. But the rest was fabricated. He never intended to accept a bribe or to give Johnson any valuable information. That was against WSGA regulation and would get him fired for certain. He may prove rogue at times, but he wasn't stupid.

Standing at the door at the top of the skinny stairway, Nick cocked an ear and listened. When he didn't hear anything, he turned the knob. The door opened easily. Grayson slipped into the stuffy room, bumping his bad knee against an unknown piece of furniture as he crossed to crack open a small window. He liked fresh air. Allowed him to think more clearly.

"Ouch," he muttered, grimacing at the old injury. He sealed the shutters and lit an oil lamp positioned upon a tidy desk, then picked up a shiny blue writing utensil, curiously rolling it between his fingers. Replacing the pen, he surveyed his surroundings.

Stockton was an orderly sort, he noted, a perfectly made bed with crisp corners and a stack of neatly folded clothing arranged in the middle. Signs of a military man. Propped at the side of the bed on the floor was a canvas sack with a multitude of straps and buckles. Pushing his hat further back on his head, a curious frown imprinted Grayson's brow as he lifted the bag and surveyed it from every angle, curious of the thin ties made from a shiny material, with a type of closure he had never seen before.

"Well, I'll be," he mouthed quietly, gripping a small handle and sliding it down to open the canvas sack, sliding it up again to close it. "Damnedest thing," he said, repeating the action with the other handle. He opened a small compartment at the top and fished out a chain with two metal medallions, displaying them flat in his palm. Identical, the embossing on each one read Kaden D. Stockton, followed by a series of letters and numbers.

Returning the metal tags where he found them, he fished into other pockets and found a series of tools folded into one another: a knife, scissors, a pick, and some he couldn't identify. Next, he sorted through miscellaneous papers without any obvious significance and more clothing. In the last compartment, he found something that gave him pause. A black, thin, brick-type object, it appeared to be constructed from a sort of lightweight metal and possibly glass. After careful inspection, he pressed a soft protrusion on the side and the contraption lit up while holding it in his palm.

"What the—?" He tossed it, the object landing with a bounce on the perfectly made bed. Frowning, Grayson studied the mesmerizing series of colorful lights flashing letters and symbols, reminding him of fireworks.

"What's this, a strange Edison or Tesla contraption?" he questioned under his breath, wondering if Stockton hailed from the East where electrical advancements were typically introduced first.

This line of thinking brought more questions to mind: was Stockton truly a military man, and *why* did he show up on the Bar C ranch? In his investigation, he learned the surname of Stockton was listed on the 1880 Wyoming census, but nowhere near the northwestern quadrant, which meant no one close enough to question.

Then, a curiosity: Did Stockton's sudden appearance have any connection to the strange disappearance of Colton Chase back in '78?

A noise outside caught his attention.

He crossed to the window, extinguishing the dim oil lantern before peering through the shutters. Looked like the old man was tending to the mare and her filly and was then limping across the corral. Across the way, Nick could see a warm yellow light in the window of the cabin where Zak and his family resided.

As soon as Henry disappeared into the big house, Nick turned his attention back to the object, noting it had gone dark again. Cautiously, Grayson picked it up and returned it to the canvas sack, in the exact pocket he found it in. He blew out the oil lamp and made his way down the stairs and back to the bunkhouse where he found a comfortable place to lay his head for the night.

CHAPTER 21

Dottie's Big Surprise

K ade and Micah rose at dawn and spent an hour at the river's edge fishing, catching two more brown trout before heading back. The priority was to stop by the house, making certain Emmy had arrived home safely the afternoon before. The second priority was a shower. Something about sleeping on the hard ground in a bedroll made a man crave soap and water. Too many times in the Army he was left without the shower option, and he learned to appreciate it when he had it.

After sending Micah off to clean the fish and grab his breakfast at the chow house, Kade knocked on the door. While waiting for her to answer, he strolled the length of the porch where he saw Estelle and Henry already collecting eggs in the hen house. He lifted his hat and pushed his fingers through his hair. Then, he wiped a bandanna over his face to get rid of some dust. He was about to knock again when the curtains moved.

Emmy peeked around an ivory lace panel and a moment later the door eased open. Initially struck by the feminine pink something-or-other she wore, it had two tiny buttons at the top open, revealing a slice of smooth skin. His brain went partially blank.

"Morning," he greeted.

"Is it—already?" she asked, voice scratchy with sleep.

"Shit, I woke you."

She grimaced, and he supposed that might be the closest he'd get to a smile. He didn't blame her.

"I'm sorry if I woke you. We only wanted to make sure you made it home safely. Not like I could text or anything." He cleared his throat, coughing into his fist.

Emmy fiddled with a loose hairpin, a larger-than-usual pouf of glossy brown hair piled atop her head, crooked and sticking out every which way. She rubbed her eyes, then poked her head out of the doorway to scan the porch.

"We?" she asked, stifling a yawn. The shawl gripped to her shoulders slipped, exposing a tiny heart locket on a gold chain. And a kissable collarbone.

What the hell—since when did you turn into a creepy lecher?

The plain material was nothing special. It appeared well-worn with at least a couple hundred washes in its history. It wasn't the gown garnering his attention; it was the woman who wore it, the intimate way it lay flush to smooth, pale skin. Long fingers clasped the ugly plaid shawl tighter. Even the three tiny moles on her neck mesmerized him. A faint scent of lemons and lilacs drifted past his nose.

Holy shit, woman, you look sexy as hell. No, a voice clanged in his head in silent warning—*stay behind that door where it's safe.*

Fortunately, she moved further back inside. Too late, his mouth already went dry. Had Miller given her that tiny heart, he wondered? Or possibly another suitor. He recalled the feel of her tight embrace the day before, the memory causing him to stumble over his words.

"We?" he reiterated, then, "Uh, Micah and me." He motioned behind, but there wasn't a soul around. Nothing but a determined magpie chasing a grasshopper across the grassy yard. Even the bird appeared to have ceased its chase to observe the awkward moment.

"Looks as though Micah left you on your own," Emmy observed.

"Appears that way."

"Well, I made it home without incident. But with the detective stopping by so late, I didn't get much sleep after that," she expounded, stifling another yawn.

Kade was about to leave when her comment forced him to put on the brakes. He glanced back to see her heart-shaped face poking around the oak door and his heart sank. Lower than low. Downright painful. The worst feeling in the world.

"I smell fresh coffee coming from the kitchen," she added. "Seems as though we both could use a cup."

Nothing would've pleased him more, but now, no amount of black coffee could wash down the lump forming in his throat. Besides, stinking up her kitchen with a potent potpourri of fish, camp smoke, dirt, and who-knew-what-else, wasn't an option. Better for everyone involved if he declined.

"Appreciate it, how about a rain check? Need to hit the shower." He pressed his hat onto his head and leaped down the porch steps, two at a time, mounting Skitter and trotting the worn-out horse to the barn. He could have walked the poor animal to the barn. What was he thinking? He didn't feel like himself at all.

Pressing the door closed, Emmy leaned her back against it and gathered her thoughts, trying hard not to envision him in the shower again. Truth was, he smelled like a big stinky fish, the notion bringing a tiny smile to her lips. And was a rain check one more thing she needed to be aware of?

Sighing, she pushed her weight from the door and headed upstairs, passing a mirror along the way, and horrifying herself at her rumpled appearance. After washing up, she arranged her hair loosely atop her head with a handful of metal pins and two tortoiseshell combs, then slipped into a comfortable day dress, this one a summery peach color. She needed to order a few new dresses. Back downstairs, she poured herself some coffee and added a splash of fresh cream, snatching the last blueberry muffin from a batch Estelle had whipped up the day before.

An unusual wave of happiness and peace swept over her, lifting her heart. An elusive emotion she hadn't felt in a long time. The sensation surprised her, the lightness of it, a reminder she truly was still alive. Had the dreary clouds hanging over her head lately begun to clear?

Emmy kissed the tip of a finger and pressed it to the glass covering the photo of a dark-haired woman upon her desk in a gilded frame. Though there wasn't a smile to be seen on the woman, Emmy knew it was there behind those glittering eyes framed by arched brows and a curl of thick lashes. The ever-so-slight lift of the right side of her mouth created a distinct dimple, and Emmy knew quite well if that dimple ever disappeared then Mama was truly angry or upset. An ebony curl had fallen over her forehead right before the picture was taken, and by that time she had tired of fiddling with her hair and the netted bonnet she thought to place over it. She ordered the photographer to take the photo and be done with it. That's what ladies did for photographs, wasn't it, wear hats? Mama rarely wore hats, even when she was outdoors. Never liked the feel, preferring the breeze in her hair. That explained the splash of healthy color Emmy knew was on her face, even though the photograph showed no hues other than muted black, murky white, and sepia.

"I think I'm going to be all right, Mama," she vowed, a quiver on her lips.

Perching the spectacles used for close-up work upon her nose, she punched figures into the heavy steel adding machine perched at the corner of the desk, cranking the lever on the side to tally a total. She plucked a pencil from the knot of hair atop her head and proceeded to figure out the amounts of the bills owed to local merchants. She would cut checks and make a trip to Gunn Pass City tomorrow and deliver them personally.

Unaware of how long she had been sitting there, she set the pencil down and removed her glasses, rubbing her eyes as she leaned back, the chair screeching in protest. She made a mental note to oil the springs, then stretched her arms above her head. If her calculations were correct, by the end of the year there would be enough money for the purchase of bulls and heifers, along with a fine start to a herd of sheep. Henry had already begun cordoning off sections of pastureland. An unused barn, a much smaller one, would be a perfect area to set up operations for breeding and shearing.

The office door eased open and in waddled Dottie. Emmy swore the little dog had gained weight lately, watching her tip-tap across the wood floors to a stretch of carpet beneath the desk. She stopped short of leaping into Emmy's lap, instead stopping at her feet, panting, tongue hanging off a row of white teeth.

"For Pete's sake, Dottie, you're getting fat—"

The words stuck in Emmy's throat. As Dottie's tail thumped rhythmically on the carpet, Emmy saw that her belly was oddly wider than the rest of her body.

"You're going to have puppies!"

Dottie wiggled to her feet as if to say, "'Bout time you noticed!" Not waiting for a further invitation, she made a flying leap into Emmy's lap and licked her cheek.

"Aww, girl, you're so happy, aren't you? How exciting. Puppies! They will be so cute, just like you." Scratching the sweet spots behind the terrier's ears, she stared off into the distance. "But—" she began, wondering who the proud papa might be. Dottie was the only small dog on the ranch. Finishing with a mental inventory of possible candidates on nearby spreads, "—ah, have you been rendezvousing with that runt that snaps at my ankles whenever I visit Helen's place?"

Dottie's tail made a final thump on Emmy's leg and then hovered midair, as if in anticipation.

Emmy gasped, "Dottie, I'm quite shocked! He is the ugliest little dog I've ever seen in my life. Why he's practically hairless, and what hair he has sticks straight up on the top of his head."

Dottie's expression drooped. The average person may not notice, but Emmy detected the little dog's upset.

"I'm sorry, girl. I didn't mean it in a bad way. I'm sure he's a charming little guy once you get to know him. His eyes are quite big. But, I'm certain your pups will be adorable and look just like you."

Splaying fingers around the dog's middle, she pressed lightly to judge a possible delivery window, noting the abdomen spreading almost beyond the ribcage. She had assisted Mama with midwifery, and studied animal husbandry at the

Institute, learning more than she ever really cared to know regarding cattle and sheep reproduction. Surely dogs weren't so much different.

"You've got some time." She recalled when Sage had delivered puppies several years back, surprising them all. Sadly, the pups came far too early and none of them survived. "We must build a special box for the birth," she pointed out. "In a quiet area where nothing can bother you. Fill it with plenty of fresh straw. Maybe Kade can help."

Wiggling in newfound excitement, Dottie turned in a circle and made to jump from her lap, but Emmy stopped her, gently setting her to the floor. "None of that. You're going to be a mama soon."

A knock sounded on the front door. Emmy rose from her chair and headed down the hallway, noting a man's shadow glimmered through the beveled glass of the sidelight. Tall, broad-shouldered, and wearing a hat. *Kade?* A bolt of excitement shot through her. Why did his presence quicken her heartbeat and stir her in areas she preferred not to be stirred in? Ridiculous. However, now she could ask him if he could construct a nice birthing box for Dottie.

Emmy flung open the door.

"Oh ... good day Detective," she said, disappointment hidden by a polite smile. Dottie went to the cool stones by the fireplace and plopped down.

"Morning, Miss Bartlett. I hope it's not too early. If so, I can come back another time."

"No, please come in. I've been up for several hours thanks to Kade. I mean, Mr. Stockton." She waved off the flicker of a question in his eyes. "You know how it is, life on a ranch. Never a dull moment." She chuckled. "We can speak in my office."

He lifted his hat from his head and placed it on the corner of the desk, then took a seat across from her.

"I appreciate you sitting down with me, Miss—"

She lifted a hand, "Please call me Emmy."

He nodded. "Very well. I'd be pleased if you called me Nick."

It felt too familiar to be calling him by his given name. Not only was he quite a handsome man, but a professional lawman at that, and even though he had been so friendly and witty at the church social, today he was all business.

"So ... Nick, are there any leads in the Dibbs Riley murder?"

"Not specifically, but there are several persons of interest. I've combed the immediate area, as well as the entire county, asking questions. That's the main reason I wanted to speak with you today. Privately"

"Oh?"

"I'm hoping to get a few answers. If you're willing."

Emmy got the feeling he would be expecting answers whether or not she was able or willing. "I will do my best, Detective."

"This is never an easy subject," he began with a slight pause. "But when things like this arise, it's my opinion to bring it out in the open right away."

"I'm unsure what you're referring to."

"I understand a few months ago, there was an incident here at the ranch. One you may not have told the sheriff about." His scrutiny grew and he leaned forward in the chair. "An assault?"

Emmy's eyes widened, and she swallowed. "Who told you that?"

"Your fiancé mentioned it. I apologize for springing this on you without warning, but it's important, and something that I need to know about if—"

"I don't have a fiancé," Emmy clarified, bristling.

Did I tell Miller about the attack? I didn't tell anyone at all! No one except for Colt and Madison.

"He did mention an upcoming wedding..." Grayson paused, starting over. "That's none of my concern. What I need is to find out more about the assault that took place. What did he want, and did you recognize the man?"

"Clearly, he wanted to rob me. Wanted me to open the safe. And no, I haven't seen the man either before or since."

"Why was it you never told the Gunn Pass sheriff?"

"Didn't feel the need, I suppose. I told you I knew how to use a weapon. And I do. I scared him off."

And because I was embarrassed, that's why! I felt weak and inadequate. The entire county doesn't need to know my vulnerabilities!

"You weren't compromised?" Grayson lifted a small notebook from the pocket of his jacket and began jotting notes with a lead pencil.

"Compromised?" He looked up with another pointed gaze. She shook her head then, "No. No, of course not."

"Very well. Can you describe this man?"

Emmy squeezed her eyes shut and drew an image of his face once again in her mind. All this time and effort to forget it, and now she must grasp for a remembrance. She described him to Grayson: Mustache, black or dark brown, long on the sides. Mostly black. Did it have silver in it? No, but his hair was scraggly, sticking out from beneath his hat, The sideburns definitely were sprinkled in silver. She noticed that because they were large. His hat was a grayish color, wasn't it? And one eye had a scar zigzagging across it to extend over his nose. Could he see out of that eye? Maybe that was why he tripped on the coat rack, or it could have been his unsteadiness because of the limp. Yes ... he had a limp! Was the limp before or after she stomped his foot?

She was terrible at this.

Emmy took a breath and opened her eyes, bathed in a sense of freedom just from describing the scoundrel.

"I see," he said, lips tightening, pencil lead scratching across the pad. She thought she had done moderately well in providing a description, though he didn't seem impressed. "And he disappeared that night without removing any property?"

"I never even opened the safe. And I haven't noticed anything missing. He was just gone, left the door hanging open."

"I'd like to know how you came about hiring Kade Stockton to work as a hand on the ranch—he is a hand, is that correct? Not a hired gun?"

"A hired gun? Heavens, no," Emmy said. "Wherever did you hear that?" Becca had come to that conclusion, she recalled, and perhaps she had passed on her theory. *For sure she had—it's Becca, for goodness sake.* "I've heard rumors, but I can assure you, Kade Stockton is not a hired gun."

"Where did he come from? Back east?"

"I heard him mention North Carolina. I met him through Colton Chase."

"The man who deeded the ranch to you? Where is he living now?"

"Colt Chase is the previous owner of the Bar C. He now lives in Colorado with his wife," Emmy answered quickly. "And being that he can't be here himself, he trusted Kade to handle things efficiently in his absence. At least for a bit. While the range wars are in full swing." She cringed. Though she had only been in the future a few days, she had picked up some unusual speech habits.

"I see." That inquisitive lift of his eyes again. Pencil scribbling. "Protection, then? Military man, is he?"

"I've heard he was a soldier, yes."

"You can understand why I would be asking these questions, with the unrest going on. Then a stranger shows up." One brow arched up at her.

"Certainly do," Emmy said. "You wouldn't be doing your job if you didn't. I can assure you, Colt only wanted an extra set of hands on the ranch to help Zak and the others. Keep an eye out. Good cowboys, trustworthy ones, are hard to come by."

Grayson smiled then, the familiar humor lighting his eyes, and Emmy breathed a sigh of relief to see the charming man from the church social emerge. She felt sure he had to be hiding in there somewhere. He sure could be intimidating when he chose to be.

"Very well, Emmy, I won't take up any more of your time," he said, indicating the ledgers and other papers littering the desk. "I appreciate your speaking with me. There is one more thing."

"Oh?" She stood.

"You promised a jar of blackberry jam next time I came through." That grin again.

"Yes! It's in the pantry. Follow me, I know exactly which kind, especially if you're fond of lemons."

"That I am. My wife used to make lemon curd, when we had access to lemons, that is."

Emmy rummaged through Mason jars on the bottom shelf of the pantry, and when she came to her feet, a bead of sweat had popped out on her brow. She handed the jar to Nick, then went to wrap up a small portion of the bread. "Take this, too."

"Are you sure?"

"Can't have jam without bread, now can you?"

CHAPTER 22

Used To The Pain

A *cloud of filth hangs low, the air thick with smoke and the stench of burning oil. Sounds of automatic rounds strike a beat in the distance, the glow of artillery lighting the night sky.*

Chaos.

Soldiers crisscross in front of him. Orders are shouted, exact words muffled, and he strains to hear, to make sense out of them.

"Americans 3 o'clock. C'mon, we're going in!" a voice calls out.

Not a combat engineer's job. Just the same, they train hard for it because it's war, and you never know. Word is a woman, and an unknown number of children are inside the gutted building in front of them. So, this time, all hands on deck.

"Cody, you're up!" Kade orders, the dust and smoke obscuring his vision. "Wyatt, you're second."

Squad stacked at the door, Cody steps up and thrusts his M4 into the jamb and fires. Shrapnel flies, striking helmets, and night goggles. Once the door is breached, Cody spins around and kicks it open, making way for Wyatt to enter at the first point position, sweeping of the room. The second point follows with a sweep in the opposite direction. Movement is staggered as the third moves in. The first point falls behind and the queue repeats at each successive doorway along the skinny hallway.

"Clear, clear," each soldier calls out in succession, the rooms illuminating with the green haze of night vision.

As team leader, Kade enters last, a security soldier directly behind him, making sure no one sneaks behind.

Go, go, go!—Kade orders with the motion of his arm and the chirp of his radio. *Wyatt, you got this!*—he thinks.

Wyatt issues a nod of understanding. Though he loses sight of him after that. The squad proceeds to the second room, and then a third. *Where's Wyatt?*

Like clockwork. One after the other in a sweeping motion.

"Clear."

"Clear."

At the next doorway, all hell breaks loose. A woman screams. An Afghani soldier materializes from the shadows with an AK47 in his hands, shuffling across the middle of the room, using a young girl as a shield.

"Tango to the right!" someone shouts.

Pandemonium. More screams and shouts.

Then a light comes on, disrupting the night vision, and Kade tears off his goggles. The silhouette of an old woman, lunging from behind a tapestry that hangs on the far wall, wailing, chattering something in Arabic. The Afghani soldier holds fast to the younger woman and yells something back—then raises the AK47 and sprays bullets across the room.

Kade dives behind a stone wall, his lungs on fire with a mix of adrenaline and a burning stench. Bullets strike the stone above his head, causing chinks of mud to fly.

"Fuck!" he growls, sliding to the floor. Through the dust, he's able to discern two of his men crumpled on the ground, one onto the other, their positions unnatural.

Another Afghani soldier materializes from behind the tapestry. Kade takes aim and fires. The soldier with the hostage drops from an unknown bullet and takes the young girl down to the floor with him. The old woman shrieks again and dashes toward her. Left arm protecting his M4, Kade bounces up to his haunches and dashes out to grab both women to pull them to safety. But one is uncooperative. She tugs and grabs at his arm, unrelenting. Grips and shakes. Shaking.

Emmy tucked her legs under the pink cotton nightgown and curled her toes inside her favorite cotton socks. She typically wore them to bed in the winter months, and even though it was July, she felt a chill that didn't have anything to do with the weather.

A pre-dawn mist swallowed the front porch in a sheer gray blanket as she sat in a rocker on the front porch. Thunder rumbled far in the distance. She remembered a bank of gray clouds against the horizon the evening before and wondered if the storm had decided to retreat.

Otherwise, there wasn't a sound. Even the bullfrogs and crickets had managed to find slumber. Not so for herself. Lying awake with a million and one thoughts in her head, she had finally flipped the covers aside and made her way to the kitchen for a cup of tea, hoping for solace in the night air. Though she felt confident with the tally of numbers in the ledgers, she was having trouble turning off her thoughts. She was worrying about possibly missing something in the books when a noise in the night jolted her to the present.

Emmy dropped her sock feet to the wooden slats of the porch and scooted to the edge of the chair, cocking an ear. Was it an owl, or something else? She clutched the stock of her trusty Winchester rifle.

The agitated call came again, sifting into the night, seemingly originating from the direction of the bunkhouse. She stood, legs carrying her down the stairs. Half a moon balanced at the eastern horizon, providing light enough to find a path to the barn, sidestepping stickers and rocks.

"Wyatt! Damn you! Where—? Help—"

A man's voice, a guttural growl, sifted toward her through the mist, growing louder and then fading.

Concern etching her face, she upped her step. She didn't recall a ranch hand by the name of Wyatt. As she passed the side door to the barn, the baritone diction grew louder and she slowed, easing open the side door, glancing to the upper level of the carriage house before entering. Where in hell was Kade when he was needed? It was so dark, she stubbed her toe, leaning to rub it with an inward curse before leveling her weapon on the blackness before her. She advanced in slow steps.

"Where ... why the fuck...!"

Startled at the intensity of the voice, Emmy stopped, eyes wide in the darkness. "Who's there?" she hissed. "Show yourself before I shoot first and ask questions later."

The pain imbued into the mumbling made her think of the cry of a wounded animal. Then, she made out the form of a man lying in the straw, a single shaft of moonlight glancing through a window above him, illuminating the light color of his shirt. Kade had worn a white undergarment shirt that day, she recalled, irritated for once again having taken note of the man's clothes—or rather, the intriguing way his torso filled them out.

"Kade?" she said again, inciting another indecipherable grumble. "Why are you sleeping in the barn?" Propped at his side was what looked to be a bottle of whiskey. "That answers a few questions," she muttered.

"Get down!" he barked.

She jumped, taking an automatic step back, "It's me—Emmy!"

Then it occurred to her. He wasn't speaking to her. Likely didn't even know she was there; talking in his sleep—a drunken sleep.

"Kade, wake up, you're dreaming. It's well past midnight. Go to bed. You'll get a crick in your neck lying there like that." She bent forward and reached out to shake his shoulder. When he didn't respond, she shook harder. "Wake up...."

In a swift breath, the man sat upright, at a speed she couldn't fathom, powerful fingers aiming to close at her throat and catching only air instead. With a cry, she gave a thrust with her legs and heaved herself backward, out of his reach. The rifle dropped to the hard-pack dirt floor with a clatter.

In a wide sweep of power, he came to his knees, taking her down to the straw and pinning her there, leaving her no option for movement except for the futile kick of one leg. Her heels scraped the dirt and pebbles littered with straw.

"Who are you?" Kade growled, his face hovering above her, contorted into jagged angles by the shadows.

"Me ... it's me!"

The murderous glare softened, slowly, and he gradually shifted his weight to the side. Breath sizzled between clenched teeth. Those lips she normally found so enticing were twisted in some faraway agony, one she couldn't assume to understand. A vague scent of whiskey touched her nostrils.

He doesn't know who you are. Doesn't even know what he's doing.

Twisting to the side, Emmy bucked with every ounce of energy she possessed, to no avail. This man held her life in his hands. Up until that sliver of time, she had had no reckoning just how strong he was. Arms of steel, corded in muscle, pinned her completely.

At his mercy.

Calculated breaths expanded his chest, and she felt each one, unable to move her arms. How had he managed to imprison her so perfectly—her legs helpless under the cross of a muscled thigh?

"Kade," she tried again, this time soft and soothing. "It's Emmy. I'm here." She sucked in a breath. "You had a nightmare. You were talking and I came to see who—what was going on. But it's all right now." Every breath she took lifted her breasts into his powerful ribcage, a torrid heat, the vibration of his life force. Finally, his features had calmed, returning his visage to one she recognized.

That oh-so-beautiful face in the blue light of darkness. Only now, that face is etched in pain, his expression tortured.

Finally, he blinked in recognition.

"*Emmy?* For chrissakes, you okay?"

Mesmerized by the indigo blue of his eyes, concern, inches above hers, she nodded weakly.

"I think ... I'm fine."

"I could have hurt you!"

Sucking in a ragged breath, he rolled off her to sit upright, rubbing the heels of his palms into his eye sockets. He then braced his arms over his knees, and stared off into the darkness, focusing on the upper reaches of the great barn as if he had nothing left to give, and never expected to. Once the epitome of strength and vigor, now his face is drawn with defeat. Emmy pushed up to sit beside him, brushing the straw from her shoulders.

"Don't *ever* wake me up like that," he growled with an accusatory glance. "The closest you want to get is touching my foot. Got that? *Jesus!*" Finally, he shook his head. "I'm sorry I frightened you. Tell me the truth. Did I hurt you?"

"No," she whispered, shaking her head. "It's the war, isn't it? In your mind?" Though she asked, she already knew: Night terrors. A soldier, a warrior, reliving the horror while he slept. Now that she had witnessed it firsthand, she remembered his mention of it. He had warned her. How was a soldier supposed to deal with it all? Not like they could prevent the nightmares from invading their sleep any more than she could chase away hers. Only she couldn't possibly imagine the terror a soldier faced—while awake and asleep.

Kade managed a nod. Hands fisted, he sunk back into the straw and stretched onto his back, head propped to a forearm. Lost once again, far away, someplace she had no hope of reaching. Long moments passed and he didn't speak. The sound of rain descended in a pitter-patter onto the rooftop. So much for the rainstorm passing on by. She would wait until the rain stopped. She wasn't about to leave him alone like this.

"Who is Wyatt?" she asked then, voice barely above a whisper. "I heard your shouts, and when I came out to investigate, I thought I heard the name, Wyatt." Kade's gaze pierced her then. He didn't speak right away, and she immediately regretted asking. It was none of her business.

His jaw clenched, the tendons in his throat cording again. She longed to reach out to touch him. Relaxing her legs, she folded them to the side, tightening her shawl against the cool air. Kade's expression focused into the darkness upon something she couldn't see. He lifted the wool blanket by his side and passed it to her.

"Here. You look cold."

"Thank you."

"Wyatt is—was a teammate. Was my third tour of duty. A long night, almost dawn, and we were all beyond tired. Word was, Americans were being held inside a vacant building. Not something my team usually did, but infantry was across the way in the process of breaching an urban building. So...." He paused, rubbing his eyes again. "Wyatt was the youngest in the platoon. But he was a go-getter, eager to learn. Reminded me of myself. Eager for that chance." He shook his head with an attempt at a chuckle, failing miserably.

Emmy reached out and touched his hand, her fingers pale in contrast to his sunned skin, barely spanning the breadth of his knuckles. She squeezed, aware of her own anxiety calming with the simple connection.

He continued.

"Went okay at first. Then halfway into it, it all went south." Kade took to talking then, describing the operation in detail, and Emmy listened intently.

"But what happened to Wyatt?" she asked at last, fearing what his answer would be. When Kade dipped his head, she knew. "I'm so sorry. Nobody should have to go through that."

Kade shrugged, "And yet, they do. It's war. And it sucks."

After a bit, his chest rose a fell rhythmically. At last, it seemed he would get some peaceful sleep, though she didn't want to leave him alone, not quite yet. Exhausted now, Emmy scooted closer, moving the blanket to share with him. Just for a bit longer, or at least until she knew he would rest well.

A few moments later, Sage and Brush came moseying through a small slide in the back door created for just that purpose, one after the other, tails wagging as they plopped down beside her. Not long after, Dottie trotted in and joined them.

"Now where did you come from, girl?" She patted her thigh with an invitation and gave the spotted terrier a scratch. "Did Estelle let you out? C'mon, stay here with me."

Emmy leaned back a bit, thoughts wandering as she stroked Sage's ears, thinking random thoughts of how she had always loved the scent of hay. And of horses. Not so much pigs. Or chickens. Or dogs who had been rolling in who-knew-what. She made a mental note to give all three dogs a warm bath with lye soap.

Kade's painful words filtered into her thoughts again. What a horrible experience war was. Figuring she should go back into the house, she made to rise and then stopped when Sage groaned in disapproval, stretching out across one leg. Dottie snuggled in closer.

"Not going to let me move, are you?" she whispered. She glanced at the man breathing evenly beside her, adjusting the blanket over his arms. Though the interior of the barn was dark, she could see him well—strong cheekbones and straight jaw, shadowed with a day or two of beard. His nose was straight, a slash of thick brows dark, like the hair on his head. And those lips. So perfect and downright kissable. Stopping herself, she averted her gaze, hoping he hadn't somehow noticed her staring at him. Her face flamed hot, though there wasn't a soul to see it.

Then, she reached for the half-empty whiskey bottle and grimaced, swirling the amber liquid curiously. She wondered if it tasted anything like the fruited brandy cordials served at Zak and Hanna's wedding. Those were the first real liquor she had ever tasted, except for the nasty skunk beer Easton Ryker brought to school on the last day, more than six years ago. After that experience, she didn't care if she ever took a drink of liquor again. Both she and Becca had stupidly taken a dare, gagging at the disgusting liquid and promptly spitting it out. Then, there was the white wine the Shaffer family drank with desserts when they could acquire it, that is. Fancy wines weren't easy to come by in these parts. Emmy remembered its taste to be fruity and sweet.

She slanted the bottle, giving the contents another slosh, studying the caramel color, and wondering at the taste. With a little shrug, she gave the dogs another scratch before popping the cork and tipping the bottle, eyes squeezing shut when the liquid touched her lips. How bad could it be?

Like inhaling fire, that's how bad.

Pulling her knees upward, she propped her forehead, stifling a choke before swallowing the offensive liquid and waiting for the fiery sensation to vacate her nose. Her eyes watered, and finally, the burn subsided. In its wake came a pleasant and welcome warmth. A lofty serenity. She tipped the bottle again, this time taking a more delicate sip. And then another.

After a bit, she felt so relaxed, she thought to lay back and rest on the hay. Only for a few moments. Then she would return to the house. Besides, Sage had curled up into a ball, her large, soft head resting on her hip. If she moved too much, she would disturb the dog.

Straw crackled at her ears, and she hardly felt the little pokes of broken ends as she snuggled within the circle of heat nearer to Kade. Before she knew it, her eyes fluttered shut. She thought of his distress, the nightmares, wishing there was something she could do. Amid the ruminations, she reached out, drawn to the warmth of his hand, taking hold. A tiny smile tugged at her lips. The last thing she remembered was the even breathing and soft snores, unsure if they came from a dog or a man.

Kade watched her sleep as the sky outside grew pale, the light inside the barn turning a milky color. He didn't want to disturb her. Any moment now the cowhands would trickle into the barn for odds and ends, saddling up to begin their day. With any luck she'd sleep right on through it, unlikely to be detected in this far corner. He'd make sure of it.

He studied Emmy's peaceful face, alabaster skin flushed with peach, lashes fanning over her cheekbones, an imprint of straw creasing her cheek when she shifted. A strand of hair fluttered near her nostril when she breathed, making him grin. He particularly liked the way her body curled toward him, how she gripped the blanket up to her chin with one hand.

The two retrievers had left, but the little black and white terrier still huddled into the V between that fine ass and delicate ankles. Her feet, wrapped in frumpy white socks, poked out from beneath the blanket. A long, thick braid coiled like a shiny boa over her shoulder. He imagined lifting it gingerly in his fingers and bringing it to his nose, inhaling, capturing the essence of her. Wildflowers, sweet forest berries—and woman. It was her scent, had lingered in his memory from when she had hugged him tight after the bear chase.

The shy sparkle in her eyes after she let go hung in his memory, too.

The night before, when the nightmarish haze of war had left his senses, the possibility of having hurt her had thrust into him like the blade of a dull knife.

His own fault. Had he gone up to his bunk at the top of the carriage house in the first place, maybe she wouldn't have heard his cries in the night—wouldn't have come searching for the source. Wasn't that the whole idea of insisting upon a bunk away from everyone else?

But it was cooler in the barn. And after what was supposed to be a simple fence repair and relaxing fishing trip, instead, they're chased by a pissed-off grizzly. Then he chances upon the group of riders and overhears an unsettling conversation between Miller and Grayson. As if that weren't enough, last night he got the bright idea to seek Emmy out for a conversation he had been avoiding, only to catch sight of Grayson and Emmy laughing it up in her kitchen. He didn't even bother to knock at that point. The vision made something sting in his gut.

What was this feeling he had whenever he saw her? He couldn't get past the thought he didn't belong here and was interfering in her life. No wonder his brain wouldn't shut down. Now, he longed to lift the blanket to see if she had marks on her neck but couldn't bring himself to do that either. Had he grabbed her by the neck, or was it all a dream?

The evening before had begun with bad choices—intentions of drinking off a crappy mood. Thing was, he rarely drank. Liquor had never been his thing, not that he didn't appreciate a shot of Tennessee whiskey now and again. When Scout offered him a half-empty bottle of rotgut after dinner, seemed like a good idea at the time. The bottle was small. But after one taste, he concluded the term "rotgut" to be disturbingly accurate. How did anyone drink that shit? Maybe a better question: what in the hell did they make it out of? Probably best not to know.

Didn't help matters either, when caustic memories of Tori wormed into his head every July, the anniversary of their wedding. Women weren't to be trusted and he should have followed his own advice from the start. What had destroyed his marriage? Maybe it was too many tours of duty. Looking back, nothing could have changed his mind at the time, and Tori hadn't understood. Or maybe she had, and simply didn't care. They'd had some wicked arguments. Would she have cheated if things were different with his career? Had he listened to her reasoning, worked harder at understanding her loneliness, and stayed stateside when he had the chance, then maybe his marriage would have survived. What ifs. Maybe his teammates would still be alive, too. As they say, hindsight is 20/20. Then again, maybe it was his own heart that had changed.

Beneath the blanket, he felt the flutter of her hand. He wove his fingers through hers and squeezed gently, then broke contact. Careful so as not to wake her, he pushed himself out of the cozy straw bed.

You're only here for a short time to do a job, then you'll be gone for good. Best thing for all involved. She is an enigma. Not the first time you've brought out the worst in a woman. Problem is, you're having issues finding reasons not to like her.

CHAPTER 23

Nightgowns & Whiskey

M en's voices, a commotion. The scuff and clomp of horse hooves on gravel.

"Need a minimum of three men riding watch at the eastern border, and another three on the west. Lukas spotted unknown riders yesterday just off the property line. Scout and I are leading the pack horses with some supplies, the rest of you boys head out to the north pastures. Start bringing the herds in closer."

Kade's voice, along with the mumble of others.

Emmy cracked open an eye, greeted by a shaft of sunlight slanting through a break in the shutters. Dust motes happily danced in its rays. She sat up with a start, brushing hair and straw from her face. Hadn't Micah fixed all the shutters? She made a mental note to tell him about this one.

Wait ... happenings of the night before slammed into her consciousness. Kade had been having nightmares. She checked on him. Had she fallen asleep out here? How could she have been so irresponsible? The entire night. In the barn. In the straw with ... *him?*

What time was it? Emmy turned so suddenly, that she spurred a crick in her neck as everything came back to her in an avalanche of despair. All that remained of the man who had slept beside her was a divot in the hay. Even Sage, Brush, and Dottie had deserted her, she thought sadly, remembering how the dogs had curled up beside her before...

Before what?

The empty pint bottle caught her eye, and she fished it out of the loose straw, horrified as she held it up with two fingers.

"Good lord, did I drink it all?" she bemoaned.

A dull throb in her head confirmed the unthinkable.

"I've done some thoughtless things, but this ices the proverbial cake," she muttered. Pushing to her feet, she brushed off her nightgown and shook the straw from her braid. Somehow, she had to get to the house without anyone seeing her.

Snatching up her trusty rifle, she padded across the dirt floor, aiming for the west door and away from the sound of voices. Blast it, more men's voices greeted her on that side. As a last hope, she crept to the rear of the barn, past Kade's shower. Content the path was clear, she upped her step and ducked out the door, making a hasty turn and up a slight incline, dodging rocks through knee-high grass. Strides brisk, she focused on the house ahead of her. Could it be no one would notice? Home free! Relief was short-lived.

"Emmy—that you? Everything all right?"

Sucking in a breath, she went perfectly still, praying the action might magically render her invisible. With a valiant inhale, she plastered a smile on her face and forced herself to turn. Not only was Zak at the pump filling his canteen, but Kade stood alongside waiting his turn.

Drat!

Zak's expression was one of concern. Kade, on the other hand, had a casual sling to his stance. With one finger, he poked his hat up to see her better. Was he mocking her?—and was that a wink she saw? Teeth bright, he flashed a cheery smile.

If I were close enough, I'd slap it clean off his face. At the very least he should have woken me, so I could make an exit to the house before everyone and their dog was out here!

"I'm well, Zak," she managed tightly. "And how are Hanna and the children? I plan to visit them later." She gestured to the Tompson family cabin, mortified to see she still held fast to the empty whiskey bottle. Dropping her arm, she tucked the bottle behind the folds of her gown. Nightgown! She was standing out in front of God and everyone in her nightgown!

"The family's fine..." he responded, focused on her hand. "Is there something I can help with?"

"Nope, I've accomplished quite enough on my own. By the way, there's a goat on the roof," she said, pointing with the hand that didn't contain an empty bottle.

Both men looked up to see the Billy goat balanced on a shingle, apparently surveying the eligible does in the barnyard below. Emmy dashed for the house, stopping once to yank a painful cocklebur from the heel of a cotton sock. She chanced a glance back to see that Kade watched her. He nodded, tugging the brim of his hat.

Sarcastic ass.

And if her humiliation wasn't enough to satisfy the gods, as soon as she got to the porch steps, a familiar voice spoke from the sky, causing her to nearly leap out of her skin.

"Fine morning, Miss Bartlett."

Shielding her eyes from the sun, she looked up to see Detective Grayson crouched on a gentle slope of the porch roof, surmising Zak had taken him up on his offer to work off his room and board. The detective's shirt sleeves were rolled up, exposing tanned skin and fuzzy muscled forearms, and he held a hammer in his right hand. When he smiled, it was around a row of nails pressed firm between his lips. He wiped his brow with a kerchief before stuffing it into a back pocket.

"Hello, Detective."

"Gonna be a warm one today," he said.

The breeze whipped at the hem of her night dress, drawing her attention to her nakedness beneath it. Dare she attempt modesty, cross her arms and risk waving the dratted whiskey bottle in the air for him to see as well?

Fortunately, he looked away to set his hammer aside and reposition his footing and Emmy snagged the opportunity to pitch the bottle into a teacup rosebush. Hastily, she folded her arms over her breasts and when he looked up, she tilted her head and delivered a radiant smile.

"It appears you've had a good sleep," Grayson observed with a flash of teeth.

What was that supposed to mean? Had he seen her sleeping off the whiskey like a bumbling idiot in the barn?

"I'm not so sure about that. The state of affairs weighs on me, I'm afraid."

"Sorry to hear that. I understand completely." Grayson cocked his head with an inquisitive smile. "Um, you have something in your hair ... right there." He motioned to the rumpled tumbleweed of a braid flopped over her shoulder.

With a grimace, she picked out the remaining sprigs of offending straw, hoping he didn't notice the embarrassment licking at her cheeks.

Time for a polite getaway.

"You must be thirsty, Nick. I'll fetch something cold—"

As she turned to mount the steps, a shadow fell over her. Accompanying it was a muscled arm circling her waist and reeling her into a sturdy frame. She gasped, a commanding voice against her ear silencing any more protest.

"Miss Bartlett, allow me to escort you indoors."

The bottle in her hand said it all. One of them had either spilled the whiskey or drank it, and he didn't think he had taken more than one sip from that bottle. He didn't blame Emmy one bit if she had. Last night she hadn't realized what she was walking into when she investigated the sounds of his nightmares. She could have asked someone else to check. But she hadn't. She came alone.

Kade sat astride Skitter, readying to ride out to the bluff with Scout, where they would spend the day strategically positioning explosives, stopping anyone who dared to cross the choke point from the south. Unwilling to risk telling anyone else about this part of his mission, including Zak, he elected to trust Scout.

Kade's mood soured as he watched Emmy chatting it up with Grayson, her face tipped toward the sky where the lawman squatted on the roof. The detective had insisted upon earning his keep by fixing a breach in the roofing, or so he heard. But judging by his apparent interest in the Bar C matriarch, he wasn't convinced that was Grayson's sole intention.

Then he pictured Emmy with Miller, and the idea rankled him even more. Not a pleasant picture. Maybe it wasn't Miller she fancied at all, could be it was the man on the roof. That idea raised Kade's hackles even more. The detective wasn't a bad-looking dude, if she were partial to the flashy, pompous sort. But who was he to pass judgment? His gripe was he didn't think the man could be trusted, and in his opinion, Emmy was too flirtatious with him at the church social.

None of your concern, and not for you to say. You'll be gone soon.

Was that a smile on Emmy's face? She hadn't smiled at him like that. Not that it mattered, he reminded himself. Worse still, that only-sexy-on-her pink nightgown billowed around shapely legs in the breeze, sunlight filtering through the gauzy material to illuminate every curve—at least from his perspective. His brows jammed together in exasperation.

Dammit!

In a blink of an eye, Kade's boots struck the ground, pounding dirt as he stalked toward the porch, unsure of a plan. Or even if he needed one. All he knew was he had to get her into the house and away from Grayson's predatory eyes.

Looping his arm about her waist, he ignored the feeble protest as he guided her up porch steps toward the front door. From the corner of his eye, he spotted Henry and Estelle busy pulling weeds in the garden. Good. Right then he felt irritable and angry, and as far as he was concerned, nobody else needed to see what he intended on doing.

Taking one step to her two, his boots were dusty and big compared to her cute sock-covered feet. Awareness spiked through him. The feel of her curvaceous waist under his hand and the feminine sway of her walk nearly did him in. His fingers tightened as he escorted her to the front door. Desire niggled at his gut,

a stinging awareness shooting to his core. He gritted his teeth, resisting the urge
to consume her in an embrace.

Before she gathered the breath to form an argument, he reached for the knob
and pushed open the door, ushering her inside.

"Listen here, you had better...." Emmy began, expressive eyes sparking in the
low light.

Kade closed the gap.

"Did I hurt you last night?" he asked.

"No, of course not."

"I didn't grab your neck?"

Shaking her head, she stood her ground. More intimate thoughts of the night
before returned to him. Her touch. Her feel. Even though it was only sensations
of her nearness. His imaginings.

He reached for her before he lost the nerve, threading his fingers into the
provocative disorder of her hair. Was that a sigh he heard? Kade cupped her face
in his palms and inhaled her feminine scent, all morning sun and flowers. He
closed the gap between them. Something about her made him feel alive and long
to experience more. *Made him appreciate.* The sensation was lost to him and he
accepted he would never feel it again.

He stroked a thumb over her jaw, searching her eyes.

Emmy's gaze lifted, wide with wonder—a kaleidoscope in shades of forest
green. Had she drunk the remainder of the whiskey? The likelihood almost
made him grin. Almost. Right now, his motive was to leave her with something
else to think about. Something far more compelling.

When her lips parted to speak again, he chucked her chin with an index finger
and lowered his mouth possessively to hers, silencing her. He didn't need to hear
whatever it was she intended to say. Only wanted to feel. Lingering, he drank
in the honeyed, pliant texture of her lips, as sumptuous as his imagination had
portrayed them to be. Playing. Tasting. Acutely aware of her surrender, the way
she leaned into him, a tentative touch of her hand to his shoulder.

This is crazy, you do realize that?

In a blast of sanity, Kade released her and turned for the door, tossing the words over his shoulder.

"For the record, I didn't desert you this morning. You were sound asleep, even snoring a little." She let out a horrified gasp, and he continued, "I didn't have the heart to disturb you. My fault you were up most of the night, and I figured you needed your rest. We'll talk when I get back. There are a few things I've got to set straight. Right now, there's work to do."

"Don't you dare tell anyone you kept me up all night!" she hissed, tailing him to the door.

As soon as he cleared it, she slammed it behind him.

There was a bounce to his step as he trotted down the porch steps back to his horse, and he wasn't doing a very good job of suppressing a grin. Zak waited astride his horse. No surprise when the foreman's stare practically burned a hole into his forehead. He didn't know if Zak had seen him enter Emmy's place, but he sure enough saw the exit.

"Emmy helped me out last night," Kade explained before Zak had a chance to ask, cringing at his choice of words.

"How's that?" Zak bumped up the brim of his hat, erasing the shadow and bringing his glower into the light.

"Remember those night terrors I mentioned? Emmy heard me talking in my sleep, is all. She came out to the barn and woke me up."

"Thought you said to never do that?"

"There are right ways and wrong ways."

"She did it the right way, that what you're saying?"

Kade hesitated, nodding. "More or less. I had to explain the correct way." Christ, that sounded worse still. "Look, Zak, last night was an especially bad one. Probably a culmination of all that's going on around here. But Emmy elected to hang around and get my mind off things with some conversation, and I was more than grateful to fall back into a dreamless sleep. What she did last night was noble, and brave."

She had a way about her; difficult to put into words. That part he kept to himself.

Confusion knotted Zak's brow. "Yeah, that's Emmy. Still don't know why she was sashaying around here this morning in a nightgown. Not like her. She's modest, ya know? I'll check on her this afternoon."

With any luck, Kade would get to Emmy first. For now, the memory of her lips under his hung sweet in his mind. What was wrong with him? Not something he needed to get caught up in. And yet he couldn't seem to stop. Memories of waking up to the warm sensation of her body beside his. Filled his head. He had made plenty of mistakes in his life, and judging by last night, he wasn't through making them.

But now, he had work to do.

Kade forced his focus to the blueprint of explosives imprinted on his brain. He and Scout had worked long into the night several times, carefully making sure their actions wouldn't be discovered. Was too dangerous if the information got out to the wrong people. If all the hands knew about the explosives, their efforts would be futile. And now it was time to bring Zak into the fold, along with more choice men.

"Better get a move on." Zak motioned to the chain of stacked bluffs in the distance. "There something you wanted to show me?"

"Yup. Only a few trusted men are to know, got that? Follow me." Kade nudged Skitter into an energetic trot, slowing when he reached Lukas, hair the color of straw poking out around his hat as he rode a chesty sorrel quarter-horse.

Things were fast coming to a head. He didn't have proof but felt any day now those men Miller had with him would be breaking past the Bar C borders, and the hands needed to be ready. Worse still, Kade didn't know how closely involved Grayson might be, or why the detective had been involved with the group out in the middle of nowhere alongside. At this point, he didn't trust Miller or Grayson any further than he could throw them. At the first opportunity, he would single Grayson out and ask a few questions.

Movement from an approaching rider flickered in the horizon and Kade and Lukas slowed, waiting.

"Who's that?" Lukas asked.

"Looks like Scout," Kade responded after a moment.

Scout was a talented tracker, the best Kade had ever known, having grown up in the wilderness of Montana hunting bears, elk, deer, and fox to feed his family. Now, Scout crested the rise, galloping toward them and reining in beside Kade.

"Hey-ho Stockton," Scout said. "Caught sight of riders. Maybe 20 or 25. I suspect they cut through the northwest corner of Bar C land and were heading south toward the gulch in the direction of Miller's land. With all the drizzling rain we had last night, there wasn't any dust, and I didn't see where they disappeared to. I can find them but wanted to tell you first."

Kade stared into the distance, gathering his thoughts. "Exactly what I was afraid of."

"Could be setting up to take a run at the Bar C. Better we prepare."

"I think you're right." Kade heeled Skitter around to face six riders as they approached: Zak, Micah, and four additional trusted hands. They formed a loose circle around him.

"Ok, boys, listen up." Kade began. He went on to explain the location of extra ammunition, along with the specific use of the trenches, which had been lined in ax-sharpened logs to discourage entry and guide them toward the bluffs. Today he planned to share the precise placement and sequencing of explosives along the upper reaches of that bluff.

"Keep tabs on where all our men are. Beginning tonight, nobody is to get past the gulch. Understand? No excuses."

"Yes, sir," Lukas and the others voiced.

"Miller's behind this, ya think?" Zak asked.

Kade stared toward the bluff, jaw clenched. "You're reading my mind."

CHAPTER 24

Kräuterlikör and a Kiss

"Y ou ever have a toothache?" Emmy asked.

"Who hasn't?" Hanna retorted.

"Whiskey works wonders on pain. And see, today it's all gone." Emmy flashed a toothy smile to prove it, though the entire toothache story was fabricated. Now if only her head didn't feel like a massive, throbbing boulder resting on her shoulders.

"A poultice works well, too." Hannah gave her friend the side-eye. "He's a mighty handsome man, ya know."

"Who?" Emmy shot back.

As if creating a piece of art, Emmy stood in Hanna's kitchen arranging sliced ham on yesterday's bread, followed by a thin layer of soft goat cheese, and finally a dollop of the creamy sauce she had seen Madison use on sandwiches. To recreate it, Emmy experimented with egg yolks, vinegar, butter, and an assemblage of spices, whipping up a comparable substitute. Proud of her creation, she cut precise portions of the sandwiches and passed them out to Hanna and the girls. Eli was down for a nap, still too young for much solid food.

"Mr. Stock-ton, silly." Hannah clarified with a teasing pull of syllables. She finished beating a bowl of muffin batter, pushing it aside, and draping a dishtowel over the top.

"Kade?" Emmy asked with a wave of a hand. "Now you're being silly. He's only here to help out with securing the ranch."

"On a first-name basis, are we? Don't tell me you haven't noticed his muscled arms, capable hands—and oh my, those hypnotizing eyes. Don't recall ever seeing such a spicy blue—"

"Mm, most delicious, Miss Emmy!" Beatrice gushed after the first bite; eyes fluttering shut to relish the flavors. With an elaborate dab of a napkin at the corners of her mouth, she folded it primly into her lap before glancing at her mother for approval, satisfied to receive Hannah's nod to her display of good manners.

Without any such considerations, Julie's mouthful threatened to burst her cheeks as she chewed.

"Julie!" Hannah admonished. "Ladylike bites, missy. And use your napkin to wipe your mouth, not your sleeve. Remove your elbows from the table, please."

Beatrice rolled her eyes triumphantly at her younger sister, instigating a swift kick under the table from Julie.

"Mama!" Beatrice began in a whine.

"Shush! Behave or I'll send ya both to bed after your meal. The adults are having a conversation." Her attention went back to Emmy.

"Where did Zak and the others head off to so early this morning?" Emmy tried to change the subject, relieved at young Beatrice's interruption.

"T'wasn't early at all. Hear tell, by the time you came sashaying out of the barn in nothin' but your frilly night rail, it was nigh on eight o'clock. They left soon after. I should think Mr. Stockton would have mentioned something to ya about the day's plans?" She gave Emmy a saucy wink and popped a fresh raspberry into her mouth.

"Hanna!" Lowering her voice so the girls wouldn't hear, Emmy continued, "I suspect Zak told you that."

"No, I *saw* you."

Emmy cringed. "As I said, I heard a noise last night, found Kade in the barn having one of those night terrors he gets, and when I woke him ..."

"Yes, yes?" Hanna leaned closer.

"He grabbed me," she finished in a hushed tone, glancing at the girls to make sure they weren't paying attention to the conversation.

Hanna's light blue eyes flashed and her nose pinkened. "Oh, my. Do tell!"

Deciding the conversation to be quite boring, Beatrice and Julie asked to be excused from the table. They bounced from their chairs and plopped down on needlepoint cushions in front of the front room window overlooking the porch and then the pastures in the distance. They proceeded to draw on a black chalkboard balanced between them on their knees.

Hanna rapped her fingers on the table, eyebrows jutting upward while waiting for further explanation.

Emmy rolled her eyes. "Mercy sakes, there's nothing to tell."

"Huh." Hanna sighed, "Well then, you're leaving me to believe he grabbed you, and you both went on to enjoy a bottle of the fancy juice. And who knows what else may have taken place in between."

"That is not what happened!"

"We're friends, eh? Not fair to keep me at arm's length. Heavens, I could use a bit of girlie gossip in my life. What with three babes to care for, mountains of filthy laundry to wash, and cooking meals, and a loving husband who spends the better part of the day out on the range—"

"Okay, but it's between me and you. Understand?" When Hanna propped her chin to her palm and delivered a sharp nod of agreement, Emmy continued. "Last night in the wee hours, I woke up. Couldn't sleep."

"Again? This has been happening for a while, has it not?"

Emmy nodded. "Anyway, I went out on the porch to get some air and heard voices—or, precisely, a man's voice in the distance. I had my weapon in hand like I always do, and so I followed the sound into the barn."

"Now why on earth didn't ya come by the cabin and alert Zak? He could 'a—" She bit her lip when Emmy shot her a glare, knowing full well her friend's stubbornness and doing things on her own.

Emmy continued. "I entered the side door and looked around. When my eyes adapted to the dark, I recognized Kade sleeping in the straw with a bottle next to him. It took a moment before I realized he was dreaming and unaware of my presence. I remembered him mentioning night terrors. When I went to wake him..." Her words trailed off.

"And?" Hanna prompted, concern hooding her eyes. "Go on, what happened?"

Emmy inhaled, "He grabbed me."

"Grabbed you ... how?" Hanna touched her fingers to her mouth.

"Went for my throat but missed thank goodness. It's my fault. I should have known."

She scooted to the edge of her chair and reached for Emmy's hand. "But how could you have known? You've never fought in a war. You sure you're fine?"

"Scared me is all. Worse was ... the look in his eyes."

Hanna shook her head. "What do you mean?"

"It wasn't him behind those eyes. Almost like he was someone else, fighting a demon I know nothing about. I felt moved to help him in the fight. If that makes sense." She shrugged. "Finally, he recognized me and came to his senses. But he was plenty mad. I expect more at himself than me, but who knows? I'm not proud of what happened next."

Hanna gave a comforting squeeze to Emmy's clenched hands and made a tsking sound, urging her to continue.

"Kade groused at me for touching his shoulder, explained it was dangerous to approach him that way, and I should only get close enough to shake his foot. We talked for a bit. Then he closed his eyes and slept like a baby from what I could tell. It's me I'm ashamed of. It didn't feel right leaving him alone after that, so I made myself comfortable in the straw. Figured it best to keep an eye on him for a bit, you know?" Hanna nodded in understanding, and Emmy continued. "The dogs moseyed in and curled up beside me. I spotted that disgusting bottle of whiskey and thought, what harm would a sip or two be? Kade was sleeping. I was alone with my thoughts, and I'd never tasted it. Brandy and wine yes, but never whiskey."

Hanna harrumphed, leaned back in her chair, and folded her arms. "And how did you enjoy it? Like rancid dog piss, eh?" Both women snorted, dissolving into laughter.

"Like drinking nasty, bitter fire. Bites your tongue and burns a hole in the throat."

Hanna threw her head back with another laugh, slapping a palm to the table. "Whiskey … pshaw. I dare you to try my special kräuterlikör, yes?"

Emmy waved a hand in protest, "No, my head hurts bad enough as it is." But Hanna was already on her feet, fishing for two miniature glass tumblers from the cabinet.

"Exactly why you need a sip of my mutter's special tonic, silly. Mends the soul and whatever else ails ya. Herbal liqueur is potent medicine for your head. It'll liven you right up," Hanna informed, dragging a stool across the kitchen, and balancing herself to access the top cabinet. She returned holding an emerald-green glass jug containing the precious contents, placing it proudly on the table. "My mutter makes it superior to any found in Germany proper. She adds fruits, alpine flowers, herbs, and a menagerie of spices, and mixes it all up to ferment. Has a few secret ingredients, too. Pure magic, it 'is. Wouldn't surprise me none if gnomes and fairies helped out." Popping the well-seasoned cork, she poured a demure serving into each tiny glass, pushing one toward Emmy. "No excuses, hear? As the English say, cheers!"

Hanna's bright blue eyes sparkled when she lifted a glass to her lips, convincing Emmy to try a small taste. What could it hurt? Bringing the glass up in toast, she sipped, squeezing her eyes shut as it passed her lips, fully expecting another invasive burning liquor. What she got was a heady swirl of cherry, spice, honeysuckle, and even a hint of lavender, or maybe it was violet. Not exactly sweet, the flavor rested on the pungent side, but not enough to make you want to set the glass down. The fact was, after a few sips, it was downright delicious. As comforting as a warm blanket placed around the shoulders.

"That man has the eyes for ya." Hanna winked, waggling a brow as she settled back in her chair.

"What do you mean?" Emmy asked with a swallow.

"I've seen how he looks at you."

"He kissed me." Emmy blurted, touching a fingertip to her lips as her eyes rounded in horror. She had no intention of ever voicing that particular occurrence out loud. If she never spoke of it, then it wouldn't be real, right? But somehow the words had a mind of their own, tumbling out of her mouth like marbles from a holey sock.

Must be the kräuterlikör. Stuff is like an evil truth serum.

"Is it true, Emmy?" Hanna squeaked with a gasp, smacking a palm to her forehead which might have left a red mark, though wasn't visible with the flush of the kräuterlikör. "Ya see, I was right! I knew it! The man has an eye for ya." She jabbed a finger into Emmy's face. "You need to kiss him back, that's all there is to it."

Emmy grimaced, shaking her head fiercely as she nibbled on the last bit of sandwich, not tasting it. It was simply something to do with her fingers. "I certainly have no intention of returning ... um, a *kiss.*"

"Why not? Was it good—the kiss I mean?"

"How should I know?"

Hanna tsked again, "All the more reason to do some more experimenting. He's a good man. Hard working. Big and strapping, plenty fine to look at, too, if I do say so myself. And he's clearly enamored with you. Knows his way around a ranch and probably around other things as well." Hanna's grin turned sly. "C'mon now, tell me you don't find the man handsome." She elbowed Emmy in the side, making her friend twist her lips in a reluctant smile.

"He is easy on the eyes, I'll give you that," Emmy lifted her glass and took another sip, each one tasting a bit better than the one before. Her head was feeling better already. An expression of consideration crossed her face. "Kade is here to do a job, and I have work to do as well. I'm afraid it's more work than I ever imagined."

"All these range war shenanigans are worrisome, I'll give ya that. But we have a good number of cowhands at the Bar C this summer. More than ever before. Between Zak and the others, we will succeed in protecting this ranch. Mark my words. We must keep our wits about us. Those bastards from down south won't get over on us!" She emphasized her words by thrusting a fist into the air.

Hanna's churlish comment sent them both into giggles.

When Emmy recovered, "Oh, Hanna, it's more than that. Running the ranch, keeping the ledgers in order, the receivables and payables, oats, sweet grain or alfalfa—the repairs, and now we need new equipment. Henry left a list on my desk. It's overwhelming. The fencing on the southeast end is breached and needs repair. And I've been researching the purchase of sheep."

"Sheep?" Hanna parroted excitedly. "I think that's a fine idea."

"Just a dozen or so to begin with. I think that would be a good idea for the future of the Bar C." She looked down, twisting the napkin in her lap before looking Hanna in the eyes again. "How did Bud do it all after Colt left? And how did Mama do it after Bud died? I respect her more than ever, now that I know what she went through. Things have been backlogged ever since Mama got sick, and I don't know how I'm ever going to catch it all up."

Hanna scooted her chair closer, leaning to embrace Emmy in a hug, and rubbing her shoulders. "There, there, it will all work out in time. Your schooling taught you well, and so did your mama. I never met Bud, but from what Zak has told me, he did a fine job of taking over the business when Colton left with his new wife.

"However, our first order of business is to secure the ranch from these hoodlums coming up from the south—and from the bureaucrats in Cheyenne aiming to run over us ranchers. Once that's taken care of, you'll have plenty of help with the books. There's me and Zak, and both Henry and Estelle have experience with that sort of thing. They ran a mercantile in their younger years, didn't they?"

Emmy nodded. "That's a good point. I've got the desire. College was easy compared to the reality of it, but both Bud and Mama taught me all they knew. I just need to eradicate my fear and uncertainty. There's so much to learn. What if I fail?"

"Ah, listen, this is how it's going to go." Hanna leaned across the table until her face was inches from Emmy's. She drummed her index finger to the table. "Trust me, this is what you'll do."

Emmy eyed her friend suspiciously.

"As soon as the men ride back to the ranch this evening, you march on out there as if you own the world, in front of God and everyone, and plant a big ol' kiss right on Mr. Stockton's mouth."

The blood drained from Emmy's face. Her eyes went wide, then her cheeks grew so hot she thought she might have to run outside.

"Hanna! I can't—"

"No? First off, he took his liberties and startled you with a kiss you weren't prepared for. Let him have a taste of the bitters right back. Give him a big smack in front of the boys. That'll teach the cocky man what you're made of." Hanna winked with a curt nod.

"And how is that going to help with my fears of running this ranch?"

"Missy, if you manage to get up the nerve to snatch up that pretty hunk of man and plant a good long smooch on his mouth in front of dozens of dusty cowboys, you can do *anything*. Now, let's get busy baking these muffins before the batter goes bad."

Early evening brought the bawl of calves and the whinnies of horses anxious for their nightly grain, followed by the banter of worn-out men happy to be at the end of a workday.

Emmy stood, arms folded, on the front porch of Hanna and Zak's cabin where she had a clear view of the corral. She chewed on her lower lip. One cowboy caught her attention: taller than the others, he perched on the top rung of the corral fence, legs splayed, an easy sling to his posture. He removed his hat and slapped it to his thigh, knocking off the dust, throwing his head back, and laughing at something said to him.

If she considered it for too long, she would surely talk herself out of it. With Hanna's urging, Emmy went to the washstand and splashed her cheeks, patting them dry with a linen cloth. She fluffed her hair and poked a few wayward curls back into the chignon at the back of her head.

"Hanna, you're right. In front of God and everyone, I'll show Kade Stockton exactly who runs the show around here."

Hanna bounced up and down on her toes and squeaked with joy. "And don't forget to pass out the goodies," she reminded, pushing a basket of fresh spice muffins into Emmy's arms.

Outside, Emmy lifted her chin proudly. She took a shortcut through swales of grass, her violet skirts swirling at her legs as she made her way to the group of twenty or so hands congregated in conversation at the corral gates.

"Evening, Ma'am," voiced Scout and Cornelius in unison, stepping aside and making way for the mistress to pass. Noses lifting to sniff the air, the men followed.

"A good evening to you," she responded. Weaving her way into the center of the garrulous group, she lifted the checkered cloth to reveal plump muffins with delightful crusty tops and began passing them out. She nodded to Lukas, Micah, and one of the newest hires, Chester, encouraging them to help themselves.

Emmy set the basket aside, crossed her arms, and stopped before Kade. Perched upon the top rung of the split-rail fence, he stopped mid-sentence in a conversation with Scout, turning to acknowledge her. His strong jaw was dusted with a day's worth of whiskers, beneath a look of surprise, and a non-smile that made you think he knew something you didn't.

"Do I get one of those muffins?" he asked.

Emmy paused, her tongue sliding along her mouth, teeth worrying her lip again.

"I imagine you do, but first...." she said, breath catching. Hitching a boot onto a rail, she grabbed a post and hoisted herself up, eye-level, face perfectly aligned to his. He didn't flinch, though a quizzical expression of dismay did cloud those icy blue eyes, which she rather enjoyed.

CHAPTER 25

So Into You

K ade barely saw her coming. In a flash, she appeared in front of him, all flowery smelling. Instinctual reflex had him reaching for her arm to steady her, though he knew the last thing she needed was stabilizing. She was the most athletic woman he knew. And then she closed in, arms braced on either side of the rail, her mouth landing on his, soft, sweet, insistent—lips closed as tight as a sprung mousetrap.

What the hell kind of kiss was that?

Damn, but she smelled good. She tasted like sugar and blackjack gum. Automatically, he set his hands on her waist. Firm, bringing to mind the feel of her beneath his hand earlier that morning. A pleasant throb signaled all was well and still alive in his pants. He didn't close his eyes when she kissed him, wouldn't risk missing a second of this, which was how he knew she closed hers. Tight. Like a little kid anticipating a shot at the doctor's office. A curl worked free, blowing in the breeze and tickling his cheek.

A collective mix of gasps, oohs, ahhs, and excited murmurs churned around them. Finished, she pulled back and he saw her cheeks were washed in red, her eyes churning gray, as wild as the Wyoming rains.

It all lasted a few seconds. A bolt of heat shot up his spine, his arousal thickening in his jeans. He shifted uncomfortably on the top rung of the fence. If he were dealing out scores—and he wasn't—he recalled better kisses in second grade. She may not know the mechanics of a knock 'em-dead kiss, but she had all the provisions to work with.

"We need to talk," she murmured with a pointed look.

All he could do was nod.

As quickly as she popped up in front of him, she dropped smartly to the ground, propping her hands to her hips. Her expression was one of triumph and she lifted her chin a notch. Milk-chocolate hair shot with golden lights wisped across her face, and she pushed it back impatiently, clearing her throat.

"Well. There. I expect that'll teach you," she announced. With a curt nod, she spun around in a grand flourish before marching off.

Struggling to suppress a grin that embodied both pleasure and admiration, he focused on the sway of shapely hips under yards of material. After having seen her in pants when she rode horseback, he knew those curves existed. And right now, he struggled to keep his imagination in check.

Yeah, you showed me. I deserved that. Now get out of my head. Please....

Emmy vanished around the corner of the barn and though he tried not to care, he wondered where she was off to. That wasn't the way back to the house. Then it occurred to him. She planned to do the one thing she most always did when she needed to clear her mind. At least he understood that about her—and knowing he took up real estate inside her head pleased him to no end.

The atmosphere was dense enough to be chopped in two with a meat cleaver. Silence coagulated around the normally rambunctious cowhands, though as soon as Emmy disappeared out of earshot, the men exploded into a ruckus of banter.

"Knock me over with a feather," one said.

"Woohoo! What was that all about?" another asked.

Kade shrugged. "That's a question for Miss Bartlett."

He dropped to the ground and heaved his saddle to his shoulder, heading toward the barn to put away the tack. An enticing aroma of a beef and potato dish wafted through the air, and the conversation behind him diverted to the subject of food. Kade chuckled inwardly at their minuscule attention span when it came to the evening meal. Conversing about other subjects, they shuffled in the direction of the chow house.

Zak walked alongside Kade for a bit, diverting toward the cabin he and Hanna shared. He glanced over his shoulder, lips quirked, a sparkle in his eyes, "I would ask what that was all about, but I'm guessing it's none of my business." He dipped his head in goodnight before cutting a path up to the top of the berm. Beatrice and Julie raced from the front porch and leaped into his outstretched arms, both jabbering excitedly about the day's highlights. Hanna waited patiently with young Eli perched on her hip, a welcoming smile on her face.

Kade returned the goodnight, watching the way the foreman's posture straightened in a burst of energy, steps livening the closer he got to his waiting family. Then the protective way he looped an arm around Hanna, pulling her in for a lingering hello kiss. Those three kiddos sure loved their dad. And his wife loved her husband.

A sense of longing ate at him, sitting like a hollow, hungry thing in his core. Brushing it off, Kade focused his attention on the east pasture where he spotted the silhouette of a lone woman leading a horse up to the corral. He had business to tend to.

"Thank you."

Emmy jumped and spun around, instantly lost within unfathomable blue eyes—sparkling, crinkling at the corners to match the cheeky smile he wore. The boar-bristle brush she gripped in one hand stilled, and Obie glanced back as if to say, *don't stop now!*

"Why thank me?"

Kade took a step, pushing fingers into the front pockets of his blue jeans while he spoke. Studying his boots, he kicked at the grassy dirt before looking up.

"Because I felt like a schmuck after I took liberties and kissed you this morn-ing. I deserved what you did."

"So, my kiss negated your kiss. We're even then," she said.

Not even at all. He's happy, and I'm more miserable than ever.

He gave a casual shrug of his shoulders, "No, not exactly."

Tilting her head, "What do you mean then?"

"I apologize for my kiss. I appreciate you sitting with me last night. I'm impressed with you, Emmy."

Pleased, a tiny smile graced her lips as she went back to work, pushing the bristle brush over Obie's back and withers with long strokes.

"Not with your kissing abilities, that's for sure," he added.

She stopped then, embarrassment zipping through her veins. She lobbed the brush into the bucket that held the grooming tools and faced him, arms folded. He flashed another charming grin and she couldn't decide if she should laugh or be hurt by the remark.

How hard is it to lay a kiss on someone? Only she could mess it up.

"What's that supposed to mean?"

"You have grit, stamina, and smarts. Your heart is as big as the world." He shuffled closer until she became aware of his body heat. "And you have what it takes to grow this ranch into something bigger than what it is. And you'll do it, too. I know it. You're a force to be reckoned with, Emmy. Not that impressing me is anything special. But I thought you should know. As far as the kissing goes, I don't give a rat's ass if your kiss needs some improvement. Like I always say, practice makes perfect...."

He lifted his shoulder in a shrug and stepped closer, his presence swallowing her. A big hand lifted to cup her jaw tenderly, the contact sending shivers down her neck, arms, and back. She tilted her face nearer to his, inhaling the manly scent of him.

"May I?" he asked, lips a breath from hers.

Did she want to know more? Yes, yes, she did.

All it took was a feeble nod. Kade lowered his mouth to hers purposefully, stroking her cheek with the pad of his thumb as he did. Like a brush of air, his tongue grazed past her lips, encouraging them to part. Like a sturdy rock, he stood before her and Emmy tentatively extended her arms to him, feeling as though she were melting. She opened for him. Accepted his creative play, losing herself in the sensation of it. The joy! His other hand came around to cradle her head, and after too few delicious moments, he broke contact.

He lifted his head, lips curving into a lazy grin.

"Now we're even," he said.

Emmy breathed a little laugh, shaking her head. "I—I feel stupid and so naive."

"Why?"

"That was very nice," she admitted, dipping her head in a blush. "So that's what all the fuss is about. I had no idea."

He chucked her chin, dropping a second, and then a third promising example to her lips, "No need to feel bad. I'm more than happy ... being your first ... real kiss."

Then, Kade loosened Obie's lead rope.

"Let's get this boy in for supper, and we can talk." He looped his other arm around her waist as they walked. "There are a few things I'd like to clear up. Now that we're even." He slanted her a wink.

As they strode to the barn, Emmy gazed up at his strong jaw and an expression hidden by the shadow of his hat. The warmth of his arm strengthened her. What did he want to talk about? Was it something to do with his going back home—to his own time? She didn't want to talk about that. Not now. She couldn't bear it!

With Obie secure in his stall munching happily on grain, Kade turned to her. "First off, what's this I hear about you and Miller tying the knot?"

She scowled, "Now where—no, I know exactly where you heard that! Probably from anyone who has ever spoken to Miller right?" She shook her head, "He doesn't seem to want to take no for an answer."

"Good enough. Needed to hear it from you is all." He leaned against the stall door. "Second, this is difficult to ask, and I had hoped you might bring it up first."

"What's that?"

"Several months ago—you were assaulted. That right?" The question glittered along with another emotion in his eyes.

Emmy's jaw dropped. First, Detective Grayson confronts her, and now Kade. She was beginning to feel like the guilty party here. Wasn't it a woman's prerogative to choose whether to discuss personal things? Colt and Madison were the only two people she had told, and that was out of necessity. Thank goodness the attack hadn't been worse. Either way, she didn't enjoy reliving it.

"You told Nick Grayson, didn't you?"

Kade's jaw hardened. "Why would I tell Grayson anything?"

"All I know is that he was in my home yesterday asking me these same questions. I assume Colt filled you in, which I understand. But there's no way Grayson would know unless you told him! Who else knows? Joy writes a gossip column in the Gunn Pass paper. You might want to keep that in mind when you're talking to people."

"Hold on," Kade lifted a hand. "Before you go getting all worked up, I haven't told a soul. I'm only asking you about it now because I need details, seeing as I'm trying to get to the bottom of all this. I had hoped you would tell me on your own. This guy could still be lurking around."

"He's not."

"How do you know that?"

"Because I saw what he looked like, and this area is a relatively small community." Emmy shook her head to rewind her thoughts. "So, you haven't mentioned it to anyone?"

"No. I swear, Emmy. I know none of these people. I'm from another time, remember?"

Yes, she remembered well, and it continually taunted her. Especially now, having experienced the sensory bliss of his kiss, his touch, she must accept the bitter knowledge of his eventual return home, to his own time.

"Then how...." She pressed a fingertip to her mouth in thought.

"What else did Grayson ask about? I noticed you two had a few laughs."

"Were you spying?" She gasped, placing her hands on her hips.

"I came by to talk, but you were already entertaining the Lone Ranger in your kitchen, so I left."

"*Who* is this ranger you keep referring to? Never mind," she relinquished in exasperation, continuing, "The detective dropped by to question me. I merely offered him the jams I promised the day of the social."

"All that aside, how about you fill me in on the evening you were assaulted? Colt told me what he knew, but I'd like to hear it from you."

Emmy sighed, moving to sink upon the bales of straw stacked against a wall, and Kade followed. She related all she remembered.

"I understand how hard it is, and regret I had to ask. But I'm happy you got one over on him. At least I have an idea what he looks like."

"I still wonder how Grayson knew."

"Maybe the culprit is still around and likes to talk."

Emmy sighed, "Maybe." She leaned her head to his shoulder, so cozy and inviting, and she suddenly felt sleepy. Probably the remnants of Hanna's special liquor. She wondered what it might be like to curl up in his arms and drift into a delightful slumber.

On a real bed this time.

Kade folded her hand in his, "If anyone tries to hurt you again, he'll be dealing with me. And just so you're aware, Scout spotted riders on the northwestern forty earlier today."

"Any idea who?" Miller crossed her mind then. He was up to something. She felt it in her gut, though somehow still had difficulty believing it. As Kade spoke, her reflections turned to him. She loved watching his expressions and was having trouble concentrating on a serious conversation.

"Not yet. Wanted to make you aware, and it's best if you don't go out riding by yourself for a while."

Emmy nodded, tracing a fingertip along his knuckles. She also fancied his masculine hands. The look of them. And now the feeling. Persistent images crept into her psyche: broad shoulders, an inked image of a blue, green, and gold dragon slithering over his chest and abdomen, arms corded with muscles, slender, powerful hips, and butt, the stream of water in his bathing shower sluicing water over his nude body....

Kräuterlikör still affecting your head? Can't go blaming it forever.

Her attention fell to the triangular collar area of his shirt, where a dusting of hair curled into the unknown. She longed to touch him there.

Before she knew it, her face tilted to his again in a silent plea. And when his visage became too blurry, she closed her eyes, relishing the commanding feel of his lips finding hers again.

Teach me. Everything.

CHAPTER 26

A Toast to Innocence

K ade kissed her then, the way he promised himself he never would. All those nights he lay on his cot in the carriage house apartment with thoughts of her warming him on chilly mountain nights, knowing she wasn't far away in her own bed.

Emmy opened her lips beneath his, shyly at first, allowing his worship, the way she shouldn't if she knew what was good for her. And worship he did, toying and teasing with his tongue. Gathering her into his arms, he held her head firm and brought his mouth to hers again.

Her arms circled him, looping around to grasp his shoulders tight, pulling him into her. When Emmy's mouth opened under his, he feared his pants may explode from the pressure of his arousal. She responded to his unspoken lessons, slanting her head to meet his lips as eagerly as he sought out hers.

Then, her eyes opened dreamily.

"Are you okay?" Kade inquired, voice husky, lips a mere breath above hers. He placed a stray kiss on the tip of her nose.

She nodded. "Don't stop the lessons."

"I'll teach you whatever I can."

And he would. Though he shouldn't—he knew that, too.

He caught her mouth again, gently tearing at her lips in a devilish dance.

"I feel hot. And dusty. Kade?"

"Hm?"

"Show me how your shower works."

Kade's breath caught as he pulled back to look at her, comprehension rooting in his brain. And his pants. Especially his pants. Her words set him on fire.

And yet, he would do the right thing, though it may be the most difficult.

"Emmy," he began, "How about I see you back safely to the house where you can have a hot bath in the privacy of your new water closet?" He added a confident smile to the suggestion.

Don't envision her naked. And don't imagine that delicate gold locket nestled in between her breasts, submerged (mostly) under a sea of bubbles lazily lapping pink—

She shook her head in the negative, lips curving sexily.

"I've never been quite this certain. I'm a grown woman. Everyone talks about that shower. We're alone, and I want to experience it firsthand. Please?"

She stood, holding out her hand.

He wanted to be with her in the privacy of his worm-holed planked wood apartment above the carriage house, in the too-skinny bed he claimed as his own for the time being. A simple mattress, painfully flat pillows, a sheet of flannel, and the wool blanket he hated— utilizing its scratchy warmth by laying it on top of two more soft sheets. It wasn't Bed, Bath & Beyond comfort, but it worked for now.

He didn't want to be with her in the spider-webbed back corners of the cluttered barn amongst the prying eyes of curious barn cats and the occasional ballsy mouse, shielded only by hanging tarps and threadbare blankets, some with holes big enough to stick an arm through.

At least it was nightfall. Everyone had disappeared into their hovels for a hot meal and a night's rest, windows glowing with low lights.

And yet, there she stood contemplating his creation in the milky rays of moonlight, staring curiously at the tangled mess of pipework above her head. With a frown of consternation, she reached for a handle.

"No, not that one. This one here." He stood beside her now. "It releases the water from the barrel on the roof. But you don't want to start it until you're ready." She tilted her head inquiringly, and he continued. "It's warm from being in the sun all day, but it runs out pretty quick."

Emmy smiled in understanding, "It's ingenious."

He appreciated the compliment. "I wouldn't go that far." She did have a knack for bringing out the little boy in him. He didn't mind. It made him rather happy.

She brings out the man in you even more.

"What will you do in the winter?"

It was an extraneous question, for surely, she didn't expect him to still be there through the change in seasons. The idea brought reality a little too close and made him sad to think he would be back in his own time by then, alone, provided all this range war nonsense was sorted out. And that meant he wouldn't see her anymore. No longer aggravated by her disregard for rules. And she wouldn't be irritated by his constant appearance in her kitchen. The thought caused him to chuckle inwardly, but then Miller Johnson's image popped into his head alongside Detective Grayson's. He should remain here just to make sure those jackasses didn't move in on her. She deserved better than that.

She deserves better than me.

When Kade looked down, she tilted her face up, her eyes shimmering gray in the reflection of the moonlight.

"I'd like to know. Will you shower with me ... and show me?"

The blood drained from Kade's face, his head, coursing down, through his neck, and into his chest, and belly, pooling in his gut and beyond, bubbling there, boiling with desire for her. Even that disappointed him. She didn't need some horny ass like himself taking advantage of the situation.

Is that what you're doing, taking advantage? Or are you teaching her what she longs to know, and allowing her to trust, when trust is what she needs? You're both as different as you are the same. Maybe it's you that needs teaching....

Kade felt an urgency fall over him then, a desperation to explore the sparring needs between them. And afterward, he would return to his life. Plain and simple. It was all that could be.

The need for her overwhelming, he wrapped her in his arms and pressed his lips to the top of her head, then her forehead, cheek, at last her mouth. Claiming her.

Emmy's arms locked around his neck, and she kissed him back, a little moan escaping her throat when his hand lowered, splaying across her buttocks and squeezing, drawing her firmly into the hardest part of him.

"Oh," she blurted, surprised.

He kissed her neck. She thrust her fingers into his hair, holding on tight as he lifted her against him.

"Your clothes need to come off. I can assist," he offered helpfully.

"And I can as well," she retorted, unsure fingers working at the front of his chambray shirt. "You will join me?" she asked shyly. "Don't think I'm going to stand here naked with you being fully clothed." He laughed, his answer coming in the form of another kiss, this one hard with intent.

With buttons unbuttoned, fasteners unfastened, ties untied, and Emmy standing before him, her eyes limpid pools of fascination as she looked down at herself, then back up to him, he realized all he ever wanted was her. This moment. The grasp of it shocked him. A long while since he'd been with a woman. In a world full of wrongs, something about that seemed very right.

He gathered her skirts in his hands and lifted her dress from her body until she stood before him in only her chemise and pantaloons, material so fragile and thin it did little to hide the intriguing shadows of her perky nipples and the enticing V between her legs. He longed to slide his hand between those legs and feel her heat, but he refrained, at least for the moment.

Emmy's fingers traced the lines of his tattoo, tickling his skin as she went, from where it began on his upper arm, along his collarbone, and then sweeping down to nearly cover his left pectoral muscle, lower over his abdomen, a flame from the dragon's mouth dipping into his waistband. She looked up at him.

"You'll have to wait," he instructed. "First...."

Unable to wait any longer, Kade worked a hand between her legs, gently, inquiring. The feel of her velvet, moist sex bare between a delicate slit of material, caused an illicit groan to pass his lips. He knew the style was Victorian and the norm for the time period, and yet, the idea of it turned him on beyond belief. He couldn't have sat down right then without busting out the zipper in his jeans.

Fascinated, he stroked her velvety skin softly, almost imperceptibly, aware of her soft moans, when she angled her thigh just so to allow him better access. Finally, she leaned fully against him to keep her legs from buckling.

When her nails dug into his arm and she began to moan in earnest, he slowed. A free hand rose and captured her jaw, lowering his mouth and stealing her breath and the soft moans passing her lips. As he removed the remainder of her clothes, her arms coiled about his neck and held fast, molding her body to his.

Kade stopped only long enough to kick out of his boots and jeans and shrug out of his shirt. The weight of his sex belied his excitement and Emmy's expression heightened, a new sparkle in her eyes. He wasn't exactly sure if she was surprised, scared, aroused, or all three.

"And so," she observed with pause, chewing at her lower lip, voice breathy, "that's where the dragon's flame goes."

He reached above her head and twisted the lever, releasing a stream of water and she giggled, clasping her arms around his neck, allowing the pleasant heat to trickle over them both. Carefully, he removed the pins from her hair and set them aside so they wouldn't be lost, nuzzling first her neck and then those beautiful, naked shoulders. Waves of thick hair tumbled down her back to caress that pleasing ass, while cascades of water sluiced over her breasts, spilling over the nubs of her nipples and dropping in splashes upon his belly. He leaned over and took one into his mouth, lightly sucking. Emmy pushed her fingers through his hair, gripping his head in a shocked "oh!"

"I can stop," he offered in all seriousness, looking up.

"I-I would like you to continue," she professed, her words and tone turning him on even more.

Kade drew each nipple into his mouth in equal turns, laving gently. He kissed his way back up, holding her head as he feasted on her neck, bodies slick, molded together. Emmy threw her head back, a languishing smile on her face. Then she picked up the square of soap, beginning by smoothing it over his chest, fingers traveling to explore his rigid flat stomach, a mat of fur, and then shyly, his sex. He let out a muffled growl.

"Is it all right? Should I stop?" she asked, concerned.

"Hell no, don't stop. Emmy, you're...."

"I'm what?"

"...amazing," he expelled on the tail of a pleasured sigh, squeezing his eyes shut.

"I've never ... seen this before. A penis. On a man, I mean. Horses, yes. Dogs, pigs, even rabbits. But rabbits fall over like they're dead after completion of ... the act." A worried frown passed over her face and she studied his face for clarification.

"I can't speak for all men, but I don't anticipate falling over dead afterward." Kade's words drifted off when he leaned in for another taste of those damp, pursed-in-curiosity, irresistible lips.

"Does it happen that fast?" she asked, apparently still concerned with rabbits.

Kade's head fell back in subdued laughter, and he speared her with a promising gaze, snatching the brick of soap from her sudsy hands.

"Let's just say, one doesn't intend for it to happen as fast as rabbits. That isn't the goal. My turn, milady," he commanded. "Turn around."

She slipped around in his embrace and Kade sudsed up his hands before pushing her hair aside and kneading her shoulders. He massaged the soap into her back, then lower to concentrate on that fabulous butt. She sighed with pleasure and leaned into him, dragging her slickened butt along his rigid cock. He suppressed another long groan for fear of alerting the neighbors. Then he nudged aside a hank of damp hair, flicking his tongue along the sensitive area behind her ear.

"I could get used to having showers instead of baths all the time," she crooned breathlessly.

"I thought most women preferred baths unless they were in a hurry."

"Baths can be lonely." Her eyes flashed up at him coquettishly.

"Ah, I see. I'm growing fonder of showers myself." His mouth discovered hers again as they rinsed off. Just in time, the water from the rooftop barrel ran dry, trickling its final droplets from the spout above their heads.

"Well, that's it. Our shower is done for tonight. I'll refill the barrel tomorrow." He reached for a large ivory sheet kept handy on a hook nearby, wrapping her shoulders and scrubbing her arms and legs dry. Emmy's gaze followed his movements closely before she spoke once again.

"Kade?"

He paused, once again lost in those intense pools of pale green and gray, her voice an almost imperceptible whisper.

"I want you to make love to me."

Like a couple of mischievous tom cats on the prowl, one at a time they poked their heads out of the far rear door of the barn, eyes darting both ways before dashing partway up a grassy berm, one after the other, then around to the outside stairway leading to the apartment situated above the carriage house. Emmy suppressed a delighted giggle, sheet floating from her shoulders, clothes wadded into a ball in her arms.

"We must look a sight," she said, amending, "if anyone were to see us, that is, which of course they mustn't. See us, I mean."

Kade lifted the brass latch and pushed open the door, ushering her inside. He took her clothes from her arms and arranged them neatly across the back of a chair. On the desk in the far corner sat a small hurricane lamp. He struck a match. The lamp was inadequate, barely exuding enough light to do any sort of reading or paperwork. Not that he cared a whit about that right now.

Mesmerized, she fidgeted, toes curling from beneath the sway of the sheet. She chewed at her lip. He sauntered toward her, his smooth skin corded in muscle, the colorful ink dragon bathed in a golden glow.

"You're gorgeous," he said, a wicked grin lighting his face.

Her gaze lowered, fixating on his sex. Strong, erect, and standing up like—unbidden, her thoughts went to the flagpole in front of Montana Collegiate University. She swallowed dryly at the random thought.

Kade scooped her into his arms and drew her close, erasing all thoughts except those of him, and she lost herself in his fantastical touch. The girth of him, the hard heat pressed into her belly. She sighed when his hand came around to grasp her hip and winch her closer still.

Easing her back onto the bed as if she were no more than a doll, he first straddled her and then lie beside her. He drew her close and cradled her head in the crook of his arm and looked into her eyes. The sheet still covered her, and he lifted it away, feasting on every inch of her body in the low light.

"God you're beautiful," he reiterated, voice husky. "Will you please tell me if I do something you don't want me to do?"

Emmy nodded, sliding her fingers into his hair and urging his lips to hers. She kissed him softly.

"I want you, Kade."

She wanted nothing more than to lose herself in his strong arms, this man who had dominated her thoughts and emotions since she had first seen him at the Bar C of the future. Only back then, she didn't understand what those feelings were.

Kade's head dipped, his lips closing around a nipple, causing her to arch closer to him, an expression of relinquishment washing over her face. The sensations, the teasing pull of his mouth. He crossed to her other breast and suckled it in turn until she writhed at the unique pleasure of it all.

An unknown fullness, almost a painful sensitivity throbbed in her lower body. When Kade slid a gentle hand between her legs, delicious pleasure washed over her, instigating a gasp. His subtle groans joined hers as he toyed. Then, he slid down her body further and the next thing she knew, molten hot wetness flicked between her legs, intensifying this new pleasure.

Emmy's eyes flew open and she cried out, twisting beneath the anchor of his arms.

"Oh dear, oh dear, oh … Godgodgod…!"

"Baby," he breathed, while delicately swishing his tongue over the sensitive bud of her sex.

Kade brought her to a fiery crest, one she hadn't known existed, his strong grip holding her steady, so she didn't buck herself off the bed.

Never had she ever...!

Gasping for air, she pressed her mouth to his delicious whiskery jaw as he positioned himself over her, those hips a perfect fit between her legs.

And then he hesitated. Seconds passed. He dipped his head and with a light groan, gently rolled away.

"Did you hear something?"

"No, what?" she asked, instinctively curling into him. The sheer pleasure of him was far more alluring than the fear of being found out.

"I think I heard the horses," he said, his tone somehow different. "Clementine's foal, I think. I'll go check."

With that, Kade pushed himself off the bed, shrugged into a shirt, and jumped into his blue jeans, not bothering to fasten them, not that he could have with the size of—

She blinked up at him, "But I don't hear anything."

"I'll be back before too long," he promised. "Don't worry. You can stay here."

Bewildered, she snuggled into the blankets and let him tuck them carefully around her. He placed a lingering kiss on her lips before leaving the upstairs apartment, pulling the door securely closed behind. She listened to the fade of his footfalls, replaced by the peaceful sounds of the night. Had she done something wrong? Had she disappointed him? Feelings hurt, eventually, her eyes grew heavy, and she slipped into a content slumber.

The fog of lust is a bitch to shake.

After losing count of repetitions, Kade dropped from the steel bar he used for pull-ups, heading over to a patch of grass and hammering out an undetermined number of sit-ups. Then he figured he would jog, but when the dogs started chasing him, thinking it was playtime, he stopped before he woke up the entire ranch. He passed by the paddock to check on Clementine and her new foal, scratching the sweet spot on her neck.

"I'm an idiot," he told the mare with a shake of his head. "Almost went through with it, and I'll tell ya right now, I'm amazed I could stop. If I had gone through with it, I'd never be able to look at myself in the mirror again. Emmy's a virgin! She doesn't deserve the outcome of me disappearing after...." He shook his head, brows lowering, "C'mon, don't look at me like that." Clementine whuffled and tossed her head. Was that pity in those soft brown eyes? He doubted it.

Eventually, Kade made his way back to the carriage house and climbed the stairs, looking forward to slipping into the skinny bed beside Emmy's deliciously warm body. Careful not to wake her, he curled into an excellent spooning position around her cute behind and tried to fall asleep—with his pants on.

CHAPTER 27

Trouble

Miller Johnson shoved the last of his sandwich into his mouth and pushed open the door to Pa's office. It swung around and knocked over a stack of books and other odds and ends, loose papers, a paperweight, and a plethora of dust balls. Ma's pink snuff bottle rolled across the floor, the one she purchased with extra money she had been squirreling away for at least a year or two.

He kicked aside a stack of old newspapers and last year's Sears & Roebuck catalog before stooping to pick it up, grunting as he did. Ma had been gone for over two years now, and Pa still held onto her catalogs and snuff bottle. For sentimental reasons, Miller surmised, Pa kept it perched on his desk like some kind of monument. Now that Pa had been gone nigh on a year, Miller supposed he should box up some of this junk.

He drank the last swig of cold sassafras tea, pushing the empty glass across a cluttered side table, a swath of dust smeared aside in its wake. He stood still for a moment to peruse the area thoughtfully. Rows of books lined one entire wall. It was a cramped room, and the books were on subjects he had no interest in or even a desire to know about. Mostly fanciful adventure stories and growing flowers—things Ma was interested in. She should have spent more time doing womanly things like needlepoint, sewing clothes, and cooking. Especially cleaning. But instead, she sat in that old purple chair by the cookstove reading books. If she had spent any time cooking while she was reading, it may have been more acceptable to him and Pa.

His sisters were a help when they weren't bossing Miller around. At least they kept the house reasonably clean and knew how to put together a mean venison stew and fluffy biscuits. Likely that stew was the prime reason their husbands proposed to them in the first place. For certain they weren't much to look at.

The original house was built in the '40s before Miller was born, and it was damn near falling apart. Pa didn't do much with upkeep, he was too busy with the sheep business. Or, struggling to keep from going broke. If Miller could just decipher the ledgers and make heads or tails of the business end of things, things would improve. As it was, bill collectors were hounding him about things he had no idea about.

He scanned the room, including the cluttered hallway. The entire house should be torn down and a new one built. Emmy's money would facilitate that. When his plan went into effect, this whole chunk of land would be integrated with the Bar C. One big happy, wealthy ranch. Once he was the owner, that is. Once Emmy got a look at Rosannah's last will and testament, the one her mama revised especially for him, Emmy would become compliant. Miller laughed, the solitary rumble startling the house cat and prompting it to dart from under the desk and down the hall. After all, he and Emmy had known each other nearly forever, and she would come to realize it was for the best.

Emmy would be happy here, wouldn't she? She liked to cook, at least he thought she did. He couldn't remember. Then it occurred to him, if she didn't like to cook, she would have to learn to like it. Because he sure as hell liked to eat. Soon she wouldn't have much choice. When the Triple Bar C burnt to the ground, where else could she go? The interloper Kade Stockton came to mind and Miller's smile melted into a scowl. He would make sure Stockton wasn't around to interfere.

Varnish peeled from the mahogany desk, snagging papers as he tried to slide them aside in orderly piles. The boys would be here soon, and he needed to make a good impression even though they weren't any smarter than idiots. The time had come to get some important things done. It was now or never.

With the desk straightened as well as it ever would be, he went about the room picking up old trash and rearranging chairs, deciding there wasn't enough room to accommodate everyone. Thirty or so men wouldn't fit into the house, let alone the tiny office. The barn was a better choice. Besides, it would be a quick meeting. He only intended to issue orders to the leaders of the pack and give them the responsibility of keeping the others in line.

That morning, Miller had withdrawn the last of the Johnson Ranch funds from the First National Bank in Gunn Pass City. Pa's gambling habit had ruined the family's savings. This was Miller's one last chance at increasing his holdings by 500 percent, maybe more. He never had been good at mathematics. As much as he despised admitting it, his future relied on Emmy Bartlett. And his own cunning ideas. Isolating Emmy's mama before she passed, when her mind was so far gone, hadn't been easy. Convincing her of his love for Emmy and desire to help her make the Bar C flourish was harder still. His plan of drawing up a will and convincing the old woman to her to sign her name. Now that was genius if he did say so himself—in theory. He never managed to get her to do it.

"Boss, you in there?" A voice echoed from the front porch, followed by the clomp of heavy boots to wood.

"In my office, Amos," Miller chimed back. "You alone?"

"Got the two oldest Carlson boys and Neely with me," Amos answered.

Miller heaved a sigh. "I told you to come here first—alone. Doesn't mean bringing the Carlson brats. Neely is fine."

Amos paused at the office window, folding his lean body in half to peek into the open part. He swiped his hat off his head, and his dirty-blond hair poked straight up as if it had never seen a comb. Squinting, he cupped his hands around his eyes to better see inside the room. "C'mon, the Carlson boys are good. Ah, there you are, sitting at your Pa's desk like a regular high-falutin' cattle baron. Alright if we come on in?"

"Get in here," Miller barked. He lit a cigarillo, leaned back, and propped boots to the desk. A chunk of dried mud fell from a boot heel to the floor. As

Amos Timms, both Tom and Larry Carlson, and Cornelius "Neely" Adams moseyed into the room, Miller took a long drag from his smoke and motioned them toward the chairs positioned in front of the desk.

"Before the others get here," he continued, sifting the smoke through his teeth. "I want to clarify a few items of consideration. I suspect things are comin' to a head."

" 'Bout time," Timms said, scooting to the edge of his chair. "Something needs to happen before Stockton does something stupid."

"What are you talking about?"

"Just that he's got the Bar C hands working on something. Digging and such. Packing supplies and taking them somewhere."

"Somewhere *where*? What supplies?"

"I dunno!" Timms cried in defense. "Only have so many eyes, can't see everything the man does."

Miller shook his head and dropped his boots to the floor. He crushed out the cigarillo before leaning forward across the desk.

"What about Neely, you have any insight?"

"Only that Stockton started them boys digging trenches. Was all kinda hushed. They dug for days, and then when I took a ride through, didn't see anything 'cept for rows of pointed timbers all in rows, like some kind of fence blocking the natural trails. Downright dangerous if you don't know they're stickin' up like that."

"Ya think?" Miller asked in a dry tone, shaking his head.

"Stockton is a sneaky feller," Amos said. "Maybe he's digging traps. That's what it is ... traps! Like those jungle stories I read as a kid. Pits to capture the tiger, covered with brambles & such—"

"For crying out loud," Miller barked, cutting him off. He pushed fingers through his hair. "This ain't no jungle and there ain't no tigers. So you can read, eh? That shocks me in itself."

Amos nodded smugly, "Yessir. I enjoy perusing the wanted posters in Gunn Pass. Anything you want to know about a wanted criminal, I can tell you. And me and a few of the others cut the fence on the far northwest section of the Chase land."

"Good, I like that. Didn't leave any evidence I hope."

"The boys have been moving herds up to the plateau, too," Neely added, hoping to please his boss. He'd only recently been put on the payroll and was enjoying the extra greenbacks in exchange for Bar C information he provided to Johnson.

Miller's gaze lifted, "You don't say?"

"Been at it for days now. The grass is plenty thick up there. Initially thought it was a rotation thing, but now I'm not so sure."

"I'd say it's more than rotation. Moving herds. Digging holes. Something's going down, I feel it. Gonna be far easier to rustle head from that plateau, which is good news for us. Wonder why Stockton, or Tompson for that matter, would want the herds in a less secure position?"

"Stockton was in town a while back purchasing saltpeter and somethin' else. Dynamite maybe," Tom piped in.

"What?" Amos and Miller voiced in unison, glaring at him.

"Figured you all knew about that. Wasn't long after he showed up. Sorry I didn't say nothin' before."

Miller leaned forward. "And how do you know about this particular tidbit?"

Tom shrugged, "Becca or her Pa must've told Miss Joy. Whilst I was strollin' by the flower shop one day, heard her telling Miss Florence. Upon their mention of Kade Stockton, I slowed down to hear the conversation. Those ladies said Becca is all aflutter over him—"

"Thank goodness for gossip, eh? Those chattering women are good for one thing, if not another." Miller laughed, then, "How about we make you the official informer on Stockton?"

"Me?" Tom asked, posture straightening proudly.

"Him?" Amos interjected with a scowl. "You sure about that, boss?"

Miller shot him a glare and he stood down.

Larry's gaze narrowed. "He like ta broke my neck at the church social. Grabbed me like this." He stood, demonstrating. "There's still a bruise on the back'a my neck. See? I'd like to shoot him dead as a flattened rattler."

"No need to get ahead of ourselves here. I've got my own plans for Stockton."

A legion of twenty-plus riders came into view, trotting, one after the other, through the front gate, up the lane, and past the window in a cloud of dust.

"Bout time," Amos said, thankful for the interruption. "Clive, Seth, and the boys are here now."

"Usher them into the barn so I can give orders to everyone at once. This house is too small. Won't be long, I'll be fixing all that."

Amos snickered, "You'll be sitting in the Bar C office passing out orders afore long."

"As it happens, that's not the plan after all, Amos. I've got other ideas." Miller stood, set his hat on his head, snatched up the thick envelope, and aimed for the door with Amos, Tom, and Neely following.

Moments later, Miller stood in the center of a group of dusty cowpokes, hired Pinkertons, and rough riders—all hailing from a questionable past, most having ridden up from Texas in the previous weeks.

First thing he noticed was the absence of Detective Grayson. Just as well, he supposed. The detective had mentioned preferring to keep his profile low, saying as much when he reported back on the items he found in Stockton's quarters.

"This is how it's going to go. Looks as though things are moving faster than I originally anticipated."

"You got that right," one of the Pinkertons said. "Crossed paths with a band of fifty or more soldiers heading up here from Kansas. A rough-looking bunch from down Mexico way. The last thing I want is to get caught in their path. I have a family back home in Missouri."

Miller's blood ran cold. Exactly what he feared. With the political corruption in Cheyenne, they weren't the only ones with sights set on the big spreads in Wyoming. Either with violence or bureaucracy, someone would come out ahead. He wanted it to be him.

"No time to waste. Seth, tomorrow night, as soon as the sun sets, you and your boys head onto Bar C land. Make certain you ride undetected. I don't care how you figure it out, or what you do, but make sure *all* the buildings burn. *Nobody leaves Bar C land until every damn structure is on fire. Got it?*" He slammed a fist onto the barn wall.

The group stared at him wide-eyed for a moment. One, then more began to converse, heads nodding.

"What's in it for us?" one asked.

"Yeah," more chorused in. "We ain't workin' for charity here."

Miller reached into the inner pocket of his vest, whipping out the chunky envelope and slapping it to his left palm. "Each one of you gets a hefty down payment. Fifty bucks to start. When the work is done on the Bar C, there's plenty more where this came from."

The men looked at one another in a murmur of words. Miller suppressed a cringe, recalling the image of a zero balance in the Johnson Ranch account when the teller pushed the ledger across the desk for him to sign.

Good thing Emmy's bank accounts are fat and healthy. Once she realizes her precious Mama signed it all over to him, she'll become far less disagreeable.

"What about this Stockton feller? Hear tell he's one of them soldiers. Fought in some wars. It made him go crazy they say."

Miller turned to the man who spoke, his scowl softening when he met the ebony stare of a Mexican vaquero. He wore a low-crowned black hat, a shirt accented in gold and blue threaded swirls, a red sash, and a plethora of ammunition across his chest. He wore leather leggings down to buckskin boots and large roweled spurs.

"No need to concern yourself with Stockton," Miller assured. "He's mine. I'll make sure he's out of the way. Listen, everyone, this part is important. Do not torch the main house until I give the word. I'll be there to make sure my bride is safe. Once I get her out, then I'll give the sign. Got it?"

Amidst a cacophony of conversation, agreements, questions, and guffaws, Miller began to move about the group, counting out bills.

"What about the Bar C hands? They're going to cause problems." someone called out.

"Kill'em. Don't need any of them left alive."

After everyone was paid and the group had celebrated by passing around the whiskey, Miller took Neely and Tom Carlson aside.

"I have assignments for you two, how's that sound?"

CHAPTER 28

Cowboy Take Me Away

K ade reeled his horse around and swung out of the saddle, looping the reins at a hitching post between the Livery and mercantile, the watering trough in reach. For the entire ride into town, he couldn't get Emmy out of his head. Specifically, her lips, every bit as tasty as her blackberry cobbler. He enjoyed the spot she occupied in his head, more as time went on, and that worried him. As soon as this mission is over, he will have gone back to his own time, to the modern Bar C and his position as a horse trainer. Just as well, though not something he enjoyed thinking about. Therefore, he needed to make certain all was well before he left. ***

Leaving Emmy to fend for herself. Gone to you. Forever.

Nerves strung tight, he sensed things would go down soon. Someone had rummaged through his belongings in the carriage house and Kade's habits were precise. Something was off. A crease on the blanket covering his bed. The straps on his backpack were askew, one fastened backward. When he went to turn on his phone, the battery was dead. Always careful to preserve the battery life, he only used it to educate himself on the history of this time period or listen to the occasional playlist: country, 70s rock, metal, depending on his mood. There were book and article downloads and screenshots of maps—where invaders had come into the state, who they were, and how many. Nothing was etched in stone, he knew that. But it never hurt to be educated on a historian's account of the Wyoming range wars.

The spare battery was depleted, and he was on the last charge of his phone. This he knew for certain. He also knew he had powered the phone down after his last use and it was at 92%. He was too careful to leave it on. Someone else did that—someone who was snooping. Now, all contact with his own time was gone, and whatever information his phone contained was lost to him.

That morning one of the hands, Neely Adams, singled him out with the news that Becca Wilkes needed to speak with him right away. He said she had searched him out at the saloon, mentioning it was important. Kade decided on the fly to ride on into Gunn Pass to speak with Becca, and hopefully the sheriff to see if there were any new developments. Might even grab a flower arrangement from the Flower Emporium for his best girl.

When Kade opened the door of the mercantile, a bell sounded and Russell Wilkes was first to greet him, extending a hand. Kade shook it heartily.

"Was hoping to have a word with Becca. Is she available?"

A dawning smile eased across the older man's jaw, eyes twinkling when he spotted the flowers in Kade's hand. "I reckon she's in the back working on mid-year inventory, but I'm sure she can spare a moment."

"I don't want to interrupt, but it is important. Won't take long."

"I'll let her know you're here."

Russell disappeared into the back while Kade idly perused aisles of housewares, farm equipment, nuts, bolts, nails, fabric, and thread, stopping to examine a curious glass jar with holes at the top. "Fly Catcher" read its label.

"Why Kade Stockton, I'm surprised to see you here!" Becca gushed, approaching from behind. Standing erect, arms folded across her middle, she rocked to and fro on stylish pointy-toed boots.

She stood so near, Kade's first impulse was to step back. If he weren't in danger of knocking over the entire fly catcher display, he would have. Becca's dark eyes, rimmed in abundant black lashes, flashed up at him, tiny crinkles at the sides when she smiled. No doubt about it, she was a beautiful woman, and she didn't need war paint to make her that way. One more thing he appreciated about the past. Women were real.

Just looking into Becca's suggestive gaze sent Kade's thoughts racing back to Emmy: *Smart, determined, thoughtful, feminine, athletic. Sexy as hell. Great butt. Lips capable of lifting a man to heaven and back....*

Kade cleared his throat, removing his hat in afterthought.

"Good to see you, Becca. Been awhile. Life treating you well?"

"I'm superb," Becca assured. "What brings you to town? Is there something you need?" She flashed another signature smile, wetting her lips with the tip of her tongue.

Kade saw her gaze resting upon the small bouquet in his left hand. In retrospect, he should have waited to pick the flowers up from Joy's place *after* he stopped at the mercantile.

My bad.

"What's that in your hand, Kade?" she asked excitedly. "You don't mind if I call you Kade, do you?" Becca sucked in a breath and pushed her palms down the apron she wore over her skirt as if preparing for something monumental.

"It's my name, last time I checked." *Don't be a smart ass.* He hated to douse the excitement in those pretty brown eyes, but... "These?" He glanced at the flowers and feigned surprise, "Just a little something for Emmy. She made some awesome muffins the other night." *Now that sounded stupid.*

"Oh. I see," Becca said, voice deflating. "I'm sure she'll be happy to receive them."

"Neely mentioned you needed to speak with me?"

Confusion crossed her brow. "Neely ... Adams? Isn't he employed by the Bar C?"

Kade dipped his head, "That's correct. He mentioned you had something important you needed to see me about ... um, he spoke with you at the saloon, last night?"

Becca gasped, a hand lifting to her breast.

"Mr. Stockton, I was *not* at the saloon, last night or any other night!" With that, Becca looped her arm through his, swiftly leading him to the back. "Don't want any wagging tongues, now do we?" she added, raising her voice an octave as they passed Winifred Godfrey, affectionately dubbed the town gossip and clearly competing with Joy Warner for the title. The older woman hovered over the sewing thread, pretending fascination with a new stock of bright colors, ducking her head sheepishly as they passed. "Good afternoon, Winifred. Nice weather we're having."

Outside of a strangled cough, Winifred didn't respond.

"She pretends to be hard of hearing, but everyone knows she hears better than most everyone in town. Isn't that right, Winifred?" Becca called over her shoulder. Something clattered to the floor, and Winifred was last seen chasing spools of thread around a corner.

Becca escorted Kade to a door, flung it open, and stepped out onto the dock area where shipments were routinely delivered by wagons, the train, traders, and local vendors. The platform area was vacant, at least for the time being. She pressed the door shut and faced him, hands on hips.

"I don't know what this is about," she continued, tone hushed, "but I don't appreciate being accused of being at the saloon!"

The young seamstress who operated the dress shop wasn't much older than Emmy. An expert in her field, Fanny Picard had been tutored by her mother—not only sewing, but design, creation, and the procurement of fine materials from around the world. During her two-hour fitting appointment, Emmy learned that Fanny's mother, Madame Picard, had fitted Madison's wedding gown all those years ago in Laramie. Small world, Emmy reflected, as Fanny worked diligently on the hem of one of her new dresses, this one a buttery-soft fabric the color of cranberries. Fanny pulled the last straight pen from between her lips and worked it into the hem.

"*Ooh-la-la, vous êtes belle, Mademoiselle!*" Fanny went on, mimicking her *maman's* crooning French as she pushed to her feet, dusting her hands together.

"Who is the lucky gentleman, if you don't mind my asking?" she pressed, lifting a perfectly sketched brow.

Emmy heard Fanny's question, though couldn't stop looking at her reflection staring back at her from the mirror—as if she viewed someone else, maybe an elegant model from a catalog. Granted, the creamy patterned carpets beneath her, a silk damask chaise lounge to her side, as well as velvet wallpaper and vases overflowing with flowers all added ambiance. Even so....

When exactly did I grow up?

"I apologize," Emmy said finally, "what was that you asked?"

"Ah, your mind wanders. I wish to know the *monsieur* you think of while wearing my creation. What is his name?"

"Monsieur...?" Emmy repeated, lifting her gaze to the ceiling where a crystal chandelier sparkled, tinkling above her head in the breeze crossing from an open window. She shrugged, snapping her attention back to Fanny. "No man," she lied. "It's just that I am pleased, and in such need of new clothes. Attending the institute in Bozeman, I rotated three practical dresses, two wool and one a plain chambray in an ugly shade of blue. I hated that dress. All were drab and plain in design. But at least they were warm. The heat registers in that building barely worked. I'd go back to the rooming house after classes and wrap up in blankets to restore body heat."

Emmy returned to staring at her visage, the slender nip of her waist, and the blossom of womanly hips. She hadn't thought twice about her shape prior to arriving for her appointment that morning.

Not exactly true. Since Kade arrived, you've thought about it quite a lot. Your figure. Your hair. Your face....

Fanny Picard worked magic with her creations, no doubt about that. No wonder she and her mother were the talk of the western territories, having procured a profitable millinery business in the state. Hear tell, women traveled from California to be fitted for a special gown. Emmy remembered when a military general's bride from Colorado made the trip to Gunn Pass City for a wedding trousseau. Joy Warner wrote about it in her gossip column and jabbered on about it for weeks. Emmy thought she'd never shut up.

She turned this way and that, fiddling with a curl, twirling it around her finger and arranging it first over her forehead, then tucking it behind her ear. She had hastily piled her hair into a loose bun that morning, pushing in hairpins and several tortoiseshell combs to secure it. Now, the sides had begun to droop, cascading in thin veils around her face. No time to fix it now. Maybe she should consider cutting it? Wouldn't that create a scandal? In a Paris fashion magazine in Fanny's parlor, she noticed women with short hairstyles. She supposed when you're in Europe and glamorous enough to appear in a magazine, you could do whatever you damn well pleased.

She blinked, examining her face, eyes smoky green in this light, cheeks, and lips a muted mauve, likely brought out by the hue of the dress. Ensconced behind delicate ruffles rows of pearlized buttons extending down the bodice, the skirt itself flowing over her legs and not quite to the floor.

"A skosh above the ankle is all the rage in Paris, paired with a smart pair of kitten-heeled boots," Fanny explained with a knowing wink. She made a tsking sound, "So ... no monsieur, eh? *C'est tres belle, et dommage de gaspiller. Very beautiful. A shame to waste such a dress."* Fanny went on to organize and put away her sewing supplies. "I'm pleased to see you've forgone the mourning colors. How have you been since your *maman* passed?"

Emmy ducked behind a changing screen and slipped out of the dress, draping it over the top. "Every day improves," she said, "though I miss Mama. Funny, I even miss caring for her when she was sick in bed. We had some of our best conversations then, I think."

Emmy lifted another dress from a satin-lined hanger and pulled it over her head, this one a similar material in a teal color, with a V-yoke and subtle ruffles, quite practical for everyday wear. It also needed no additional alterations and so she decided to wear this one home.

"I completely understand," Fanny replied. "I miss my *maman*, too, and she is only a few towns away. We are both busy with the shops, but soon I hope she will travel here. When she does, we should get together for tea, yes? *Maman* told me you were fortunate to visit with Mr. and Mrs. Chase not long ago."

Emmy blanched at Fanny's words. One of the benefits of Joy's gossip column again. "Yes, it was quite a nice visit. And tea sounds lovely."

Perching her serviceable straw hat atop her head, she popped out from behind the screen, arms full of intended purchases—the cranberry dress, two practical day dresses, one in a light-yellow stripe and the other a pale seafoam green, along with an assortment of soft cotton underthings Fanny recommended. And stockings. Mustn't forget those. Her thicker stockings wouldn't work with these gorgeous creations.

The purchases that didn't need alterations were wrapped, and Fanny stacked the bundles neatly on the counter.

"Can I interest you in a bauble to match?" Fanny asked, indicating rows of jewelry items in every tone and style imaginable, winking alluringly beneath the glass.

"I couldn't," Emmy said. "Where do I ever go that requires jewelry?" Captivated by rows of sparkles on velvet, she leaned in, drawn to a particular set of earrings with delicate gold filigree and tiny jewels the same color as her dress.

Fanny laughed, "Pshaw. Who needs somewhere special to go? It's all about your essence. Whatever makes you joyous is of the most importance. *Non?*"

Emmy's jaw firmed and she nodded, "You're absolutely right. I'll take those," she said, pointing to the earrings.

"*Très bon!* Let's put them on your ears right away," Fanny insisted, opening the case to retrieve the petite baubles, and clipping them on Emmy's earlobes. "Now, your new dresses, the rouge and yellow will be prepared soon. Return in a week, yes? I shall have heard from *Maman* by then. And, I'm including a sample of the French perfume, L'Etoile. It's positively chic. The bottle is wrapped up in the package."

"You are too kind, Fanny."

Emmy penned a cheque for her purchases, and the two women shared a hug and kisses on each cheek. Outside, the balmy summer air refreshed her as Emmy made her way to the wagon, tucking the packages under the bench seat. She had ridden into town with Estelle and Henry so they could tend to business at the blacksmith, while Emmy stopped into the bank to pay on an installment loan, and then to her fitting at Fanny's. Now, she made her way to the Emporium to select flowers for Becca.

Something about Emmy's mood lately made her feel...

Feminine? Sensual? Thinking of his kisses again? The heated strength of his arms circling your waist and shoulders, hauling you close to his chest, to his heart. And the caresses. All she had to do was think of the evening spent in his arms, and her heart expanded, the special spot between her legs feeling toasty and....

With a fresh bouquet in hand, Emmy erased the wicked thoughts and headed to Wilkes Mercantile to say hello to Becca. She hadn't seen her since the church picnic and thought they might sit down for a chat if she wasn't too busy. After rushing Becca off the day she popped in at the ranch, Emmy felt guilty. She would invite her out to the ranch for some lemonade made from the lemons Helen Riley had given her. Turns out, a salesman from California had brought a wagon load of fresh lemons, limes, and oranges to the area, a rare and delicious treat.

Straightening her demure straw bonnet, Emmy stepped into the mercantile to the welcome aroma of coffee beans, salted bacon, as well as a tempting array of sugared candies in oversized jars. Becca's father busied himself behind the counter.

"Good afternoon, Mr. Wilkes. I thought to say hello to Becca. Is she here?"

"Ahh, Miss Emmy, look at you! Radiant as always." Russell's head popped out from behind a row of tobacco ropes. He adjusted wire spectacles, face reddening as it always did when he was pleased—but then the smile faded. He glanced to the side door. "Let's see. She was here a moment ago, and Mr. Stockton stopped in to speak to her as well. Becca sure is popular today," he continued with a forced laugh. "I'm sure she'll be right back."

Did she hear Mr. Wilkes right, Kade was here? So, it wasn't imagination when she thought she spied Skitter hitched down by the Livery, listing to the side with eyes half-closed.

The side door opened. In whooshed Becca, flushed and chattering faster than a chipmunk caught in a blizzard. Kade followed, the wide grin he wore evaporating when he saw Emmy. He held a bouquet of wildflowers in his hand.

"Emmy!" Becca squealed, racing up the side aisle and wrapping her in a hug. "So good to see you. What brings you here?"

A gust of west wind could've knocked Emmy over. Not only was she at a loss for words, her entire being deflated, as if all air seeped painfully from her lungs with no hope of plugging the hole.

Somehow she managed to speak.

"I'm in town for errands with Henry and Estelle, and a fitting at Fanny's place. I wanted to say hello. Well, I've said it. The day's not getting any younger. Here's some flowers for you." Releasing the death grip she had on her bouquet, she pushed them into Becca's hand. "Bye now, I will be getting on home."

"But you just got here! At least have a glass of cool tea before you go. Maybe Kade would like one as well?" she offered cheerfully.

"Nope. Too late for caffeine," he said, a loaded gaze fixed on Emmy.

"Sassafras doesn't have caf—um, I don't think," Becca stumbled, confusion written on her face.

"Thanks anyway, though. I'll leave you two ladies to your conversation." He spun on a heel and went for the door as if he couldn't get out of there fast enough. His excuse joined with a lift at the corner of his mouth, the very one that turned Emmy's insides to jelly. He aimed it right at her.

Why did this man affect her this way? Barely more than 24 hours ago she had lain naked in his arms, eager for him to teach her things, ways of the flesh she had only dreamt about. The memories brought on a wicked blush, and she flinched at the nagging twinge in her belly.

But he left before actually making love to you. Could someone else have been on his mind?

"A fitting? Sounds divine!" Becca prodded again. "Surely you can stay for a bit?"

Emmy shook her head. "No, but I do want to invite you out to the Bar C for lemonade. You'll come out soon I hope? Good." She didn't pause for an answer, "You like lemons? I seem to remember you do. Helen gifted me with some lemons—anyway, I need to go. See you soon."

Embarrassed, the words tumbling willy-nilly from her mouth, she forced a pleasant expression that she feared resembled more of a snarl. Blowing Becca a kiss, she went to the door where she found Kade standing outside, holding it for her.

How stupid to let Kade Stockton's actions get to you! Lies. All lies. Best for him to finish his business and go back to his own time as soon as humanly possible.

"I didn't know you were coming into town," he said, closing the door behind her.

"Obviously," Emmy bit out as she set off on a brisk walk, heels clicking to wood.

"We could have ridden in together." He jogged a few strides to catch up.

"I doubt it. I came in early with Estelle and Henry."

He frowned, "Look, it's not what you're thinking."

He moved closer and Emmy shuffled back, only to wedge herself against a wall with nowhere left to go—face him or open the door and enter the Dentist's office. Kade focused on her mouth and her breath hitched.

"New dress?" he asked. "Pretty. I like it. The earrings too. Brings out the green in your eyes. By the way, these are for you." He presented the bouquet, and she grasped it tentatively, nodding a quiet thank you.

"They're nice. But people are looking at us," she reminded. By people, she referred to Joy Warner, whose head bobbed around a display of handmade paper sunflowers in the Emporium's showcase window. Emmy fluttered her fingers in that direction and Joy ducked out of sight.

"I don't care who's watching. For some reason, I can't seem to stop thinking about the other afternoon, when you kissed me in front of everyone," Kade said.

"You kissed me first."

"Hm," he agreed with a thoughtful nod. "Then, we kissed each other. I liked that best of all." He leaned in, bracing an arm to the brick wall above her head.

Her heart did another flip-flop. A flash of heat shot from her nether regions, blossoming, sending imaginary flames upward to lick at her face. This is what she had dreamed of her entire adult life. A good and capable man who could make her feel this way. A man who instigated this reaction without her permission. The sheer rightness of it made her insides go all liquidy.

And yet, nothing is right with Kade. You found him in a meeting with your best friend. And, don't forget, he will be lost to you as soon as the ranch is secured.

"Not enough to keep you from seeking out Becca Wilkes." Finding her voice, she lifted the bouquet to her nose.

"Ah, so that's what has you all fired up."

"I'm not fired up."

"Like hell, you're not. Would you like to know why I was talking to Becca?"

"She *is* the prettiest girl in Gunn Pass, not to mention the most talented. I trust you heard her sing in the choir since you've been to church numerous times since the social."

"The only time she ranks as the prettiest girl in Gunn Pass is when you aren't here. And the reason you're aware of my presence at church is that you were there as well. See a pattern here?"

That confident grin oozed with boyish charm, those carved lips a mere hair away from hers, or so it seemed. She wanted to fling her arms around his neck, laugh against his neck, lose herself in his strength. But it wasn't possible. Especially in the middle of town. She felt the weight of the stares of passersby, even those who thought they were hidden. Beyond Kade's broad shoulder, once again she caught Joy's slender form perched in the opposite store window between two tall vases of pink roses, ramrod stiff and eyes so wide they looked as though they would pop out of her head and bounce across the street. Was that Winifred Gunther's round face next to hers beside a container of daisies?

Emmy leaned around Kade and waved again. Horrified at being discovered a second time, Joy sheepishly returned the wave, pretending to adjust the display before exiting the window and yanking Winifred along with her.

"Wonderful. Now the entire town will know we're arguing," Emmy said with a heavy sigh, pressing a finger between her brows and shaking her head.

"We could kiss again, and then everyone will know we made up," Kade suggested.

"Stop it! Nobody can know about that."

"Little late, considering half the ranch hands saw it. I wonder if Joy has written her gossip column this week—"

Emmy winced, smacking Kade in the arm. "Damn Hanna's kräuterlikör. It made me brave, stupid, *and* forgetful." She lowered her voice, "Look, I don't want you to feel obligated...."

"Because we—well, almost made love?" he finished, voice low. Now he looked genuinely irritated, "Don't assume, Emmy."

"I'm an adult, and can handle my own irresponsibility and indiscretions, among other things."

"You do handle things quite well."

"Kade ... stop it."

"What?" A mischievous brow arched.

"You're teasing me." She sighed, "Why did you come into town to see Becca? You—didn't want to...," she looked around to make sure they were completely alone, ".... make love to me. If it's because you're interested in Becca, you can tell me. She is my friend. I'll understand." Jaw quivering, she looked away, worried she would embarrass herself by tearing up. And she feared she told a lie—no, she wouldn't understand at all.

Kade grew serious.

"Baby," he breathed, wanting so much to reach for her, stopping himself. "I don't know how to say this."

"Just say it," she said impatiently.

"We need to talk. Privately," he said, checking to make sure nobody was within hearing distance. Someone could be sitting in the dentist's chair, but he would take the chance. "You have my heart. *All* my heart. That's all I can say right here."

Emmy's eyes searched his, her hopes taking flight, "I do? Have your heart, I mean? You're not just saying that, are you?" For a second, she suspected he might kiss her, not bothered at all by who might see.

"You do," he said, voice low. "Your first time, I didn't want it to be ... like that. I want it to be special."

She laughed, a few tears springing forth and mixing in, "Kade, every day and night with you is special, don't you know that?"

"If we don't stop talking about this, I'm going to embarrass us both. I'm humbled as hell knowing you care enough to be mad at me. But the entire reason I'm here today is because Neely told me Becca came into the saloon yesterday while he was in town for a poker game. He said she needed to talk to me urgently."

Emmy's gaze narrowed, "You mean Cornelius Adams, the new hand?"

Kade nodded. "Yeah. Only she didn't know anything about it, and now it looks like I'm on both yours and Becca's shit lists. She didn't appreciate being 'accused' of being at the saloon."

"Oh dear, I imagine not." Emmy hid a smile, now feeling sorry for him. "If it makes you feel better, I'll remove you from my shit list, as you call it."

He laughed and tapped a finger to her nose before pushing his weight from the wall. "I'll kiss you later," he promised. He faced the street then. "Looks as though Grayson is heading into Townsend's office. I need to talk with them both, then it's back to the ranch to figure some things out."

"I'll go along."

Kade shook his head, expression serious.

"Listen, it's best if you gather up Henry and Estelle and head straight home."

"I think it's important that I'm included."

"I agree, just not right now. Things aren't adding up. It's a hunch, and I always pay attention to hunches." She walked up to stand beside him, and he slid his fingers gently across the nape of her neck, gazing into her eyes. "Trust me?"

She bobbed her head, the warm tingles of his touch almost making her forget where they were—on the boardwalk in the middle of Main Street, with who knew how many eyeballs trained on them.

"I'm not a damsel in distress, Kade. You of all people must know that by now. I must be made aware of what's happening with the Bar C."

"Damn right I know it, sweetie. You outsmarted a grizzly with cubs and came out on top."

The comment brought a chuckle, and she temporarily lost herself in the brilliant blue light of his eyes.

He called me sweetie....

Kade circled her shoulders with a protective arm and urged her to walk alongside to where Henry was finishing business with the blacksmith, the two men loading a repaired piece of haying equipment into the back of the wagon. Estelle stood off to the side talking with a woman Emmy didn't recognize.

"It's getting late. My priority is making sure you stay safe. Right now, I've got a bone to pick with Grayson. Neely is next on my list." Squinting, Kade's gaze trained at the front door to the Sheriff's Office, where Grayson now stood in conversation with one of the deputies. He chucked her chin, "This part is my war. Be careful, and I'll fill you in when I get home."

Home.

A flame blazed to life, expanding her soul and forcing her to grasp a burgeoning reality. This foreign thing inside her began as a tentative flame, grasping hold and finding itself. Yes, the ranch was her home. But there wasn't a thing in this world she wanted more than to make it really a *home*—with Kade Stockton by her side.

The revelation didn't give her happiness, didn't tempt her to rush to the highest peak and scream it to the heavens. It merely grazed the surface of a stark understanding of something that could never be.

CHAPTER 29

Heard It Through The Grapevine

While waiting for the two lawmen to join him, Kade seated himself in a hard oak chair in front of the well-used, though neat, desk of Sheriff Lloyd Townsend. The two lawmen still stood at the doorway alongside two recently deputized citizens, discussing the lynching of a woman and her partner, a man whom it was unknown if he was her husband or not—which to them, was as significant as the vile act itself.

He crossed a boot over his knee and folded arms across his chest, thoughts wandering to Emmy. Those inviting sugar-sweet lips, the healthy color of her cheeks, extra pink when she was giving him a piece of her mind. The determined and proud way she carried herself, a cute straw hat with a big bow perched on her curls in a jaunty fashion. A smile eased across his face as he recalled delicate jewels dangling from her perfect earlobes. It only drew his attention to the creamy skin of her neck—where he spent a good deal of time kissing two evenings ago. The music of her sighs echoed in his head.

Many times over the past weeks, he caught himself falling into the depths of those hazel eyes. But earlier, when she looked up at him, lashes dampened with tears, eyes so full of hurt, weighted in sadness and concern, he felt his own heart beginning to break. All he longed for when he saw her at the mercantile was to wrap her into his arms and hold on tight, assure her all was okay. He would lay down his life. Make sure of it.

Why did she have to be so alluring, so damned sexy? Catching a random flash of a rumpled stockinged leg gave him a hard-on, for chrissake.

Things had certainly shuffled around in his head these past several weeks. He had been convinced he had no interest in women or relationships ever again. An occasional good time, of course, was still on the table. Over the past year, even that didn't hold much interest. Sure, he loved his family, Dad, and Sean, but otherwise, the horses he trained were his life.

That is until you traveled back in time.

Might have started way back in modern day, when she first came around the corner of his cabin and startled him. As annoyingly sarcastic as she was, something intrigued him. Maybe it was the veiled challenge. Or their rousing mutual animosity. The disapproval on her face didn't match the playful sparkle in her eyes. Was he developing feelings for her? Panic slammed into his chest like a sucker punch. Nope, not an option. He would never hurt her, not deliberately. But a relationship? Not possible. The thought scared him enough to make a mental note not to lose himself. Kade shot a worried glance to the office window, hoping she was at that moment on her way back to the ranch.

You're falling for her. That slip of a woman has proven you wrong.

The two men returned to the desk where Kade sat, jostling him from his musings. Grayson took the chair beside him, and Townsend sat behind his desk.

"Several prominent cattle ranchers over in Sweetwater County have allegedly hanged a man and woman over a range dispute," Townsend explained to Kade. "Claimed they were rustling cattle on their land."

"I heard as much," Kade said. "Any arrests?"

"Not yet, too many stories flying around. Authorities are still trying to piece things together. Detective Grayson has been called over to Sweetwater to assist with the unrest, at least for a while."

That wasn't good. He disliked Grayson more than jock itch. Mainly because the man grated on his nerves, gave the impression of ulterior motives, i.e. interest in Emmy, and now, add to that the suspicion he rummaged through his belongings

Three strikes, you're out.

However, it was never good to lose an ally. Though it may seem things are quieting down here in Uintah County, he needed to make them both understand the desperate nature of the situation. He no longer had the information from his phone, thanks to the nosy dipwad sitting beside him, but he remembered the stories of large groups of men heading north from Texas.

"My opinion is, Grayson, as much as I'd like to see you go, you're needed here. At least for now."

Grayson dipped his head in a mirthless chuckle, "Feeling is mutual, Stockton. However, the governor has handed down the assignment. At this point, I'm locked in. If things change, I'll return, you can count on it."

"Now, there's no need to get all riled up, Stockton," the sheriff said. "I'm fully aware there are bands of rustlers in these parts, likely among us here in town if I've got my feelers on correctly. I've organized my own men. Town and country folk alike have been deputized and have instructions on what to do if problems arise—"

"I happen to know of particular groups heading this direction as we speak. If Grayson can't be our liaison to the state, then someone needs to be."

Townsend leaned forward, cocking an eye and twisting the end of his mustache absently. "May I ask exactly *how* you know these things?"

"Hard to explain. You might say I ... I heard it through the grapevine." The beat to the 70s hit song, along with Marvin Gaye's iconic voice resonated in Kade's head.

"Exactly what grapevine is this?" Grayson interjected. "Surely not Joy Warner's? I've got my own eyes and ears all over the state. I'd say mine are a damn sight more reliable. Unless you have particularly close connections with the criminal element." A thick eyebrow cocked in question.

"Let's just say I know how it works. I don't know about the sheriff, but you're an employee of the state and have an ironclad agenda. And you're not always on the side of the cattle rancher. This I know. Even though you like to give the impression that the honest, hard-working landowners and ranchers in the good state of Wyoming are your priority. Politics can be a slippery slope, and you Detective, along with the governor and other officials, are having a difficult time keeping your balance. The entire state of Wyoming has an agenda and you're a puppet. You may not feel that way currently, and it may not be purposeful, but I'd consider it if I were you. I've heard of criminals and hired Pinkertons coming up from the south to take advantage of the disruption, and they're out to get their piece of the pie."

"I don't know where in hell you get your information, Stockton," Grayson said with a scowl. "Could be I've put too much focus on the criminal element, and not enough on the stranger in front of me."

"Depends on how much integrity you have. If you want to help the landowners you've been assigned to protect, then you have the power to do so. The first step is coming clean on your intentions and being upfront with the ranchers—and Sheriff Townsend here."

"Hold on just a minute. What exactly are you accusing me of?" Grayson came out of his seat, chair legs scraping the planked wood floor. Kade was on his feet at equal speed.

"Now, now," Townsend chimed in. Both of you stallions calm down. Stockton, I don't know exactly where you've gotten your information, so how about we start with that."

After a mutual glare, both men lowered into their seats. Kade said the only thing he could that wouldn't cast him in a crazy light.

"Let's just say I accidentally stumbled across a meeting taking place on the far outskirts of the Bar C land, and it so happens, I overheard impending plans."

Grayson's expression tightened.

"Go on. Exactly who was at this meeting?" the sheriff asked.

"Several rough-looking characters I'm unfamiliar with, but two I happen to know. One was Miller Johnson. The other, Detective Grayson."

Townsend didn't flinch. "Johnson was by the office yesterday, and Grayson and I have been working together for the past month. Johnson has men running the line and is keeping me informed of all the developments. The thing is, I'm an open book, Stockton. Have no secrets from the community I'm tasked with protecting."

Kade's blood ran cold. Something wasn't right with this whole scenario, aware that neither of these men could be fully trusted. Usually a good judge of character, he now doubted his capabilities. He shifted in his seat, his brain shuffling different scenarios.

"Miller works with you then?" he asked.

"Deputized him months ago. Now, I'd be happy to work with you as well, that is, if you're serious about protecting this community and willing to take orders. I don't know you as well as other folks, but I'll take the chance seeing as we need as many men as possible."

Take orders. He'd done plenty of that in his life. He'd passed out quite a few of them, too. Emmy mentioned Miller having spent time in jail, but it seemed as if it was minor offenses, primarily drunkenness and brawling. Apparently, that wasn't an important factor in the sheriff's decision.

"Certainly," Kade replied finally. Relatively satisfied for the moment, he caught Grayson's jaw clench. He wondered if the good detective had found anything in his belongings to report to Townsend. A music box that lit up, perhaps?

"Good. Consider yourself deputized, Stockton. Doesn't give you permission to stalk and kill, but it does give you the right to protect the land and its owners, and since you've been hired by Mr. Chase and Miss Bartlett, the Bar C is considered your land for the time being. As a side note, Miss Bartlett stopped in earlier. She and Mr. Johnson are not planning to wed after all. May change the dynamics a bit," he added, with the lift of a proliferous eyebrow.

Kade flinched, in a good way, impressed as hell she had taken the time to make sure the sheriff knew the score. He glanced at Grayson, wondering if the detective was as pleased to hear the news as he was.

The sheriff stood then, shook each of their hands, and bid both men a good day. He wasn't overly concerned about something going down very soon. Kade wished he had his phone, once again irritated at Grayson. End of July and early August was a major factor in the range wars, only he couldn't recall details. It was a premonition or whatever, and something told him to get back to the ranch. He'd feel better surrounded by the familiar—call a meeting with the boys, make sure the explosives on the bottom forty were ready to go.

Kade went first, Grayson following, stepping single file out of the Sheriff's Office and out into the sunshine. Grayson paused to position his hat onto his head, adjusting it to perfection before turning to face him.

"So, Stockton," he said, "Looks as though you've gained a position as an honorary Uintah County deputy. It's not something to take lightly. And I'll still be keeping a close eye on you."

Kade chewed his cheek in thought, digesting those words first before stepping up and looking Grayson in the eye. It pleased him to look down a bit.

"You do that. But if I ever catch you going through my possessions again, it'll be the last thing you ever do. Good day." With that, Kade tipped his hat and stepped from the boardwalk. He aimed across the dusty street toward his horse, leaning against the hitching post with eyes closed, having found himself an optimal slice of shade,

"Wake up you goofy horse," Kade said with a scratch between Skitter's ears. "Time to head home."

At the opposite end of the Livery, a young man ducked behind a grouping of sheds and scrambled to mount a paint horse. He tore off in a gallop out of town.

Boxletter Canyon was positioned in such a way that anyone heading from Gunn Pass City toward the outskirts of the Triple Bar C ranch would have to ride through the center of it, otherwise, add hours to their ride time by going

around either the east or west rim. Once a rider reached the far end, the southern gates to the Bar C appeared just beyond a distinctive red rock spire, where a ledge connected it to a granite shelf and a grassy area.

Miller had always been partial to that ledge. Years back, he used to sit atop and watch for Emmy to come through those gates on her way to school each morning. Was easy to scamper down the game trail on the backside unnoticed, then circle around to meet up with her, happenstance style, as if it were a coincidence, walking alongside her to school. A few times he had gotten the nerve to hold her hand, until one day she shook free, wrinkled up her freckled nose, and proclaimed his hand was sweaty and creepy.

Once he had gotten over the insult, he attempted to invite her to picnic on the ledge. That Saturday, he had taken care preparing a lunch comprised of pork sandwiches and one of Ma's blueberry crumb cakes. Damn, he loved that cake. Made him miss her whenever he thought of it.

Emmy seemed to enjoy the picnic he'd taken such care in preparing for her, but when he had tried to be romantic, catching her unawares and laying her back in the grass for a nice kiss, she had screeched and kicked, pushing him off and making an 'ew' noise. Granted, it took place years ago when they were young, but the memory still smarted. Still felt angry and never quite got over it. Even now, he sometimes felt like grabbing her and shaking some sense into her.

How was it she didn't see the benefit of marrying and combining their land? How in the hell did she think she could run that ranch without his help? He was the only man for her, and all he had to do was convince her of it. The attack hadn't convinced her she needed protection. Or if it did, she made the wrong choice of bringing in a total stranger to protect her.

Emmy might be strong, but she was only a woman. Ain't no way she can run this ranch all on her own.

Now that the Stockton feller had moseyed into the picture, it was getting all that much harder to convince her. Something about him seemed to have put a spell on her. Maybe Colt Chase was controlling things from afar and he couldn't allow it to continue.

Kade Stockton had to go.

An hour ago, Emmy and the Rodgers couple, Henry and Estelle, came by in the buckboard wagon on the way home from town. Emmy had hopped down to open the gates. Once they pulled the wagon through, the gates were closed and they disappeared over the rise.

Now, according to Tom's information, Kade should be passing through here any time. Wouldn't be long now. The boys had their instructions to breach a section of the south Bar C border fence and execute his plans by first taking out Zak, the foreman, and whoever stands in their way, setting fires afterward.

With Kade dead, Miller would hightail it to the house and find Emmy. First things first, he aimed to find out why in hell she had made a fool of herself and kissed Kade in front of everyone. What kind of bullshit was that? Neely told him about it right after it happened. Whatever excuse she had for those wanton actions, he would deal with it later.

For now, she needed to believe he was rescuing her from the carnage. He would take her away, rescue her, save her from the ruffians. It was a plan he had worked long and hard on. She would love him forever. Every woman wanted a knight in shining armor, right? Emmy always liked fairy tales. He knew her better than anyone and would prove to her how right he was for her. He grinned at the image conjured in his head. Pictured himself standing on that wide porch, giving the 'ok' for the men to burn it down. The house could be rebuilt to his specifications. He and Emmy would ride off into the sunset together.

She would get her fairy tale ending. He would get the ranch.

Miller grinned just as a mosquito lit on the tip of his nose. He whipped off his wide-brimmed hat and swung at the insect. "Dammit—" he muttered, the faint clop of horseshoes on the gravel road below cutting into his irritation.

Smashing the hat back on his head, he hunkered low, quickly snatching up his long gun and chambering a round. When Kade rounded the bend at a brisk trot astride his palomino horse, Miller smiled, lifting the Sharps rifle to his shoulder, the image of Emmy laying a kiss on this man entered his head. With a growl, he set sights right above Kade's torso and squeezed the trigger.

CHAPTER 30

Coming Home

K ade trotted Skitter at a brisk clip toward home. *Home.* He sure liked the sound of that. The urgency of getting back and conversing with Scout and Zak about the explosives hung paramount in his mind. They had instructions to detonate the innermost series of explosives if warranted, which was if more than three riders advanced northward onto Triple Bar C land from the south. All hands diligently took shifts on 6-hour watches. If riders encroached on the detours, they'd be forced to ride up the ridge toward the honeypot.

Despite all that, checking to make sure Emmy arrived home safely topped the list. Maybe the idea of a feminine slip of a woman fighting off hardened outlaws was too much for his ego. She does have more starch than he gave her credit for. And just enough softness to go with it. Unlike any woman he had ever known, he was getting to the point where he couldn't imagine a day without her in it.

Funny, considering she was bossy.

Now, he looked forward to talking with her, telling her what he had learned. His life here was short-lived and he would be gone soon. The reality of that was clear. He couldn't give in to the urge to be with her, yet still couldn't stop thinking about the way she looked in that new aqua-green dress she wore. Sun-kissed skin. Bare arms—from the elbow down, but still. The tiny heart locket she always wore shimmered in the sun, resting lazily in that delectable spot between her breasts. Lucky locket.

What's wrong with me? I can smell her before I see her. I taste her before I inhale her scent. She's like a witch. I'll never get her out of my head, even though I'm going to have to.

He couldn't get the taste of her out of his head, the memory of a shared shower, a nude make-out session. Hadn't used that term since high school. Where did that strength come from, stopping himself before making love to her? It had been the only responsible option. Not only because of birth control but the ramifications to her life here, and her future. This wasn't the 21st century.

He promised himself then to make the most of the time left here...while keeping his distance from the obvious. Even though he couldn't get enough. Wanted to embrace her, kiss her until they both came up for air. God, he loved the passion in those mysterious kaleidoscope eyes.

The wind picked up then, twirling a dust devil on the path and sending a tumbleweed between Skitter's front legs. The horse tossed his head with a snort and Kade brought him down with a shush and a scratch to his neck. Kade had taken a shortcut. He used it often in the future, but now it was overgrown, and he had to envision it as it existed in his time. Even with the diversions, it proved quicker than riding the main road.

A noise caught his attention. High on the hill to his right.

Kade squinted into the sun, scanning a ridge lined with granite and pine trees, where grayish clouds grew in the blue skies, skimming across far peaks in the winds beginning to pick up. Looks like rain, he thought. A cry of an eagle split the air, fluffing his wings before perching on a naked pine tree, long dead.

Uneasiness settled over him.

Kade pulled back slightly on the reins and twisted in the saddle, scanning the horizon a second time. A flash of fear, then apprehension, a warning, but it was too slow. He heard it before he felt it, never a chance to avoid it. The report of a weapon, a crack followed by a sizzle splitting the air, followed by a vicious thump. A burning scrape to his temple, throwing him back. Searing fire sliced into his flesh.

A shock wave sent his hat sailing over his shoulder and the blunt force knocked him from the saddle. He careened back, crashing to the earth in a pit of blackness as his horse shied, jigging to the side in a puff of dust before bolting.

Miller scrambled to his feet, took hold of the reins, and crammed his rifle back into the scabbard.

"Wh-what now?" Tom Carlson asked, white-knuckling his paint horse's reins as he stared over the ledge at the man crumpled on the ground below. Face as white as death, the boy looked as though he might be sick. He never thought Miller would shoot Stockton.

"You did your job. Now go find Amos. He'll tell you what's next."

Mounting his horse, Miller left Tom standing there and took off toward the Bar C, purposely riding a wide berth around the lifeless form sprawled amongst the scrub. He was on his back, eyes closed, face and head bloodied.

Not wishing to get any closer, Miller scanned the horizon. Earlier, he thought he had seen wolves drinking at the river. Maybe the pack would smell the blood.

Spurring his horse, he made his way to an old oak beside a grouping of rocks, a marker where he had surreptitiously cut the wire so that he and his men could gain access to the land. Opening the gap and closing it again from his position in the saddle, he aimed up and over the hill with sights set on the sprawling house.

Shame it would soon be a pile of ashes. Certainly was a handsome bit of construction that the Chase family had created. The entire Bar C ranching empire was impressive, but all good things must come to an end; at least that's what Ma and Pa always said. Neely had passed on the word about Emmy's plans on going into town that morning with the old folks, and he watched the trio return. Maybe she would be cooking up some dinner. Too bad he didn't have time to eat.

"Emmy, you here?" Miller called out, helping himself inside through the kitchen door. When he didn't smell anything cooking, he frowned, then wondered where the old man and lady were. Last thing he needed was Henry and Estelle's interference, feeling at his side for the butt of his pistol. He would use it if he had to. Otherwise, they could die in the fire for all he cared. They may come in handy for some work around the place, but sometimes sacrifices had to be made

"Emmy? We've got some discussing to do," he called out, raising his voice. Crossing the empty parlor, Miller headed down the hallway, his heavy footfalls echoing in the silence.

"What in the world—" The office door flung open and Emmy raced out, concern on her face. "What's going on?"

He reached out and took hold of her shoulders with both hands and spun her around, pushing her back into the expansive office with the mahogany paneling, leather-bound books lining the shelves. Normally a peaceful place, except not that day.

"What has gotten into you?" Emmy dug in her heels and shook off his hold, facing him with a questioning scowl.

"I could ask you the same thing." Working his tongue in his cheek, he glared down at her. "Heard you went and kissed Stockton."

He hadn't intended on bringing that up first thing, but when he laid eyes on her standing there looking extraordinarily pretty, his thoughts went to Stockton and the reason why she may have purchased the new dress she wore. The idea of her kissing another man made him madder than a hornet. Even more than he thought it might. He felt the blood rush to his face. Ma used to say it glowed redder than a beet when he got angry, and that he scared her.

"Who ... told you that?" she asked, voice hitching. "How dare you march into my home without knocking. What I do is none of your concern, Miller."

"The hell it ain't!" He puffed his chest and moved closer.

"You don't have any holds on me. I think you better leave, come back when you've calmed down and we'll discuss it like adults."

"You better think twice before ordering me around. Won't be long and I'll be the man of the house."

Emmy set her hands to her hips, "Have you been drinking again? I have no patience for that. I told you to get out!" When Miller got close enough, he went for her shoulders. She ducked away, skirting the doorway. "I'm not playing games—"

"Either am I." Miller made a lunge and pinned her to the wall, his mouth closing over hers before she could slither away.

"Stop it!" Emmy cried, bringing her knee up in a hefty thrust. He shifted to the side just in time to avoid a painful jab, bellowing in laughter at her failed effort.

"Always been too feisty for your own good, Emmy. I like 'em spirited, and you and I used to get along good. We'll figure out a way to make it work. Ma and Pa always did fine." He recalled Pa beating up on Ma, bruising her up good now and then. Sometimes that's just what it took to get a woman's respect and encourage her acceptance of who's the boss. "Now, listen. I'll tell you how it's going to work. You probably won't like it much at first, but you'll learn to love me properly and we can grow this empire as it should be."

"What in hell are you blathering about?" Emmy hissed, gaze shooting fire as she bucked to get away. "Get off me or I'll scream—"

"No, now you don't wanna do that. The old couple might get hurt."

Emmy froze at his words.

"Now tell me why you kissed Stockton," he repeated.

Jaw set, she glared up at him, stubbornly lifting her chin, "I'm in love with him."

Miller's demeanor darkened. He moved back and scrubbed his jaw in thought. It occurred to him he should probably smack her just to get her to listen. Even as he thought it, he began to raise his arm. Then something stopped him. A humorless smile crept across his face. Why hit Emmy for loving a dead man? Not like it meant anything to him anymore. Not when the entire Triple Bar C was going to be his very soon.

"He's dead," he said as if merely reporting the weather.

Emmy blanched, then dashed for the exit, pausing when her hand touched the crystal knob. "What did you say?" she whispered into the wood-paneled door, unwilling, or maybe unable to turn around.

"Just what I said. The man died. That's why I'm here. Wanted to break the news, tell you I saw him myself alongside a ditch on my way here. Somebody must have taken a pot-shot at him, and I saw a pack of wolves over across—"

Emmy twirled to face him, her fists balled up, chest heaving. Then she came at him, clawing at his upper arms until fingernails bit through the sleeves of his shirt. She glared at him like a frenzied animal.

"Where? Answer me! *Where* is he? You're lying!"

"Ouch. Let go of me with those daggers you call fingernails. Dammit, woman!" Miller shuffled back and rubbed his arms, then shook chastising finger at her. "This war is getting closer, Emmy. I suggest you pack your bags. Get together enough clothes to get you by. Men are heading here as we speak. With torches. Wouldn't doubt if this entire place goes up in flames. I'm here to save you from that."

"You've lost your mind!" she bit out. "Get out before I shoot you dead, Miller." With that, Emmy gave him wide berth and charged to the desk, pulling open the top drawer. Locating a Colt Peacemaker revolver, she leveled the heavy piece at his chest with both hands, her shaky thumb pulling back the hammer. *"I said get out."*

"Better think twice. Your mama wanted me to have this place. She knew I had the proper knowledge, and she approved of you and I tying the knot. She wanted *me* to take over the Bar C."

"You've completely lost your mind," Emmy whispered. "Mama never cared for you much, even back in school. Said you were a mealy-mouthed coward. And I know for a fact Colt lost all respect for you after that incident with the Woods girl."

Miller blanched, "Now, now. That's not nice at all."

"It's the truth. You always were out for yourself."

"Whether you like it or not, you're going to have to honor your mama's wishes."

"Stop talking in circles and tell me where Kade is, or God help me, I'll start at your knees and use all six shots." Struggling to keep the shake from her hands, she angled the barrel toward his left knee.

"Emmy, put that thing away. Your mama—"

"Stop talking about Rosie!" she cried.

"Listen, the beneficiary was changed. I have the paperwork. She knew you would have trouble running this place all by yourself, and when she asked for my help, I was willing to step up and do my part. You're my friend, Emmy, and soon to be my wife." Though he felt like slapping some sense into her, he felt proud of himself for remaining calm and speaking gently. He shuffled closer to the desk in small steps. "When you face up to that fact, the easier all this'll be. I've already got lawyers working—"

"You're lying." She dipped the pistol and squeezed the trigger, discharging a round into the floorboards between his boots. A white splinter ricocheted into the air and disappeared.

"Shit, woman!" he growled, dancing to the side.

Then, from somewhere far away, another explosion interrupted the tension, this one much larger, rumbling the earth and the floorboards under their feet. Emmy gasped, splaying one hand on the tooled leather border of the mahogany desk to steady herself.

"That dynamite?" Miller asked, bewilderment crossing his face as he high-tailed it out the door and down the hall, sounding all the world to be an elephant in full charge. Estelle met him at the foot of the stairs, a hand clasped to her heart. Henry wasn't far behind, a clump of gray hair sticking up from an afternoon nap.

"What happened?" Estelle demanded.

"Sounds like a war out there!" Henry echoed her concern, both craning necks to see out the side window.

Emmy passed by on her way out the front door.

"Somebody tell me what's going on!" Estelle repeated.

Neither she nor Miller paused to answer, the couple trailing Emmy out to the porch where all four watched a plume of dense, black smoke roll up from the earth. Miller faced them all, his breath coming in labored snorts. Beads of sweat formed on his forehead below his hat.

"Pack up and get ready to go," he ordered, pointing a finger at Emmy. "I'm going to see what's happened down south. Looks like the rustlers are blowing up your land, eh?

"I doubt that," she snapped back, knowing full well this wasn't the work of rustlers, and likely the explosives Kade and the Bar C hands had orchestrated and arranged.

"Mark my words, your house, and every other building will be next."

He stomped down the porch steps and mounted his horse, and with a slap of reins to the hindquarters, he galloped off.

* * *

Estelle turned a startled gaze to Emmy, lips parting wordlessly.

"What's he talking about—packing for *what?*"

About that time Hanna rounded the corner of the porch with Eli perched on her hip, the one-year-old's pale blue eyes as round as rubber balls. "My god, are we being raided? Have you seen Zak?"

Emmy wasn't to be deterred. All she could think about was Kade. The revolver she held felt cold and heavy, yet provided strength, contrasting the weakness filling her insides. If anything had happened to Kade …

He can't be dead. He's hurt. Must find him.

"Try not to worry, Hanna," she said. "That's our defense line. I'm sure Zak will be riding up anytime." She faced Estelle and Henry then, "Miller's gone crazy! Everyone take refuge in the spring house. I've got to find Kade. Miller said he's … dead." Her voice caught on the last word.

Miller had always had a temper, though this time was different. He smelled of whiskey, and she had never seen him quite this belligerent. His wording when he mentioned *the old couple* rang familiar, the same wording her attacker had used several months back. Miller wasn't in his right mind. How had she not seen this side of him before? They had been casual childhood friends and neighbors, growing up together.

Without pausing to answer any more questions, Emmy crammed the pistol into her dress pocket and raced down the steps in the direction of the creek, all three dogs running alongside. She stopped, tears burning her eyes as she realized she needed a horse. Twirling back around, she broke into a run for the barn.

A sharp whistle from the pine trees at the side of the house made her skid to a stop.

Flat on his back, Kade had somehow steeled himself for the aftershock when all the precious air left his lungs in a *whoosh*. Eyes squeezed shut, he forced himself not to move.

Relax. Allow your lungs to recover. Where are you? Who is around you?

A rock dug into the small of his back. He shifted to the side. He could feel his legs. That was good. Thoughts circled in his head—the status of his injuries—of his life—the location of the enemy.

A beautiful woman with long brown hair entered his thoughts and he remembered, feeling at first relief, and then anger. Had Skitter galloped off? Yes, he felt sure of it. Didn't have a horse. Above his right temple, a fire raged, ebbing into a rhythmic and insistent throb. Hot, sticky liquid trickled over his temple and down his ear, dripping. Damned lucky.

Thump... thump... thump.

Pumping, his heart beat painfully inside his head while twisting hot against his ribs, shooting agitated blood to his brain. He must untangle his thoughts, only every time he tried to think, it intensified the pain.

Then he heard a sound, the grind of gravel to earth. Was Skitter back? Another horse and rider? He longed to open his eyes and yet didn't dare. Instead, he allowed his senses to assess the situation, and called upon skills he was once trained to use regularly.

Kade stilled his breathing, senses heightened to the point he felt as though his body was vibrating.

Emmy's in danger.

Ignoring the excruciating pain in his temple, Kade sat up, grabbed his hat, and climbed to his feet. When he had gathered his bearings, he began to walk. A movement in the distance caught his eye. A palomino horse with a brown rump, head down, blending with the swaying grasses.

He'd kiss that goofy horse right on the mouth if he came back.

He put two fingers between his lips and whistled, the shrill note sending waves of pain through his temple and down his spine. Skitter's head snapped up, and he broke into a trot.

Five minutes later, Kade rode hellbent in the direction of the main house, refusing to stop until he reached the banks of the creek that rolled through the center of the land, urging Skitter across. The wound on his head began to bleed again, dripping down into his ear and off his jaw, plop, plop onto his shirt. He wiped his face as best as he could with a bandanna, knowing it would scare Emmy to see him this way. And then his heart twisted, wondering of her whereabouts and if she was hurt. Or worse.

Across a gully and into the trees. Another shortcut. Around a hill and the house came into view past the trees. In the distance, he saw a woman with a babe in her arms racing about—Hanna. And then two others, looked like Estelle and Henry. The dogs, Sage, Brush, and Dottie were dashing in the direction of the barn. *Where was Emmy?* There, behind the dogs was a woman running in a green dress, her hair flowing free.

Kade put two fingers at his lips and whistled, cringing at the throb in his head. *Damn, that hurts.*

She stopped in her tracks and whirled around.

"Kade!" Emmy cried, voice hoarse, reversing directions and coming back. All three dogs reversed and followed.

He steered Skitter through the pines, pushing him into a canter to meet her halfway. On the ground, he gathered her in his arms, thinking this was the best day of his life.

"You're bleeding! But you're alive, thank God." She grabbed a hold of his cheeks and planted a kiss on his mouth, leaning away to see better. "Look at your head, you're hurt...."

"I can't see my head," he said, more in frustration than humor.

She examined the wound on his temple, smoothing his hair back and dabbing it with the bandanna. "You're going to have one hell of a headache, but you'll live. I think." Still teary, she paused to blow her nose on the bandanna. "I'm sorry, I'll get you another. Let's get you inside."

"No, the explosives detonated. I've gotta get down there," he began. "Where's Zak and the others? There's work to do, and you're going to the house. Where's Miller?"

"I'm going wherever you go. He took off toward the explosion—he shot you, didn't he?"

"Not sure. Think I heard someone on a horse but didn't see anyone."

"Miller's gone crazy," Emmy said, "He got violent, threatened to burn down the house, then ordered me to pack and be ready when he got back! Can you imagine?"

"Like hell that's gonna happen," Kade muttered.

Another rider approached along the main road at a fast gallop. Instinctively, Kade shifted his stance in front of Emmy, palming the pistol occupying the holster at his waist. As they watched Nicholas Grayson's approach, neither took notice of a second rider on a naked berm to the southeast. The heavyset man dismounted and positioned himself behind his horse. Then came a crack, splitting the air around them.

Emmy let out a sharp cry. Clinging to his shoulder, she slumped forward as he swung around and caught her in his arms, lowering her limp body to the ground.

CHAPTER 31

Ease My Worried Mind

K ade was on the ground, pulling Emmy into his arms and cradling her lifeless form. Her eyes were closed, and her complexion paled as blood soaked the middle of her new dress. She breathed, but it was shallow and produced a gurgling sound.

"Emmy!" He stroked her cheek, "Stay with me, you're not going anywhere!"

In a beat, everyone gathered around. Estelle hovered, a fist pressed to her mouth, while Hanna fell to her knees beside Kade. Even Hanna's girls dashed from their cabin to find out what was going on. Already holding Eli on his hip, Henry intercepted to care for the little girls.

Kade issued a string of orders.

"I need something non-porous, a piece of clean leather maybe—and strips of material for binding, lots of them—and scissors. A blanket, too. Hurry! "

About that time Grayson arrived in a cloud of dust, swinging off his mount, boots striking dirt.

"What happened?" he demanded.

"That's what I'd like to know. A shooter—from that hill," he said, indicating the open space. "Why don't you make yourself useful and go find the bastard! Likely it's Miller or one of his men."

"What makes you think that? And what was the explosion?" Grayson was on the ground, feeling her neck for a pulse and smoothing the hair from her forehead.

"Look, you're either with me or you're not," Kade growled, over-the-top fed up with the lawman. "I'm dealing with a sucking chest wound here. That explosion was *my* men defending *our* land. If you want to help and do the right thing, get a handle on Miller and his idiots. Last seen, he rode south after threatening to burn the house. Keep them under wraps until I get back, got that? I'm getting Emmy to a doctor."

Zak appeared on his horse, dropping to the ground and kneeling beside Emmy. "What happened? Dear God!"

"Gunfire from the south," Hanna explained, out of breath as she raced to Emmy's side alongside Estelle, providing a small piece of buckskin, a quilt for warmth, and a sheet ripped into strips. Estelle handed Kade the scissors, and he proceeded to cut the clothing away from Emmy's upper abdomen. He saw a bullet hole. Then, lifting her gently to the side, he spotted an exit wound and felt a modicum of relief. He folded the buckskin to the size of a deck of cards and placed it over the wound, then began the process of binding the strips taut around her torso. He applied pressure to the wound, knowing she needed more than a country doctor's care, especially one in the 19th century. The only option was to get her back to the future—to an urgent-care hospital. No telling what vital organs may have been struck by the bullet.

"We have to get her into town. I'll fetch the wagon." Zak scrambled to his feet.

"No need for a wagon. I'm taking her back," Kade said.

"Back where?" Zak argued. "Closest doctor is Gunn Pass. He's tipsy a good part of the time, but maybe we'll catch him on a good day. He's the best option."

"Not good enough." Kade bundled Emmy in the patchwork quilt, then stood to adjust Skitter's tack, mounting his horse. "I know of a much better place.

You'll just have to trust me on this one." He looked to Grayson, "Lift her and hand her to me. *Gentle.*"

The glower on Grayson's face stemmed from either worry or irritation, maybe both. But he did as he was asked, gathering Emmy into his arms and passing the bundle up to Kade. He helped to adjust her legs on either side of the pommel, upper body cradled securely against Kade's chest and left arm. She groaned with the movement, the gurgling sound in her breathing less evident.

"I got you, baby," Kade murmured into her ear, pained to see all the blood in her long, beautiful hair. He nudged Skitter into a brisk walk, heading toward the trail that would take them to Rosebush Ridge. A legion of stunned supporters remained behind, watching them go, Hanna and Estelle restraining the dogs so they wouldn't try to follow.

The sun disappeared beyond the jagged peaks. He pushed Skitter to ascend as fast as was safe, Emmy's body rolling with the motion as they traversed the rocky switchbacks. He feared her life force ebbed, unsure if it was imagination or reality. He pressed his mouth to her forehead and spoke to keep her alert.

He was pissed at his failure to stop Miller, to notice the shooter aiming from the top of that hill, or that he wasn't the one to take the bullet. That bullet was surely meant for him, he knew it.

Don't die, baby. My world will end if you die. I love you.

"Stay with me," he crooned, singing softly to distract himself. "Your favorite, remember this one?"

> *"...like a fool, I fell in love with you*
> *You turned my whole world upside down*
> *Layla, you've got me on my knees, Layla*
> *Darling, won't you ease my worried mind?"*

Her right hand rested over his, and he felt the feeble squeeze of her fingers. Or was it wishful thinking? A bittersweet joy riveted through him, and he voiced an impassioned prayer, the first time since Afghanistan. He brushed the wetness from his cheek with a shrug of a shoulder.

"Here we are, babe," he announced at the top, steering them to the bent spruce tree. He dismounted while holding her steady, then lifted her gingerly onto a bed of pine needles long enough to locate the clinging vine and pluck a rosebud.

And then he waited, scanning the dusky skies, heart thumping a beat in his head. What if she got nauseous? The heaves could further damage her injury, but there simply wasn't an option. They must take the chance.

He scooped her up once again and held her to his heart, legs braced wide, stance firm. Her head lolled to the side, and he spoke soothing words as thunder cracked and raindrops began to fall. Wind blustered. Lightning arced in the distance. Skitter positioned himself to take the brunt of the storm, dipping his head occasionally to tear at a patch of long grass.

"I'll call 911!" Madison raced into the house for her phone and keys, returning to jump behind the wheel of the truck while Colt and Kade loaded Emmy into the back seat. "Wait, she doesn't have identification."

"Authorities will ask questions we can't answer," Kade added, short of breath from a combination of exertion and stress. The slip through time had left him lightheaded and disoriented, though he felt grateful Emmy hadn't become sick as he had feared she might. As a bonus, Skitter remained close by to carry them down the trail.

"You're right." Colt said. "We'll meet the ambulance at the main gate, tell them we don't know who she is; found her alongside the road."

Angela stood at the front door with the twins watching them go as Colt jumped into the passenger seat and dialed 911. Madison hit the gas, gravel flying as they left the drive and began the five-minute trek to the timber log entrance gate.

In the backseat of the black F-250 pickup, Kade held Emmy across his lap while keeping pressure on the wound. Face a ghostly gray, she drifted in and out of consciousness, occasionally wincing in pain.

A flurry of sirens and activity descended after what seemed an eternity, yet in reality was only ten minutes—first responders including sheriff deputies, followed by fire rescue and finally an ambulance. Kade rode along as Emmy was transported to St. Anthony's in Jackson and immediately rushed into surgery. Colt and Madison met them at the hospital.

Officers and doctors inquired as to who found her and exactly where. If they had ever seen her before. Any new employees at the ranch? Were they aware of any strangers lurking around recently? Reports were written and questioning looks were shared, but Emmy was getting the care she needed, that's all that mattered. Those in charge announced she would be interviewed when she woke and felt up to it. When the time came, they must make sure Emmy knew what to say.

The first hurdle a success, Kade felt wired and exhausted at the same time, his irate inner dialog telling him to suck it up and consider what Emmy must be experiencing.

Had it taken something like this for you to realize what she means to you?

In the waiting room, the trio spoke briefly to the surgeon. Emmy had lost a lot of blood. Gunshot wounds were common, unfortunately, and they had treated this sort of thing many times. But it was still serious, and she wasn't out of the woods yet. They would do the best they could.

I'd give my own life right now, he thought, for a promise of Emmy's recovery.

Colt and Kade shared a pointed look, the realization striking home. The terror occurring back in 1888 wasn't going to end until those responsible were either apprehended ... or dead. With an unspoken oath, Colt rose to his feet. He took Madison aside in the waiting room for a hushed and serious conversation. Her expression grew stoic as he wrapped her in a long embrace, then departed with a kiss.

"Let's go, we have business to tend to," he said, striding past Kade and heading to the elevator. Madison rushed up to hug Kade, demanding he takes care of both himself and her husband, assuring him she would stay by Emmy's side.

Once in the pickup, Colt made a detour, stopping outside the city museum. "I'll be right back."

Confused, Kade watched him walk up to talk to the security guard who stood outside as the museum prepared to close for the day. The two shook hands and talked for a moment before the guard pulled out a ring of keys and opened the door, escorting Colt inside. Not five minutes later, Colt exited with something in his hands, jogging back to the truck.

"*Now* I'm ready," he said placing the bundle on the seat between them and parting the felt material to reveal a pair of matching Colt Peacemakers, an intricate rose carved into each handle.

"Nice," Kade said, impressed. The truck rumbled down the side street, and back onto the main road, heading in a northerly direction.

Back at the ranch, Colt opened the safe to retrieve some paperwork, just in case. He changed into his old standbys: leather vest, double holster along with an ammunition bandolier across his chest, a Bowie knife strapped to his leg in a hideaway sleeve, a bandanna knotted at his neck, and his usual Stetson hat. Kade donned his holster and strapped on a hunting knife Out in the barn, they saddled up the horses with Buck's assistance, tying rain slickers behind saddle cantles and tossing jerky and a few energy bars into the saddlebags.

Buck gave a low whistle, "You two look the part. Need a sidekick, maybe an old man with failing eyesight? Surely I'd be good for something." He chuckled.

"Doubt Angela would appreciate that," Colt said.

"Nope, you're right. If I made it out alive, she'd kill me when I got back. You two take care of yourselves and try not to worry about Emmy, we'll be there for her."

With that, the two gunslingers, one with a bit more experience than the other, nudged their horses into brisk canter toward the trail leading to Rosebush Ridge.

At the top, both men donned rain slickers in preparation, then Colt snagged a rosebud from the vine, pressing it to his nose in memory of the first time. Astride his horse again, he faced Kade.

"First time I did this, I rode Cinder hellbent into the storm. I'd say let's do it again, but not in the darkness. Wouldn't be the safest idea."

"You're getting old," Kade teased, and they laughed, though it did little to ease the tension vibrating the air.

Lightning struck at the far side of the valley, and the storm descended to whip furiously at the trees. They pressed their hats down, looking through sheets of rain into the lightning-lit valley below. It glowed an eerie blue.

"You game?" Kade's voice rumbled.

"Let's go," came the response beside him.

Atop the hill and overlooking an unseen portal into the past, the two men tapped heels to the horses' flanks, leaned forward, and broke into a tandem gallop. Dashing into a tunnel of pixelated light, it twisted and spun around them in a cacophony of warped sound, spitting pine needles and twigs into the air. As quickly as the tunnel formed, it dissipated. The air around them hushed, bringing about the scents of rain and pine trees. And a sense of calm.

Fighting off nausea, Kade twisted in his saddle first one way and then the other, straining to see through the fog in search of his partner. The rain continued to fall, and he swiped his face with his palm. From afar, Colt waved, and Kade trotted his horse over to meet him.

"Let's get to the house and check on the status of things," Kade said. "From there we'll formulate a plan."

They rode at a brisk clip down the dark, misty trail. On the way down, Kade filled Colt in on Detective Grayson, the explosives, the suspected 'mole', Neely, and everything he recalled transpiring in between—with the obvious exception of kisses, a sexy shower, and sharing a warm bed with Emmy Bartlett.

Riding watch by twilight, Zak and Scout intercepted their approach a few hundred feet from the house.

"How's Emmy?" Zak asked first.

"She's under the care of a team of excellent doctors," Kade assured, and Zak nodded, turning to the man who rode alongside him. His jaw fell slack.

"Colt Chase ... I'll be doggoned. *That you?* Don't look a day older."

A gladdened smile eased across Colt's face and they shook hands, "How are you, Zak? Been a long time."

"Slightly bumfuzzled right now," he admitted. "This here is Rainero, one of our better hands," he added, indicating the man on horseback beside him.

"Pleased to make your acquaintance. You can call me Scout, like Kade does. I rather like it." Rainero said, edging closer to shake Colt's hand and giving him a respectful nod.

The men chuckled, things turning to more sober subjects.

"Where's Grayson and the sheriff?" Kade asked.

"Grayson and several of the men set up watch around Miller's place. Heard there's a light inside the house, but not much in the way of activity. Likely they're waiting for daylight. The explosives and rockslide took out a bunch of Miller's cohorts, but hard to tell how many are left. With this rain, we'll have fog at dawn which could work in our favor."

Kade nodded. "Has anyone gone into town to let Townsend know?"

"Sheriff should be on his way to Miller's place. Head out now, you should meet up with him."

"Good. Zak, you keep patrolling here. Colt, Scout, and I are stocking up on ammunition, and heading to Millers."

The men disbanded, Kade and Colt watering the horses before heading out once more. Kade couldn't stop thinking of Emmy, wishing there was some magic way of checking on her. Had she gotten out of surgery yet? What if something had gone wrong? He supposed it was good he wasn't there, since his presence with a woman who was supposed to be a stranger would draw attention. The situation may appear less odd with Madison at the hospital as support. Besides, he wouldn't be able to remove his hat without displaying the half-assed bandage job on his head, creating reasons for law enforcement to ask more questions.

"Let's go. We'll shoot the shit while we ride." Astride his gray stallion, Colt rode next to Scout.

"As good as it'll ever be," Kade said, steering Skitter from the watering trough. "Let's go."

The silhouettes of three determined cowboys disappeared into the night.

∞

"What's this?" Emmy fingered the tangle of clear IV tubes snaking from the tender skin at the crook of her elbow. She winced, shifting on the mattress and splaying a hand across her middle. "...ouch."

At the sound of the shaky voice, Madison stood from the chair at the side of the bed.

"Emmy, sweetheart, it's me, Madison. Don't move too much, and don't pull at the tubes. It's for fluids and medicine to enter your body so you can heal. You were shot."

"I know that part," she grumbled, voice raspy. "Miller ... I'll ... kill him myself."

Madison's brow lifted, and she tempered a smile as relief coursed through her. Emmy was back, and she was going to be all right, she knew it.

Twisting for comfort on the stiff bed, Emmy winced again. The grimace on her forehead melted as a corner of her mouth lifted.

"Oh, hi. It's you," she said with a sigh.

"It's me. I'm here to sit with you."

"I'm glad. But ... where's Kade?" she asked then, eyes round with worry. "What about his head? He was hurt."

"Kade is with Colt. They are together. Um, working." Madison cringed at the lame comment. "I told him I would sit with you, and they will return, soon." *She hoped and prayed.*

Madison smoothed Emmy's hair from her forehead. Though she had been cleaned up somewhat, she still had dried blood on the long ends of her beautiful golden-brown locks. Emmy's jaw quivered and a tear formed in the corner of her eye. Then she fidgeted in discomfort, clutching the bandage at her stomach, face flushing.

"See this button here?" Madison lifted one of the tubes, pointing out the black rubber tip. "It's medicine called a morphine drip. When the hurting gets too much, push the button like this," she explained, demonstrating. Emmy nodded in understanding and a minute later was able to relax. An airy smile eased across her face and her eyes grew limpid.

"I miss Kade," she whispered.

Madison touched her hand, "I get it. I miss Colt."

The door opened and in walked a nurse.

"Looks like someone is awake," she said, smile cheery, her dark hair pulled back into a severe ponytail. "Let's get your vitals and check the wound." The nurse turned to Madison, who had stepped away from the bed to allow her more room. "Are you family?" she asked.

"No," Madison answered in silent panic. Emmy had only just woken up, and she hadn't thought to mention the situation with her identity. Emmy's eyes slid shut, and hopefully, she slept. "I'm sitting with her for support. No relation." The nurse's gaze rested squarely on her for a moment before breaking away.

Finished, the nurse switched out IV bags and entered some stats into a laptop, then refilled the cup of ice chips and placed it on the bedside tray. "Only ice chips for now. According to the doctor's notes, if there's no nausea, we can start a liquid diet."

As soon as the nurse left, Emmy's eyes snapped open—glassy, but as sharp as ever.

"Why didn't you tell her who you are?" Emmy asked, voice low.

"This is the plan," Madison explained, making sure the door was pulled to before returning to the bed. "We told law officers and doctors that we found you injured outside by the road. In modern day, you're required to have some kind of identification. Not only would they be trying to learn your identity, but with a bullet wound, the questions would be nonstop until they knew exactly what happened, by whom, and with what weapon. It's their job."

"And when they question me....?"

"You don't remember anything. Not your name, where you come from, or who your family is."

"All right," she agreed. "How long do I have to stay here?"

"You need to stabilize and mend. The doctors and nurses will check you several times a day and make sure everything is healing as it should. The bullet didn't hit any vital organs, which is a very good thing. I don't know how long, but when Colt and Kade get home, we'll figure out a plan."

"They went back, didn't they?" Emmy asked pointedly.

The startle, and worry, in Madison's expression, confirmed her fears. Her heart twisted. Not that Kade shouldn't have gone back. Of course, he would. But she needed to be there, too! *Damn Miller for taking a potshot and hitting her! Worse, she knew he wasn't aiming at her—he aimed at Kade.* More than anything she longed to face down her nemesis one last time. She needed to tell Colt and Kade both what they were up against—Miller's claims of Rosie signing the ranch over to him. Now it may be too late.

The thought of Kade confronting Miller sent chills through her. He wasn't fair, not at all. And Kade was one of the fairest men she had ever known.

Kade is a formidable soldier, skilled in fighting wars you can only imagine.

Steeling herself, Emmy's gaze swept the room: unfamiliar machines with blinking green and blue lights, cords and hoses holding her prisoner. A light glowed in the corner beside a window and a comfortable-looking chair.

"Try to rest. I'm not going anywhere," Madison vowed, touching her arm.

Emmy managed a weak smile, allowing her eyes to slide closed.

CHAPTER 32

Gimme Shelter

S ome time later, Kade, Scout, and Colt arrived at the base of the ridge overlooking Johnson Ranch. Slivers of early dawn fog floated along the ground as the horses picked their way up the slope.

"Who goes there?" A low whisper came from a dip between two trees.

"Grayson, that you? It's me, Stockton."

"Come on up."

They dismounted just below the crest and tied off their rides. Kade slung the Remington rifle over his shoulder. Neither he nor Scout had ever been this close to the Johnson homestead, but Colt had. This angle provided an excellent view of the front of the house. A sizable barn stood a distance from the house at the right. A small herd of sheep huddled in a corner of the corral, its gates leading into the pastures to their left. An outhouse stood at the opposing side of the house, and a chicken coop and shed skirted what used to be a vegetable garden, since taken over by wild grasses and clusters of yellow toadflax and thistle.

"How's Emmy?" Grayson asked.

"She's being cared for," Kade said, throat tightening. All he wanted was to finish this business and get back to her. But he wouldn't let himself think too far ahead. Best to stay focused on the here and now.

Scout moved away from the others, stretching out on his belly along an outcropping of rock where he had a prime view of all buildings. He pulled out a pair of field glasses and held them to his eyes. Though a mist hovered near the ground, the sky glowed with stars and a bright quarter moon, showcasing the homestead below.

"Keep an eye out for their guard," Grayson advised. "He's sitting on the porch in that shadow, but patrols now and then."

"This is Colt Chase," Kade added, turning to Grayson, and the two men shook hands.

"A pleasure, Colt," he said, leaning back to a rock. "Surprised to meet the Bar C owner. Heard a fair amount about you."

"Not my ranch any longer. Belongs to Emmy Bartlett now," Colt corrected. "You could say I'm visiting and looking forward to setting things straight with Johnson."

"Appreciate the assistance," Grayson said. "Folks are coming out of the woodwork with scores to settle with Johnson. Appears he made more than a few enemies along the way."

"Not a surprise," Kade said lowering to his haunches, eyes trained over the edge. "Where are the troops deployed?" Grayson looked a bit confused and he revised his wording, "I mean where are the men posted?"

"Got a man with a long gun on this side of the barn, and another staking out by the shed. Townsend should be here anytime with a few more deputies. Not much movement inside. A trip to the outhouse, one pissed in a bush. That's about it."

"Good," Kade said. After a moment, "I would've guessed you'd be on your way to Sweetwater County by this time."

After a long pause, Grayson adjusted his position on the ground and sucked in a breath, "I resigned."

Kade slanted a look, "Any particular reason?"

"Yep," he said, "but nothing I care to share with you."

"Fair enough," Kade responded with a shrug.

"But since you're here, and it may affect things moving forward," he began, "what you said earlier in Townsend's office stuck with me." He paused, then, "I don't know exactly where you get your information, but you're right, shady politics are going on in the capital. As a younger man, I figured if it didn't affect me, I'm no worse off. Nothing I can do to make things right anyhow. Nowadays I've come to believe differently. When it starts to affect me and those I care about, a bright light shines on the folks wrongly put in the crossfire. I suppose your words got me thinking. Sweetwater wasn't simply a reassignment, it was an order to side with big-money ranchers regardless of who was right. I won't be the state's pawn any longer. I do have scruples, Mr. Stockton." He trained his gaze ahead.

Kade nodded in understanding, "Don't know what to say, other than I wish you the best in finding something ... better." He stumbled over the words.

Shit, did I just change history? Should I not have given Grayson a piece of my futuristic mind back in Townsend's office? I have no clue what the rules are while time-traveling....

The crunch of footfalls sounded behind, and the men shifted their attention, weapons at the ready.

Sheriff Townsend identified himself as he crept up the hill and tied his horse off next to the others. Hunching down, he joined the four men already positioned behind the crest of the hill. Then, as if he had seen a ghost, he turned, his copious brows thrusting together, "Am I losing my mind, or is that Colton Chase sitting there?"

Colt grinned, thrusting out a hand for a hearty shake. "Not the time to reminisce, but we'll catch up," he promised in a whisper. "I intend to dispute the will Miller claims to have with Rosie's signature, granting the Bar C to him."

"Miller claims that?" Townsend leaned back with a grimace, shaking his head. "That's plain nonsense. Heard he threatened to burn your house to the ground, and he shot Emmy. Good enough reason to lock him up, far as I'm concerned. How is Emmy?"

"Being treated at a hospital," Kade said.

Lloyd's gaze went hard, "Tom Carlson rode into town and told me what Miller had done. The kid thought you were dead. Was plenty upset. According to him, Miller paid him to keep an eye on your movements."

Kade snorted, lifting his hat a notch to display a shoddy bandage, "Glad Miller's a crappy shot."

A scuffle of movement from the white clapboard house drew their attention and voices fell silent. A lone guard pushed to his feet and stretched, relieving himself off the side of the porch before moving up to the front door. The man fished a pouch from a shirt pocket and rolled a cigarette, striking a match and touching it to the end. With a relished inhale, he propped a shoulder to a wooden post, the tip of his smoke glowing orange. If not for the lamplight shining from a window, the man's features might have been more difficult to discern. As it was, a flamboyant mustache and eye patch stood out in sharp contrast to the rest of his face. He wore a deep-color calvary-style hat.

Grayson's posture stiffened, his heart pounding a vicious beat in his chest. Could that be the drifter who murdered his wife? The hunch wasn't set in stone. He hadn't seen this man do the deed, though he had valid suspicions, and wanted posters went up across Montana. Tightening his grip along the stock of his rifle, he stroked the trigger guard with a gloved index finger.

"What's wrong?" Kade asked, observing Grayson's demeanor morph into someone he hadn't yet met. Had seen it happen a time or two on the battlefield.

"That man is wanted in Montana for murder," Grayson said.

Kade followed his gaze, endeavoring to see what Grayson saw: Average build, dark shaggy hair poking out from beneath his hat. Bulky sideburns. Handlebar mustache. That hat! Rewinding his thoughts, he recalled Emmy's description of the man who attacked her several months back. Black or brown hair. Check. Mustache and ... was that an eyepatch? Not sure about that, but a beat-up calvary hat? Check. He would kill him. Let's go, Grayson! he thought. We'll hang him from the highest tree for what he's done! No, wait, we'll beat the shit out of him first. Then we'll hang him.

Get a grip. This isn't a Clint Eastwood spaghetti western, this is real life.

Real life in 1888, Kade argued with the know-it-all voice in his head.

He forced himself to settle down. At least two men in that house below caused Emmy harm, and by the end of the night, both would pay.

Check.

Kade lifted his gaze. The purple sky, studded with stars, had already begun to fade. "We need to get a move on before the sun rises," he said. "Sheriff, did you bring more men?"

He nodded, "Yup, two of'em. Set'em up in that grove of trees behind the well."

"Good. I need you to fill everyone in. Nobody is to light a match or anything to draw attention. You ride up to the house alone. Tell that guard you need to speak to Miller right away. Scout, you're overwatch, stay exactly where you are. I'll skirt around the barn and instruct our man down there to position up in the loft for a better view. Grayson and Colt, you two back up the sheriff, but stay out of sight for the time being."

Scout bobbed his head in understanding, embracing the rifle at his side.

Townsend frowned, looking to Colt for clarification, "He a military man?"

Colt inclined his head toward Kade, "Army. He knows his shit. Best to do what he says, Lloyd."

With Townsend leading his horse, the others followed, trekking quietly down the backside of the knoll and out of sight.

As the sheriff approached the front of the house, the roving guard came to his feet, "Hold it right there. What's your business?"

"Sheriff Townsend here. I'd like to have a word with Miller."

Silence, except for a bullfrog's croak, the scuttle of sheep in the corral, and the crow of a rooster. Suddenly, the front door swung open.

"Sheriff, boy, am I glad to see you!" Miller bounded down the porch steps. "We're caught in the crossfire here, what with explosions and potshots. These rustlers are trying to kill us! Me and my men, we're holed up in the house until things settle down."

Townsend looked over one shoulder and then the other, shrugging. "Looks rather calm now. Emmy was shot, but I expect you already knew that."

"My Emmy?" he gasped, taking another step. "Please tell me she ain't dead!"

"She's under a doctor's care. Not so for all those men downed by falling rocks on the Bar C property. Don't suppose you know anything about that?"

"My God, no, I don't!"

"Funny. I understood they all worked for you."

Three additional men trickled out the front door and spread over the porch.

"Those men terrorizing us law-abiding ranchers must be stopped," Miller proclaimed.

"I agree one hundred percent," the sheriff said. "Got a few associates with me that may be able to help."

The silhouettes of three men positioned a good twenty feet apart, identities concealed by hats, materialized from the early morning mist. Two wore rain slickers, a third dressed all in black. Bewildered, Miller blinked, straining to recognize the imposing figures hidden by the wispy fog.

Then, the sun erupted from the horizon, scintillating, slashing yellow light across his face. He squinted, lifting a palm to block it. "Who's that out there?"

"Remember me, Miller?" Colt stepped fully from the mist, his slicker billowing behind. Miller took in a gulp of air.

"Colton Chase? I'll be a monkey's uncle! Been a right smart spell since—"

"Not here for a social call. Need to set a few things straight. Make certain there are no misguided impressions on who owns the Bar C."

"About that," Miller inserted, glancing down to his boots, then up again. "Mighty sad when Rosannah passed. She and I, well, we got close during her unfortunate illness. Since you weren't around or taking part in managing the ranch business, she looked up to me to help Emmy out."

"Emmy needs no help from you, or anyone else."

"I've got papers that say otherwise. Now, where..." Patting his pockets, he produced a paper and unfolded it. "This here pretty much seals the deal on the Bar C. I'm sorry you had to find out this way, but you've been gone so long and Rosie trusted my expertise. Emmy didn't even know where you were."

Mr. Mustache descended the steps in a jingle of spurs and moved to stand beside Miller. Kade grit his teeth. What he wouldn't give to kick that man's ass right here and now.

Colt slid open his slicker, exposing the two Peacemakers holstered at his side. Kade and Grayson followed suit. The men seated on the porch slowly came to their feet.

Miller extended a palm, "Don't get jumpy. We're only talking."

"I'll have a look at that document," Townsend said. Miller passed the paper to a cowpoke standing behind him, instructing him to walk it over. The sheriff perused it, although clearly having trouble without his glasses.

"Sheriff, if it's acceptable to you, I'd like to look at that."

Nicholas Grayson emerged from the mist, clad in an exquisitely tailored frock coat, crisp white shirt, and black hat with a snakeskin band. He took the paper the sheriff passed his way, and Nick rolled Miller a cynical gaze, "Earned my law degree before I took on the more hands-on duties of law enforcement," he explained, proceeding to study the document with a frown. "Looks fraudulent to me. Doesn't have official seals or a judge's signature, and I know about every judge in the surrounding counties. He produced a match, glancing to the sheriff for approval, "May I?" With permission, he struck the match and set fire to the paper, lifting it high so all might watch it blacken and curl.

"Rosie signed that—it's my personal property!" Miller said.

Too late. The paper, engulfed in flames, drifted to the ground. Grayson ground his boot over the embers.

"Surely you've got another hidden away in a safe place, with the appropriate seals, notary, and witness signatures," the sheriff said, pleased to see Miller's face go white.

Two additional characters shuffled out the front door and Townsend stiffened, sliding his right hand from the saddle horn to his hip. "You may want to call off your dogs, Miller. Captain Stockton has a man up in your hay loft, overwatch—somethin' or other he called it. One up on the hill, two behind the house, more out by your well, and one by the chicken coop. Don't want a shootout, but one can be arranged."

Miller scowled, "Stockton's dead!"

The final figure cloaked in mist advanced a few steps. Rain slicker draping at his legs, Kade entered the clearing, stopping with a sling to his stance. Tipping up his hat, he took a moment to thoroughly enjoy the drain of color from Miller's face. "Why Johnny Ringo, you look like somebody just walked over your grave," he drawled, mimicking the iconic Tombstone movie quote.

A grin dented Colt's cheek. Grayson and the sheriff shared head-scratching looks.

Stunned, Miller glared at the ghost before him, the man he believed was dead, fingers flinching nervously near the six-gun in his holster. His mind raced. How he would love to finish the job right now in front of everyone. "Bastard has nine lives," he cursed under his breath.

"Somebody here named Johnny?" came a whisper from the porch.

"I don't have any issues with you folks up on the porch. You boys care to leave, slowly unbuckle your gun belts, and drop'em right where you're standing. Pick'em at my office in Gunn Pass later today."

Clive Monroe blustered as he watched the others shuffle off the porch, one by one, leaving their weapons and filing towards the barn, each with something to say.

"Hey, now, don't you be leavin'," Miller called after them, "you all have responsibilities, dammit ... what about me?"

"You still owe us back pay and I ain't about to die for your ass," one said.

"You and Mustache here aren't going anywhere," Townsend informed.

"Ain't takin' me alive," Clive said, bolstering his stance and puffing out his chest.

"That can be arranged," Grayson said. He took a step closer, lifting his hand to the others. "This is between me and him. You ever been to Montana, ace?"

Clive blinked, eyes shifting, "I may have."

"You remember an incident involving a pretty brunette doing laundry in her home, minding her own business? She might have been kind enough to offer you a cup of lemonade or tea, maybe not. Either way, you may have taken it upon yourself to take liberties. When she rebuffed you, you got a little too rough. That sound familiar?"

"Never been to Helena," Clive said.

"I didn't say anything about Helena. However, Mr. Monroe, I do know you're wanted for murder in the state of Montana, for this and other offenses."

Sweat popped out over his brow, shimmering in the morning sun. With the subtle crunch of boots on gravel, he shifted, and in a blur of motion, went for the six-gun at his side. At the same moment, Grayson pulled his pistol. But before he could fire, the report of several long guns reached his ears and Clive Monroe went down to his knees, then forward into the dirt.

Miller screamed, hunkered down, and covered his head.

Kade was on him first, then Colt, then Grayson. Disarmed, they jerked him to his feet and secured his hands behind his back. A wet spot spread along the front of Miller's tight pants and down one leg.

Sheriff Townsend sauntered up behind and snapped on the handcuffs.

"Miller Johnson, you're under arrest for attempted murder, fraud, and forgery, just to name a few. You may never see the light of day again. My suggestion is to enjoy the sunshine while you can on the ride to the Gunn Pass jail."

CHAPTER 33

Won't Look Back

Madison pecked on the hospital room door before entering. Emmy sat upon the cushioned chair by the window overlooking the street below, a blanket draped around her shoulders. A metal IV stand was positioned beside her, two bags of clear liquid dangling from the top.

"Good morning, Madison," she greeted with a sleepy smile.

"An especially good morning for you, me, us, *and* the Bar C," Madison said, skipping over to hug Emmy's shoulders excitedly. She pulled up a chair and sat down.

Emmy's eyes rounded and she straightened, "Have you heard from Kade and Colt?"

"Better still, they're back!"

She gasped, hand flying to her mouth, "They're safe?" She gripped one of Madison's hands and squeezed. She wanted so much to bounce up from the chair and wrap her in a hug, but the intention alone made her bruised ribs and healing bullet wound ache. "I need to hear all about what happened, *everything!*" she demanded, euphoric and fearful at the same time. What if someone had been hurt, or worse? "But where's Kade, why isn't he here?"

Emmy's heart deflated, splintered memories of the night she was shot coming back to her. He told her he loved her ... didn't he? He cradled her. He wrapped her wound. He brought her into the future, carrying her, saving her life! Was it simply an obligation, his completion of a promised job? He was an honorable man. Of course, he would do all humanly possible to make sure the job was done right. She could think of no reason why Kade wasn't here himself.

"Give me a chance and I'll tell you," Madison began with a smile. She touched on all the pertinent highlights that she had gleaned from both Colt and Kade upon their return.

"Miller's in jail?" Emmy asked.

Madison nodded, "With a lot of charges against him."

"But the ranch, what about the Bar C? Is it...."

"It's the Bar C again, not Johnson Ranch. The spell or whatever it was, was broken."

"Thank God," Emmy breathed, willing away the burn filling her eyes. "Dammit," she whispered, knowing by now it was a losing battle to fight the tears.

She flung her arms around Madison's neck and the two women embraced, though when a nurse entered Madison broke away, greeting her politely.

"Looks as though our patient is feeling better today," the nurse said. "A detective with Teton County Sheriff's Office is requesting to visit with you at two o'clock this afternoon if you're feeling up to it?"

Emmy looked to Madison, then back with a nod. "Yes, I understand. That will be fine."

"Perfect. I'll let him know. If there's anything you need, push the button." With that, she left the room.

"What will I say?" Emmy asked.

"Absolutely nothing. That's the second part of our plan," Madison began, edging in close and lowering her voice.

Kade stepped out of the shower and dried himself off, hardly able to contain his excitement at seeing Emmy again. Madison updated him and Colt on her status and progress, and he felt thankful and relieved, yet still unable to shake his feelings of failure. That bullet was intended for him, and it should have been his to suffer through. Even though Miller was out of the picture, it wasn't over, not by a long shot—Miller being merely a gnat in the ointment, as Grayson phrased it. Wasn't the expression 'fly in the ointment'? Didn't matter.

All Kade cared about was Emmy's safety and a speedy recovery from her wounds.

But what about the future?

The future he was already living and had been for almost 29 years, and it didn't thrill him, not when she couldn't be a part of it.

Keep her here in the future with you.

Now that's a stupid plan. Then who would run the ranch? Someone would go and fuck up the history of the Bar C and he and Colt would just have to go back and kick some ass ... again. A vicious circle.

Kade grinned as he stood before the mirror, scrubbing a towel over his wet head, tying it at his waist, and then lathering his face for a much-needed shave. It felt good to know he had made a difference in people's lives. A simpler time. He had made friends, likely a few enemies, and he ... fell in love.

For sure, didn't plan on that, did you?

Razor hovering mid-air, her face flashed before him—giggling, sarcastic, pissed off, happy, serious, thoughtful. Sexy. Would he allow this proud, capable woman to return to her position on the historic Triple Bar C Ranch without him by her side? And she would return, he knew that. Nothing could deter her from her duties.

Maybe the better question is, will she allow you to come along for the ride?

He finished shaving, got dressed, and jogged over to the main house to meet up with Colt in the kitchen. In his mind's eye, Emmy stood at the rectangular oak table with a rolling pin in hand, dressed in one of those threadbare working dresses, frilly apron tied around her waist, hair piled messily on top of her head, a blotch of flour on her nose. The image made him smile.

"You sure are cheerful for getting absolutely no sleep," Colt said, pouring a second cup of coffee for himself, and offering Kade his first.

"Suppose I am feeling a bit full of myself," he agreed. "There's something I'd like to discuss with you before we head over to the hospital."

"Sure," Colt said, thinking about the antique photograph of a man standing next to the old Lakota warrior and his paint pony—a man with an uncanny resemblance to the one standing before him now.

"If Emmy will have me, I'd like to go back with her," he began. "With your blessing, of course."

Madison met Colt and Kade in the hospital lobby.

"How is she?" Kade asked first thing.

"IVs removed, the doctor made his rounds, and she's doing great. She's weak, but we made two laps around the third floor so she could test her balance and stamina. I helped her with the t-shirt, sweatpants, and sneakers I brought, and she'll keep a blanket wrapped around her shoulders so nobody will be the wiser. A detective is scheduled to come by at two."

"Good," Colt said. "We drove Buck's old beater truck. Kade will park it over on the side street by the east exit where that vacant gas station is. I'll hang out in the waiting room and intercept the detective as he arrives, ask if they have any leads, small talk, that sort of thing. I'll detain him as long as I can. Can Emmy get down three flights of stairs by herself?"

"She insists she can. I'll stuff my hair into a baseball cap and put on sunglasses, then meet her at the back door and walk her to the truck." Madison knew there were security cameras, but it was impossible to avoid all of them. Just a matter of luck at this point.

An hour later, Madison ushered Emmy to the green and white truck idling in the ancient gas station parking lot, weeds poking through the asphalt. Kade met them halfway and wrapped her ever-so-gently in his arms, kissing her forehead, cheeks, and her hair.

"Your head ... how is it?" she asked.

"Hard as ever," he promised. He lifted her into his arms, carrying her to the truck and placing her on the passenger side. With help, she gingerly scooted to the middle and Madison followed. Kade hopped into the driver's side and wrapped Emmy into the fold of his arms, swallowing her into his embrace, burying his face in the hair at her neck before finding her lips with his. He kissed her long and hard.

Madison gazed out the passenger window until it became uncomfortably long, seconds ticking by, "C'mon you two, we need to go!"

Laughing, Kade slammed the column stick shift into first and sped off in the direction of Town Square, where Colt appeared sometime later, traversing under the elk antler archway and hopping into the backseat.

"Let's go," he said.

Sundown blazed pink across the sky above the grasslands, a tepid breeze gently lifting the hair from her shoulders. The long waves flowed almost to her hips. She stood in the gazebo, absorbing the scent of surrounding rosebushes. Madison had provided an attractive blue and orange print maxi dress for her to change into, much cooler than the thick pants she had worn leaving the hospital. It didn't cover as much skin as she would have liked, her arms and décolletage exposed. She clutched a thin plaid shawl over her shoulders.

"Are you sure you don't want to sit?" Kade asked, presenting her with a peach-colored rose with a long stem. "I felt confident it would send us back in time if I picked it ... so..."

She grinned, pressing it to her nose. "Thank you. I'm enjoying standing right now. It's so nice to be outside and back home, almost."

"Almost," Kade agreed. He moved up behind and looped his arms around her, mindful of her injuries, drawing her close. Her head fell back to his chest.

"I'm happy you're on the mend. I don't know how I would have handled it if ... well, if things didn't turn out so well."

"You would have done what Kade Stockton does best," she said softly. "Taken care of business. Made certain things continued as they should."

"You have a lot of faith in me."

"That I do. You could have run the Bar C exactly as it should be run, falling into rhythm with the folks in my time, rising above, creating an empire." The vibration from his chuckle soothed her.

"I'd rather not think about it." He lifted her shawl aside and dropped a kiss on her shoulder, lingering to inhale the delicate scent of her skin, needing assurance she was really here. "Turn around," he said, guiding her and drawing her into an embrace. He chucked her chin, forcing her eyes to his. "You want to know the truth? I'm nothing without you." The hitch in his voice caught him off-guard.

"Don't say that."

"It's true, Emmy." Lips grazing hers, he closed his eyes and lost himself. "I think back, and it's like, I can trace every moment of my life, see exactly where it took me, and how it led me to you. Weird, I can even see the reason why I never saw it before now."

"Kade..." she said, eyes lifting, "that's a beautiful thing to say."

"It's true, baby." His mouth took hers in a lingering kiss, caressing the sweetness with his tongue. He pulled back to stroke a cheek with the pad of his thumb. "There will be times when things get rough. I can't promise you endless rainbows, or that we won't have bad days, but I can promise to love you, to give you all I have. And I'll never look back." A tear escaped her eye, and he kissed it away.

"You said you loved me," she whispered.

"I did, and I do, love you, Emmy Bartlett."

"I love you, too," she whispered, clutching him as tightly as she dared without causing pain. "Please say you'll come home with me."

"In a heartbeat," he vowed.

"But it's not that simple. What about your family...."

Kade stroked her hair, looking past her to the rows of bunkhouses, and further to the tree-filled ridge where Dad's cabin rested on the other side. They had just finished sitting down to supper with him and the Chase family. He would take his dad aside and have a long talk with him, and he would call Ben, too. Neither knew about the roses, but they would understand his need to go.

"Life is about measured sacrifice," he said, voice low. "I don't have answers. My guess is that we all just do the best we can. I do know that I don't want a life without you in it."

"You make me so happy," she confessed, satisfied grin on her face, "and I can't imagine not finding you in my kitchen every single day for the rest of my life." Lifting her face to his, she invited a kiss from his smiling lips. And then another.

"Besides, I have to go back," he said, shaking his head in feigned upset.

"Why?"

"I left my guitar there."

She squeezed her eyes shut and concentrated on avoiding the painful process of laughing, begging him not to be so funny.

"Take me home, Stockton.

Epilogue

"I now pronounce you man and wife. You may kiss the bride." Pastor Simmons of the Crooked Creek Church closed the dogeared Bible.

Finally, having waited patiently through all the necessary passages, anxious to get to the good part, Kade lifted the veil from Emmy's radiant face. Bringing his new wife into a tender embrace, he forever locked her next to his heart. "I love you, Mrs. Stockton," he said in a voice only she could hear, before branding her lips with his kiss.

After several seconds Pastor Simmons cleared his throat, "I'm pleased to introduce, Mr. and Mrs. Kade Stockton."

Maid of Honor Hanna Tompson exhaled a little squeak, bouncing excitedly in her emerald-green taffeta dress, a bouquet of peach roses fashionably created by Joy's Flower Emporium clutched in her hand. Beatrice and Julie wore matching green dresses, each carrying a small basket of rose petals. Zak, as best man, stood stiff in his black Sunday suit and extra clean hat, a big grin on his face.

The church erupted into cheers and applause. The music began. Helen Riley, seated at the organ, played an energetic rendition of The Bellamy Brothers, Let Your Love Shine, with Becca singing the lyrics. Kade, dapper in a black suit, ivory shirt, silk tie, and spiffy black Stetson, squeezed Emmy's hand and they rotated to greet the congregation.

Estelle and Henry sat in the front pew with little Eli perched on Henry's lap. The couple was excited to be fixing up the old cabin and moving in soon. Fanny Picard and her elegant mother, Francesca, wore stunning bustle dresses in lavender and purple, respectively. Winifred Godfrey wore a straw hat decorated in gaudy sunflowers and stood alongside Joy Warner, barely able to conceal her exuberance at how fabulous her flower arrangements turned out. Florence Jenkins yanked on her husband Barney's hand until he stood and clapped. Scout, handsome in a tobacco-color suit, joined in alongside half a dozen of the bathed-and-cleaned-up Bar C hands. Even Lukas and Micah wore their Sunday finest, occupying an entire pew along with the rest of the Shaffer family. Nicholas Grayson sat at the rear beside the now-retired Lloyd Townsend, his happy wife, and six children. Word was, Nick would be taking over as the new Sheriff of Gunn Pass City.

With every seat occupied by a smiling Gunn Pass citizen, Kade and Emmy swept down the center aisle to a chorus of cheers and congratulations. Hanna, Beatrice, and Julie trotted behind caring for the train of Emmy's gown, lovingly cut, and sewn from champagne brocade silk by Fanny Picard herself, a floral design of beads and satin across the bodice.

The happy cheers dangerously overshadowed the music. Becca, only a tiny bit frustrated, wasn't having any of that. She maneuvered her way to the center front and sang louder still, instigating Helen to rapidly pump pedals while cranking open the organ shutters for more volume.

"That woman has some lungs," Kade whispered, and Emmy giggled.

The double doors of the church swung open to an invigoratingly sunny fall afternoon, and the congregation poured out and down the church steps behind the couple. Leaves drifted lazily from the cottonwoods circling the pond, the path to the shiny black Phaeton carriage carpeted in yellow and orange.

Tom Carlson hurriedly finished draping flower garland, ribbons, and a noisy cowbell or two, to the carriage. He stepped up to proudly escort the newly married couple to the vehicle that would whisk them home to their new life. According to Joy's gossip column, Tom was mending his ways by completing his education and assisting schoolmarm, Maryann Fletcher, with intentions of one day becoming a schoolteacher himself.

Emmy stopped and twirled around, tossing her bouquet into a high arc directly into the crowd. Becca nearly mowed down Faye Judd to get to it. Just as well. According to Becca, Faye was far too young anyway.

Kade assisted Emmy and the voluminous dress onto the carriage. As he circled to the driver's side, from the corner of his eye he saw Tate Wind Spirit astride his paint horse on the other side of the river. Raising a hand in salutation, the elder smiled, and Kade responded in kind.

When the couple arrived home, they were greeted by two yellow retrievers with graying muzzles, and a small black, white, and tan terrier followed by three yipping ragamuffin puppies.

Braced on his elbows Kade, threaded fingers through Emmy's hair and watched her face, placing searching kisses upon her lips in a teasing rhythm. "Tell me if you'd like me to stop," he reminded, careful of her healing injuries, but also her innocence, even though they hadn't been apart a single night since returning from modern day.

Emmy fell into indigo blue eyes brimming with unspent passion. She brushed a piece of thick brown hair from his brow. "I want you," she murmured with a naughty grin, lifting her hips to his, "always ... my love."

That's all it took.

Fitting together like two lost puzzle pieces, they found their way home at last. A gentle move bathed his sex in her moisture, and he sheathed himself inside her, slowly at first, strength building. With a gasp, Emmy reveled in the pleasure and lost herself in the mesmerizing dance. She especially loved the way he kissed her, toying with her tongue at the same time he rotated strong hips, filling her completely. Eventually, the lovers pulled away to gasp their pleasure.

Then, clinging to one another, they rocked back and forth until their hearts had calmed.

An hour later, Emmy perched in their cozy double bed and hugged her knees, back nestled against pillows propped to the brass headboard. She cuddled beneath a quilt pulled to her chin as a cheery fire crackled in the hearth. Kade sat beside her with nothing on but a pair of faded blue jeans, his guitar slung around his neck.

"Sing that song to me, what is it....?" She pressed a finger to her chin and pondered.

"You're going to have to give me more clues than that," he said, chuckling.

Unsure of the words, she hummed a refrain, "We drank a toast to innocence—mmm—mm, the snow, it turned into rain."

"Now where did you hear that?" Kade asked, amazed at her memory.

She toyed with the locket around her neck—a locket he learned once belonged to Emmy's mother, given to Rosie by Emmy's father.

"You were singing it one time, and your window in the carriage house was open. I was in the paddock with Obie. I liked it."

Kade's expression turned thoughtful. As a testament to the pure love in his heart, he gazed at his wife a long while before speaking.

"It's a Dan Fogelberg song. His music was genius. My opinion, of course." Fingers strumming the strings of the guitar, he began to softly sing:

> "We drank a toast to innocence,
> we drank a toast to now,
> And tried to reach beyond the emptiness,
> but neither one knew how."

"You have a nice singing voice."

"Don't know about that. But I do enjoy music."

"That song makes me sad."

"Well, I don't want you to be sad," he said, lightening the mood with a John Lennon ballad, the eccentric lyrics making them both laugh—tolerable now that her ribs had mostly healed.

"Mm, I sure do like it when you laugh," Kade proclaimed, propping the guitar to the wall, and climbing over to kiss her nose first, biting her neck playfully. She fell back into the pillows and pulled him along by wrapping her legs around his middle.

"Have mercy!" she squealed, squirming like an out-of-water fish. When he stopped, she flung her arms around his neck and reciprocated the mellow kiss he pressed to her lips, testing at first, then growing with passion and need.

About Author

Bonita Clifton is a bestselling and award-winning author. She grew up in the shadows of the Rocky Mountains in Colorado, where the majestic beauty and rich history filled up her heart. Bonita also writes bold and sensual historical romance alongside her own macho hero, T.K. Rogers, under the pseudonym of **Sindee Harlow**.

A Spotify playlist is now available, created especially for **Journey of the Rose**. For more information, to catch up with this series, and to learn about other books, visit www.bonitaclifton.com.

If you enjoyed **Journey of the Rose**, Book 2 of the *Twisted Rose Saga*, please leave a review on Amazon and/or Goodreads. A star rating is invaluable, and a written review is even better, as it helps readers to make informed choices.

You can also join **Bonita's Insider Newsletter** on her website at www.bon itaclifton.com for the inside scoop on almost everything (except for how to keep houseplants alive; she knows absolutely nothing about that.)

Follow Bonita Clifton on Bookbub and/or Amazon to be notified of new releases.

Also By Bonita Clifton

Time of the Rose
Twisted Rose Saga, Book 1

She loves all things antique and longs to experience the olden days. He's a legendary gunslinger who is destined to die young. Can they change history with their passion?

Madison Calloway has become too well acquainted with despair. Still reeling from a divorce, the heartbroken travel agent steps out of her routine to embrace an intriguing work trip to a Wild West tourist town. And when a magnetically masculine gunslinger shows up at the shooting exhibition, he captures her imagination with his skillful display...and outlandish claims of being from 1878.

Colton Chase is too busy pursuing a murderer to pause for love. Yet after a mysterious rose hurtles him over one hundred years into the future, a beautiful and feisty stranger catches his eye. When she is unwittingly caught in the storm that whisks him back to his own time, he vows to protect her from danger, but how can he explain her to his family?

Caught up in the hardships of the rancher's rough-and-tumble life, Madison wavers between her yearning for the familiar and the joys of their growing relationship. Though it breaks her heart all over again, she knows she must leave. And with the man who slaughtered his parents still on the loose, Colton is willing to sacrifice his happiness to see her safely returned home.

Can the lovestruck pair turn an impossible meeting into happily ever after?

Coming Soon!
Origin of the Rose – **A Prequel**

www.ingramcontent.com/pod-product-compliance
Lightning Source LLC
Chambersburg PA
CBHW031937210726
48290CB00006BA/1637